They're back from Pocket Books—the classic novels of
Ed McBain's 87th Precinct series, "one of the great
literary accomplishments of the last
half-century" (Pete Hamill, New York *Daily News*).

PRAISE FOR

LULLABY

"McBain is a superior stylist, a spinner of artfully designed
and sometimes macabre plots." —*Newsweek*

"Staccato dialogue and authentic characters . . . a page-turner."
—*Publishers Weekly*

"A very difficult book to put down." —Stephen King

VESPERS

"A master clearly is at work!" —*Chicago Tribune*

"One of the best in the 87th saga . . ." —*People*

"Exciting, absorbing, and surprising . . . A stunner."
—*The Washington Post Book World*

WIDOWS

"Phenomenally good." —*Los Angeles Times Book Review*

"Splendid . . . You're in for a treat." —*Cosmopolitan*

"Honest and chilling." —*The Plain Dealer* (Cleveland)

D0053113

"[A] howlingly funny send-up."
—*The New York Times Book Review*

"Fresh and vibrant . . . Only McBain can write like this. . . ."
—*Library Journal*

MONEY, MONEY, MONEY
Edgar Award nominee!

"Crisp and fresh . . . savagely brutal . . . [with] unexpected and amusing twists."
—*Los Angeles Times*

"Tight plotting, crackling police work, and bizarre people . . . a witty tale of counterfeit money that grows before the reader's eyes."
—*The Plain Dealer* (Cleveland)

"Captivating stuff."
—*St. Petersburg Times* (FL)

THE LAST DANCE

"This is McBain in classic form . . . a cop story that's as strong and soulful as the urban heart of America he celebrates so well."
—*Publishers Weekly* (starred review)

"McBain forces us to think twice about every character we meet . . . even those we thought we already knew."
—*The New York Times Book Review*

"McBain remains simply at the top of his game. . . . [A] great piece of writing."
—Larry King, *USA Today*

THE BIG BAD CITY

"As good as it gets . . . compulsively readable."
—*The Seattle Times-Post Intelligencer*

Written by Evan Hunter

Novels

The Blackboard Jungle (1954) *Second Ending* (1956) *Strangers When We Meet* (1958) *A Matter of Conviction* (1959) *Mothers and Daughters* (1961) *Buddwing* (1964) *The Paper Dragon* (1966) *A Horse's Head* (1967) *Last Summer* (1968) *Sons* (1969) *Nobody Knew They Were There* (1971) *Every Little Crook and Nanny* (1972) *Come Winter* (1973) *Streets of Gold* (1974) *The Chisholms** (1976) *Love, Dad* (1981) *Far from the Sea* (1983) *Lizzie* (1985) *Criminal Conversation** (1994) *Privileged Conversation* (1996) *Candyland** (2001) *The Moment She Was Gone** (2002)

Short Story Collections

Happy New Year, Herbie (1963) *The Easter Man* (1972)

Children's Books

Find the Feathered Serpent (1952) *The Remarkable Harry* (1959) *The Wonderful Button* (1961) *Me and Mr. Stenner* (1976)

Screenplays

Strangers When We Meet (1959) *The Birds* (1962) *Fuzz* (1972) *Walk Proud* (1979)

Teleplays

The Chisholms (1979) *The Legend of Walks Far Woman* (1980) *Dream West* (1986)

*Available in paperback from Pocket Books
**Available in hardcover from Simon & Schuster

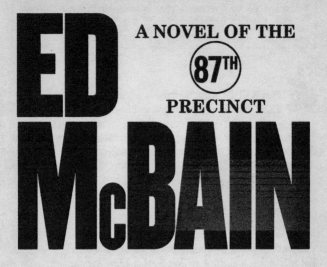

A NOVEL OF THE 87TH PRECINCT

ED McBAIN

LULLABY

POCKET BOOKS

New York   London   Toronto   Sydney

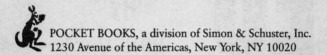
POCKET BOOKS, a division of Simon & Schuster, Inc.
1230 Avenue of the Americas, New York, NY 10020

This book is a work of fiction. Names, characters, places and incidents are products of the author's imagination or are used fictitiously. Any resemblance to actual events or locales or persons, living or dead, is entirely coincidental.

Copyright © 1989 by Hui Corporation

All rights reserved, including the right to reproduce this book or portions thereof in any form whatsoever. For information address Pocket Books, 1230 Avenue of the Americas, New York, NY 10020

ISBN: 0-7434-7074-5

First Pocket Books paperback edition September 2004

10 9 8 7 6 5 4 3 2 1

POCKET and colophon are registered trademarks of Simon & Schuster, Inc.

Front cover design by Rod Hernandez
Front cover photo by Brian Velenchenko

Manufactured in the United States of America

For information regarding special discounts for bulk purchases, please contact Simon & Schuster Special Sales at 1-800-456-6798 or business@simonandschuster.com.

This is for Julian and Dorothy Pace

The city in these pages is imaginary.
The people, the places are all
fictitious. Only the police routine is based
on established investigatory technique.

LULLABY

1.

BOTH DETECTIVES had children of their own.

The teenage baby-sitter was about as old as Meyer's daughter. The infant in the crib recalled for Carella those years long ago when his twins were themselves babies.

There was a chill in the apartment. It was three o'clock in the morning and in this city most building superintendents lowered the thermostats at midnight. The detectives, the technicians, the medical examiner, all went about their work wearing overcoats. The baby's parents were still dressed for the outdoors. The man was wearing a black cloth coat and a white silk scarf over a tuxedo. The woman was wearing a mink over a long green silk gown and high-heeled green satin pumps. The man and the woman both had stunned expressions on their faces. As if someone had punched them both very hard. Their eyes seemed glazed over, unable to focus.

This was the first day of a bright new year.

The dead sitter lay sprawled on the floor midway down the hallway that ran the rear length of the apartment. Baby's bedroom at the far end, off a fire escape. Tool marks on the window and sill, they figured this was where he'd come in. Mobile with a torn cord lying on the floor beside the crib. Monoghan and Monroe stood looking down at the dead girl, their hats settled low on their heads, their hands in the pockets of their overcoats. Of all the men in the room, they were the only two wearing hats. Someone in the department once said for publication that the only detectives who wore hats in this city were Homicide detectives. The person who'd said this was a Homicide detective himself, so perhaps there was some truth to the ancient bromide. In this city, Homicide detectives were supposed to supervise each and every murder investigation. Perhaps this was why they wore hats: to look supervisory. By department regulations, however, a murder case officially belonged to the precinct catching the squeal. Tonight's double murder would be investigated by detectives in the local precinct. The Eight-Seven. Detectives Meyer Meyer and Steve Carella. Lucky them.

The M.E. was crouched over the teenager's body. Monoghan guessed he would tell them any minute now that the girl was dead from the knife sticking out of her chest. Monoghan had been called out from a party. He was still just drunk enough to find all of this somehow comical. Dead girl on the floor here, blouse torn, skirt up around her ass, knife in her chest. A lapis pendant on a broken gold chain coiled like a blue-headed snake on the floor beside her. Monoghan looked down at the M.E. and smiled mysteriously. Monroe was cold sober, but he found all of this a little comical, too, perhaps because it was New Year's Day and in this rotten business if you didn't laugh and dance away all your troubles and cares—

"She's dead," the M.E. said.

Which made it official.

"Shot, right?" Monoghan asked, and smiled mysteriously.

The M.E. didn't bother answering him. He snapped his satchel shut, got to his feet, and then walked into the living room, where Carella and Meyer were still trying to get some answers from the baby's dazed parents.

"We'll do the autopsies soon as we can," he said, and then, in explanation, "The holidays. Meanwhile you can say one was stabbed and the other was smothered."

"Thanks," Meyer said.

Carella nodded.

He was remembering that years and years ago, whenever he got up in the middle of the night to feed the twins, he would hold one in his arms and prop the other's bottle on the pillow. Alternated the routine at the next feeding. So that one of them would always be held.

There was a dead baby in the bedroom at the far end of the hall.

"Mrs. Hodding," Meyer said, "can you tell me what time you got back here to the apartment?"

Gayle Hodding. Blonde and blue-eyed, twenty-eight years old, wearing eye shadow to match the green gown, no lipstick, the dazed expression still on her face and in her eyes. Looking at Meyer blankly.

"I'm sorry?"

"Two-thirty," her husband said.

Peter Hodding. Thirty-two. Straight brown hair combed to fall casually on his forehead. Brown eyes. Black bow tie slightly askew. Face a pasty white, shell-shocked expression in his eyes. Both of them walking-wounded. Their baby daughter was dead.

"Was the door locked?" Meyer asked.

"Yes."

"You had to use a key to get in?"

"Yes. I was drunk, I fumbled with the lock a lot. But I finally got the door open."

"Were the lights on or off?"

"On."

"When did you notice anything out of the ordinary?"

"Well, not until . . . we . . . Annie wasn't in the living room, you see. When we came in. So I called her name . . . and . . . and when I . . . I got no answer, I went to look for her. I figured she might be in with the baby. And didn't want to answer because she might wake up the baby."

"What happened then?"

"I started for the baby's room and . . . found Annie there in the hallway. Stabbed."

"Could we have her last name, please?"

"Annie Flynn."

This from the woman.

Coming alive a bit. Realizing that these men were

detectives. Here to help. Had to give them what they needed. Carella wondered when she would start screaming. He wished he would not have to be here when she started screaming.

"You've used her before?" Meyer asked. "This same sitter?"

"Yes."

"Pretty reliable?"

"Oh, yes."

"Ever any trouble with boyfriends or . . . ?"

"No."

"Never came home and found anyone with her, did you?"

"No, no."

"Because kids . . ."

"No."

"Nobody she was necking with or . . . ?"

"Never anything like that."

All this from Hodding. Drunk as a lord when he'd walked in, sober enough the next minute to be able to dial 911 and report a murder. Carella wondered why he'd felt it necessary to tell them he'd been drunk.

"Excuse me, sir," Meyer asked, "but . . . when did you learn that your daughter . . . ?"

"I was the one who found her," Mrs. Hodding said.

There was a sudden silence.

Someone in the kitchen laughed. The Crime Scene technicians were in there. One of them had probably just told a joke.

"The pillow was on her face," Mrs. Hodding said.

Another silence.

"I took it off her face. Her face was blue."

The silence lengthened.

Hodding put his arm around his wife's shoulders.

"I'm all *right*," she said.

Harshly. Almost like "Leave me *alone,* damn it!"

"You left the apartment at what time?" Meyer asked.

"Eight-thirty."

"To go to a party, you said . . ."

"Yes."

"Where was that?"

"Just a few blocks from here. On Twelfth and Grover."

This from Hodding. The woman was silent again, that same numb look on her face. Reliving that second when she'd lifted the pillow off her baby's face. Playing that second over and over again on the movie screen of her mind. The pillow white. The baby's face blue. Reliving the revelation of that split second. Over and over again.

"Did you call home at any time tonight?" Meyer asked.

"Yes. At about twelve-thirty. To check."

"Everything all right at that time?"

"Yes."

"Was it the sitter who answered the phone?"

"Yes."

"And she told you everything was all right?"

"Yes."

"She was okay, the baby was okay?"

"Yes."

"Did she sound natural?"

"Yes."

"Nothing forced about her conversation?"

"No."

"You didn't get the impression anyone was here with her, did you?"

"No."

"Did you call again after that?"

"No. She knew where to reach us, there was no need to call again."

"So the last time you spoke to her was at twelve-thirty."

"Yes. Around then."

"And nothing seemed out of the ordinary."

"Nothing."

"Mr. Hodding, does anyone except you and your wife have a key to this apartment?"

"No. Well, yes. The super, I guess."

"Aside from him."

"No one."

"Your sitter didn't have a key, did she?"

"No."

"And you say the door was locked when you got home."

"Yes."

In the hallway, one of the technicians was telling Monoghan that the knife in the sitter's chest seemed to match the other knives on the rack in the kitchen.

"Well, well," Monoghan said, and smiled mysteriously.

"All I'm saying," the tech said, "is that what you got here is a weapon of convenience. What I'm saying . . ."

"What he's saying," Monroe explained to Monoghan, "is that your killer didn't walk *in* with the knife, the knife was *here,* in the *kitchen,* with all the *other* knives."

"Is what I'm saying," the tech said. "For what it's worth."

"It is worth a great deal, my good man," Monoghan said, and nodded gravely.

Monroe looked at him. This was the first time he had ever heard his partner sounding British. He turned to the technician. "Michael was out partying when I called him," he said.

"Which may perhaps explain why he seems a little drunk," the tech said.

"Perhaps," Monoghan said gravely.

"Which, by the way, I didn't know your name was Michael," the tech said.

"Neither did I," Monoghan said, and smiled mysteriously.

"So what it looks like we got here," Monroe said, "is an intruder finds a knife in the kitchen, he does the sitter, and then he does the baby."

"Or vice versa," the tech said.

"But not with the knife," Monroe said.

"The baby, no," the tech said.

"The baby he does with the pillow," Monroe said.

Monoghan shook his head and clucked his tongue.

"What a terrible thing," he said, and began weeping.

He was weeping because he had suddenly remembered a very beautiful, dark-haired, dark-eyed woman who'd been at the party tonight and the terrible thing was that he'd forgotten her name. He was also weeping because he'd had his hand up under her skirt when Monroe telephoned. Lying on a lot of coats on the bed, his hand up under her skirt when the telephone rang. Scared him half to death. He took out his handkerchief and wiped at his eyes. Monroe patted him on the shoulder. The technician went back into the kitchen again.

A pair of ambulance attendants came into the apartment, took a look at the dead teenager, and asked Monroe if he wanted them to leave the knife in her chest that way. Monroe said they should check with the officers investigating the case. One of the ambulance attendants walked over to where Hodding still had his arm around his wife.

"Leave the knife in her or what?" he asked Carella.

Which was when Mrs. Hodding began screaming.

IT WAS FOUR O'CLOCK in the morning when Carella knocked on the door to the Flynn apartment. Both detectives had the collars of their coats pulled up. Both detectives were wearing mufflers and gloves. Well, Carella wore only *one* glove, since he'd taken off the right glove before knocking on the door. Even inside the building, vapor plumed from their mouths. It was going to be a cold year.

Meyer looked colder than Carella, perhaps because he was entirely bald. Or perhaps because his eyes were blue. Carella's eyes were brown and they slanted downward, giving his face a slightly Oriental cast. Both men were tall, but Meyer looked cold and burly whereas Carella looked warm and slender. It was a mystery.

They had obtained the baby-sitter's address from Hodding, and now they were here to break the news to her parents. This would have been a difficult thing to do on *any* day of the year. Bad enough that a child had died; it was not in the natural order of things for parents to outlive their children. Bad enough that death had come as the result of a brutal murder. But this was the beginning of a new year. And on this day, two strangers dressed for the freezing cold outside would stand on the Flynn doorstep and tell them their sixteen-year-old daughter was dead. And forevermore, the first of every year would be for the Flynns an anniversary of death.

Meyer had handled the questioning of the Hoddings. Carella figured it was his turn. He knocked on the door again. Knocked long and hard this time.

"Who *is* it?"

A man's voice. Somewhat frightened. Four o'clock in the morning, somebody banging down his door.

"Police," Carella said, and wondered if in that single word he had not already broken the news to Annie Flynn's parents.

"What do you want?"

"Mr. Flynn?"

"Yes, what is it? Hold up your badge. Let me see your badge."

Carella took out the small leather case containing his shield and his ID card. He held it up to the peephole in the door.

"Could you open the door, please, Mr. Flynn?" he asked.

"Just a minute," Flynn said.

The detectives waited. Sounds. A city dweller's security system coming undone. The bar of a Fox lock clattering to the floor. A chain rattling free. Oiled tumblers clicking, falling. The door opened wide.

"Yes?"

A man in his mid-forties was standing there in striped pajamas and tousled hair.

"Mr. Flynn?"

"Yes?"

"Detective Carella, Eighty-Seventh Squad," Carella said, and showed the shield and the ID card again. Blue enamel on gold. Detective/Second Grade etched into the metal. 714-5632 under that. Detective/Second Grade Stephen Louis Carella typed onto the card, and then the serial number again, and a picture of Carella when his hair was shorter. Flynn carefully studied the shield and the card. Playing for time, Carella thought. He knows this is going to be bad. It's four o'clock in the morning, his baby-sitting daughter isn't home yet, he knows this is about her. Or maybe not. Four A.M. wasn't so terribly late for New Year's Eve—which it still was for some people.

At last he looked up.

"Yes?" he said again.

And with that single word, identical to all the yesses he'd already said, Carella knew for certain that the man already knew, the man was bracing himself for the words he knew would come, using the "Yes?" as a shield to protect himself from the horror of those words, to deflect those words, to render them harmless.

"Mr. Flynn . . ."

"What is it, Harry?"

A woman appeared behind him in the small entry-way. The detectives had not yet entered the apartment. They stood outside the door, the cold air of the hallway enveloping them. In that instant, the doorsill seemed to Carella a boundary between life and death, the two detectives bearing the chill news of bloody murder, the man and the woman warm from sleep awaiting whatever dread thing had come to them in the middle of the night. The woman had one hand to her mouth. A classic pose. A movie pose. "What is it, Harry?" and the hand went up to her mouth. No lipstick on that mouth. Hair as red as her dead daughter's. Green eyes. Flynn, indeed. A Maggie or a Molly, the Flynn standing there behind her husband, long robe over long nightgown, hand to her mouth, wanting to know what it was. Carella had to tell them what it was.

"May we come in?" he asked gently.

THE SQUADROOM at a quarter past five on New Year's morning looked much as it did on any other day of the year. Dark green metal filing cabinets against apple green walls. The paint on the walls flaking and chipping. A water leak causing a small bulge in the ceiling. Cigarette-scarred wooden desks. A water cooler in one corner of the room. A sink with a mirror over it. Duty chart hanging on the wall just inside the wooden slatted rail divider that separated the squadroom from the long corridor outside. A sense of dimness in spite of the naked hanging light bulbs. An empty detention cage. Big, white-faced clock throwing minutes into the empty hours of the night. At one of the desks, Detective/Third Grade Hal Willis was typing furiously.

"Don't bother me," he said the moment they came into the room and before anyone had said a word to him.

Willis was the shortest man on the squad. Curly black hair. Brown eyes. Hunched over the machine like an organ grinder's monkey, he pounded at the keys as if he'd been taught a new and satisfying trick. Battering the machine into submission. Both fists flying. The reports Willis submitted were no masterpieces, but he didn't realize that. He would have made a good lawyer; his English composition qualified him for writing contracts no one could understand.

Neither Carella nor Meyer bothered him.

They had business of their own.

They had learned little of substance from either the Hoddings or the Flynns; they would question them again later, when the shock and subsequent numbness had worn off. But they had been able to garner from them some definite times that pinpointed Annie Flynn's whereabouts and activities while she was *not* being murdered. Starting with all the negatives, they hoped one day they might get lucky enough to fill in the positives that would lead to the killer. Cops sometimes got lucky, Harold.

Meyer sat behind the typewriter.

Carella sat on the edge of the desk.

"Quiet, you two," Willis called from across the room.

Neither of them had yet said a word to him.

"Eight P.M.," Carella said. "Annie Flynn leaves her apartment at 1124 North Sykes . . ."

Meyer began typing.

". . . arrives Hodding apartment, 967 Grover Avenue, at eight-fifteen P.M."

He waited, watching as Meyer typed.

"Okay," Meyer said.

"Eight-thirty P.M. Hoddings leave Annie alone with the baby . . ."

Meyer kept typing.

A COLD GRAY DAWN was breaking to the east.

He had shared bacon and eggs with Eileen in an all-night diner on Leland and Pike and then had jokingly but hopefully asked, "Your place or mine?" to which she had given him a look that said, "Please, Bert, not while I'm eating," which was the sort of look she always gave him these days whenever he suggested sex.

Ever since she'd blown away that lunatic last October, Eileen had sworn off sex and decoy work. Not necessarily in that order. She had also told Kling—who, she guessed, was still her Significant Other, more or less—that she planned to leave police work as soon as she could find another job that might make use of her many-splendored talents, like for example being able to disarm rapists in the wink of an eye or put away serial killers with a single shot. Or, to be more accurate, *six* shots, the capacity of her service revolver, the first one in his chest, the next one in his shoulder, the third one in his back, and the others along the length of his spine as he lay already dead on the bed. I gave you a chance, she'd said over and over again, I gave you a chance, blood erupting on either side of his spine, I gave you a chance.

"Now I want a chance," she'd told Kling.

He hoped she didn't mean it. He could not imagine her as a private ticket, tailing wayward husbands in some imitation city, of which there were many in the U.S. of A. He could not imagine her doing square-shield work in a department store somewhere in the boonies, collaring shoplifters and pickpockets. I'm quitting the force, she'd told him. Quitting this city, too. This fucking city.

Tonight, they'd left the diner and he'd gone up to her apartment for another cup of coffee, greet the new year. Kissed her demurely on the cheek. Happy New Year, Eileen. Happy New Year, Bert. A sadness in her eyes. For what had been. For the Eileen who'd been his lover. For the Eileen who'd been a fearless cop before the city and the system burned it out of her. Ah, Jesus, he'd thought and had to turn his head away so she wouldn't see the sudden tears flooding his eyes. Still dark outside when he'd left the apartment. But as he'd driven home through silent deserted streets, a thin line of light appeared in the sky in the towers to the east.

He turned the corner onto Concord.

Oh, shit, he thought, I don't need this.

There were four men on the street corner.

Three huge black men and a small Puerto Rican.

The streetlamp was still on over their heads. They struggled silently in the morngloam, natural light min-

gling with artificial, the three black men wielding baseball bats, the little Puerto Rican trying to defend himself
with nothing but his hands. Blood spattered up onto the
brick wall behind him. This was in earnest.

Kling yanked up the hand brake and came out of the
car at a run, hand going for his gun, rules and regs racing through his mind, felony in progress, substantial
reason to unholster the piece. "Police officer," he
shouted, "freeze!"

Nobody froze.

A bat came spinning out of the half-light, moving
like a helicopter blade, horizontal on the air, twirling
straight for his head. He threw himself flat to the pavement, a mistake. As he rolled over and brought the gun
into firing position, one of the black men kicked him in
the head. In the dizziness, he thought Hold on. In the
dizziness, he thought Shoot. Blurred figures. Someone
screaming. Shoot, he thought. And fired. One of them
fell to the pavement. Someone else kicked him again.
He fired again. Knew he was okay by the book, piece as
a defensive weapon, tasted blood in his mouth, not a
means of apprehension, lip bleeding, how the hell,
almost choked on something, a tooth, Jesus, and fired
again, blindly this time, angrily, and scrambled to his
feet as one of the men swung a baseball bat for his head.

He took a step to the side, the thick end of the bat
coming within an inch of his nose, and then he
squeezed the trigger again, going for the money, catching the batter too high, five inches above the heart,
spinning him around with a slug in the shoulder that
sent him staggering back toward the blood-spattered

brick wall of the building where the third black man was busily beating the shit out of the little Puerto Rican, swinging the bat at him again and again, long-ball practice here on the corner of Concord and Dow.

"Put it down!" Kling shouted, but his words this morning were having very little positive effect, because all the man seemed intent on doing was finishing off the little Puerto Rican who was already so bloody he looked like a sodden bundle of rags lying on the sidewalk. "You dumb *fuck!*" Kling shouted. "Put it *down!*"

The man turned.

Saw the gun. Saw the big blond guy with the gun. Saw the look in his eyes, knew the man and the gun were both on the thin edge of explosion. He dropped the bat.

"Hey, cool it, man," he said.

"Cool *shit!*" Kling said, and threw him against the wall, and tossed him, and then handcuffed his hands behind his back.

He knelt to where the little Puerto Rican was lying on the sidewalk, bleeding from a dozen wounds.

"I'll get an ambulance," he said.

"Gracias por nada," the Puerto Rican said.

Which in Spanish meant, "Thanks for nothing."

2.

A RECONSTRUCTED TIMETABLE can only be veri-
fied by the one person who cannot possibly verify it:
the corpse.

It appeared, however, that Annie Flynn had left her
home on North Sykes, seven and a half blocks from the
Hodding apartment, at eight o'clock and had taken a
Grover Avenue bus (she'd told this to the Hoddings)
down to Twelfth Street, arriving there at eight-fifteen.
The Hoddings had left for their party at eight-thirty
sharp, taking a cab to their friends' apartment only four
blocks downtown on Grover; Mrs. Hodding said she
hadn't wanted to walk even such a short distance
because of the high heels and the long gown.

From eight-thirty P.M. until approximately twenty
minutes past midnight neither the Hoddings nor the
Flynns had talked to Annie. As was usual on New Year's
Eve, all circuits were busy after midnight and it took
Annie's father a while to get through to her. Both he and
his wife wished her a happy new year and then chatted

with her for five minutes or so. Hodding was trying to reach his home at about that same time. Kept getting a busy signal. It was around twelve-thirty when finally he got through. He ascertained that the baby was okay, wished Annie a happy new year, and then hung up. It was certain, then, that she was still alive at twelve-thirty in the morning. She was not alive at two-thirty, when the Hoddings came back to the apartment. There was no way of knowing whether Annie Flynn—as was often the case with sitters—had made or received any other calls on the night of her murder. The telephone company did not keep records of local calls. Period.

It was now ten minutes past eight.

Meyer and Carella had been relieved officially at a quarter to, but this was a homicide and the first twenty-four hours were the most important. So once again they put on their overcoats, and their mufflers, and their gloves, and they went back to the Hodding building, this time to knock on doors. This was the tedious part. No cop liked this part. No cop liked getting shot at, either, but given the choice many cops would have preferred a good old-fashioned chase to the sort of leg-work that required asking the same questions over and over again.

With only one exception, each and every resident of 967 Grover Avenue wanted to know whether it was necessary to be asking these questions so early in the morning. Didn't they know this was New Year's Day? Didn't they realize that a lot of people had been up late the night before? What was so important that it couldn't wait till later in the day? With only one excep-

tion, everyone in the building was shocked to learn that
the Hodding baby and her sitter had been murdered
last night. This was such a good neighborhood, they
could understand if something like this had happened
farther uptown, but *here?* With a doorman and everything? With only one exception, everyone the detectives interviewed had neither heard nor seen anything
strange or unusual between the hours of twelve-thirty
and two-thirty last night. Many of them hadn't even
been *home* during those hours. Many of them had gone
to sleep shortly after midnight. The one exception—

"You're a little late, aren't you?" the man said at
once.

"What do you mean?" Meyer said.

"The big show was last night," his wife said. "We had
the whole damn police department here."

"Well, two uniformed cops and a detective," the man
said.

As opposed to all the other tenants in pajamas and
robes, the Ungers—for such was the name on their
doorbell—were fully dressed and ready to take their
morning walk in the park, *despite* what had happened
last night. What had happened last night . . .

"We were robbed last night is what happened," the
wife said.

Her name was Shirley Unger. She was a good-looking brunette in her late twenties, wearing a gray sweatshirt with a University of Michigan seal on it, gray
sweat pants to match, red Reeboks. Hair springing from
her head like a tangle of weeds. Red sweatband on her
forehead. Luminous brown eyes. A Carly Simon mouth.

She knew she was gorgeous. She played to the cops like a stripper on a runway.

"We got home at about one-thirty," she said. "The robber was just going out the window. In the TV room. Actually a second bedroom."

She rolled her eyes when she said the word "bedroom," as though there'd been something licentious about a burglar going out the window. She seemed to be enjoying the thrill of all this criminal activity, although—like most honest citizens—she confused burglary with robbery. To your honest citizen, somebody stole something from you, it was robbery. Any cheap thief on the street knew the difference between burglary and robbery. Any garden-variety crook could reel off the penal-code numbers for each crime, the maximum prison terms. Just like a cop. In this business, you needed a scorecard to tell which player was which.

"We called the police right away," Unger said.

"They were here in three minutes flat," Shirley said. "Two cops in uniform and a detective. A little short guy with curly hair."

Willis, they both thought.

"Detective Willis?" Carella asked.

"Yes," Shirley said. "That's the one."

"Must have picked it up on the car radio," Meyer said.

Carella nodded.

A police department was a big organization. There were close to twenty-eight thousand cops in this city. Even in the same squadroom, you didn't always get a chance to cross-check one case against another. Willis had probably been making a routine run of the sector when he'd caught the 10-21. Burglary Past. Figured he'd run on over, save the responding blues the trouble of calling it back to the precinct. The report Willis had been typing so furiously when Meyer and Carella got back to the squadroom may have been on the Unger burglary. They hadn't told him they'd caught a double homicide at 967 Grover. He hadn't told them he'd caught a burglary at the same address. Nobody asked and nobody offered. Sometimes you had to go the long way around the mulberry bush.

"So what's this?" Shirley asked. "The follow-up?"

They told her what this was.

She did not seem terribly impressed. She was more interested in whether the police were going to get back the emerald ring her husband Charlie had bought for her eight years ago on their honeymoon in Calle di Volpe, Italy, on the island of Sardinia. She was also interested in whether the police were going to get back the new VCR Charlie had bought her for Christmas this year. "Well, *last* year already, am I right?" she said and smiled a radiant smile that said I would love to kiss your pectorals. She also wanted to know how long this was going to take because she wanted to go out for her walk and she was beginning to get hot here in the apartment, dressed for the outside as she was.

Carella told her that any questions regarding the burglary would have to be answered by Detective Willis, but that he and his partner wanted to know a little more about this man they'd seen going out the window . . .

"Yes, onto the fire escape," Shirley said.

. . . because the burglary here in the Unger apartment on the sixth floor of the building might have been
related somehow to the double homicide downstairs on
the fourth floor.

"Oh," Shirley said.

"Yes," Meyer said.

"Then would you mind if I took off my sweatshirt?"
she asked. "Because, really, it *is* very warm in here."

Without waiting for their permission, which she
didn't need anyway, she pulled the U-Mich sweatshirt
over her head, revealing fat red suspenders and a flimsy
white cotton T-shirt. She was not wearing a bra under
the T-shirt. She smiled modestly.

"You say this was around one-thirty?" Carella said.
"When you came into the apartment?"

"Yes," Shirley said shyly. Now that she was half-
naked, she was playing a novitiate nun at a cloister in
the mountains of Switzerland. Her husband was still
wearing a ski parka. He had begun to perspire visibly,
but he did not take off the parka. Perhaps he figured he
could inspire the detectives to cut this short if he did
not remove the parka. Let them know he wanted to get
the hell out of here, go take his walk in the park. Subtly
hint to them that he didn't give a flying fuck about the
baby who'd got snuffed in the apartment downstairs.
Or her baby-sitter, either. What were they going to do
about getting back his camel hair coat that had been
bought at Ralph Lauren for eleven hundred bucks was
what *he* wanted to know.

"And you say the burglar was in the bedroom,
going out the window . . ."

"Yes. The robber," Shirley said. "With my VCR under his arm."

"What did he look like?" Meyer asked. "Did you get a good look at him?"

"Oh, yes," Shirley said. "He turned to look back at us."

"As we came into the bedroom," Unger said.

Carella had already taken out his pad.

"Was he white?" he asked. "Black? Hispanic? Orient . . . ?"

"White."

"How old?"

"Eighteen, nineteen."

"Color of his hair?"

"Blond."

"Eyes?"

"I don't know."

"Neither do I."

"How tall was he?"

"That's difficult to say. He was all hunched over, you know, going out the window onto the fire escape."

"Can you guess at his weight?"

"He was very thin."

"Well, he was wearing black," Shirley said. "Black makes a person look thinner."

"Even so, he was thin," Unger said.

"Was he clean-shaven? Or did he have a beard, a mustache . . . ?"

"A mustache."

"A small mustache."

"Well, a *scraggly* mustache. He was just a kid, you know."

"Like it was just growing in."

"You know the kind of mustache a kid has? Like fuzzy?"

"That's the kind of mustache this was."

"When you say he was wearing black . . ."

"A black leather jacket," Unger said.

"Black slacks."

"And sneakers."

"White sneakers."

"And my coat," Unger said.

"Your what?"

"My camel hair coat Shirley bought for me at Ralph Lauren for eleven hundred bucks."

Must be some coat, Meyer thought.

Carella was thinking the same thing. The first *car* he'd owned had cost eleven hundred bucks.

"What color was the coat?" Meyer asked.

"I told you. Camel hair. Tan."

"And he was wearing this over the black leather jacket . . ."

"Yes."

"And the black slacks . . ."

"Yes, and the white sneakers."

"Any hat?" Meyer asked.

"No."

"Did you say anything to him?"

"Yes, I yelled 'Take off my coat, you fucking crook!'"

"Did *he* say anything to you?"

"Yes."

"What did he say?"

"He said, 'If you call the cops, I'll come back!'"

"Very scary," Shirley said.

"Because he was pointing a gun at us," Unger said.

"He had a gun?" Carella said.

"Yeah, he pulled a gun out of his pocket."

"Very scary," Shirley said again.

"So I called the police right away," Unger said, and nodded for emphasis.

"Do you think he'll be back?" Shirley asked.

Carella didn't know what she was playing now.

Maybe the expectant rape victim.

"I don't think so," he said.

"Did Detective Willis examine that fire escape?" Meyer asked.

"Yes, he did."

"Would you know if he found anything out there?"

"Nothing belonging to *us*, that's for sure," Shirley said.

DETECTIVE HAL WILLIS was in bed with a former hooker when the telephone rang at ten minutes past twelve that afternoon. He was sleeping soundly, but the phone woke him up and he grabbed for the receiver at once. Every time the phone rang, Willis thought the call would be from some police inspector in Buenos Aires, telling him they had traced a murder to the city here and were planning to extradite a woman named Marilyn Hollis. Every time the phone rang, even if he was asleep, Willis began sweating. He began sweating now.

Not many cops on the squad knew that Marilyn Hollis had done marijuana time in a Mexican prison or that she'd been a hooker in B.A. Willis knew, of course.

Lieutenant Byrnes knew. And Carella knew. The only cop who knew that Marilyn had murdered her Argentine pimp was Willis.

"Willis," he said.

"Hal, it's Steve."

"Yes, Steve," he said, relieved.

"You got a minute?"

"Sure."

"This burglary you caught last night . . ."

"Yeah."

Beside him, Marilyn grunted and rolled over.

"We're working a double homicide in the same building."

"Oh boy," Willis said.

"Occurred sometime between twelve-thirty and two-thirty."

"Mine was at one-thirty," Willis said.

"So the Ungers told us."

"How'd you like her tits?" Willis asked.

Beside him, Marilyn rammed her elbow into his ribs.

"I didn't notice," Carella said.

"Ha!" Willis said.

"The Ungers told us you were poking around on . . ."

"Who's us?"

"Me and Meyer. Poking around on the fire escape."

"Yeah."

"Did you find anything?"

"A vial of crack."

"So what else is new?"

"Plus there looked like a lot of grimy prints on the windowsill, where he was working with a jimmy to get in. I called in for the van, but nobody showed. This was only a two-bit burglary, Steve. On New Year's Eve, no less."

"If it's linked to a homicide . . ."

"Oh, sure, they'll dust the whole damn city for you. *Two* homicides, no less."

"You mind if I give them a call?"

"Please do. We bust the burglar, I'll have an excuse to go see Shirley again."

Marilyn gave him another poke.

"Did you file your report yet?" Carella asked.

"It's probably still sitting on Pete's desk."

"Mind if I have a look at it?"

"Go right ahead. Let me know what happens, okay? I bust a big burglary, I'll maybe make Second Grade."

"Don't hold your breath," Carella said.

"Talk to you," Willis said, and hung up.

IN THIS CITY, if your apartment got burglarized, the police sometimes sent around a team of technicians to see what they could find by way of latent finger-prints. This was if the burglary involved big bucks. A dozen fur coats, negotiable securities, expensive jewelry, cash, like that. In smaller burglaries, which most of them were, the technicians never showed. This was not negligence. Close to a hundred and twenty-five thousand burglaries had been committed in this city during the preceding year, and there were only one lieutenant, six sergeants and sixty-three detectives in the Crime Scene Unit. Moreover, these people were more urgently needed in cases of homicide, arson, and rape.

So your average responding uniformed police officer would tell the burglary victim that a detective would be handling the case, and that they could expect a visit from him within the next day or so. Which was normally true unless the detective's case load was backed up clear to China, in which event the victim wouldn't be getting a visit from him until sometimes a week, ten days, even two weeks after the burglary. The detective would then take a list of what was stolen and he would tell the victim, quite honestly, that unless they caught the perpetrator in the act of committing another burglary or else trying to pawn the stuff he'd stolen here, there wasn't much chance they'd ever find him *or* their goods. And then the detective would sigh for the dear, dead days when cops used to have respect for burglars.

Ah, yes, there once was a time when burglars were considered the gentlemen of the crime profession. But that was then and this was now. Nowadays, most burglars were junkie burglars. Your more experienced junkie burglars usually jimmied open a window, the way the Unger burglar had done, because they knew that nothing woke up neighbors like the sound of breaking glass. Your beginning junkie burglars didn't give a shit. *Whap,* smash the window with a brick wrapped in a dish towel, knock out the shards of glass with a hammer, go in, get out, and then run to your friendly neighborhood fence (who was most often your dope dealer as well) and pick up your ten cents on the dollar for what you'd stolen. Only the most inexperienced burglar went to a pawnshop to get rid of his loot.

Even a twelve-year-old kid just starting to do crack knew that cops sent out lists of stolen goods to every pawnshop in the city. To take your stuff to a pawnshop, you had to be either very dumb or else so strung out you couldn't wait another minute. Either that, or you were visiting from Mars.

So the chances of the Crime Scene Unit showing up at the Unger apartment were very slight, when one considered that the only items stolen were an emerald ring purchased in Italy for the sum of $2000, which gave you some idea of the quality of the emerald; a VCR that had cost $249 on sale at Sears; and an admittedly expensive cloth coat which was, nonetheless, merely a cloth coat. In a city crawling with addicts of every color and stripe, in a city that was the nation's drug capital, the dollar amount of your average burglary haul fell somewhat lower than what had been stolen from the Ungers, but this was still nothing to go shouting in the streets about and nobody down at the lab was about to dispatch the van for a garden-variety *burglary,* for Christ's sake, when people were getting killed all *over* the place, for Christ's sake!

Until Carella called in to say they had a double homicide and that one of the victims was a six-month-old baby.

IN THE PRIVATE SECTOR, if a CEO asked for an immediate report on something which in his business would have been the equivalent of a homicide, that report would have been on his desk in the morning. All two hundred and twenty pages of it. Otherwise, heads would have rolled. But this was not the private sector. This was civil service work. Considering, then, that New Year's Day was a Sunday and that the holiday was officially celebrated on a Monday, Carella and Meyer were hoping that by the end of the week—maybe— they'd have some urgently needed information from the Latent Print Unit. If one of the forty-three examiners assigned to that unit could come up with a match on the prints the Crime Scene boys had lifted from the Unger windowsill; if they could further match the prints on the handle of the Flynn murder weapon with prints in the Identification Section's files, everybody could go to Lake Como for a vacation.

On Tuesday morning, the third day of the New Year, they had a long talk with Annie Flynn's parents. Harry Flynn worked as a stockbroker for a firm all the way downtown in the Old City; the walls of the Flynn apartment were covered with oils he painted in whatever spare time he managed to salvage from his rigorous routine. His wife—neither a Molly nor a Maggie but a Helen instead—was secretary to the president of a firm in the garment district; she mentioned the name of the clothing line, but neither of the detectives was familiar with it. This was now ten o'clock in the morning. The Flynns were dressed to go to the funeral home. He was wearing a dark suit, a white shirt, and a black tie. His wife was wearing a simple black dress, low-heeled black pumps, and dark glasses.

The detectives did not yet know where to hang their hats.

The Flynns came up with a possible peg.

"Scott Handler," Flynn said.

"Her boyfriend," Mrs. Flynn said.

"Used to be, anyway."

"Until Thanksgiving."

"Broke off with him when he came down for the Thanksgiving weekend."

"The long weekend they had in Thanksgiving."

"Broke off with him then."

"Came down from where?" Carella asked.

"Maine. He goes to a private school in Maine."

"How old is he?" Meyer asked.

"Eighteen," Mrs. Flynn said. "He's a senior at the Prentiss Academy in Caribou, Maine. Right up there near the Canadian border."

"They'd been going together since she was fifteen," Flynn said.

"And you say she broke off with him in November?"

"Yes. Told me she was going to do it," Mrs. Flynn said. "Told me she'd outgrown him. Can you imagine that? Sixteen years old, she'd outgrown somebody." Mrs. Flynn shook her head. Her husband put his hand on her arm, comforting her.

"Called the house day and night," Mrs. Flynn said. "Used to burst into tears whenever I told him she didn't want to talk to him. Spent hours talking to me instead. This was long distance from Maine, mind you. Wanted to know what he'd done wrong. Kept asking me if he'd done something. I really felt sorry for him."

"He came by again just before Christmas," Flynn said.

"Home for the holidays."

"Caught Annie here in the apartment, she was the one who answered the door."

"We were in the back room, watching television."

"Started begging her to tell him what he'd done wrong. Same thing he'd kept asking my wife on the phone. What'd I do wrong? What'd I do wrong? Over and over again."

"Annie told him it was over and done with . . ."

"Said she didn't want him to come here ever again . . ."

"Said she wanted nothing further to do with him."

"That's when he raised his voice."

"Began hollering."

"Wanted to know if some other guy was involved."

"We were in the back room, listening to all this."

"Couldn't hear what Annie said."

"But *he* said . . ."

"Scott."

"*He* said, 'Who is it?'"

"And then Annie said something else . . ."

"Couldn't quite make it out, her back, must've been to us . . ."

"And he yelled, 'Whoever it is, I'll *kill* him!'"

"Tell them what else he said, Harry."

"He said, 'I'll kill you both!'"

"Those exact words?" Carella asked.

"Those exact words."

"Do you know his address?" Meyer asked.

SCOTT HANDLER'S MOTHER was a woman in her late forties, elegantly dressed at eleven-thirty that Tuesday morning, ready to leave for a meeting with clients for whom she was decorating an apartment. She looked a lot like Glenn Close in *Fatal Attraction*. Meyer thought that in this day and age, he would not like to be any woman who looked like the lady in that movie. If Meyer had been a woman with naturally curly blonde hair, he'd have paid a fortune to have it straightened and dyed black just so he wouldn't have to look like the woman in that movie. Luckily, he was bald and didn't look like her in the slightest. On the other hand, Mrs. Handler had a problem. Right down to a somewhat chilling smile.

"My son left for Maine early this morning," she said.

"Went back to school, did he?" Meyer asked.

"Yes," Mrs. Handler said, and smiled that slightly psychotic, hair-raising smile, although Meyer did not have any hair.

"The Prentiss Academy," Carella said.

"Yes."

"In Caribou, Maine."

"Yes. Why do you want to see him? Does this have something to do with the little Irish girl?"

"Who do you mean?" Meyer asked innocently.

"The one who got killed on New Year's Eve. He broke off with her months ago, you know."

"Yes, we know," Carella said.

"If their relationship is why you came here."

"We just wanted to ask him some questions."

"About where he was on New Year's Eve, I'd imagine." The chilling smile again.

"Do you *know* where he was?" Carella asked.

"Here. We had a big party. Scott was here."

"All night?"

"All night."

"What time did the party start?"

"Nine."

"And ended?"

She hesitated. Merely an instant's pause, but both detectives caught it. They guessed she was trying to remember if she'd read anything about the time of Annie Flynn's death. She hadn't because that was one of the little secrets the detectives were keeping to themselves. But the hesitation told them that her son had *not* been at the party all night long. If he'd been there at *all*. Finally, she chose what they figured she thought was a safe time to be saying goodbye to the old year.

"Four in the morning," she said.

"A late one," Meyer said, and smiled.

"Not very," she said, and shrugged, and returned the smile.

"Well, thank you very much," Carella said.

"Yes," she said, and looked at her watch.

ON WEDNESDAY MORNING, the fourth day of January, both murder victims were buried.

The detectives did not attend either of the funerals.

The detectives were on extension phones to the Prentiss Academy in Caribou, Maine, talking to an English professor named Tucker Lowery, who was Scott Handler's advisor. They would have preferred talking to Scott himself; that, after all, was why they had placed the long distance call. Both men were wearing sweaters under their jackets. It was very cold here in the city, but even colder in Caribou, Maine. Professor Lowery informed them at once that it was thirty degrees below zero up there. Fahrenheit. And still snowing hard. Carella imagined he could hear the wind blowing. He decided that if his son ever wanted to go to the Prentiss Academy, he would advise him to choose a school on the dark side of the moon. His daughter, too. If Prentiss ever began admitting females. Who, being the more sensible sex, probably would not want to go anyplace where it got to be thirty degrees below zero.

"I don't know where he is," Lowery said. "He's not due back until the ninth. Next Monday."

"Let me understand this," Carella said.

"Yes?" Lowery said.

Carella imagined a tweedy-looking man with a pleasant, bearded face and merry brown eyes. A man who was finding this somewhat amusing, two big-city detectives on extension telephones calling all the way up there to Maine.

"Are you saying that classes won't resume until next Monday?" Carella said.

"That's right," Lowery said.

"His mother told us he'd gone back to school," Meyer said.

"Scott's mother?"

"Yes. We saw her yesterday morning, she told us her son had already gone back to school."

"She was mistaken," Lowery said.

Or lying, Carella thought.

THE PUERTO RICAN'S NAME was José Herrera. There were tubes sticking out of his nose and mouth and bandages covering most of his face. One of his arms was in a cast. Kling was there at the hospital to try to learn when Herrera would be released. He had come here upon the advice of Arthur Brown, one of the black detectives on the squad.

Brown had said, "Bert, you have shot two men, both of them black. Now every time a cop in this city shoots a black man, you got deep shit. A cop can shoot seventeen honest Chinese merchants sitting in the park minding their own business, no one will even raise an eyebrow. That same cop sees a black man coming out of a bank with a .357 Magnum in his fist, he just stole fifty thousand dollars in cash and he shot the teller and four other people besides, your cop better not shoot that man or there's going to be an outcry. All kinds of accusations, racial discrimination, police brutality, you name it. Now, Bert, I would love to see what would happen if one day I *myself* shot a black man, I would love to see how *that* particular dilemma would be resolved in this city. In the meantime, my friend, you had best get over to that hospital and talk to the man whose brains were getting beat out on that street corner. Get him to back up your word that you were following departmental guidelines for drawing and firing your pistol. That is my advice."

"Go fuck yourself," Herrera told Kling.

The words came out from under the bandages, somewhat muffled, but nonetheless distinct.

Kling blinked.

"I saved your life," he said.

"Who asked you to save it?" Herrera said.

"Those men were . . ."

"Those men are gonna kill me anyways," Herrera said. "All you done . . ."

"I almost got killed *myself!*" Kling said, beginning to get angry. "I lost a goddamn *tooth!*"

"So next time don't butt in."

Kling blinked again.

"That's what I get, huh?" he said. "That's the thanks I get. I save a man's goddamn life . . ."

"You know how much pain I got here?" Herrera asked. "If you'da let them kill me, I wouldn't have no pain now. It's all your fault."

"*My* fault?"

"You, you, who you think? I get outta this hospital, they'll kill me the next minute. Only this time I hope you ain't there. This time I hope they finish the job."

"Nobody's gonna kill you," Kling said. "Only one of them's out on bail . . ."

"How many does it take? You don't know these people," Herrera said. "You got no idea how they operate."

"Tell me all about it."

"Sure. Big fuckin' brave cop, knows everything there is to know. You don't know shit. These people are gonna *kill* me, you understand that?"

"Why?"

"Go ask *them*. You're the big hero, go talk to who you busted. They'll tell you."

"Since I'm here, why don't you just save me the time?" Kling said.

"Go fuck yourself," Herrera said again.

3.

THE LATENT PRINT UNIT reported back on Thursday morning. That very same morning, Meyer and Carella received reports from both the police lab and the Medical Examiner's Office. This had to be some kind of record. The Hat Trick, for sure. Every other detective on the squad was astonished and envious. Cotton Hawes, who was himself working a burglary, asked if he could use the Hodding-Flynn murders as an excuse to get the lab to do some work for *him*. Hawes looked furiously angry when he asked this question, perhaps because he was a huge man with fiery red hair except for a white streak over his left temple where once he'd been knifed. The streak made him look even more furious, like a vengeful bride of Frankenstein. Unintimidated, Willis told him to go find his *own* double murder.

The lab reported that the tool marks found on the fire-escape window and sill in the sixth-floor Unger apartment did not match the tool marks found on the fire-escape window and sill in the fourth-floor Hodding apartment.

The lab reported that the cord attached to the mobile discovered on the floor in the baby's bedroom matched a cord fastened to a hook in the ceiling over the baby's crib. This suggested that the mobile had been torn loose from the ceiling. The mobile was made of tubular metal painted red and blue. It emitted a chime-like sound when one section of it struck any other section. There were no fingerprints on any section of the mobile.

The lab reported that the hairs vacuumed from Annie Flynn's body and clothes were foreign pubic hairs.

The Medical Examiner's Office reported finding fresh seminal fluid in Annie Flynn's vaginal contents.

Had she been resisting rape?

They had not, until this moment and despite the girl's torn blouse, considered the possibility that this might be a rape-murder.

But . . .

The M.E.'s report went on to note that within a few minutes after female orgasm, spermatozoa normally was spread throughout the somewhat alkaline cavities in the uterus and fallopian tubes. The spermatozoic spread at the time of the Flynn autopsy—begun half an hour after the body reached the morgue—had been well-advanced, indicated not only penetration but orgasm as well. Absent orgasm, as was normal in most rape cases, the spread often took as long as six hours. The M.E. was not conclusively ruling out rape. He was merely pointing out that the girl had apparently achieved orgasm. The report further noted that semen samples had been sent to the laboratory for identification and group-typing in the event of later comparison with isoagglutination groups in the blood of the accused—God willing, Meyer thought.

The Latent Print Unit reported that Annie Flynn's fingerprints were the only good ones found on the handle of the knife that had killed her. There were foreign prints as well, but these were too smudged to be useful in a search. Regarding the burglary in the Unger apartment, the unit had done what was called a *cold* search. No suspect's prints against which to compare. No names to check. Nothing but the latents lifted from the Unger window and sill. Find out who had left them there. A cold search on the local level could sometimes take weeks. On the state level, it often took months. Carella had once asked the FBI to do a cold search for him, and they had not come back to him until a year later, after the case had already gone to trial. But on this fifth day of January, the LPU reported that the latents on the Unger window and sill had been left there by a man named Martin Proctor—alias Snake Proctor, alias Mr. Sniff, alias Doctor Proctor—who had a record going back to when he was twelve years old and first arrested for breaking into a candy store in Calm's Point. His B-sheet, as supplied by the Identification Section, filled in the rest.

At the time of his first arrest, Proctor belonged to a street gang called The Red Onions, comprised of daring young bandits between the ages of eleven and fourteen,

all of them with an apparent craving for chocolate.
Snake (as Proctor was then known) had been elected to
break into the candy store and steal a carton containing
a full gross of Hershey bars—with almonds, the president of The Red Onions S.A.C. had specified. The
S.A.C. stood for Social and Athletic Club, a euphemism
most street gangs affected.

The cop on the beat had caught him coming out of
the back of the store. Snake had grinned and said, "Hi,
want a Hershey bar?" The arresting officer had not
found this comical. The judge, however, thought
Snake's casual remark indicated a good sense of humor,
which he felt was the prime requisite for making a
worthwhile contribution to society. He let Snake off
with a warning.

First mistake.

Six months later, Snake . . .

He was called Snake, by the way, because there was a
python tattooed on his left biceps, beneath which, lettered in blue, were the words LIVE FREE OR DIE, the
motto for the state of New Hampshire, though by all
indications he had never been there.

Six months later, Snake was arrested for a jewelry
store smash-and-grab and this time the judge was a
lady who frowned upon such activities even if they net-
ted only a pair of eighteen-karat-gold wedding bands
and a digital wristwatch selling for $42.95. Snake, a
juvenile offender, was sent to a juvenile detention facility upstate, from which he was released at the age of
fourteen. By then, he had learned how to do cocaine,
which for a price was readily available at the facility,

and had acquired the name "Mr. Sniff," which was a *nick*name as opposed to the earlier "Snake," which had been a *street* name. The new name was apparently premised on Mr. Sniff's insatiable need for sucking up into his nostrils however much cocaine he could purchase or steal.

Drugs and stealing go together like bagels and lox.

Your white collar drug users may not necessarily be thieves, but down in the streets, baby, your user is a hundred times out of a hundred stealing to support his habit.

Over the years, Proctor managed to avoid imprisonment again until he was nineteen years old and got caught red-handed inside somebody's house in the nighttime. Burglary One, for sure, in that the dwelling was also occupied and Proctor threatened the person with a gun, little knowing the house was wired with a silent alarm, and all of a sudden two cops were on him with guns bigger than his own, so goodbye, Charlie. A Class B felony this time. State penitentiary this time. Big time this time. The D.A. flatly refused to let Proctor cop a plea—well, why the hell should he? They had the man cold. But the court sentenced him to only half the max, and he'd been paroled from Castleview two years ago, after having served a third of his term.

The name "Doctor Proctor" had been acquired in prison.

Proctor had a habit as long as the Pacific Coast Highway. Every thief in the world knew that Castleview was as tight as a virgin's asshole. You wanted to cure a dope habit, you got yourself sent to Castleview because, man, there was no way of getting even a shred of grass inside there. Unless you were Doctor Proctor.

No one knew how he did it.

It had to be some kind of miracle.

But if you were hurting, baby, Doctor Proctor could fix you. If you needed what you needed, Doctor Proctor could get it for you. Always ready to help a friend in need, that was Doctor Proctor. A confirmed junkie, and a prison dope dealer. But none of that mattered. He had a *title* now, which was better than either a nickname *or* a street name. Doctor Proctor. Who for the past two years had been on the streets again. Apparently doing burglaries again. Or perhaps worse.

His mug shot showed a round clean-shaven face, dark eyes, short blond hair.

The Ungers had described him as thin and blond and growing a mustache.

The date of birth on his records made him twenty-four last October.

The Ungers had said he was eighteen, nineteen.

The last address his parole officer had for him was 1146 Park Street, in Calm's Point. But he had long ago violated parole, probably figuring if he was going to go back to work at his old trade it certainly didn't pay to waste time with parole-officer appointments. If a man was going to break parole by stealing, then why check in with the P.O.? If he got caught stealing, he'd go back to prison anyway. Besides, he wasn't going to *get* caught.

No criminal ever thinks he's going to get caught. Only the *other* guy gets caught. Even criminals who've already been caught and sent to prison believe they won't get caught the next time. The reason they got caught the first time was they made a little mistake. The next time, they wouldn't make any mistakes. They would never get caught again. They would never do time again.

It never occurred to a criminal that a sure way to avoid doing time was to find an honest job. But why should a man take a job paying $3.95 an hour when he could go into a grocery store with a gun and steal four thousand dollars from the cash register! Four fucking thousand dollars! For ten minutes' work! Unless he got caught. If he got caught, he'd be sent up for thirty years, and when you divided the four grand by thirty, you got two hundred a year. And when you broke that down to a forty-hour week for every week in the year, you saw that the man had earned a bit more than six cents an hour for his big holdup.

Terrific.

He marches in there with a big macho gun in his big macho fist, and he scares the shit out of Mom and Pop behind the counter, and he never once thinks, not for a minute, that what he's doing is betting thirty years against that money in the cash register—which, by the way, might turn out to be *four* dollars instead of four *thousand.*

Smart.

But who says criminals have to be brilliant?

And, anyway, he's not going to get caught.

But even if he does get caught, even if he does make another teeny-weeny little tiny mistake the second time around, and even if the judge throws the book at him because now he's a habitual criminal, he can do the time standing on his head, right? The Castleview Penitentiary S.A.C. Lots of old buddies from the street in there. Hey, Jase! How ya doin', Blood? Lift a lot of weights in there. Shoot the shit in the Yard. Get some fish in the gym to suck your cock, your buddies standing watch and then taking their turns. Send away for correspondence courses can make you a lawyer or a judge. Shit, man, you can do the time with one hand tied behind your back.

The signs tacked up in every police precinct in this city read:

> If you can't do the
> TIME—
> Don't do the
> CRIME!

Criminals laughed at those signs.

Those signs were for amateurs.

Martin Proctor had been to prison and enjoyed it very much, thanks, and he was out again, and had at least burglarized one apartment on New Year's Eve, and perhaps done something more serious than that. But the cops had an address for him. And when you had an address, that was where you started. And sometimes you got lucky.

1146 Park was in a section of Calm's Point that had once been middle-class Jewish, had gone from there to middle-class Hispanic, and was now an area of mostly abandoned tenements sparsely populated by junkies of every persuasion and color. Nobody in the building had ever heard of anyone named Proctor—Martin, Snake, Mr. Sniff or even Doctor.

Sometimes you got lucky, but not too often.

"I SHOULD BE in Florida right this minute," Fats Donner said.

He was talking to Hal Willis.

Willis had dealt with him on many a previous occasion. Willis did not like him at all. Neither did any of the cops on the Eight-Seven. That was because Donner had a penchant for young girls. In the ten- or eleven-year-old age bracket; for Donner these days, twelve was a little long in the tooth. Willis was here only because he'd worked with Donner more often than had any other cop on the squad. Donner, being such an expert ear, might have heard something about Proctor's recent whereabouts, no?

"No," Donner said.

"Think," Willis said.

"I already thought. I don't know anybody named Martin Proctor."

Donner was a giant of a man, fat in the plural, fat in the extreme, Fats for sure, an obese hulk who sat in a faded blue bathrobe, his complexion as pale as the January sky outside, his fat hairless legs resting on a hassock, one obscenely plump hand plucking dates from a basket on the end table beside his easy chair, the hand moving to his mouth, his thick lips sucking the meat off the pit. Standing beside him, Willis—who was short by any standards—looked almost tiny.

"Doctor Proctor," he said.

"No," Donner said.

"Mr. Sniff."

"Four hundred people named Mr. Sniff in this city, you kidding?"

"Snake."

"*Eight* hundred Snakes. Give me something easy like Rambo."

He smiled. He was making a joke. Rambo was another popular name. A piece of date clung to his front upper teeth, making it look as if one of them was missing. Willis really hated being in his presence.

"It's your burglary," Carella had told him.

"You've worked with him before," Meyer had said.

And was working with him again now.

Or trying to.

"You think you can listen around?" he asked.

"No," Donner said. "I think I can go to Florida. It's too fucking cold here now."

"It's cold in Florida, too," Willis said. "But it can get hot both places."

"Oh, look, Maude," Donner said to the air, "here comes the rubber hose."

They both knew that the only reason an informer cooperated with the police was that the police had something on him that they were willing to forget temporarily. In Donner's case, the something wasn't child abuse. No cop in this city was willing to forget child abuse, even temporarily. Dope, yes. Murder, sometimes. But child abuse, never. There was a criminal adage to the effect that the only thing you couldn't fix in this city was a short-eyes rap.

The main thing the police had on Donner was the long-ago murder of a pimp. The way the police looked at it, the city was better off without pimps in general, but this did not mean that they could condone murder. Oh, no. They had the goods on Donner and could have sent him to prison for a good long time. Where there were no girls, by the way. Young or otherwise. But the cops chose to work this one six ways from the middle. They didn't give a damn that the city had lost another pimp. And they wouldn't have minded sending Donner up for the crime. But they figured there were other ways to make him pay for what he'd done.

A tacit deal was struck, no handshakes sealing the bargain—you did not shake hands with murderers and especially not with child abusers—not a single word spoken, but from that day forward Donner knew he was in the vest pocket of any cop who wanted him, and the cops knew that Donner for all his bullshit would deliver or else.

Willis merely looked at him.

"You got a picture of him?" Donner asked.

THIS IS the way it worked.

A hearing-impaired person like Teddy Carella—who'd been deaf since birth and who had never uttered a single word in her entire life—had finally and reluctantly been convinced by her husband to purchase and have installed one of these newfangled gadgets that had only been on the market for the past God knew how long. The gadget she'd resisted all this time—

Listen, I'm an old-fashioned girl, she'd signed with her hands and mimed with her face.

—was called a Telecommunication Device for the Deaf and was known in the trade as a TDD.

It looked like a typewriter that had married a telephone and given birth to a character display and an adding machine. When the TDD was in use, a telephone rested at the very top of the unit, where two soft, molded cups were shaped to fit the handset. Between these was a roll of paper some two and a quarter inches wide, upon which printed messages appeared in upper-case type. Beneath this, and running horizontally across the face of the unit, was the display line. Twenty-character display. Blue-green vacuum fluorescent illumination. Half-inch character height. Angled so it could be read from above. Just under the display screen was a forty-five key, four-row keyboard with almost the same lettering layout as on a typewriter.

State of the art was not yet able to translate voice to type or vice versa. This would have made things simple indeed for any hearing- or speech-impaired person in the world. But, listen, it was simple enough the way it was. In the Carella house, there was a TDD on the kitchen counter under the wall phone. On Carella's desk at the office, there was an identical TDD alongside *his* phone. Either of the telephones could be used for normal use, but when Teddy—or any other hearing-impaired person, for that matter—wished to make a call, she first turned the TDD power switch on, placed the handset of her phone onto the acoustic cups, waited for the steady red light that told her she had a dial tone, and then dialed the number she wanted. A slow-flashing red light on the unit told her the phone was ringing. A fast-flashing red light told her the line was busy.

Whenever the phone on Carella's desk rang, he picked up and said "Eighty-seventh Squad, Carella." If the call was from a hearing, speaking person, the conversation continued as it normally would. But if this was Teddy calling—as it was at three o'clock that afternoon, while Willis was mildly intimidating Fats Donner—Carella would hear beeping that sounded like a very rapid diddle-ee-dee. This was caused by Teddy repeatedly hitting the space bar on her machine to let the person on the other end know this was a hearing-impaired caller.

If Carella had been calling *her*, a master ring-signal jacketed to the telephone line and linked to remote receivers throughout the house would flash lamps in several different rooms, letting Teddy know the phone was ringing. A similar device told her when someone was ringing the doorbell. But meanwhile, back at the Eight-Seven Corral, when Carella heard that rapid beeping—as he did now—he immediately knew it was Teddy calling, and he cradled the handset of his phone onto the TDD, and switched on the power, and by golly Moses, what you got was two people talking!

Or, to be more exact, two people typing.

HI HON, he typed, GA.

The words appeared on both his display line and the

one Teddy was watching at her kitchen counter all the way up in Riverhead. It was magic. Moreover, a printer on each machine simultaneously printed out the message on the roll of paper. GA was the abbreviation for Go Ahead. On many TDD units—as was the case with theirs—a separate GA key was on the right-hand side of the keyboard. To save time, TDD users often abbreviated commonly used words or expressions.

Teddy typed HI SWEETIE HV U GOT A MIN GA.

Carella typed FOR U I HV HRS GA.

RMBR BERT/EILEEN TONITE, Teddy typed, GA.

Carella typed YES 8 O'CLOCK GA.

PLS WEAR TIES, Teddy typed, GA.

They continued talking for the next several moments. When Carella pulled the printout from the machine later, the twenty-character lines looked like this:

```
HI  HON  GA  HI  SWEETIE
HV  U  GOT  A  MIN  GA  FO
R  U  I  HV  HRS  GA  RMBR
BERT/EILEEN   TONITE   G
A  YES  8  O'CLOCK  GA  PL
S   WEAR   TIES   GA   I'LL
TELL  BERT  HV  TO  GO  N
OW  SEE  YOU  LTR  LUV  Y
OU  SK  LUV  YOU  TOO  SK
SK
```

The letters SK were also on a separate key. SK meant Signing Off.

They were both smiling.

* * *

PETER HODDING hadn't gone back to work yet.

"I don't think I could stand looking into people's eyes," he told Carella. "Knowing they know what happened. I had a hard enough time at the funeral."

Carella listened.

The sky outside was darkening rapidly, but the Hoddings had not yet turned on the lights. The room was succumbing to shadows. They sat on the living room couch opposite Carella. Hodding was wearing jeans, a white button-down shirt, a cardigan sweater. His wife Gayle was wearing a wide skirt, a bulky sweater, brown boots.

"He'll go back on Monday," she said.

"Maybe," Hodding said.

"We have to go on," she said, as if to herself.

"I wonder if you can tell me," Carella said, "whether Annie Flynn ever mentioned a boy named Scott Handler."

"Gayle?" Hodding said.

"No, she never mentioned anyone by that name."

"Not to me, either," Hodding said.

Carella nodded.

He and Meyer were eager to talk to the Handler boy—if they could find him. But where the hell was he? And why had he fled? Carella did not tell the Hoddings that they'd been looking for the boy for the past two days. There was no sense in building false hopes and even less sense in implicating someone before they'd even talked to him.

Gayle Hodding was telling him how strange life was.

"You make plans, you . . ."

She shook her head.

Carella waited. He was very good at waiting. He sometimes felt that ninety percent of detective work was waiting and listening. The other ten percent was luck or coincidence.

"I quit college in my junior year," she said, "oh, this was seven, eight years ago, I went into modeling."

"She was a very good model," Hodding said.

Carella was thinking she still had the good cheekbones, the slender figure. He wondered if she knew Augusta Kling, Bert's former wife. He did not ask her if she did.

"Anyway," she said, "about a year and a half ago, I decided to go back to school. Last September a year ago. How long is that, Peter?"

"Sixteen months."

"Yes," she said, "sixteen months. And I was about to enroll for the new semester in September when the agency called and my whole life changed again."

"The modeling agency?" Carella said.

"No, no, the adoption agency."

He looked at her.

"Susan was adopted," she said.

"I'd better put some lights on in here," Hodding said.

HE'D HAD TO come down from the roof.

Security in the building, he knew this, twenty-four-hour doorman, elevator operator, no way to get in unobserved through the front door. You had to do gymnastics. Go up on the roof of the connecting building, no security there after midnight, go right on up in the elevator, break the lock on the roof door, cross the roof and climb over the parapet to the building you wanted, 967 Grover.

Down the fire escapes.

Past windows where you could see people still partying, having a good time. He'd ducked low on each landing, sidling past the lighted windows. Counting the floors. Eighteen floors in the building, he knew which window he wanted, a long way down.

Fourth-floor rear.

He'd eased the window open.

The baby's bedroom.

He knew this.

Dark except for a shaft of light spilling through the open doorway from somewhere else in the apartment. The living room. Silence. He could hear the baby's soft, gentle breathing. Two o'clock in the morning. The baby asleep.

The master bedroom was at the other end of the apartment.

He knew this.

In the middle, separating the sleeping wings, were the kitchen, the dining room, and the living room.

He leaned in over the crib.

Everything changed in the next several seconds.

In the next several seconds, the baby was screaming.

And a voice came from the living room.

"Who is it?"

Silence.

"Who's there?"

More silence.

And suddenly there she was. Standing there. Standing in the door to the baby's room, a knife in her hand.

He had to go for the knife.

4.

OSTENSIBLY, Kling was eating and enjoying the cannelloni on his plate while listening to Carella tell him about the several approaches he and Meyer were taking to the Hodding-Flynn murders. But he caught only snatches of what Carella was telling him. His mind and his ears were on what Eileen was saying to Teddy.

He had never heard her so bitter.

They sat on opposite sides of the round table.

Eileen with her red hair and her green eyes, blazing now, her hands flying all over the place as the words tumbled from her mouth.

Teddy listening, her head cocked to one side, dark hair falling over one cheek, brown eyes open wide and intently watching Eileen's mouth.

". . . find this Handler kid," Carella was saying, "then maybe we can . . ."

"And your cop comes home at last," Eileen said, "and he's watching television after a long, hard day of dealing with a wide variety of victimizers, and he sees a news broadcast about the rioting in this or that prison wherever in the United States, and the convicts are saying the food's terrible and there aren't enough television sets and the equipment in the gymnasium is obsolete, and the cells are overcrowded, and you know what that cop *thinks,* Teddy?"

From the corner of his eye, Kling saw Teddy shake her head.

". . . cause why would he have run if he hasn't got something to hide?" Carella asked. "On the other hand . . ."

"That cop sits there shaking his head," Eileen said, "because *he* knows how to rid the streets of crime, man, *he* knows how to make sure the guy he arrested two years ago isn't out there again right this minute doing the same damn thing all over again, *he* knows *exactly* how to get kids thinking that serving up burgers at a drive-in is more attractive than a life of criminal adventure—and, by the way, the answer isn't Just Say No. That's bullshit, Teddy, Just Say No. That lays the guilt trip on the *victim,* don't you see? If only you'd have said No, why then you wouldn't have got addicted to heroin, and you wouldn't have been molested by some weirdo in the street . . .

Here it comes, Kling thought.

". . . and you wouldn't have been raped or murdered, either. All you have to do is just say no. Have a little willpower and nobody'll hurt you. Where the hell does Mrs. Reagan live? On the moon? Did she think the streets of America were in Disneyland? Did she think all it ever came to was politely saying No, thank you, I've already had some, thank you? I'm telling you, Teddy, someone should have just curtsied and said no to *her,* told her that cute little slogan of hers *sucked,* lady, that just isn't the way it is."

Teddy Carella sat there listening, wide-eyed.

Knowing.

Realizing that Eileen was talking about her *own* rape. The time she'd got cut. The time she'd said *Yes.* Because if she'd have said No, he'd have cut her again. Just say no, my ass.

"Every cop in this city knows how to keep criminals off the street," Eileen said. "You want to know the answer?"

And now she had Carella's attention, too.

He turned to her, fork in mid-air.

"Make the time impossible to do," Eileen said. "Make *all* time *hard* time. Make it back-breaking time and mind-numbing time. Make it senseless, wasted time. Make it the kind of time where you carry a two-hundred-pound boulder from point A to point B and then back to point A again, over and over again, all day long, day in and day out, with no parole, Charlie."

"No parole?" Carella said, and raised his eyebrows.

"Ever," Eileen said flatly. "You catch the time, you *do* the time. And it's hard, mean time. You want to be hard and mean? Good. Do your hard, mean time. We're not here to teach you an honest job. There are plenty of honest jobs, you should've found one *before* you got busted. We're here to tell you it doesn't pay to do what you did, what*ever* you did. You wouldn't be here if you hadn't done something uncivilized, and so we're going to treat you like the barbarian you are."

"I'm not sure that would . . ."

But Eileen was just gathering steam, and she cut Carella off mid-sentence.

"You want to go out and do another crime after you've served your time? Good, go do it. But don't let us catch you. Because if we catch you for the same crime again, or a different crime, what*ever* crime you do, why, the next time you're going to do even *harder* time. You are going to come out of that prison and you are going to tell all your pals on the street that it doesn't pay to do whatever illegal thing they're thinking of doing. Because there's nothing funny or easy about the kind of time you're going to do in any slammer in the country, you are going to do hard, hard time, mister. You are going to carry this ten-thousand-pound rock back and forth all day long, and then you are going to eat food you wouldn't give a *dog* to eat, and there'll be no television, and no radio, and no gym to work out in, and you can't have visitors and you're not allowed to write letters or make phone calls, all you can do is carry that goddamn rock back and forth and eat that rotten food and sleep in a cell on a bed without a mattress and a toilet bowl without a seat. And then maybe you'll learn. Maybe once and for all you'll *learn.*"

She nodded for emphasis.

Her eyes were shooting green laser beams.

Carella knew better than to say anything.

"There isn't a cop in this city who wouldn't make prison something to *dread,*" she said.

Carella said nothing.

"Mention the word prison, criminals all over this city would start shaking. Mention the word prison, every criminal in the United States would just say *no*, Mrs. Reagan! No! Not *me!* Please! Do it to Julia! Please!"

She looked at Carella and Kling.

Daring either of them to say a word.

And then she turned to Teddy, and her voice lowered almost to a whisper.

"If cops had their way," she said.

There were tears in her eyes.

ON HER DOORSTEP Eileen said, "I'm sorry."

"That's okay," Kling said.

"I spoiled it for everyone," she said.

"The food was lousy anyway," he said.

Somewhere in the building, a baby began crying.

"I think we ought to stop seeing each other," she said.

"I don't think that's such a good idea."

The baby kept crying. Kling wished someone would go pick it up. Or change its diaper. Or feed it. Or do whatever the hell needed to be done to it.

"I went to see somebody at Pizzaz," Eileen said.

He looked at her, surprised. Pizzaz was the way the cops in this city pronounced PSAS, which initials stood for the department's Psychological Services and Aid Section. Calling it Pizzaz gave it a trendy sound. Made it sound like the In thing to do. Took the curse off psychiatric assistance, which no cop liked to admit he needed. Psychiatric assistance often led to a cop losing his gun, something he dreaded. Take away a cop's gun, you were putting him out to pasture. The Tom-Tom Squad. Indians with bows and arrows, no guns.

"Uh-huh," Kling said.

"Saw a woman named Karin Lefkowitz."

"Uh-huh."

"She's a psychologist. There's a pecking order, you know."

"Yes."

"I'll be seeing her twice a week. Whenever she can fit me in."

"Okay."

"Which is why I thought you and I . . ."

"No."

"Just until I get my act together again."

"Did *she* suggest this?"

He was already beginning to hate Karin Lefkowitz.

"No. It's entirely my idea."

"Well, it's a lousy idea."

"I don't think so."

"I do."

Eileen sighed.

"I wish somebody would pick up that fucking baby," Kling said.

"So," Eileen said, and reached into her bag for her key. He could see the butt of her revolver in the bag. Still a cop. But she didn't think so.

"So what I'd like to do," she said, "if it's okay with you . . ."

"No, it's not okay with me."

"Well, I'm really sorry about that, Bert, but this is *my* life we're talking about here."

"It's my life, too."

"You're not drowning," she said.

She put her key into the latch.

"So . . . let me call you when I'm ready, okay?" she said.

"Eileen . . ."

She turned the key.

"Good night, Bert," she said, and went into the apartment. And closed the door behind her. He heard the lock being turned, the tumblers falling with a small oiled click. He stood in the hallway for several moments, looking at the closed door and the numerals 304 on it. A screw in the 4 was loose. It hung slightly askew.

He went downstairs.

The night was very cold.

He looked at his watch. Ten minutes to ten. He wasn't due at the squadroom until a quarter to twelve.

"WHAT I THINK you should do," Lorraine said, "is go to the police."

"No," he said.

"Before *they* come to you."

"No."

"Because, Scott, it looks very bad this way. It really does."

Lorraine Greer was twenty-seven years old. She had long black hair and a complexion as pale as moonstone.

She claimed she had violet-colored eyes like Elizabeth Taylor's, but she knew they were really only a sort of bluish-gray. She affected very dark lipstick that looked like dried blood on her lips. She had good breasts and good legs, and she wore funky clothes that revealed them to good advantage. The colors she favored were red and yellow and green. She dressed like a tree just starting to turn in the fall. She figured this leggy, busty, somewhat tatterdemalion look would immediately identify her once she became a rock star.

Her father, who was an accountant, told her there were *thousands* of busty, leggy girls in this country. *Millions* of them all over the world. All of them dressed in rags. All of them thinking they could be rock stars if only they got a break. Her father told her to become a legal secretary. Legal secretaries made good money, he said. Lorraine told him she was going to be a rock star. She'd never had any formal musical training, that was true, but he had to admit she had a good singing voice and besides she'd written hundreds of songs. The lyrics to them, anyway. Usually she worked with a partner who put music to her words. She was writing songs all the time, with this or that partner. She knew the songs were good. Even her father thought some of the songs were pretty good, maybe.

Years ago, she'd been Scott Handler's baby-sitter.

She'd been fifteen, he'd been six. That was the age difference between them. Nine years. She used to sing him to sleep with lullabies she herself wrote. The lyrics, anyway. At that time her partner used to be a girl she knew from high school. Sylvia Antonelli, who when she was nineteen years old married a man who owned a plumbing supply house. Sylvia now had three children and two fur coats and she lived in a big Tudor-style house. She never wrote songs anymore.

Lorraine's partner nowadays was a woman who'd been in *Chorus Line*. On Broadway, not one of the road companies. She'd played the Puerto Rican girl, whatever her name was, the one who sang about the teacher at Music and Art. Be a snowflake, remember? Gonzalez? Something like that. She wrote beautiful music. She wasn't Puerto Rican, she was in fact Jewish. Very dark. Black hair, brown eyes, she could pass easily for Puerto Rican, Lorraine could visualize her in the part. She had also played one of Tevye's daughters in a dinner-theater production of *Fiddler*. In Florida someplace. But her heart was in writing songs, not in singing or dancing. She was the one who'd told Lorraine she was robbing the cradle here. Starting up with a kid nine years younger than she was. Lorraine had merely shrugged. This was only last week.

He'd come to her a few days after Christmas.

She was living in an apartment downtown in the Quarter. Her father paid the rent, but he kept warning her that pretty soon he'd turn off the money tap. She knew he didn't mean it; she was the apple of his eye. She'd once written a song, in fact, called "Apple of My Eye," which she'd dedicated to her father. Rebecca— that was her new partner's name, Rebecca Simms, née Saperstein—had written a beautiful tune to go with Lorraine's lyrics.

Apple of my eye . . .
Lovely child of yesterday . . .
Little sleepy eye.

Hear my lullaby . . .
Sleepy girl as bright as May . . .
Little lullaby.

And so on.

The song brought tears to Lorraine's eyes whenever she sang it. Rebecca thought it was one of their better efforts, though her personal favorite was a feminist song they'd written called "Burn," in which Joan of Arc was the central metaphor. Rebecca wore her dark hair in a whiffle cut. Sometimes, Lorraine wondered if she was gay. She'd seemed inordinately angry about Scott moving in.

Lorraine hadn't expected to go to bed with Scott.

He'd just shown up on her doorstep, his eyes all red, his face white, she'd thought at first it was from the cold outside. He told her he'd got her address from her father, who'd remembered when she used to baby-sit for him, and she'd said Oh sure, that's okay, come on in, how are you? She hadn't seen him now in it must have been three, four years. Since he'd gone off to school in Maine. He'd looked like a kid then. Pimply-faced, lanky, you know. Now he looked like . . . well . . . a man. She was really surprised by how handsome he'd turned out. But of course he was still a kid.

He told her he remembered how he used to tell her everything when he used to sit for him, how he used to trust her more than he had his own parents.

She said, "Well, that's very nice of you, Scott."

"I mean it," he said.

"Thank you, that's very nice of you."

She was wearing a short red skirt with red tights and yellow leg warmers. Short, soft, black leather boots. She was wearing a green blouse, no bra. She was sitting on the couch, long legs tucked under her. She had offered him a drink, which he'd accepted. Apple brandy. Which was all she had in the house. He was on his third snifterful. The snifters were a birthday gift from Rebecca. This was the twenty-eighth day of December. It was very cold outside. Wind rattled the windows in the small apartment. She was remembering how she used to take him to the toilet in his Dr. Denton's. Hold his little penis while he peed. Sometimes he had a little hard-on. Six years old, he'd have a little hard-on, he'd piss all over the toilet tank, sometimes the wall. She was remembering this fondly.

He told her this girl he'd been going with had suddenly ended their relationship. She thought this was cute, his using a very grown-up word like relationship. But, of course, he was eighteen. Eighteen was a man. At eighteen, you could vote. When he was home for Thanksgiving, he said. Some Thanksgiving present, huh? She wondered if people exchanged gifts for Thanksgiving. Maybe the Indians and the Pilgrims had. She wondered if there was an idea for a song in that. He was telling her the girl had made it final last week. He'd gone over to see her the minute he'd got home for the Christmas break. She'd told him she never wanted to see him again. He'd been crying for the past week,

well, actually nine days now. She hoped he didn't think
he was a baby, coming here like this. And then he
started crying again.

She'd held him in her arms.

The way she'd done when he was six and she was fifteen and he woke up crying in the middle of the night.

She'd kissed the top of his head.

Comforting him.

And next thing she knew . . .

Well, one thing just sort of led to another.

His hands were all over her.

Under the short red skirt, down the front of the
green silk blouse.

Christmas colors.

Falling away under his rough, manly hands.

That was on the twenty-eighth.

He'd been living here since. Today was the sixth of
January. Not five minutes ago, he'd told her what he'd
said to Annie the last time he'd seen her. Annie Flynn,
that was the girl's name. About killing them both. Annie
and her new boyfriend, whoever he was. And now someone had *really* killed Annie and he was afraid the police
might think it was him.

"Which is why you have to go to them," she said.

"No," he said.

Nibbling at his lower lip. Handsome as the devil. She
got damp just looking at him. Wanted him desperately,
just looking at him. She wondered if he knew what
effect he had on her.

"Unless, of course, you *did* kill her," she said.

"No, no," he said.

He wasn't looking at her.

"*Did* you?" she asked again.

"I told you no."

But he still wasn't looking at her.

She went to him.

Twisted her hand in his hair. Pulled his head back.

"Tell me the truth," she said.

"I didn't kill her," he said.

She brought her mouth down to his. God, such sweet lips. She kissed him fiercely.

And wondered if he was telling the truth.

Somehow, the idea was exciting.

That maybe he *had* killed that girl.

JOSÉ HERRERA was sitting on a bench in the second-floor corridor when Kling came in that night. Head still bandaged, face still puffy and bruised, right arm in a cast.

"*Buenas noches,*" he said, and grinned like one of the Mexican bandits in *Treasure of the Sierra Madre*. Kling wanted to go hide the silver.

"You waiting for *me?*" Kling asked.

"Who else?" Herrera said. Still grinning. Kling wanted to punch him right in the mouth—for the way he was grinning, for the way he'd behaved at the hospital the other day. Finish off what those black guys had started. He went to the railing, opened the gate, and walked into the squadroom. Herrera came in behind him.

Kling went to his desk and sat.

Herrera came over and took a chair alongside the desk.

"My head still hurts," he said.

"Good," Kling said.

Herrera clucked his tongue.

"What do you want here?" Kling asked.

"They let me out this afternoon," Herrera said. "I think they let me out too soon, I may sue them."

"Good, go sue them."

"I think I may have a good case. My head still hurts."

Kling glanced at a Ballistics report he had requested on a shooting that had taken place during the four-to-midnight on Christmas Eve. A family dispute. Man shot his own brother on Christmas Eve.

"I decided to help you," Herrera said.

"Thanks, I don't need your help," Kling said.

"You told me at the hospital . . ."

"That was then, this is now."

"I can get you a big drug bust," Herrera said, lowering his voice conspiratorially, glancing over to where Andy Parker was on the telephone at his own desk.

"I don't *want* a big drug bust," Kling said.

"These guys who were trying to dust me? I'll bet you thought they were just regular niggers, am I right? Wrong. They were Jamaicans."

"So?"

"You familiar with Jamaican posses?"

"Yes," Kling said.

"You are?"

"Yes."

The Jamaican gangs called themselves posses, God knew why, since traditionally a posse was a group of people deputized by a sheriff to assist in *preserving* the public peace. Kling figured a little bit of Orwellian doublethink was in play here. If War was Peace, then surely Bad Guys could be Good Guys and a Gang could be a Posse, no? The Jamaicans couldn't even pronounce the word correctly. Rhyming it with Lassie, they called it passee. Then again, when they wanted to say "man," they said "mon." Either way, mon, they would break your head as soon as look at you. Which they had successfully but not fatally done to Herrera.

And now he was ready to blow the whistle.

Or so it seemed.

"We're talking here a posse that's maybe the biggest one in America," he said.

"Right here in our own little precinct, huh?" Kling said.

"Bigger than Spangler."

"Uh-huh."

"Bigger than Waterhouse."

"Uh-huh."

"You know Shower?"

"I know Shower."

"Bigger even than Shower," Herrera said. "I'm talking about dope, white slavery, and gun-running. Which this posse is muscling in on all over the city."

"Uh-huh," Kling said.

"I'm talking about a big dope deal about to go down."

"Really? Where?"

"Right here in this precinct."

"So what's this big posse called?"

"Not so fast," Herrera said.

"If you've got something to tell me, tell me," Kling said. "You're the one who came here, I didn't come knocking on your door."

"You're the one who wanted me to back your story about . . ."

"That's a thing of the past. They're convinced downtown that I acted within the . . ."

"Anyway, it don't matter. You owe me."

Kling looked at him.

"*I* owe *you?*" he said.

"Correct."

"For what?"

"For saving my life."

"*I* owe *you* for saving *your* life?"

"Is what I said."

"I think those baseball bats scrambled your brains, Herrera. If I'm hearing you correctly . . ."

"You're hearing me. You owe me."

"What do I owe you?"

"Protection. And I'm not gonna let you forget it."

"Why don't you take a walk?" Kling said, and picked up the Ballistics report.

"I ain't even talking cultures," Herrera said.

"That's good, 'cause I'm not even listening."

"Where if you save a person's life, you are responsible for that person's life forever."

"And which cultures might those be?" Kling asked.

"Certain Asian cultures."

"Like which?"

"Or North American Indian, I'm not sure."

"Uh-huh," Kling said. "But not Hispanic."

"No, not Hispanic."

"You're just muscling in on these cultures, correct? The way this Jamaican posse is muscling in on dope and prosti . . ."

"I told you I *ain't* talking cultures here."

"Then what the fuck *are* you talking, Herrera? You're wasting my time here."

"I'm talking human decency and responsibility," Herrera said.

"Oh, dear God, spare me," Kling said, and rolled his eyes heavenward.

"Because if you hadn't stopped them Jakies . . ."

"Jakies?"

"Them Jamaicans."

Kling had never heard this expression before. He had the feeling Herrera had just made it up. The way he'd made up his cockamamie Asian or North American Indian cultures that held a man responsible for saving another man's life.

"If you'd have let them Jakies kill me," Herrera said, "then I wouldn't have to be worrying they would kill me now."

"Makes perfect sense," Kling said, shaking his head.

"Of course it makes sense."

"Of course."

"This way I'll probably have a nervous breakdown. Waiting for them to kill me all over again. You want me to have a nervous breakdown?"

"I think you already had one," Kling said.

"You want them Jakies to kill me?" Herrera asked.

"No," Kling said honestly. If he'd wanted them to

kill Herrera, he'd have let them do it the first time around. Instead of getting a tooth knocked out of his mouth. Which he still hadn't gone to the dentist to see about.

"Good, I'm glad you realize you owe me," Herrera said.

Kling was neither a Buddhist monk nor a Hindu priest nor an Indian shaman; he didn't think he owed Herrera a goddamn thing.

But if a strong Jamaican posse really *was* about to do a big dope deal right here in the precinct . . .

"Let's say I do offer you protection," he said.

5.

THE ORIENTAL GANGS in this city had difficulty pronouncing his name, which was Lewis Randolph Hamilton. Too many L's and too many R's. The Hispanic gangs called him *Luis El Martillo.* Which meant Louie the Hammer. This did not mean that his weapon was a hammer. Hamilton was strapped with a .357 Magnum, which he used liberally and indiscriminately. It was said that he had personally committed twenty-three murders during his several years in the States. The Italian gangs called him *Il Camaleonte,* which meant The Chameleon. That was because hardly anyone knew what he looked like. Or at least what he looked like *now.*

There were Miami P.D. mug shots of Hamilton wearing his hair in an exaggerated Afro, mustache on his upper lip. There were Houston P.D. pictures of Hamilton wearing his hair in Rastafarian style, so that he looked like a male Medusa. There were N.Y.P.D. pictures of him with his hair cut extremely short, hugging his skull like a woolly black cap. There were L.A.P.D.

pictures of him with a thick beard. But here in this city, there were no police photographs of Lewis Randolph Hamilton. That was because he'd never been arrested here. He'd killed eight people here, and the underworld knew this, and the police suspected it, but Hamilton was like smoke. In Jamaica, as a matter of fact, he had for a number of years been called Smoke, a name premised on his ability to drift away and vanish without a trace.

Hamilton's posse was into everything.

Prostitution. Exclusively Mafia in the recent dead past, increasingly Chinese ever since a pair of lovely sisters named Tina and Toni Pao moved from Hong Kong to San Francisco and began smuggling in girls from Taiwan via Guatemala and Mexico, their operation expanding eastward across the United States until it was now fully entrenched and—because of its local-tong and overseas-triad connections—virtually untouchable here in this city. Hamilton had discovered the enormous profits to be made in peddling ass on carefully selected, police-protected street corners. Nothing high-class here. No Mayflower Madam shit. Just a horde of young, drug-addicted girls standing out in the cold wearing nothing but *Penthouse* lingerie.

Gun-running. The Hispanics were very big on this. Maybe because, like cab drivers coming back from the airport, they didn't like to ride deadhead. Bring up a load of Colombian coke, you didn't want that ship going back empty. So you filled it with guns—high-powered handguns, automatic rifles, machine guns—which you then sold at an enormous profit in the

Caribbean. Hamilton already knew how to bring up the dope. He was now learning—way too damn fast to suit the Hispanics—how to send down stolen guns.

And, of course, drugs.

Unless a gang—*any* gang, any nationality, any color—dealt drugs, then it wasn't a gang, it was a ladies' sewing circle. Hamilton's posse was heavily into dope. With enough weaponry to invade Beirut.

All of this was why the slants, the spics and the wops wanted him dusted.

Which amused Hamilton. All those contracts out on him. If they didn't know what he looked like, how could they reach him? Unless one of his own people turned, there wasn't no way anybody could be out there squatting for him. All highly amusing. Their dumb gang shit. Contracts. What was he, a kid playing in the mud outside a shack? The concept of a Hollywood hood with a broken nose looking high and low for him made him laugh.

But not today.

Today he wasn't laughing.

Today he was annoyed by the way three of his people had mishandled the José Herrera thing.

"Why baseball bats?" he asked.

The word "bats" sounded like "bots."

Very melodious. Heavy bass voice rumbling up out of his chest. Bots. Why baseball bots?

A reasonable question.

Only one of the three was standing there in front of him. The other two were in the hospital. But even if the cop hadn't jammed them, they'd have been denied bail.

Assaulting a police officer? Terrific. The one who'd been sprung looked shamefaced. Six feet three inches tall, weighing in at two hundred and twelve pounds, big hands hanging at his sides, he looked like a schoolboy about to be birched. Like back in Kingston when he'd been a kid.

Hamilton sat there patiently and expectantly.

At an even six feet, he was smaller than the man he was addressing. But he emanated even in his reasonableness a sense of terrible menace.

He turned to the man sitting beside him on the couch.

"Isaac?" he said. "Why baseball bats?"

The other man shrugged. Isaac Walker, his confidant and bodyguard—not that he needed one. A confidant, yes. It could get lonely at the top. But a bodyguard? Wasn't anyone ever going to take out Lewis Randolph Hamilton. *Ever.*

Isaac shook his head. He was agreeing that baseball bats were ridiculous. Baseball bats were for spics out to break a man's legs. For chasing after a man's woman. Very big thing with the spics, their women. There were women attached to the posse, of course. Camp followers. There when you needed them. But nobody was going to get into a shootout over a mere cunt. Big macho thing with the spic gangs, though. Even the Colombians, who you thought would have more sense, all the fuckin' green involved in their operation. Mess with a spic's woman, it wasn't maybe as serious as messin' with his shit, but it was serious enough. Break the man's legs so he couldn't chase no more. But who had given these three the order to use baseball bats on Herrera?

"Who told you baseball bats, man?" Hamilton asked.

It came out "Who tole you baseball bots, mon?"

"James."

Like a kid telling on his best friend.

James. Who was now at Buenavista Hospital where they had dug the cop's bullet out of his shoulder. At the hospital, James had whispered to Isaac that he'd knocked out one of the cop's teeth. He'd sounded proud of it. Isaac had thought he was a fucking dope, messing with a cop to begin with. A cop showed, they should have split, saved Herrera for another day. Which they were having to do anyway. Jump up and down on a cop? Had to be fucking crazy. James. Who, it now turned out, had told them to go after Herrera with baseball bats.

"James told you this?"

Hamilton speaking.

"Yes, Lewis. It was James for certain."

The Jamaican lilt of his words.

Andrew Fields was his name. Giant of a man. He could have broken Hamilton in half with his bare hands, torn him limb from limb, the way he'd done other people without batting an eyelash. But there was deference in his voice. When he said "Lewis," it somehow sounded like "sir."

"Told you to use baseball bats on the man?" Hamilton asked.

"Yes, Lewis."

"When I specifically said I wanted the man put to sleep?"

"That message did come down, Lewis."

"But you used baseball bats *anyway,*" Hamilton said.

Andrew was hoping he believed him. He didn't want Hamilton thinking that he himself, or even Herbert, had been acting on their own initiative. Had somehow taken it in their heads that the way to do the little spic was with ball bats. Herbert had been the third man on the hunting party. The one who'd thrown his bat at the cop. The first one the cop had shot. He'd had nothing at all to do with deciding on the ball bats. James had made that decision. Maybe because the person they were about to do was a spic and spics understood baseball bats. But if the whole idea was to put the man to sleep, then what difference did it make *how* they did it? Was he later going to remember in his grave that it was a gun or a knife or three ball bats had done him? James's reasoning on this had eluded Andrew. But in a posse, as in any kind of business, there were levels of command. The man had said ball bats, so ball bats it had been.

"Was it James's notion to merely *harm* the man?" Hamilton asked.

"I think to box him," Andrew said.

"Not just to break a few bones, eh?"

"He told us you wanted the man boxed, Lewis."

"Then why baseball bats?" Hamilton asked reasonably, and spread his hands before him, and lifted his shoulders and his eyebrows questioningly. "If we are looking to put this man in a box in a hole in the ground, why take the long way home, Andrew, why take the dusty road by the sea, do you understand what I'm ask-

ing? Why not short and sweet, *adiós, amigo,* you fuck
with us, you kiss your sister goodbye? Am I making my
point?"

"Yes, Lewis."

"Did James have an explanation? Did he say I want
to use bats for this or that reason?"

"He didn't offer no reason, Lewis."

"Oh my my my," Hamilton said, and sighed, and
shook his head, and looked to Isaac for possible guid-
ance.

"Shall I go to the hospital and ask him?" Isaac said.

"No, no. The man's been denied bail, there's a
policeman outside his door. No, no. Time enough to
talk to him later, Isaac."

Hamilton smiled.

The smile was chilling.

Andrew suddenly did not want to be James. It seemed
to Andrew that the best thing that could happen to James
was to be sent away for a long, long time. Where Hamilton could not get to him. Although Andrew couldn't
think of a single prison in the United States that Hamilton could not reach into. Andrew didn't know why
Hamilton had wanted the little spic killed, nobody had
told him that. But he knew James had fucked up badly
and the spic was still out there walking around.

"Andrew?"

"Yes, Lewis."

"I'm very troubled by this."

"Yes, Lewis."

"I send three men to do *one* little spic . . ."

"Yes, Lewis."

". . . a man who could have been blown away with a fucking twenty-*two* . . ."

Those eyes.

Blazing.

"But instead the three of you decide to use . . ."

"It was James who . . ."

"I don't *give* a fuck who! The job wasn't done!"

Silence.

Andrew lowered his eyes.

"Do I have to go do this myself?" Hamilton asked.

"No, Lewis. You still want the job done, I can do it."

"I want the job done."

"Fine then."

"No mistakes this time."

"No mistakes."

"We are not trying to win the World Series, Andrew."

A smile.

"I know, Lewis."

"Go sing the man his lullaby," Hamilton said.

THE SOCIAL WORKER who had handled the adoption for the Hoddings was a woman named Martha Henley. She had been working for the Cooper-Anderson Agency, a private adoption agency, for the past fourteen years now. In her late sixties, a trifle stout, wearing a dark brown suit, low-heeled walking shoes, and gold-rimmed eyeglasses that demanded to be called spectacles, she warmly greeted the detectives at ten o'clock that Monday morning, and offered them seats on easy chairs facing her desk. A bleak wintry sky edged with skyscrapers filled the corner windows of her office. She told them at once that she loved children. She told them that nothing brought her greater happiness than to find the right home for a child needing adoption. They believed her. They had told her on the telephone why they wanted to see her. Now she wanted to know why they felt information about the adoption of Susan Hodding was important to their case.

"Only in that it's another possible avenue," Meyer said.

"In what way?"

"We're investigating *two* possibilities at the moment," Carella said. "The first is that the murders may have been felony murders—murders that occurred during the commission of another crime. In this case, a burglary. Or a rape. Or both."

"And the second possibility?"

She was making notes on a lined yellow pad, using an old-fashioned fountain pen with a gold nib. She was left-handed, Meyer noticed. Wrote with her hand twisted around peculiarly. Meyer figured she'd been growing up when schoolteachers were still trying to change all left-handers into right-handers. He imagined this had something to do with Good vs. Evil, the right hand of God vs. the sinister left hand of the Devil. All bullshit, he thought. Those exercises at changing a person's handedness had in many cases led to stuttering and a whole carload of learning disabilities. Carella was still talking. Mrs. Henley was still writing.

". . . who wanted the *sitter* dead, the Flynn girl. In

which case, the murder of the infant was a side effect, if you will, an offshoot of the other murder. That's the second possibility."

"Yes," she said.

"But there's a third possibility as well," Carella said.

"Which is?"

"That the murderer wanted the *baby* dead."

"A six-month-old child? That's difficult to . . ."

"Admittedly, but . . ."

"Yes, I know. In this city . . ."

She let the sentence trail.

"So," Carella said, "the reason we're here . . ."

"You're here because if the baby *was* the primary target . . ."

"Yes . . ."

". . . you'll need to know as much about the adoption as possible."

"Yes."

"Where shall I begin?" she asked.

The Hoddings had first come to her a bit more than a year ago, on the recommendation of their lawyer. They'd been trying to conceive ever since Mrs. Hodding . . .

"She used to be a model, you know," Mrs. Henley said.

"Yes."

. . . quit modeling some three or four years back. But although they'd assiduously followed their physician's directions, their efforts merely proved fruitless and bitterly disappointing, and they had ultimately decided to seek legal assistance in finding a reputable adoption agency.

Those were Mrs. Henley's exact words. She had a

rather flowery way of speaking, Carella noticed, as old-fashioned as her gold-nibbed fountain pen and her gold-rimmed spectacles.

"Their lawyer recommended us," she said, and nodded as if in agreement with the lawyer's good taste. "Mortimer Kaplan," she said, "of Greenfield, Gelfman, Kaplan, Schuster and Holt. A very good firm. We did all the home studies, obtained all the necessary references, prepared the Hoddings in advance for the sort of baby that might realistically turn up . . ."

"What do you mean?" Carella asked.

"Well, many of them want what we call a Gerber Baby, do you know? Blue eyes and blonde hair, cute little smile, chubby little hands. But not all babies look like that. We get all sorts of babies put up for adoption. We place all of them."

"All of them?" Meyer said.

"All of them. We've placed babies born with handicaps. We've even placed babies born with AIDS. There are a great many decent, caring people out there, I'm happy to say."

Carella nodded.

"Anyway," she said, "to cut a long story short, in July of last year I telephoned the Hoddings to say we had a newborn infant for them to look at. Well, not quite newborn. The baby at that time was two weeks old. That's the initial grace period we give the birth parents. Two weeks. Agency policy is to place the infant in a foster home, give the birth parents an opportunity to change their minds about adoption, if that's what they wish. At the end of the two weeks, they can either reclaim the baby or else sign a legal surrender that transfers custody to the agency. In this case, I had little doubt that the mother—this was the only birth parent involved—would allow the adoption to proceed. In any event, I called the Hoddings and asked them to come see the baby. A little girl. They were—as I'd expected—thoroughly enchanted with her. A beautiful baby, truly. A storybook child, a little princess. Well, a Gerber Baby. I gave them all the facts about her . . ."

"What facts would those be, Mrs. Henley?"

"Background information about the birth mother and birth father—in this case, not much was known about him—medical, religious, educational, all that. Hospital record on the infant. Hospital record on the birth mother. And so on. Everything they needed to know. The foster mother and I spent about twenty minutes with the Hoddings and little Susan . . . that was the name we'd given her here at the agency, Susan; the mother hadn't cared to name her. The Hoddings, as I'm sure they told you, still don't know the birth mother's name. It's here on record at the agency, of course, but the court records of the adoption are sealed and so is the original birth certificate. At any rate, as I say, the Hoddings loved the child on sight and agreed to take her home for the ninety-day trial period."

"This was when, Mrs. Henley?"

"Early in August. That's when they took Susan home with them. Little Susan."

Mrs. Henley shook her head.

"And now this," she said.

Now this, Carella thought.

"When did the actual adoption take place?" he asked.

"Early in December."

"Who was the child's natural mother?" he asked.

"I'll have the records sent in," Mrs. Henley said, and pressed a button on her telephone console. "Debbie," she said, "would you bring in the Hodding file, please? Mr. and Mrs. Peter Hodding. Thank you," she said, and released the button. "This won't take a moment," she said, looking up at the detectives again.

A knock sounded on the door five minutes later.

"Yes, come in," Mrs. Henley said.

A dark-haired girl wearing a long skirt and a ruffled white blouse came in carrying a manila folder. She put the folder on Mrs. Henley's desk . . .

"Ah, thank you, Debbie."

. . . turned, smiled at Carella, and then walked out again. Mrs. Henley was already riffling through the papers in the folder.

"Yes, here we are," she said. "But you know, gentlemen, I really can't release this information without . . ."

"Of course," Carella said. "You've been very kind, Mrs. Henley, and we don't want to place you or the agency in jeopardy. We'll be back in a little while with a court order."

THE BIRTH MOTHER'S NAME was Joyce Chapman.

Last June, when she'd first gone to the agency, she'd given her address as 748 North Orange, apartment 41.

"The Three-Two," Meyer said. "Down near Hopscotch."

Carella nodded.

On the Cooper-Anderson background information form, she had listed her age as nineteen, her height as five feet ten inches, her weight as one hundred and fifty-two pounds . . .

COLOR OF HAIR:	Blonde.
COLOR OF EYES:	Green.
COMPLEXION:	Fair.
BEST FEATURE:	Pretty eyes.
PERSONALITY:	Cheerful.
NATIONALITY:	American.
ETHNIC ORIGIN:	Scotch-Irish.
RELIGION:	Catholic.
EDUCATION:	High-school degree. One year college.
WORK EXPERIENCE & OCCUPATION:	None.
TALENTS OR HOBBIES:	Tennis, scuba diving.
HEALTH HISTORY ILLNESSES:	Measles, whooping cough, etc.
ALLERGIES:	None.
OPERATIONS:	None.

No, she had never been confined to any mental institution . . .

No, she was not addicted to any controlled substance . . .

No, she was not an alcoholic . . .

And No, she had never been arrested for a felony

or sentenced to imprisonment in a state penal institution.

Among the papers released by the court order was an agreement Joyce had signed shortly after the baby was born. It read:

AGREEMENT WITH
THE COOPER-ANDERSON AGENCY

I, Joyce Chapman, do hereby consent to the release of my child, Female Baby C, to a representative of the Cooper-Anderson Agency and do hereby direct the proper officers of the St. Agnes Hospital to permit the removal of said child by a representative of the Cooper-Anderson Agency.

I hereby authorize the Cooper-Anderson Agency to consent on my behalf to any medical, surgical or dental services which in the opinion of the doctor or doctors selected by the Cooper-Anderson Agency are deemed necessary for the well-being of said child. I further agree to the testing of said child for exposure to the human immunodeficiency virus (HIV) which can cause AIDS, and any other necessary and related tests. The Cooper-Anderson Agency will inform me of the test results.

I hereby agree to plan for my child with the Cooper-Anderson Agency and to keep

the Agency informed at all times of my
address and whereabouts until such time
as final plans have been completed with
the Agency for adoption, or until (or
unless) I should decide to take said child
back into my care and custody.

Dated this . . .

And so on.

Joyce had also sworn and subscribed to—before a
notary public—a document that read:

AFFIDAVIT OF NATURAL MOTHER
CONCERNING INTEREST OF ALLEGED
NATURAL FATHER

Before me, the undersigned authority, personally appeared Joyce Chapman, who,
being first duly sworn, deposes and says:

1. That she is the natural mother of:
Female Baby C.

2. That the natural father of said child is:
UNKNOWN. Residence: UNKNOWN

3. That the natural father has never con-
tributed to or provided said child with
support in a repetitive and customary

manner, nor has he shown any other tangible sign of interest in said child.

4. Due to the aforesaid statements, it is affiant's belief that the natural father has no interest in said child and would not have any objection to the adoption of said child.

Signature: *Joyce Chapman*
Affiant

And yet another document that read:

The Cooper-Anderson Agency wishes to advise each parent who releases a child for adoption that at some time in the future your child may wish to know your name and whereabouts. The Agency will not release this information without your consent, unless required by law to do so.

To help your child in the future, the Agency asks you to keep us advised of any health problems which may develop with you or your family which could later affect your child.

I would_____ I would not__X__ want to be notified if my child wishes to contact me at a later date.

I do not_____ wish at this time to
make a decision on this matter.

I understand that my decision may be
changed at any time in the future by
writing to the Agency.

Signed:

Joyce Chapman

"Let's go see her," Carella said.

748 NORTH ORANGE was in the area of the city that
sounded like a Chamber of Commerce promo for a
small Florida town. Narrow, twisting little streets with
names like Lime, Hibiscus, Pelican, Manatee and Heron
lay cheek by jowl with similarly narrow streets like
Goedkoop, Keulen, Sprenkels and Visser, which had
been named by the Dutch when you and I were young,
Maggie.

The center of the Three-Two was in Scotch Meadows
Park, which opened at its westernmost end onto Hopper
Street, hence the ellipsis "Hopscotch" for the now-vogu-
ish area where many of the city's artists and photogra-
phers had taken up residence. Orange Street itself was
hardly voguish. Too far uptown to be Lower Platform,
too far downtown to be Hopscotch, it meandered
almost to the Straits of Napoli and Chinatown on its
eastern end and then veered sharply north to run into
the warehouses hugging the River Harb. 748 North was

in a building that used to be a shoe factory, was later a warehouse for the storage of heavy machinery, and was now divided into lofts occupied not by artists—as were those in the Quarter and in Hopscotch—but by people who called themselves actors, playwrights, musicians and dancers. Most of these people were students. The *real* actors, playwrights, musicians and dancers lived farther uptown in a recently renovated neighborhood near the theater district, but don't get confused, Harold.

The young woman who answered the door to apartment 41 was named Angela Quist.

The detectives told her they were investigating a homicide and asked if they could talk to Joyce Chapman.

She told them Joyce didn't live there anymore, and then said that she herself was on the way out. She was wearing a loden coat, blue jeans, boots, and a red wool cap pulled down over her ears. She told them she was really in a hurry, class started at one, and she didn't want to be late. But she took off her coat and hat and said she could give them a few minutes if they really made it fast. They sat in a small living room hung with framed Picasso prints.

Angela Quist was an actress.

Who lived in a loft.

But Angela Quist was in reality a waitress who took an acting course once a week on her day off, and her loft was a twelve-by-twenty space sectioned off with plasterboard partitions from a dozen similar small spaces on the floor.

It did, however, have a high ceiling.

And Angela did, in fact, have a beautifully sculpted face with high cheekbones, an aristocratic nose, a generous mouth and eyes like star sapphires. And her hair was the color of honey and her voice sounded silken and soft, and who said Cinderella *couldn't* go to the ball and live in a palace?

She had known Joyce Chapman in Seattle, Washington, where they'd both grown up.

Went to high school with her.

They'd both come to this city after graduation, Angela to seek a career in the theater, Joyce to study writing at Ramsey U.

"With Parker Harrison," Angela said.

Carella said nothing.

"The poet," Angela said. "And novelist."

Carella felt he was supposed to say, "Oh, *yes,* of course! Parker Harrison!"

Instead, he cleared his throat.

"He's *quite* famous," Angela said.

Meyer cleared his throat, too.

"It's very difficult to get accepted for his course," Angela said.

"But apparently he accepted Joyce," Carella said.

"Oh, yes. Well, she's marvelously talented, you know."

"And is she still studying with him?" Meyer asked.

"Joyce? Well, no."

"What's she doing now?" Carella asked.

"I really don't know," Angela said.

"Do you know where she's living?"

"Yes."

"Can you give us her address?"

"Well, sure. But . . . I mean, if this has to do with something that happened *here* . . ."

"Yes, it . . ."

". . . in this city, I don't see how my giving you Joyce's address is going to help you."

"What do you mean, Miss Quist?"

"Well, she's in Seattle. So . . ."

The detectives looked at each other.

"I mean, she went back there shortly after the baby was born. Well, actually, as soon as the baby was placed."

"Uh-huh. That would've been in August sometime."

"Around the fifteenth, I think it was. Well, the baby was born in July . . ."

"Yes."

"And I think arrangements were made right away for . . ."

"Yes."

"So as soon as she was clear . . ."

"Clear?"

"Well, she didn't want to be saddled with a baby, you know. I mean, she's only nineteen. We talked about it a lot. She's Catholic, so abortion was out of the question, but she certainly didn't want to *keep* the baby. I mean, Joyce is *enormously* talented. She's got a tremendous future ahead of her, she never even once considered keeping the baby."

"Did she consider marriage?" Meyer asked.

"Well, I don't think this was that kind of relation-ship."

"What do you mean?"

"I mean, she picked him up in a bar. A merchant sea-man. He was on his way to the Persian Gulf. He doesn't even know he's a father."

"What's his name?"

"I don't know."

"Does Joyce know?"

"I guess so. I mean, this was an *extremely* casual encounter, believe me."

"Uh-huh," Meyer said.

"I think she was stoned, in fact. I mean, I was here asleep when she came in with him. Usually we, well, we made arrangements if we planned to be with someone, you know."

"Uh-huh."

"Asked the other person to spend the night someplace else, you know."

"Uh-huh."

"So there'd be some privacy."

"Uh-huh. But she just came home with this sailor . . ."

"Yeah. Well." Angela shrugged. "She's a little impetu-ous sometimes, Joyce. But she's very talented so, you know." She shrugged again.

"She can be forgiven her little oddities," Meyer said.

Angela looked at him as if suspecting sarcasm.

"What'd he look like?" Carella asked.

"I have no idea. I told you. I was asleep when they got here, and still asleep when he left the next morning."

"And you say she was enrolled in this man's course . . ."

"Yes. Parker Harrison."

"Then why'd she go back to Seattle?"

"Her father's sick."

"Uh-huh."

"Dying, in fact. He owns a big lumber company out there. Chapman Lumber."

"Uh-huh."

"Cancer of the liver. I've been meaning to call her, see how he's coming along."

"When's the last time you spoke to her?" Meyer asked.

"She called from Seattle on New Year's Eve."

The detectives looked at each other.

"She was in Seattle at that time?" Carella asked.

"Yes. That's where she called from. Seattle. To wish me a happy new year."

"Could we have the number there, please?" Meyer asked.

"Sure, let me get it," Angela said. "But what's this homicide got to do with Joyce?"

"Her baby got killed," Carella said.

THE TWO MEN were in a diner on Longacre and Dale.

This was now one-thirty in the afternoon, but they were just having breakfast. One of the men was eating buttered French toast over which he'd poured syrup. The other man was eating eggs over easy with sausage and home fries. Both men were drinking coffee.

This was a little early for either one of them to be up and around. One-thirty? Very early when you had a night job. Usually, their separate days didn't start till two, three in the afternoon. Roll out of bed, have a cup of coffee in the apartment, make a few calls, see who wanted to meet you for a bite, take your time showering and getting silked up, have your first meal of the day maybe around four, four-thirty.

"You sure got enough syrup on that," the one eating the eggs said.

"I like it wet."

"Tell me about it."

The man eating the French toast looked at the other man's plate. "What you're eating there is enough cholesterol to give you six heart attacks," he said. "The eggs. There's more cholesterol in a single egg than there is in a whole steak."

"Who told you that?"

"It's true."

"So who cares?"

"So it could kill you, cholesterol."

"So what do you think they make French toast with?"

"What do you mean?"

"French toast, French toast, what you're eating there all covered with syrup. French toast. What do you think they make it with?"

"They make it with bread."

"And what else?"

"They fry the bread."

"*Before* they fry the bread."

"What do you mean?"

"I mean what do they *dip* it in?"

"I don't know. What *do* they dip it in?"

"Eggs."

"No, they don't."

"Yes, they do."

"Are you tryina tell me there's eggs in this?"

"What do you *think* that stuff is?"

"What stuff?"

"All over the toast. Both sides of the toast."

"I thought it was what they fried it in."

"No, that's the eggs, is what it is. I'm surprised you don't know that."

"How'm I supposed to know that? I never cooked French toast in my life."

"So now you're gonna have a heart attack. All that cholesterol."

"No, I'm not."

"Sure you are. There's more cholesterol in a single egg . . ."

"Yeah, yeah . . ."

". . . than there is in a whole steak, isn't that what you said?"

"Let me eat in peace, okay?"

They ate in silence for several moments.

"What'd you do last night?" the one eating the eggs asked. He had lowered his voice. They were sitting in a booth at the far end of the diner, with only one other person in the place, a man in a booth near the door, but he had lowered his voice nonetheless. The man sitting across from him soaked up some syrup with a piece of the toast and brought it dripping to his mouth. He chewed for a while, licked his lips, and said, "A supermarket." He had lowered his voice, too.

"Where?"

"In Riverhead. A lay-in job. I worked it with Sammy Pedicini, you remember him?"

"Sure, how is he?"

"He's fine. It was his job, he called me up on it."

"What'd you get?"

"There was only two grand in the safe. I figure this was like to put in the cash registers in the morning, get them started, you know. I'll tell you the truth, I wouldn'ta took the job if I knew Sammy was talkin' a grand apiece. I wasted the whole fuckin' night in there. First I had to knock out the alarm so I could let him in, and then we spent I don't know how long on the safe, it was one of those old boxes with a lead spindle shaft, a real pain in the ass. With the locknuts away from the shaft, you know the kind? For two lousy grand! We got through it had to be four in the morning. I told Sammy he ever calls me again with a dog like that one, I'll piss on his leg. How about you?"

"I done a private house in Calm's Point. I was watching it the past week, I figured the family was away on a trip."

"You go in alone or what?"

"How long you know me to ask a question like that? Of course I went in alone."

"What'd you come away with?"

"A couple of nice coats."

"The one you're wearing?"

"No, no, I got this one New Year's Eve. This is a Ralph Lauren coat, it's worth eleven hundred bucks."

"It don't look like eleven bills, Doc, I gotta tell you the truth."

"That's what it costs, go check it out. It's camel hair."

"I believe you. I'm just saying it don't look the money."

"There's a Ralph Lauren on Jefferson, go in and price the coat."

"I told you I believe you, Doc. It's just that a cloth coat . . ."

"These two I got last night are furs."

"What kind?"

"A raccoon . . ."

"Which ain't worth shit. I don't waste time with raccoons no more. What was the other one?"

"A red fox."

"That's a nice fur, red fox."

"Yeah."

"You said Calm's Point, huh? Where you got the coats?"

"Yeah, the furs. Not the one I'm wearing."

"You oughta be careful, Calm's Point."

"What do you mean?"

"According to Sammy, anyway."

"Why? What's the matter with Calm's Point?"

"There were cops came around your old building."

His voice lower now.

"What are you talkin' about?"

His voice lowering, too.

"According to Sammy. Park Street, am I right?"

"Yeah?"

"His girlfriend lives on Park. She told him some cops came around lookin' for you."

"What the fuck are you saying?"

"This is according to Sammy."

"He said some cops were *looking* for me?"

Both men virtually whispering now.

"Yeah, is what his girlfriend told him. She lives in an apartment with two other hookers, she said some detectives . . ."

"When was this?"

"Last night. While Sammy was workin' the spindle, it took *forever* with that fuckin' . . ."

"I mean when did they come around *looking* for me?"

"Coupla days ago? You gotta ask Sammy. I think he said Friday. Give him a call, he'll tell you."

"Did his girlfriend say *why* they were looking for me?"

"This is all secondhand, Doc. The cops weren't questioning *her*, they were talking to people in your old building."

"On Park?"

"Yeah."

"1146 Park?"

"Whatever. But when the cops were gone, she wandered over, you know . . ."

"Yeah?"

"And asked what the fuck was happening. So this guy in the building says they were lookin' for you."

"For me."

"Yeah."

"Why?"

"To ask you some questions."

"About what?"

"I don't know, Doc," he said, and smiled. "You done something bad lately?"

6.

CARELLA PLACED THE call at two o'clock his time.

The receptionist who answered the phone at Chapman Lumber in Seattle was surprised to be receiving a call from a detective in the east. Carella told her that he was trying to locate Joyce Chapman, and the receptionist asked him to hold, please. Another woman came onto the line.

"Yes, may I help you?" she asked.

Carella explained all over again who he was and why he was calling. He had tried the number he'd been given for Miss Chapman . . .

"What did you wish to talk to Miss Chapman about?" the woman asked.

"Who am I talking to, please?" Carella said.

"Mr. Chapman's secretary. He's been in the hospital . . ."

"Yes, I know."

"So if you can tell *me* what . . ."

"I don't want to talk to Mr. Chapman," Carella said. "I

have some business with his daughter. But the number I have for her doesn't seem to be a working number . . ."

"Yes, what sort of business?"

"What did you say your name was, ma'am?"

"*Miss*. Ogilvy. Miss Pearl Ogilvy."

Figures, Carella thought.

"Miss Ogilvy," he said, "I'm investigating a double homicide here, and I'd like very much to talk to Joyce Chapman. If you have any knowledge of her whereabouts, you'd save me the trouble of calling the Seattle police, who, I'm sure . . ."

"Miss Chapman has been staying at the Pines."

"Is that a hotel there in Seattle?"

"No, it's Mr. Chapman's home. The Pines."

"I see. Do I have the correct number there?" he asked, and read off the number Angela Quist had given him.

"No, the last digit is a nine," Miss Ogilvy said, "not a five."

"Thank you very much," Carella said.

"Not at all," Miss Ogilvy said, and hung up.

Carella pressed the receiver rest on his phone, got a fresh dial tone, dialed the 206 area code again, and then the number, with a nine this time. The phone on the other end kept ringing.

And ringing.

He was about to give up when—

"Hello?"

A muffled, sleep-raveled voice.

"Miss Chapman?"

"Mmmm."

"Hello?"

"Mmmm."

"This is Detective Carella of the 87th Precinct, I'm calling from . . ."

"Who?"

"I'm sorry if I'm waking you up," he said, "is this Joyce Chapman?"

"Yes, what time is it?"

"A little after eleven your time."

"Who did you say this was?"

"Detective Carella, I'm calling from Isola, Miss Chapman, we're investigating a double homicide here, I wonder if . . ."

"A *what?*"

"A double homicide."

"Jesus."

"We spoke earlier today to a woman named Angela Quist . . ."

"Angie? Is she involved in a murder?"

"No, Miss Chapman. We talked to her because she was the person we found at the last address we had for you."

"For *me?*"

"Yes."

"The last address you had for *me?*"

"Yes."

"What've *I* got to do with a homicide? And where'd you get my last address?"

"From the Cooper-Anderson Agency," Carella said.

There was a long silence on the line.

"Who got killed?" Joyce finally said. "Mike?"

"Who do you mean?" Carella asked.

"Mike. The baby's father. Did somebody kill him?"

"Mike who?" Carella said.

There was another silence. Then:

"Is he dead or isn't he?"

"He may be, for all I know," Carella said. "But he's not one of the victims in the case we're investigating."

"Then what is he? A suspect?"

"Not if he was on a ship in the Persian Gulf on New Year's Eve. May I have his last name, please?"

"How'd you know he was a sailor?"

"A merchant seaman," Carella said.

"Same thing."

"Not quite. Miss Quist mentioned it."

"Is she the one who told you I'd put the baby up for adoption?"

"No."

"Then how'd you know about Cooper-Anderson?"

"The baby's adoptive parents told us."

"And Cooper-Anderson gave you my *name?* That's a fucking violation of . . ."

"Miss Chapman, it was your baby who got killed."

He thought he heard a small sharp gasp on the other end of the line. He waited.

"She is not my baby," Joyce said at last.

"Not legally perhaps . . ."

"Not emotionally, either. I gave birth to her, Mr. Carella, is that your name?"

"Yes, Carella."

"That was the extent of my involvement with her."

"I see. But she is nonetheless dead."

"I'm sorry to hear that. Why are you calling me, Mr. Carella?"

"Miss Chapman, we know you were in Seattle on New Year's Eve . . ."

"Is that when she was killed?"

"Yes."

"Who else was killed? You said a double . . ."

"Her baby-sitter. A young girl named Annie Flynn. Does the name mean anything to you?"

"No."

"Miss Chapman, can you tell me the father's full name?"

"Why do you want to know? If you think he's the one who . . ."

"We don't think anything yet. We're merely trying to . . ."

"He didn't even know I was pregnant. I was with him on a Saturday night, and he sailed the next day."

"Where'd you meet him, Miss Chapman?"

"At a disco called Lang's. Down in the Quarter."

"Yes, I know the place. And you took him back to the Orange Street apartment?"

"Yes."

"And spent the night with him?"

"Yes."

"Did you see him again after that?"

"No. I told you. He sailed the next day."

"For the Persian Gulf."

"To pick up Kuwaiti oil. At least, that's what he told me. It may have been bullshit. Some guys try to impress girls by saying they do dangerous work."

"Do you know if he's still in the Persian Gulf?"

"The last time I saw him was at eight o'clock on the morning of October eighteenth, fifteen months ago."

"You keep track of time nicely," Carella said.

"So would you if you gave birth nine months after you kissed somebody goodbye."

"Then Susan was conceived that . . ."

"Is that what they named her?"

"Susan, yes."

"Susan," she repeated.

"Yes."

"Susan," she said again.

He waited.

Nothing more came.

"That weekend," Carella concluded.

"Yes," she said.

"What's his last name?" Carella asked. "The father."

"I don't know," Joyce said.

Carella raised his eyebrows.

"You don't know his last name," he repeated.

"I do not know his last name."

"He didn't tell you his . . ."

"Sue me," she said.

Carella nodded to the squadroom wall.

"What'd he look like?" he asked.

"Tall, dark hair, blue eyes, who knows?"

"Uh-huh," he said.

"I'm not promiscuous," she said.

"Okay," he said.

"I was stoned."

"Okay."

"We were having a good time, I asked him to come home with me."

"Okay. Was he white, black, Hispanic . . . ?"

"White."

"And he never mentioned his last name?"

"Never."

"And you never asked."

"Who cared?"

"Okay. Did he tell you what ship he was on?"

Silence.

"Miss Chapman?"

"Yes, I'm thinking."

He waited.

"A tanker."

"Yes?"

"Do they name them after generals?"

"I guess they can."

"The General Something?"

"Maybe."

"Putnam? Or Putney? The General Putney? Could that be a tanker?"

"I can check it out."

"But how could he have killed her?" Joyce asked. "He didn't even know she existed."

"Well, we *would* like to talk to him, if we can find him," Carella said. "Miss Chapman, does the name Scott Handler mean anything to you?"

"No."

"He isn't anyone you might have known?"

"No."

"Or might have met somewhere even casually?"

"Like at a *disco?*" she said, her voice turning suddenly hard and mean. "I told you, Mr. Carella, I'm not promiscuous."

"No one said you were, Miss Chapman."

"You stressed the word 'casually' . . ."

"I didn't intend to."

"But you did! How the hell am I supposed to know who this Scott Hampton . . ."

"Handler."

"Who*ever* the fuck, how am I supposed to know him?"

"I was only asking if his name sounded . . ."

"No, you wanted to know if I'd met him *casually* . . ."

"Yes, but I . . ."

"The way I'd met *Mike!*"

Carella sighed.

"I don't know him," Joyce said.

"Okay," he said.

There was a long awkward silence.

"Listen," she said.

"Yes?"

"If you . . . if you find who . . . who . . . who killed . . ."

It was hard for her to say it. It seemed as if she would never say it. But at last the name formed on her lips and came over the telephone wires like a whisper.

"Susan," she said. "If you find who killed Susan . . ."

Her voice caught.

"Let me know, okay?" she said, and hung up.

* * *

EILEEN WAS taking her measure.

This was only the second time she'd seen the woman, and she wasn't sure she'd be seeing her again. Like a cop studying a suspect, she scrutinized Karin Lefkowitz.

Big-city Jewish-girl looks. Barbra Streisand, but prettier. Brown hair cut in a flying wedge. A sharp intelligence in her blue eyes. Good legs, she probably looked terrific in heels, but she was wearing Reeboks. A dark blue business suit—and Reeboks. Eileen liked what she saw.

"So," Karin said. "Shall we begin with the rape?"

Straight for the jugular.

Eileen liked that, too—she guessed.

"It's not the rape I want to talk about," she said.

"Okay."

"I mean, that's not why I'm here. The rape."

"Okay."

"The rape was a long time ago. I've learned to live with it."

"Good. So what *did* you want to discuss?"

"As I told you last week . . . I want to quit the force."

"But not because you were raped."

"The rape has nothing to do with it." Eileen crossed her legs. Uncrossed them again. "I killed a man."

"So you told me."

"That's why I want to quit."

"Because you killed a man in the line of duty."

"Yes. I don't want to have to kill anyone else. Ever again."

"Okay."

"I think that's reasonable."

"Uh-huh."

Eileen looked at her.

"What are we supposed to do here?" she asked.

"What would you like to do?" Karin asked.

"Well, first off," Eileen said, "I'd like you to understand I'm a cop."

"Uh-huh."

"A Detective/Second Grade . . ."

"Uh-huh."

". . . who knows a little bit about interrogation."

"Uh-huh."

"As for example answering questions with questions to get a suspect talking."

"Uh-huh," Karin said, and smiled.

Eileen did not smile back.

"So when I ask you what we're supposed to do here, I don't like you asking me what *I'd* like to do here. You're the trained person, you're the one who's supposed to *know* how to proceed here."

"Okay," Karin said.

"And by the way I know the Uh-Huh-Okay routine, too," Eileen said. "You got yourself a suspect? Good. Just keep him talking, just okay and uh-huh him to death."

"But you're not a suspect," Karin said, and smiled.

"What I'm saying . . ."

"I understand what you're saying. You'd appreciate my treating you like the professional you are."

"Yes."

"Good. I will. If you'll extend the same courtesy to me."

Eileen looked at her again.

"So," Karin said. "You want to quit the force."

"Yes."

"And that's why you're here."

"Yes."

"Why?" Karin asked.

"I just told you. I want to . . ."

"Yes, quit the force. But that doesn't tell me why you're here. If you want to quit the force, why did you come to see me?"

"Because I was talking to Sam Grossman at the lab . . ."

"Yes, Captain Grossman."

"Yes, and I was telling him I forget what now, something about, I don't remember, I guess looking for a job in some other line of work, and we got to talking, and he asked me if I knew about Pizzaz, and I said I did, and he suggested that I give Dr. Lefkowitz a call, she might be able to help me with this problem I seemed to have."

"And what is this problem you seem to have?"

"I just told you. I want to quit the force."

"So why don't you?"

"Well, that's the problem. Every time I'm about to hand in my resignation, well, I . . . I can't seem to do it."

"Uh-huh. Have you actually written a resignation letter?"

"No. Not yet."

"Uh-huh. And this shooting occurrence took place when?"

"This *killing* occurrence, you mean. I *killed* a man, Dr. Lefko . . . what am I supposed to *call* you, anyway?"

"What would you like to call me?"

"You're doing it again," Eileen said.

"Sorry, but it's habit."

Eileen sighed.

"I'd still like to know what I should call you," she said.

"Are you uncomfortable with Dr. Lefkowitz?"

"Yes."

"Why?"

"I don't know why. Do you plan to call me Detective Burke?"

"I don't know what I plan to call you. What would you like me to . . . ?"

"I don't think this is going to work," Eileen said.

"Why not?"

"Because I realize you've got to ask a question every time I ask a question, but that's the same game we play with any cheap thief off the street."

"Yes, but this isn't a game here," Karin said.

Their eyes met.

"The same way questioning a thief isn't a game," Karin said.

Eileen kept looking at her.

"So maybe you should concentrate less on my technique and more on our getting comfortable with each other."

"Maybe."

"That is, if you can overlook my clumsiness."

Karin smiled.

Eileen smiled, too.

"So," Karin said. "What would you like me to call you?"

"Eileen."

"And what would *you* like to call *me*?"

"What would *you* like me to call you?" Eileen said.

Karin burst out laughing.

"Karin, okay?" she said.

"Karin, okay," Eileen said.

"Will you be comfortable with that?"

"Yes."

"Good. Can we get to work now?"

"Yes."

"All right, when did you kill this man?"

"On Halloween night."

"This past Halloween?"

"Yes."

"Less than three months ago."

"Two months and nine days," Eileen said.

"Where did it happen?"

"In a rented room in the Canal Zone."

"On the docks?"

"Yes."

"Over in Calm's Point?"

"Yes."

"The Seven-Two?"

"That's the precinct, yes. But I was working with Annie Rawles out of Rape. It gets complicated. Homicide called her in, and she contacted me because they needed a decoy." Eileen shrugged. "I'm supposed to be a good decoy."

"Are you?"

"No."

"Then why'd Annie call you in?"

"I was then."

"A good decoy."

"Yes. But I'm not anymore."

"Is that why you want to quit the force?"

"Well, if I can't do the job right, I might as well quit, no?" She shrugged again. "That's the way I look at it, anyway."

"Uh-huh. What was this man's name?"

"The one I killed?"

"Yes. Why? Who did you think I meant?"

"I thought you meant the one I killed. That's what we were talking about, wasn't it? Halloween night?"

"Yes."

"His name was Robert Wilson. Well, Bobby. He called himself Bobby."

"Why did you kill him, Eileen?"

"Because he was coming at me with a knife."

"Uh-huh."

"He'd already killed three hookers here in this city."

"Nice person."

"He was, actually. I mean . . . this sounds stupid, I know . . ."

"Go on."

"Well, I had to keep reminding myself I was dealing with a killer. A man who'd killed three women. One of them only sixteen years old. They showed me pictures up the Seven-Two, he'd really done a job on them. I'm talking genital mutilation. So I knew this, I knew he was very dangerous but he seemed *charming*. I know that's crazy."

"Uh-huh."

"Kept telling jokes."

"Uh-huh."

"Very *funny* jokes. It was strange. I was sitting there with a killer, and I was *laughing*. It really was strange."

"What did he look like?"

"Bobby? He was blond. Six-two, six-three, in there. Two hundred pounds or so, well, a bit over. Maybe two-ten, fifteen. A big man. With a tattoo near his right thumb. A blue heart outlined in red."

"Anything in it?"

"What do you mean?"

"The heart. Any lettering in it?"

"Oh. No. Nothing. I thought that was strange, too."

"At the time?"

"No. Later on. When I thought about it. A heart without a name in it. Usually there's a name, isn't there?" Eileen shrugged. "All the thieves I've dealt with, if they've got a heart tattoo, there's always a name in it. But not him. Strange."

"So let me understand this. He was telling jokes while you were in this rented room with him?"

"No, earlier. In the bar. They planted me in a bar. In hooker's threads. Because . . ."

"Because the previous three victims were hookers."

"Yes. And he hit on me in the bar, and I had to get him out of there so he could make his move. So we went to this rented room."

"Where he came at you with a knife and you had to shoot him."

"Yes."

"Where were your backups?"

"I lost them. But that's another story."

"Let me hear it?"

"Well," Eileen said, and sighed. "My S.O. thought I needed a little help on the job. So he . . ."

"What's *his* name?"

"Kling. Bert Kling. He's a detective up in the Eight-Seven."

"Do you think of him as that?"

"As what? A detective?"

"No, your Significant Other."

"Yes. Well, I did."

"Not any longer?"

"I told him I didn't want to see him for a while."

"Why'd you do that?"

"I figured while I was trying to sort things out . . ."

"Uh-huh."

". . . it might be best if we didn't see each other."

"When did this happen?"

"Well, I told him Friday night."

"How'd he take it?"

"He didn't like it very much."

"What'd he say?"

"First he said he didn't think it was such a good idea, and then he said it was a lousy idea. He also wanted to know whether you were the one who'd suggested it."

"And what'd you tell him?"

"I said it was my own idea." Eileen paused, and then said, "*Would* you have suggested it?"

"I really couldn't say at this point."

"But do you think it's a good idea? Until I get myself straightened out?"

"How long have you known him?" Karin asked.

"Quite a while now. I was doing a job for the Eight-

Seven, and we met up there. A laundromat. This guy was holding up laundromats. They planted me like a lady with a basket full of dirty laundry."

"Did you catch him?"

"Oh, yeah."

"And this was when?"

"A long time ago. I sometimes feel I've known Bert forever."

"Does he love you?"

"Oh, yes."

"And do you love him?"

Eileen thought about this.

"I guess so," she said at last.

"I'm assuming you've been intimate . . ."

"Oh, sure. Ever since . . . well, I had another job shortly after the laundromat, some guy who was raping nurses in the park outside Worth Memorial. The Chinatown Precinct, you know?"

"Uh-huh. Did you catch him, too?"

"Oh, yeah."

"Then you *must* have been very good."

"Well, I was okay, I guess. But that was then."

"But you were saying . . ."

"Only that when it was over, the thing in the park, I went up to Bert's place and we, you know."

"And that was the start of it."

"Yes."

"And you've been intimate since."

"Yes. Well, no."

"No?"

"Not since . . ."

Eileen shook her head.

"Not since when?"

"Halloween," Eileen said. "But *that's* another story, too."

"Maybe they're all the same story," Karin said.

ANDREW FIELDS was waiting outside José Herrera's apartment building when he came downstairs at three o'clock that Tuesday afternoon. It was a cold, gray shitty day like the ones you always got in January in this city. In Jamaica, you never got days like this. Never. It was always sunny and bright in Jamaica. Even when it rained it was a different kind of rain than you got here in this shitty city. There were times when Fields was sorry he'd ever left Jamaica except for the money. Here there was money. In Jamaica, you wiped your ass on last year's newspaper.

Herrera was wearing his overcoat like a cloak, thrown over his shoulders, unbuttoned to accommodate the cast on his left arm. Fields wondered what he had on under the coat. A sweater with only one sleeve? After he shot him, he would take a look under the coat, see what he was wearing. He would also steal the wristwatch he saw glinting on Herrera's left wrist, which looked like gold from this distance, but which may have been only junk. Lots of spics wore fake jewelry.

Fields planned to approach Herrera soon as he found an opportunity, fall into step beside him, tell him in English—if the fuckin' spic *understood* English—that this was a gun here in Fields's pocket and that he should walk very nice and quiet with him and keep walking till they came to 704 Crosley, which was an abandoned building in this lovely spic neighborhood Herrera lived in. Fields planned to walk him up to the third floor of that building and shoot him in the back of the head. Very clean, very simple. No fuss, no muss.

Herrera stood on the front stoop, looking up and down the street.

Playing it like a cool television gangster.

Only ten thousand blacks in his immediate vicinity, so the dumb spic was trying to pick his exterminator from the bunch.

Fields smiled.

On New Year's Day, when they'd gone after him with the baseball bats, they were wearing jeans and leather jackets, boots, red woolen watch caps, they'd looked like some kind of street gang. Today, Fields was dressed like a banker. Dark suit and overcoat, black shoes, pearl gray stetson, black muffler. Briefcase in his left hand. So his right hand could be on the piece in his coat pocket when he caught up with Herrera and advised him that they were about to take a healthful little morning walk.

Herrera, apparently satisfied that no one on the street was life-threatening, came down the steps in front of the building, and then stopped to talk to an old man standing near a fire in a sawed-off gasoline drum. It took Fields a minute to figure out what Herrera wanted. He was showing the old man the package of cigarettes he had just taken from his coat pocket. He was asking the old man to light a cigarette for him. The old man nodded in comprehension, took the matchbook Herrera handed him, struck several matches unsuccessfully against the wind, finally got one going, and held it to the tip of the cigarette dangling from Herrera's mouth.

Enjoy it, Fields thought.

It'll be your last one, man.

Herrera thanked the old man, retrieved his matchbook, and put it in the same pocket with his cigarettes. He looked up and down the street again. It'll be a terrible shame if nobody assassinates this dude, Fields thought, seeing as he's looking for it so bad.

Herrera was in motion now.

So was Fields.

Following behind him at a safe distance, waiting for a good time to make his approach, didn't want too many people around, wanted the street populated enough to provide cover, but not so crowded that anyone brushing by could hear what he was telling Herrera. They had come maybe five, six blocks when Fields saw up ahead a nice break in the sidewalk traffic. Two, three people in Herrera's immediate orbit, moving in the same direction, half a dozen more up ahead, walking toward him. Time to move on the man.

He stepped out smoothly and quickly, planning to come up fast on Herrera's left, the side with the bad arm and also the side closest to the gun in the right-hand pocket of his coat. He was half a dozen paces behind him when Herrera suddenly veered in toward a door on his right. Fields stopped dead. The little spic was going into a bar. The name of the bar was *Las Palmas*. Fields peeked in through the plate glass window.

The big blond cop who'd done all the shooting on New Year's Day was sitting at the bar.

Herrera took the stool alongside his.

FELICE HANDLER was standing against a zebra-striped wall. With her frizzied blonde hair and her amber eyes, she looked somewhat like a healthy lioness posing against the hides of a herd she had stalked, killed and eaten. The other walls in the apartment's den were black. As she had already mentioned, Mrs. Handler was an interior decorator.

Workmen were still trotting through the apartment as Meyer and Mrs. Handler talked. It made their conversation difficult. He suspected she welcomed the interruptions; he was there, after all, to ask further questions about her son. For Mrs. Handler, everything else took precedence over the business of bloody murder. Did the wallpaper with the tiny floral pattern go in the master bedroom or the second bedroom? Which wall in the master bedroom got the floor-to-ceiling mirror? (Meyer knew the answer to that one.) Where did the gold metallic paper with the purple flecks go? Would she like to see a dipstick sample of the red for the ceiling in the study? Did the rocket ship paper go in the nursery? What was this roll of yellow paper that wasn't indicated anywhere on the floor plan? Where should they put it? (Meyer had an answer to that one, too.)

"Mrs. Handler," he said at last, his patience virtually exhausted, "I know it's important that you give all these people the answers they're . . ."

"Yes, it is," she said.

"I realize that," he said. "But we have a lot of people waiting for answers, too."

"Oh?"

One eyebrow raised. Her expression saying What in the world could *possibly* be more important than what I'm doing here?

"Yes," he said. "So, you know, I'd hate to have to get a subpoena just to *talk* to you, but . . ."

He let the sentence trail.

She looked at him.

Was he really about to subpoena her?

Amber eyes flashing with intelligence.

Considering whether to tell him to go ahead and get his goddamn subpoena if *that's* how he wanted to be.

Instead, the smile from *Fatal Attraction*.

"I do apologize," she said, "I know you must be getting a lot of pressure. The case is all over everything, isn't it?"

He wished he could have said that the pressure from upstairs had nothing to do with his eagerness to solve the case. But this wasn't entirely true. Television and the tabloids were having a holiday with this one. A six-month-old baby? Murdered in her crib? If a baby wasn't safe from the maniacs in this city, then who was?

The calls to Lieutenant Byrnes had started on the morning the story broke. First a captain from Headquarters Division downtown. Then the Chief of Detectives. Then Howard Brill, one of the Deputy Police Commissioners, and then the First Dep himself, and finally the Commissioner, all of them politely inquiring as to whether Byrnes felt the investigating detectives were making reasonable headway or did he think Homicide should enter the case in something more than an advisory capacity? Or perhaps Special Forces? Just checking, of course, please let them know if the squad needed any help. Meaning please let them know if his men were ready to admit to failure before they'd even done the preliminary legwork.

"Do you think we could step out into the hall?" Meyer said. "For ten minutes, okay? Without your people bothering us? That's all I ask."

"Certainly," she said, and looked at her watch. "It's time for a cigarette break, anyway."

They went out into the corridor, and walked down to the end of it, where there was an emergency exit. Mrs. Handler shook a cigarette free from a package of Pall Malls, and offered the package to Meyer. He had smoked Pall Malls for years. The familiar red package filled him with craving. He shook his head. And watched as she lighted her cigarette. And inhaled. And exhaled in deep satisfaction. Chinese torture.

"Mrs. Handler," he said, "you know, of course, that your son's not back at school yet."

"No, I didn't know."

"I called Prentiss this morning, shortly before I spoke to you."

"I see. And now you want to know if I've heard from him."

"Have you?"

"No."

"When we spoke to you last Tuesday . . ."

"Yes."

"You said your son had left for Maine early that morning . . ."

"Yes."

"But of course he hadn't."

"I didn't know that at the time."

"He told you he was going back to school."

"Yes."

"Mrs. Handler, do you have a school calendar?"

"What do you mean?"

"Didn't you know that classes would not resume until the ninth?"

"Yes, I knew that."

"But you didn't think it odd that your son was going back on the *third*. Almost a full week before he was *due* back."

"Scott is a very good student. He was working on a difficult science project and he wanted to get back early."

"Then you saw nothing odd about . . ."

"Nothing. He's a graduating senior. The top colleges look favorably on student initiative."

"So when he said he was going back . . ."

"I had no reason to believe he did *not* go back."

She inhaled and exhaled smoke every two or three sentences. Meyer was getting a nicotine fix just standing beside her.

"And do you find it odd that he isn't there at the school now? The day *after* classes started again?"

"Yes, I find it odd."

"But you don't seem very concerned," Meyer said.

"I'm not. He's a big boy now. He knows how to take care of himself."

"Where do you think he might be, Mrs. Handler?"

"I have no idea."

"He hasn't called you . . ."

"No."

"Or written to you."

"No."

"But you're not concerned."

"As I told you . . ."

"Yes, he's a big boy now. Mrs. Handler, let's talk about New Year's Eve."

"Why?"

"Because your son had a relationship with one of the victims, Mrs. Handler, and now we can't find him. So I'd like to know what he was doing on New Year's Eve."

"I already told you . . ."

"Yes, you had a party that started at nine o'clock . . ."

"Yes."

". . . and ended at four in the morning."

"That's an approximate time."

"And your son was there all night long."

"Yes."

"Are you sure about that?"

"I'm positive."

"I suppose the other guests at the party would be willing to corroborate . . ."

"I have no idea whether anyone else noticed Scott's comings or goings. He's my son, I'm the one who . . ."

"*Were* there comings and goings?"

"What do you mean?"

She dropped her cigarette to the floor and ground it out under her sole. Then she opened her handbag, reached for the package of Pall Malls again, shook one free, and lighted it. A delaying tactic, Meyer figured.

She'd already made her first mistake, and she knew it. But so did he.

"You said he was there all night long, Mrs. Handler."

"Yes, he was."

"Well, when he's home, he *lives* with you, doesn't he?"

"Yes?"

Cautious now. The lioness sniffing the air.

"So he didn't have to *come* to the party, did he? He was already *there,* wasn't he?"

"Yes?"

"And he didn't have to *go* anywhere after the party, did he? Since, again, he was already where he lived. So what did you mean by his comings and goings?"

"That was merely a figure of speech," she said.

"Oh? Which one? Simile? Meta . . . ?"

"Listen, you," she said, and hurled the cigarette down like a gauntlet.

"Yes, Mrs. Handler?"

Her eyes were blazing again.

"Don't get smart with me, okay?"

She stepped on the cigarette, ground it out.

And looked challengingly into his eyes.

Taxpayer to civil servant.

Meyer figured it was time to take off the gloves.

"I'll need a guest list," he said.

"Why?"

"Because I want to know if everyone at that party will swear that your son was there all night long. While a six-month-old baby and her sixteen-year-old sitter were getting *killed,* Mrs. Handler. If you want me to go get a court order, I will. We can make it easier by you just giving me, right here and now, the names, addresses and telephone numbers of everyone who was there. What do you say? You want to save us both a lot of time? Or do you want to protect your son right into becoming the prime suspect in this thing?"

"I don't know where he is," Mrs. Handler said.

"That wasn't my question," Meyer said.

"And I don't know where he went that night."

Meyer pounced.

"Then he *did* leave the party."

"Yes."

"What time?"

"About . . ."

She hesitated. Trying to remember when the murders had taken place. Covering her son's tracks again. Counting on the faulty and perhaps drunken memories of whoever had seen him putting on his coat and hat and—

"Okay, forget it," Meyer said. "I'll go get my subpoena while you work up that guest list. I just want you to know you're not helping your son one damn bit, Mrs. Handler. I'll see you later."

He was starting for the elevator when she said, "Just a minute, please."

7.

THEY FOUND Colby Strothers at two o'clock on Wednesday afternoon, the eleventh day of January. He was sitting on a stone bench in the Matisse Wing of the Jarrett Museum of Modern Art on Jefferson Avenue, making a pencil sketch of the huge Matisse painting that hung on the white wall in front of him. For several moments, so intent was he on what he was drawing, he didn't even know the detectives were standing there. When finally he looked up, it was with a surprised look on his face.

"Mr. Strothers?" Meyer asked.

He looked pretty much the way Felice Handler had described him. Nineteen years old, with startlingly blue eyes, a cleft chin, a shock of dark brown hair falling over his forehead. He had the strapping build of a football player but apparently the soul of an artist, too: Strothers was a freshman at the Granger Institute, one of the city's more prestigious art schools.

"Detective Meyer, 87th Squad," Meyer said, and

showed his shield and ID card. "My partner, Detective Carella."

Strothers blinked.

Mrs. Handler had directed Meyer to the Granger Institute. He had gone there this morning and spoken to someone in the Registrar's Office, who had passed him on to the head of the Art Department, who had told him that Strothers would be at the Jarrett that afternoon. Now Meyer and Carella stood with a Matisse at their backs and a puzzled art student directly in front of them, looking up at them from a stone bench and probably wondering if it was against the law to sketch in a privately owned museum.

"Want to come someplace where we can talk?" Meyer asked.

"Why? What'd I do?" Strothers said.

"Nothing. We want to ask you some questions," Carella said.

"About what?"

"About Scott Handler."

"What'd *he* do?"

"Can we go outside in the garden?"

"In *this* weather?"

"Or the cafeteria. Take your choice."

"Or we can sit right here," Meyer said. "It's up to you."

Strothers kept looking at them.

"What do you say?" Carella asked.

"Let's go to the cafeteria," Strothers said.

They walked like three old buddies through corridors lined with Picassos and Van Goghs and Chagalls and Gauguins. They followed the signs past the glass wall overlooking a sculpture garden dominated by a magnificent Chamberlain, and then up the escalator to the second floor and the newly installed Syd Solomon exhibition, and on up to the third floor where the signs led them past the museum's movie theater (which was currently running a Hitchcock retrospective that included *The Birds*) and finally into the cafeteria itself, only mildly busy at ten minutes past two in the afternoon.

"Would you like some coffee?" Carella asked.

"Sure," Strothers said tentatively. He looked as if he was wondering whether they would dare use a rubber hose on him in a public place.

"What do you take in it?"

"Sugar and a little cream."

"Meyer?"

"Black."

Carella went to the counter. Meyer and Strothers sat at the table. Meyer smiled at him, trying to put him at ease. Strothers did not smile back. Carella returned, transferred the coffee cups and spoons from the tray to the table, and then sat with them.

"So," Meyer said, and smiled again.

"Tell us where you were on New Year's Eve," Carella said.

"I thought this was about Scott."

"It is. Were you with him?"

"Yes."

"Where?"

"At his house. His folks gave a party. Scott invited me."

"What time did you get there?"

"What'd Scott do?"

"Nothing. Have you talked to him lately?"

"No."

"What time did you get to the party?"

"About nine-thirty, ten o'clock."

"Alone."

"No, I had a girl with me."

"What's *her* name?"

"Why?"

"Mr. Strothers, this is a routine questioning, all we . . ."

"Well, thank you, but I'd like to know why you're . . ."

"We're trying to pinpoint Scott Handler's whereabouts on New Year's Eve," Meyer said.

"So why do you need my girlfriend's name? If this is about Scott, why . . . ?"

"Only because she would have been another witness," Carella said.

"A witness to what?"

"To where Scott Handler was at what time."

"What time are you trying to pinpoint?" Strothers asked.

Carella noticed that he still hadn't given them his girlfriend's name. He guessed he admired that. He wondered now if he should level with the kid. Tell him they were interested in knowing where Handler was between twelve-thirty, when Annie Flynn received her last phone call, and two-thirty that same morning—when the Hoddings came into their apartment to find her dead. His eyes met Meyer's briefly. Meyer nodded with his eyelids. A blink. Go ahead, risk it.

"We're investigating a double homicide," Carella said. "One of the victims is a girl Scott Handler knew. We're trying to establish his whereabouts between twelve-thirty and two-thirty in the morning."

"On New Year's Eve," Strothers said.

"Yes. Well, New Year's *Day,* actually."

"Right. So this is pretty serious, huh?"

"Yes, it's pretty serious."

"But if those times are critical . . ."

"They are."

"Then Scott isn't your man."

"Why do you say that, Mr. Strothers?"

"Because I know where he was during those hours, and it wasn't out killing anybody."

"Where was he?"

"With me. And my girl. And his girl."

"Do you want to tell us their names?"

"Isn't my word good enough?"

"Sure," Carella said. "But if two other people can swear to it, your friend would . . ."

"Who says he's my friend?"

"I thought . . ."

"I hardly know him. I met him at a gallery opening around Thanksgiving. He was down from Maine, he goes to a private school up there."

"Uh-huh."

"He'd just broken up with some girl, he was really . . ."

He stopped dead.

There was sudden understanding in his eyes.

"Yes?" Meyer said.

"Is that who got killed?"

The detectives waited.

"The girl who dumped him?"

"What'd he tell you about her?"

"Only that she'd shown him the door. It couldn't have been too serious a thing, he seemed to be over it by New Year's Eve."

"Had you seen him at any time between Thanksgiving and . . ."

"No. I told you. We met at this opening, and then him and me and my girl went to a party afterward. At this loft an artist friend of mine has down in the Quarter. Scott seemed very down, so we asked him to come along. Then he called me just before New Year's Eve, told me there was going to be a party at his house, could I come and bring Doro . . ."

He cut himself short.

"Is that your girlfriend's name?" Carella asked. "Dorothy?"

"Yes."

"Dorothy what?"

"I'd like to leave her out of this, if that's okay with you," Strothers said.

"Sure," Carella said. "So you got to this party at about nine-thirty, ten o'clock . . ."

"The pits," Strothers said. "If he'd told me we were gonna be the only young people there . . . I mean, everybody there was thirty, forty years old!"

Meyer's expression said nothing.

"How long did you stay there?" Carella asked.

"We left a little after midnight."

"You and Dorothy, and Scott and his girlfriend."

"No, his girl wasn't there. That's where we *went*. To *her* place."

"She wasn't at the Handler party?"

"No."

"Any idea why not?"

"Well, she's older than Scott, maybe he wasn't too keen on having his mother meet her."

"How *much* older?" Meyer said.

"Well, she's pretty old," Strothers said.

"Like what?" Meyer asked. "Thirty? Forty?"

His expression still said nothing.

"Close to it, that's for sure. She's got to be at least twenty-seven, twenty-eight."

"What's *her* name?" Carella asked.

"Lorraine."

"Lorraine what?"

"Greer."

"Her address?"

"I don't know. Someplace down in the Quarter. We went by taxi from Scott's apartment."

"But you don't remember the address?"

"No, I'm sorry."

"What does she do, do you know?"

"She's a waitress. Wants to be a rock star."

Strothers shrugged elaborately, rolled his eyes, and then grimaced, making it abundantly clear what he thought her chances were.

"What time did you get to her place?" Meyer asked.

"Maybe a quarter to one? Something like that."

"You left Scott's apartment at a little past midnight . . ."

"Around twenty after."

"And you got downtown at about a quarter to one."

"Yes."

"And what time did you leave Miss Greer's apartment?"

"A little after five. Some of the people were already having breakfast."

Meyer asked the big one.

"Was Scott Handler with you all that time?"

"Yes."

"You're positive about that?"

"Well . . ."

"What is it, Mr. Strothers?"

"Well . . . we were together when we left his apartment, of course . . ."

"Of course."

"And we were together when we got to Lorraine's place . . ."

"Yes?"

"But it was sort of a big party there, you know . . ."

"Did you lose track of him, is that it?"

"Well, Dorothy and I sort of drifted off, you know . . ."

"Uh-huh."

"So we were sort of . . . well . . . *out* of it, you know, for maybe . . . well, an hour or so."

"By *out* of it . . ."

"In the bedroom, actually."

"Uh-huh. From when to when?"

"Well, I'd say maybe from around one o'clock to maybe two-thirty or so."

"So then you don't really know for *sure* that Scott Handler was there all that time."

"Well, he was there when we went in the bedroom and he was there when we came out, so I've got to assume . . ."

"There at one o'clock, and there at two-thirty."

"Well, a little later than that, maybe."

"Like what?"

"Like maybe three."

"Uh-huh."

"Or even three-thirty. I guess."

"So, actually, you were *out* of it for two and a half hours."

"Well, yeah. I guess."

Which would have given Handler plenty of time to have run back uptown.

"You said she's a waitress," Meyer said.

"Scott's girlfriend? Yeah."

"Did she mention where she works?"

LEWIS RANDOLPH HAMILTON was pacing the floor.

"You hear this?" he asked Isaac.

Isaac had heard it. Fields had just told them both.

"You're sure it's the same cop?" Hamilton asked.

"The same," Fields said. "The one shot Herbert and James and was ready to shoot me, too, I hadn't lain down the bat."

"Together in this bar, huh?"

"*Las Palmas.* On Walker."

"Sitting together in this bar, talking like old friends."

"Like brothers," Fields said.

"Now what do you suppose little Joey was telling the man?" Hamilton said.

Isaac looked at him meaningfully.

Hamilton walked to Fields and threw his arm around his shoulder.

"Thank you, Andrew," he said. "You were wise to back off when you did. Forget little Joey for a while, okay? Forget little José for now."

Fields looked at him, puzzled.

"You don't want him done?" he asked.

"Well, now, Andrew, how can you get *near* him, man? With fuzz growing on him? No less fuzz that has looked you in the eye and knows you?"

Fields was suddenly concerned. Was Hamilton blaming him somehow? Was Hamilton saying he had fucked up? The way James had with the ball bats?

"They didn't see me, Lewis," he said. "Neither one of them. Not the spic nor the cop neither."

"Good," Hamilton said.

"So if you still want me to dust him . . ."

"But what has he already told the cop?" Hamilton asked.

A FAIRY TALE.

Kling was almost embarrassed to report it to the lieutenant.

This was the story according to Herrera:

A ship was coming in on the twenty-third of January. A Monday night. Scandinavian registry, but she was coming up from Colombia. There would be a hundred kilos of cocaine aboard that ship. Normal purchase price would have been fifteen to twenty-five thousand a key, but since the posse was taking delivery on the full shipment, the price was a mere ten grand per. A kilo was two point two pounds, ask any kid on the block. A million dollars in cash would be exchanged for two hundred twenty pounds of cocaine. That was a lot of coke, friend. That was a great big mountain of nose dust. On the street, that huge pile of flake would be worth twelve and a half million bucks.

So far it sounded within the realm of reason. The normal return on a drug investment was five to one. The return here would be twelve and a half to one. So, okay, the stuff was being discounted.

But this was where the brothers Grimm came in.

According to Herrera, the posse had made arrangements for the cocaine to be delivered to an address right here in the city, which address he didn't know as yet, but which he would find out for Kling if Kling made sure the posse didn't kill him in the next few days. The million dollars was supposed to be turned over at that time, after the customary testing and tasting. That was where Kling and his raiders would come in, busting up the joint and confiscating the haul—as soon as Herrera found out where delivery would take place, of course.

"Of course," Kling said.

He was wondering what was in this for Herrera.

He didn't ask him as yet.

He asked him instead what the name of this posse was.

Herrera said again that it was bigger than Shower or Spangler, bigger even than the Tel Aviv posse, which was a strange name for a gang run by Jakies, but it happened to be real nonetheless. As a side excursion, Herrera told Kling that the way the Jakies decided to call their gangs "posses" was from watching spaghetti Westerns down there in the Caribbean, which were a very popular form of entertainment down there, the Westerns. Kling thought that was very interesting, if true. He still wanted to know the name of the posse.

"I don't know the name of this posse," Herrera said.

"You don't."

"I do not," Herrera said.

"These guys want to kill you, but you don't know who they are."

"I know the people you arrested were trying to kill me."

"Did you know those people *before* they tried killing you?"

"Yes," Herrera said. "But not who they were."

And here the fairy tale began to grow and grow like Jack's beanstalk.

Or Pinocchio's nose.

According to Herrera, he'd been sitting in this very same bar, *Las Palmas*, where he and Kling were sitting at the time of the tale, in one of the booths there across the room, when he overheard a discussion among three black men sitting in the adjoining booth.

"Uh-huh," Kling said.

"These three men were talking about the shipment I just told you about."

"Talking all the figures and everything."

"Yes."

"The hundred kilos . . ."

"Yes."

"The discounted price . . ."

"Yes, all of that."

"And the date of delivery. All the details."

"Yes. Except where. I don't know where yet."

"You overheard all this."

"Yes."

"They were talking about a shipment of cocaine, and they were talking loud enough for you to hear them."

"Yes."

"Uh-huh," Kling said.

But, according to Herrera, they must have seen him when he was leaving the bar, and they must have figured he'd been listening to everything they'd said, so they probably asked the bartender later who he was, and that was how come they'd tried to kill him on New Year's Eve.

"Because you knew about the shipment."

"Yes."

"And, of course, you could identify these men."

"Of course."

"Whose names you didn't know."

"That's true, I didn't know their names."

"James Marshall, and Andrew Fields and . . ."

"Well, yes, I know the names *now*. But then, I didn't know the names."

"You didn't."

"I did not."

"So why were they worried about you? You didn't know who they were, you didn't know where delivery would be made, why should they be worried about you?"

"Ah-ha," Herrera said.

"Yeah, ah-ha, tell me," Kling said.

"I knew the delivery date."

"Uh-huh."

"And how much cocaine would be on the ship."

"Uh-huh. What's the name of the ship?"

"I don't know. Swedish registry. Or Danish."

"Or maybe Finnish."

"Maybe."

"So they got very worried, these three guys in this posse—they *did* mention a posse, huh? When you were listening to them?"

"Oh, yes. The posse this, the posse that."

"But not the *name* of the posse."

"No, not the name."

"Too bad, huh?"

"Well, that I can find out."

"The way you can find out where delivery's gonna take place, huh?"

"Exactly."

"How?" Kling asked. "These guys are trying to kill you, how do you plan to find out where they're gonna take delivery of this shit?"

"Ah-ha," Herrera said.

This was some fairy tale.

According to Herrera, he had a cousin who was a house painter in Bethtown, and this man's wife cleaned house for a Jamaican whose brother was prominent in posse circles, who in fact reputedly belonged to the Reema posse, which wasn't the posse in question here. Herrera knew that if his cousin's wife, who was his cousin-in-law, asked a few discreet questions about the person—Herrera himself—who'd almost got killed on New Year's Eve, she could find out in three minutes flat the name of the posse the three assassins belonged to. And once she told Herrera the name, the rest would be easy.

"How do you know this isn't the Reema posse?" Kling asked.

"What?" Herrera said.

"You said the Reema posse was not the posse in question."

"Oh. I know that because my cousin's wife *already* asked some questions, and it wasn't this posse that tried to do me."

"So once you learn the name of the posse in question, why is the rest going to be easy?"

"Because I have connections," Herrera said.

"Uh-huh," Kling said.

"Who know such things."

"What things?"

"Posse business."

"Uh-huh."

Kling looked at him.

Herrera ordered another Corona and lime.

Kling said, "So what's in this for you, José?"

"Satisfaction," Herrera said.

"Ahhh," Kling said, "satisfaction."

"And, of course . . . protection. You owe it to me."

Here we go with the owing again, Kling thought.

"You saved my life," Herrera said.

Kling was wondering if there was even the tiniest shred of truth in anything Herrera had told him.

THE STEAMBOAT CAFE was in a newly created mall-like complex directly on the River Dix. South and west of the midtown area, Portside had been designed with an adult trade in mind. Three restaurants ranging from medium-priced to expensive to *very* expensive. A dozen better shops. But, alas, the teenagers who discovered the area weren't interested in eating at good restaurants or buying anything in up-scale shops. They were interested only in meeting other teenagers. Portside was a good place to do that. Day and night, teenagers began flocking there from all over the city. In no time at all, thousands of them were wandering through the beautifully landscaped area, congregating on the benches, holding hands on the walks, necking under the trees on the cantilevered riverside platforms.

In this city, adults did not like teenagers.

So the adults stopped going to Portside.

And all the boutiques, and the bookshop, and the florist, and the jewelry stores were replaced by shops selling T-shirts, and earrings, and blue jeans and records and sneakers. The *very* expensive restaurant closed in six months' time, to be replaced by a disco called Spike. The merely expensive restaurant also closed; it was now a thriving McDonald's. The Steamboat Cafe, the medium-priced restaurant, had managed to survive only because it actually *was* a transformed steamboat floating there on the river and docked alongside one of the platforms. Teenagers loved novelty.

According to Colby Strothers, Lorraine Greer worked as a waitress at the Steamboat Cafe.

The detectives got there at twenty minutes past four.

The manager told them the girls on the day shift would be leaving as soon as they set the tables, filled the sugar bowls and salt and pepper shakers, made sure there was enough ketchup out, generally got things ready for the next shift. That was part of the job, he explained. Getting everything ready for the next shift. He pointed out a tall young woman standing at the silverware tray.

"That's Lorraine Greer," he said.

Long black hair, pale complexion, bluish-gray eyes that opened wide when the detectives identified themselves.

"Miss Greer," Carella said, "we're trying to locate someone we think you know."

"Who's that?" she asked. She was scooping up knives, forks and spoons from the silverware tray. Dropping them into a basket that had a napkin spread inside it. "Don't make me lose count," she said. Meyer figured she was multiplying the number of her tables by the place settings for each table, counting out how many of each utensil she would need.

"Scott Handler," Carella said.

"Don't know him," she said. "Sorry."

She swung the basket off the stand bearing the silverware tray, and began walking across the restaurant. The detectives followed her. The floor—the *deck*—rolled with the motion of the river. Carella was trying to figure why Strothers might have lied to them. He couldn't think of a single reason.

"Miss Greer," he said, "we feel reasonably certain you know Mr. Handler."

"Oh? And what gives you that impression?"

Fork on the folded napkin to the left of the plate. On the right, she placed a knife, a tablespoon, a teaspoon, in that order. Working her way around the table. Six place settings. Eyes on what she was doing.

"We talked to a young man named Colby Strothers . . ."

"Don't know him, either. Sorry."

River traffic moving past the steamboat's windows. A tugboat. A pleasure craft. A fireboat. Lorraine's eyes sideswiped the entrance door amidships. Both detectives caught the glance.

"Mr. Strothers told us . . ."

"I'm sorry, but I don't know either of those people."

Eyes checking out the door again.

But this time . . .

Something flashing in those eyes.

Both detectives turned immediately.

The young man standing in the doorway was perhaps six feet two inches tall, with blond hair, broad shoulders, and a narrow waist. He was wearing a red team jacket with ribbed cuffs and waistband, brown leather gloves, brown trousers, brown loafers. He took one look at them standing there with Lorraine, and immediately turned and went out again.

"Handler!" Carella shouted, and both detectives

started for the door. Handler—if that's who he was—
had already crossed the gangplank and was on the dock
when they came out running. "Police!" Carella shouted,
but that didn't stop him. He almost knocked over a
teenybopper eating a hamburger, kept running for the
streetside entrance to the area, and reached the sidewalk as Carella and Meyer came pounding up some
twenty yards behind him. Handler—if that's who he
was—then made a left turn and headed downtown, par-
alleling the river.

The streetlights were already on, it was that time of
day when the city hovered between dusk and true darkness. A tugboat hooted on the river, an ambulance siren
raced through the city somewhere blocks away, and
then there was a sudden hush into which Carella again
shouted, "Police!" and the word shattered the brief still-
ness, the city noises all came back again, the sounds of
voices and machines, the sound of Handler's shoes slap-
ping against the pavement ahead—if that's who he was.

Carella did not like chasing people. Neither did
Meyer. That was for the movies. In the movies, they
filmed a chase in forty takes that were later edited to
look like one unbroken take where the hero cop is running like an Olympics gold-medal track star and the
thief is running like the guy who won only the bronze.
In real life, you did it all in one take. You went pounding along the sidewalk after a guy who was fifteen to
twenty years younger than you were, and in far better
physical condition, and you hoped that his red team
jacket wasn't for track or basketball. In real life, the
calves of your legs began to ache and your chest caught

fire as you chased after someone you knew you'd possibly never catch, watching the back of that disappearing red jacket, barely able to make out the white lettering on it, *The Prentiss Academy,* which in the gloom and with your thirty-something-eyes you couldn't have deciphered at all if you weren't already familiar with it. In real life, you watched the beacon of that red jacket moving further and further—

"We're losing him!" Carella shouted.

But then suddenly, Harold, in this city of miracle and coincidence, a police car came cruising up the street from the opposite direction, and Handler—if that's who he was—spotted the car, and made an immediate hundred-and-eighty-degree turn and began running diagonally across the traffic. Toward them. On the other side of the street. Running for the corner, where he undoubtedly planned to turn north. They anticipated his route, though, and came racing for the same corner, Carella getting there an instant before he did, Meyer getting there an instant later, so that they had him boxed between them. He saw the guns in their hands. He stopped dead. Everyone was out of breath. White puffs of vapor blossomed on the air.

"Scott Handler?" Carella said.

That's who he was.

THE TWO WOMEN were white hookers of a better grade than those Hamilton's people placed on the street every day of the week. Hamilton had in fact ordered these two from a lady named Rosalie Purchase, which happened to be her real name. Rosalie was a dame in her sixties whose call-girl operation had survived the inroads of the Mafia, the Chinese, and now the Jamaican and "other exotic punks," as she defiantly called them. Rosalie dealt in quality flesh. Which might have accounted for her survival. In a day and age when two-buck whores were turning vague tricks for holier-than-thou ministers in cheap roadside motels, it was nice to know that if a *real* sinner wanted a racehorse, Rosalie Purchase was there to provide one.

Rosalie wore hats as a trademark.

On the street, in the house, in restaurants, even in church.

The cops called her Rosalie the Hat.

Or alternately Rosalie the Hot, despite the fact that she had never personally performed even the slightest sexual service for any one of her clients. If, in fact, she *had* any clients. For a lady who'd been openly running a whore house for a good many years now, it was amazing how little the police had on her. For all the police could prove, Rosalie might just as easily have been a milliner. Nobody could understand why she had never been busted. Nobody could understand why a wire had never been installed on her telephone. There were rumors, of course. Hey, listen, there are rumors in any business.

Some people in the department knew for a fact that Rosalie had grown up in East Riverhead at the same time Michael Fallon was coming along, and that as teenagers they'd been madly in love with each other. It was also true that Rosalie later moved to San Antonio, Texas, after Fallon ditched her to marry a girl named Peggy Shea. The rest, however, was all surmise.

Was it true, for example, that poor, brokenhearted Rosalie had learned how to run a cathouse out there in the Wild West? Was it true that the reason she'd never been busted in this city was that she'd become Fallon's mistress the moment she came back here to make her fortune and buy a lot of hats? Was it true that she was *still* Fallon's mistress? In which case, this might have explained why she'd never been busted, since Michael Fallon happened to be Chief of Detectives.

All this was whispered around the water coolers down at Headquarters.

The two girls were named Cassie and Lane.

These were not their real names. They were both from West Germany, and their real names were Klara Schildkraut and Lottchen Schmidt, but here in the land of opportunity they were Cassie Cole and Lane Thomas. They were both in their early twenties, both blond, both wearing ankle-strapped spike-heeled slippers and teddies—Cassie's was red and Lane's was black—and both stoned out of their minds on cocaine and champagne. So were Hamilton and Isaac.

This was a nice little sundown party here in the penthouse Hamilton owned on Grover Park North. This was also a little business meeting here on the twenty-first floor, but there was nothing Hamilton liked better than mixing business with pleasure. The two girls had been trained by Rosalie Purchase to dispense pleasure by the cartload. Isaac was dispensing a little pleasure himself, by way of refilling the girls' glasses and heaping fresh mounds of very good coke onto their mirrors. The girls sniffed with their legs widespread, the better to see you, my dear. In the west, the sun was almost completely gone, its dying stain visible only peripherally through the apartment's south-facing windows.

The two girls spoke with heavy German accents.

"This is very good shit here," Cassie said.

It sounded like, "Das ist vehr gut schidt hier."

"We have connections," Hamilton said, and winked at Isaac.

Both of them were all silked out for the girls. Hamilton was wearing green silk pajamas and a yellow silk robe and black velvet slippers with what looked like the crest of the king of the Belgians on the instep. He looked like Eddie Murphy playing Hugh Hefner. Isaac was wearing a red silk, V-necked, short-sleeved top over what looked like red silk Bermuda shorts. He was barefooted. He was wearing eyeglasses. He looked like a trained monkey with an enormous hard-on.

"Come do me here, sweetheart," he said to Lane.

Lane was busy snorting a mountain of coke. With her free hand, she reached down to unsnap the crotch of her black teddy. Snorting, she began stroking herself. Isaac watched her working her own lips.

"But why do you feel the cop takes precedence?" he asked.

"For what Herrera may have told him," Hamilton said.

"But what does the little spic *know?*"

"Naughty, naughty," Cassie said, at last raising her head from the mirror. Rosalie had taught her that calling Hispanics spics was a no-no in this business where so many of her customers were Colombian dealers up from Miami.

"You finished with that shit?" Hamilton asked.

"For now," Cassie said, grinning.

Oh my, she was stoned. Oh my, these two niggers had glorious shit here.

"Then come do me," Hamilton said.

"Oh, yeah," she said.

It sounded like, "Ach, ja."

She went to him, and settled down on the carpet between his knees, making herself comfortable. The strap of the teddy fell off her right shoulder. She was about to put it back when Hamilton said, "Leave it."

"Okay," she said, and lowered the strap completely, pulling the front of the teddy down over her right breast. Hamilton cupped her breast in his hand. He began kneading it, almost absentmindedly. The nipple actually stiffened, she was that stoned.

"He likes tits," she said to Lane.

Lane was on Isaac's lap now, facing him, straddling him. Both her breasts were in his hands.

"He does, too," she said.

They were talking German now, which Rosalie had warned them against ever doing in the presence of customers. Customers didn't like to think they were being discussed in a foreign language. But in this case it was okay because now Hamilton and Isaac fell into a Jamaican Creole patois neither of the girls could understand. So Cassie and Lane chitchatted back and forth in German like hausfraus gossiping over the back fence except that one had Hamilton in her mouth and the other was riding Isaac hell-bent for leather. Hamilton looked down at Cassie's bobbing blonde head and sipped at his champagne and sang out the riffs of the patois to Isaac who sipped his champagne and then told Lane in perfectly understandable English to turn around the other way, which she did at once, commenting to Cassie in German that if he tried any backdoor stuff all bets were off, this was getting to be a dirty party.

Dirty in more ways than one.

Isaac and Hamilton were discussing murder.

Hamilton was saying that if José Herrera, in gratitude or for whatever reason imaginable, had told the blond cop anything at all about their operation, why then they were *both* dangerous, the cop more so than Herrera. In which case, the cop had to be dusted very quickly. To silence him if he hadn't yet discussed the posse with anyone else in the department. Or, if he had already shared the information, to dust him as a warning to the others.

"We have to make a statement, man," Hamilton said in the patois.

Let the police know that where millions of dollars were at stake, no one could be allowed to interfere.

"Especially not with all the money we're paying them," Isaac said in the patois.

"Was his name in the newspaper?" Hamilton asked.

"I'll find it."

Lane was standing in front of him, her legs widespread, bent over, hands on her thighs, looking straight at Hamilton while Isaac pumped her from behind.

There was a blank expression on her face. Hamilton suddenly desired her fiercely.

"Come here," he said.

"Me?"

"No, Adolf Hitler," he said, making a joke.

Lane was twenty-two years old. She had only vaguely heard of Adolf Hitler. But she knew who the boss was here. She eased Isaac out of her, giving him a promising backward glance, head turned over her shoulder. Smiling, then, she licked her lips the way Rosalie had taught her and walked the way Rosalie had taught her to where Hamilton was on the couch with Cassie.

Isaac knew better than to complain.

He poured himself another glass of champagne and watched as the two girls began working Hamilton.

In the patois, Hamilton said, "I'll take the cop out myself."

"Why?"

"Because none of them knows what I look like," Hamilton said, and smiled. In English, he said to the girls, "Yeah, good, I like that."

"He likes it," Lane said in German.

"I'll *bet* he likes it," Cassie said in German.

"And then we take out the spic," Hamilton said in the patois. "For what he stole from us."

"You finish him off," Lane said in German.

"Ick," Cassie said in English.

CARELLA TALKED to Lorraine in the Interrogation Room.

Meyer talked to Scott in the squadroom.

Lorraine thought she was playing to a packed house at the London Palladium. A star at last. All this attention focused on her. There were probably a hundred other cops in the next room, behind that fake mirror on the wall. She had seen a lot of movies and she knew all about two-way mirrors. Actually, no one was watching her and Carella through the admittedly two-way mirror, but Lorraine didn't know this, and she was doing a star turn, anyway. Big performance here at the old station house. Give the cops the show of their lives. Cop, as the case actually happened to be.

On the other hand, Scott thought he was talking to his priest.

He guessed Meyer was Jewish, but this was a confessional scene anyway.

All contrite and weepy.

Waiting for Meyer to dispense penance.

"I didn't kill her," Scott said.

"Did someone accuse you?" Meyer asked.

He *almost* said, "Did someone accuse you, my son?"

With his bald head, and in Scott's abject presence, he felt like a tonsured monk. He felt like making the sign of the cross on the air and saying "Dominus vobiscum."

Instead, he said, "Why'd you run?"

"I was scared."

"Why?"

"Because I knew exactly what you'd be thinking."

"And what was that?"

Stopping himself before he added, "My son?"

"That I'd done it," Scott said. "Because she bounced me."

"Do you want to tell me where you were on New Year's Eve?"

"HE WAS with *me,*" Lorraine said.

She was on her feet, facing both Carella and the mirror behind which the Police Commissioner and the Chief of Detectives and all the high-ranking departmental brass were undoubtedly standing, watching her performance. She had changed out of the waitressing costume and into her street clothes before leaving the Steamboat Cafe. Short denim skirt, red sweater, red tights, short black boots with a cuff turned down above the ankle. She was strutting for Carella and everybody behind the mirror. Carella knew that she knew she possessed long and spectacularly beautiful legs.

"From what time to what time?" he asked.

He was sitting on the opposite side of the long table that ran the vertical length of the room. The mirror was behind him.

"He got to the party at around twelve-thirty," Lorraine said.

Strothers had said a quarter to one.

"Was he there all night?" Carella asked.

"ALL NIGHT, YES," Scott said.

"Until when?"

"Well, I spent the *night* there. I mean, I slept over. With Lorraine."

That'll be another fifty Hail Marys, Meyer thought.

"I've been staying there," Scott said. "With Lorraine. When I found out about the murder . . ."

"How'd you find out?"

"On television."

Nobody reads the newspapers anymore, Meyer thought.

"I figured I'd . . . I knew you'd think I did it. Because her parents would've mentioned the argument we had. And what I said. And I knew . . ."

"What was it you said?"

"THAT HE WAS GOING to kill her," Lorraine said.

"Uh-huh," Carella said.

"Her and her new boyfriend both."

"Uh-huh. And this is what he told you that day he came to your apartment?"

"No, no. This was later. When he came to the apartment, she'd just broken up with him. A few days earlier."

"This was . . . ?"

"Three days after Christmas. When he came to me. Because I used to be his baby-sitter. And he could tell me anything."

"And he told you Annie Flynn had broken up with him."

"Yes."

"But he didn't mention the death threats."

"Well, I wouldn't call them death threats."

"What would you call them, Miss Greer?"

"Well, would *you* call them death threats?" she said, looking directly into the mirror behind Carella and above his head.

"Yes, I would call them death threats," Carella said.

"When a person threatens to kill someone, we call that a death threat."

"Well, he didn't mean he'd *actually* kill them."

"THAT WAS JUST an expression," Scott said.

"That you'd kill her and her new boyfriend."

"Yes. I was angry, I just . . . I was just saying anything that came to my mind. Because I was angry, and hurt and . . . do you understand what I'm telling you?"

Yes, my son.

"Yes, I understand," Meyer said. "What I *don't* understand is why you thought it was better to hide instead of . . ."

"HE WAS SCARED," Lorraine said. "He figured her parents would tell you what he'd said, and you'd get him up here and wring a confession out of him. I don't mean *beat* a confession out of him. I mean *outsmart* him, get him to say things he didn't really *want* to say. Don't you go to the movies?"

"Sometimes," Carella said. "When did he tell you all this?"

"Last Friday. I advised him to turn himself in."

"Uh-huh."

"Otherwise you'd think he killed her."

"And what'd he say?"

"He said he *didn't* kill her."

"Then why wouldn't he come in?"

"I told you. He was scared."

"I don't see why. He had a perfect alibi."

"Sure, alibis," she said to the mirror, dismissing the

possibility of an innocent man being able to protect himself from a roomful of clever, aggressive cops. Like the ones behind the mirror.

"Well, he *does* have an alibi, doesn't he?" Carella said.

She looked at him. Was *he* starting to get clever?

"You said he was with you all night . . ."

"That's right."

Flatly. Challengingly. You don't like the idea of my sleeping with a nineteen-year-old kid? Tough. Rock stars can do whatever they want to do.

"Didn't leave the apartment at any time, is that right?"

"He was there all night long. We had breakfast around five, five-thirty. Then everyone left, and we went to bed."

"So there you are," Carella said.

" . . . **SCRAMBLED EGGS** and bacon, coffee, hot rolls. I guess everybody cleared out by seven, seven-thirty. Then Lorraine and I went to bed."

Meyer nodded.

"Tell me about this new boyfriend," he said.

"Huh?"

"Annie's new boyfriend. The one you said you were going to kill."

"I told you, that was just an ex . . ."

"Yes, I know. But did she say who he was?"

"She said I was crazy."

"Meaning what?"

"I guess . . . well, meaning there *wasn't* anyone else."

"And did you believe that?"

"No."

His eyes met Meyer's.

"I think she dropped me because of another guy."

NEW APARTMENT BUILDING and all, he'd had to present himself in the sales office as somebody looking to buy. So he could get floor plans. He knew which apartment the Hoddings were in, he'd got that from the directory in the lobby the first time he'd gone to the building. Doorman said Yes, sir, can I help you? Told him he was looking for the sales office, which it turned out was on the third floor in an apartment that had been furnished as a model. One of the bigger apartments, the salesperson said it was going for $850,000, because of the parkside view. Same apartment higher up in the building—there were eighteen stories in all—went for a million-six. There were less expensive apartments without a view of the park, all of them facing the side street, and these started at five and a quarter, it wasn't cheap living in this part of the city, the salesperson told him.

He'd asked for floor plans of the different apartments being sold. Each apartment had a name. Like ordering from a menu. There was the Cosmopolitan and the Urbanite and the Excel and the Luxor and the most expensive of them all, the Tower Suite, which shared the entire eighteenth floor of the building with an identical apartment flipflopped. The building on the right was also only eighteen stories high, and there were height restrictions built into the zoning, so there was no question of ever being overshadowed. And, of course, on the left there was the side street.

He'd gathered up the floor plans for all the different apartments and then asked for a plan showing the location of the apartments on each floor. He knew the Hoddings were in apartment 4A. All of the A apartments were Urbanites.

So he had the floor plan right there in his hand.

Knew exactly where the fire escapes were.

Knew exactly how to get in.

Exactly how to get to her.

The salesperson thought she had a live one.

8.

DANNY GIMP WAS OFFENDED.

"How come you went to Donner?" he asked.

The two men were sitting on a bench facing the ice-skating rink that had been named after Louis Weiss, the noted mountain climber. In this city, it was common knowledge that no mountain in the world was too high for Weiss to assail. With the help of his faithful shleppers—faithful *sherpas*—and with a god-given sense of humor and a ready smile, Weiss continued climbing to ever loftier heights, suffering frostbite of the nose only once. It was perhaps in memory of this single mishap in the Himalayas that an ice-skating rather than a roller-skating rink had been named after him. On occasional Saturdays, Weiss himself could be seen gliding over the ice, cheerfully asking children not to scatter candy bar wrappers on his rink. He was not there this Saturday.

It was already the fourteenth day of January.

Exactly two weeks since the murders were committed.

Eight days since Hal Willis had first contacted Fats Donner.

Now Danny Gimp wanted to know why.

Carella said, "How do you know we went to Donner?"

"My *job* is listening," Danny said, even more offended. "I really am upset, Steve. Truly."

"He has a short-eyes history," Carella said.

"That is no reason to have gone to him."

"If a baby and a sixteen-year-old are the victims, it's a very *good* reason."

"This is a very big case, Steve, it's all over the papers, you can't turn on your TV without seeing something about it."

"I know," Carella said wearily.

"So instead of giving me a shot at a whammer, you give it to Donner. I can't understand that, Steve, I really can't."

"Also," Carella said lamely, "it may be linked to a burglary Willis is working. So he went to Donner. Because he's worked with him before. Willis."

Danny looked at him.

"Okay," Carella said.

"I mean, you know, Steve . . ."

"I said okay."

Both men fell silent. On the rink, children of all ages flashed by in a rainbow of color. A young girl who thought she was Katarina Witt leaped into the air, did a triple jump, beamed happily in mid-air, and fell on her ass. Without embarrassment, she got up, skated off, and tried another jump—a double this time.

"Does it hurt when it's cold like this?" Danny asked.

Carella knew instantly what he was talking about.

" 'Cause the leg does," Danny said. "From when *I* got shot."

This was a lie. Danny had never been shot. He limped because he'd had polio as a child. But pretending he'd been wounded in a big gang shootout gave him a certain cachet he considered essential to the business of informing. Carella was willing to forgive the lie. The first time he himself got shot, Danny came to the hospital to see him. This was unusual for an informer. Carella guessed he actually liked Danny. Gray and grizzled and looking chubbier than he actually was because of the layers of clothing he was wearing, Danny sat on the bench and watched the skaters. He and Carella might have been old friends sitting in the park on a wintry day, remembering good times they had shared, complaining about small physical ailments like a leg that hurt when the temperature dropped.

" 'Cause I heard you got shot again," Danny said.

"Yeah," Carella said.

"On Halloween, I heard."

"That's right."

"So I was wondering if it hurts when it gets cold like this."

"A little."

"You got to stop getting shot," Danny said.

"I know."

"That can be a bad failing for a cop."

"I know."

"So be more careful."

"I will."

"And give me a call every now and then when you got a whammer. Instead of *I* have to call *you* and beg for a meeting here in the park where I'm freezing my ass off."

"The park was your idea," Carella said.

"Sure, all I need is to get spotted in a bar someplace, talking to a cop. Especially one who gets himself shot every other weekend. You're starting to be like that other guy you got up there, what's his name?"

"O'Brien."

"O'Brien, right. He's got a reputation for that, ain't he? Getting himself shot every time he gets out of bed in the morning."

"He's been shot a fair amount of times," Carella said drily.

"So what're you trying to do? Break his record?"

Carella suddenly realized that Danny was truly concerned.

"I'll be careful," he said gently.

"Please do," Danny said. "Now tell me who you're looking for."

"A man named Proctor."

"The Doctor?"

"You know him?"

"I know the name. He ain't into murder, Steve. He's a two-bit burglar and a sometime-dealer."

"We're thinking maybe a felony murder."

"Well, maybe," Danny said dubiously.

"Because we know he did a burglary in the same

building on the night of the murders. If he was doing *another* one, and the sitter surprised him . . ."

"Well, sure, then you got your felony murder."

"Because he used a knife."

"Yeah, I saw that on television."

"A weapon of convenience."

"Yeah."

"Which could happen if a person is surprised. He grabs a knife from the rack . . ."

"He don't have to be surprised to do that."

"Well, nobody goes in *planning* to use what he finds on the spot."

"I suppose," Danny said, and shrugged. "Proctor, Proctor, where did I hear something about him lately? Did he just get out?"

"Two years ago."

"Did he break parole or something?"

"Yes. Where'd you hear that?"

"Shmuck breaks parole it's all over the street. Captain Invincible, right? Nobody can touch him. But that's not it. I mean, this was something new. Where the hell did I hear it?"

The men fell silent again.

Danny was thinking furiously.

Carella was waiting.

There were two figure skaters out on the ice now. They floated like sugar plum fairies among the children churning furiously around them. An ice hockey game, strictly against the rules, was in its formative stages, two rosy-cheeked boys choosing up sides while half a dozen others circled them.

"They always picked me last," Danny said.

He never misses a trick, Carella thought.

"Because of the leg."

"They picked me last, too," Carella said.

This was a lie. He'd always been a fairly good athlete.

"Who you think has the better legs? The one in blue or the one in red?"

Carella looked out over the ice.

"The one in red," he said.

"Really. You know what I call those kind of legs? I call them Chinese legs."

"Why?"

"I don't know why. It's the kind of legs Chinese girls have. Did you ever make it with a Chinese girl?"

"Never."

"That's the kind of legs they got. My money's on the one in blue."

"Okay," Carella said.

"Salzeech his own, huh?" Danny said, and smiled.

Carella smiled, too.

"That's a pun," Danny explained.

"I know."

"You know the expression 'To each his own'?"

"Yes."

"That's the pun," Danny explained. "The Italians say *salsiccia,* which means sausage. Salzeech for short. I ain't Italian, but you ought to know that."

"I do know it."

"So that's the pun. Salzeech his own."

"I got it already, Danny."

"So how come you didn't bust out laughing?" he said, and smiled again.

Carella smiled with him.

They fell silent again.

Danny was still thinking.

"It'll come to me," he said at last.

THE MAN SITTING at Kling's desk was obviously Jamaican.

One of the Jakies, as Herrera had labeled them. As if this city needed more ethnic labels than it already had.

His speech rolled from his tongue like the sea nudging the shores of his native island.

He was telling Kling that his wife had threatened to kill him.

He was asking Kling to come back to the apartment with him, to warn his wife—whose name was Imogene—not to say such things to him anymore. And especially not to *do* such things, if that was what she really planned to do. Which he strongly believed was her plan since she had recently purchased from a street vendor a .22-caliber pistol for sixteen dollars and change.

The man talking to Kling said his name was Dudley Archibald.

He was, Kling supposed, in his early thirties, with a very dark complexion, soulful brown eyes, and a thin-lipped mouth. He wore his hair in a modified Afro. He was dressed conservatively in a tan suit that appeared a bit tropical for the frigid temperatures outside. You told somebody in the Caribbean that it was cold up here, he nodded knowingly, figured all he had to do was pack a sweater. Like for when it got a bit chilly at night in the islands. Just like that. Sure. Came up here, immediately froze to death. Tan tropical suit with the temperature outside at twenty-one degrees Fahrenheit and the squadroom windows rimed with ice.

Archibald told Kling he was a postal worker. This was his day off. Saturday. He'd come up here on his day off because he was truly worried that his wife Imogene would take it in her mind to use that pistol one of these days.

"I would appreciate it, sir," he said, "if you came home with me and told her that wouldn't be such a good idea, sir."

"You know," Kling said, "people sometimes say things they don't really . . ."

"Yes, sir, but she bought a pistol, sir."

"Even so."

"I don't think you would want my murder on your head, sir."

Kling looked at him.

What the hell *was* this?

First Herrera, now Archibald. Telling Kling if he didn't take care of them, their murders would be on his head.

"How'd you happen to come to me?" he asked.

He really wanted to say Of all the detectives on this squad, why the fuck did you pick me?

"You did a burglary in the neighborhood," Archibald said.

Kling realized he wasn't suggesting that Kling had *committed* a burglary. He was merely saying that Kling had *investigated* one. Of several hundred, Kling imagined. In this precinct, burglaries were as common as jaywalking.

"Which one?" he asked.

"I forget her name," Archibald said. "A fat lady."

"Uh-huh."

"She said you were very good."

"Uh-huh."

"So I asked the sergeant downstairs for you. Gloria Something?"

"Well," Kling said, and shrugged.

"Gloria, I think."

"Well, in any event, Mr. Archibald, I don't think it would be appropriate for me to come to your home and to intrude on what doesn't even appear to be a family dispute as yet. I would suggest . . ."

"A pistol *is* a family dispute," Archibald said. "If she has threatened to kill me with it."

"Did she use those exact words? I'm going to kill you?"

"She said she would shoot me with the pistol. A .22-caliber pistol."

"Was this during an argument?"

"No, it was calmly. Over breakfast."

"When?"

"Every day this week."

"Every day."

"Yes."

Kling sighed.

"She keeps the pistol in the bread box," Archibald said.

"I see."

"In the kitchen."

"Uh-huh."

"She probably plans to shoot me while we're eating." Kling sighed again.

"I can't come with you . . ."

"Then my murder . . ."

". . . just now," Kling said. "I've got a showdown to run, some women are coming in at one o'clock." He looked at his watch. "I should be done around two, two-thirty. I can maybe get over there around three. Will your wife be home then?"

"Yes, sir. Thank you, sir."

"Where do you live?"

"337 South Eustis. Apartment 44."

"You make sure your wife's there, okay? I'll come by and talk to her. Does she have a license for that pistol?"

Archibald looked as if he suddenly realized he'd bought more trouble than he'd bargained for.

"No, sir," he said. "But I don't want to . . ."

"Gives me a reason to take the gun away from her, right?" Kling said, and smiled.

Archibald did not return the smile.

"Relax, nobody's going to hurt her," Kling said.

"Thank you, sir," Archibald said.

"I'll see you at three," Kling said.

It never occurred to him that in this city certain types of Jamaicans sometimes shot policemen.

* * *

THERE WERE TIMES when the irony of the situation amused Teddy.

She was deaf. She had been born deaf. She had never heard a human voice, an animal's cry, the shriek of machinery, the rustle of a fallen leaf. She had never spoken a word in her life. A woman like Teddy used to be called a "deaf mute." A label. Intended to be descriptive and perhaps kind. "Dummy" would have been the cruel word. Now she was called "hearing-impaired." Progress. Another label. She was, after all, merely Teddy Carella.

What sometimes amused her was that this deaf mute, this hearing-impaired person, this *dummy* was in fact such a good listener.

Eileen Burke apparently understood this.

Perhaps she'd understood it all along, or perhaps she'd only reached her understanding last Friday night, when during dinner she had seized upon Teddy as a sympathetic ear.

"I've always thought of you as my best friend," she said now, surprising Teddy. Their relationship had, at best, been a casual one. Dinner out with their respective men, an occasional movie, a football game, a private party, a big police affair. But best friend? Strong words. Teddy was a woman who chose her words carefully. Perhaps because her flying fingers could only accommodate so few of them in a single burst. Best friend? She wondered.

"I wouldn't tell this to anyone else," Eileen said. "I've been seeing a shrink, Teddy. I go twice a . . ."

She hesitated.

There was a puzzled expression on Teddy's face.

One of the words had thrown her.

Eileen thought back for a moment, and then said, "Shrink," exaggerating the word on her lips. Then, to nail it down, she said, "Psychologist."

Teddy nodded.

"I go to her twice a week."

Without saying a word, merely by slightly raising her eyebrows and opening her eyes a trifle wider, Teddy said—and Eileen understood—a multitude of things.

And?

How's it going?

Tell me more.

"I think she's going to be okay," Eileen said. "I mean, I don't know yet. It bothers me that she's younger than I am . . ."

Teddy began signing.

And caught herself.

But she used her hands, anyway, signaling Eileen to go on, to elaborate, to tell her exactly . . .

"Twenty-six or -seven," Eileen said.

Teddy pulled a face.

"Yeah," Eileen said, "that's just it. She seems like a kid to me, too."

The restaurant was crowded with Saturday shoppers taking a break away from the Hall Avenue department stores. Eileen was wearing jeans, a bulky green sweater, and brown boots. A dark blue car coat was draped over the back of her chair. Her service revolver was in her shoulder bag, on the floor under the table. Teddy had taken the subway in from Riverhead. She, too, was dressed for a casual afternoon in the city. Jeans, a yellow turtleneck with a tan cardigan over it, Adidas jogging shoes. A black ski parka was draped over the back of her chair. Her small handbag was on the table. At a nearby table, two women noticed that she was using her hands a lot, making exaggerated facial expressions. One of them whispered, "She's deaf and dumb," another quaint label Teddy would have found offensive had she heard it. She did not hear it because she was too busy talking and listening.

Eileen was telling her that she'd stopped seeing Kling.

"Because I don't think he understands what I'm trying to do here."

Teddy watched her intently.

"Or how much . . . how . . . you know . . . I don't think he . . . he's a man, Teddy, I don't think any man in the world can really understand what . . . how . . . you know . . . the effect that something like . . . like what happened . . . how traumatic it can be to a woman."

Teddy was still watching her.

Dark brown eyes luminous in her face.

Listening.

Waiting.

"Rape, I mean," Eileen said.

Teddy nodded.

"That I was raped."

Tears suddenly sprang to Eileen's eyes.

Teddy reached across the table, took her hands in her own.

"So . . . so you . . . I figure if I have to cope with *his* goddamn feelings while I'm trying to understand my own . . . I mean, it's just too much to handle, Teddy."

Teddy nodded. She squeezed Eileen's hands.

"I mean, I can't worry about his . . . his . . . you know . . . *his* sensitivity, he's not the one who got raped. Aw, shit, I don't know, maybe I did the wrong thing. But don't *I* count, Teddy? Isn't it important that I . . . aw, shit," she said again, and reached down into her bag for the package of Kleenex tissues alongside her gun.

"Excuse me," a man said, "are you all right?"

He was standing alongside the table. Tall. Brown eyes. Dark hair. Craggy good looks. Perhaps thirty-seven, thirty-eight years old. Wearing a brown overcoat and brown gloves. Obviously just leaving the restaurant. Obviously concerned about Eileen's tears.

"I'm fine," she said to him, turning her head away, drying her eyes.

He leaned over the table. Gloved hands on the table.

"Are you sure?" he said. "If there's any way I can help . . ."

"No, thank you, that's very nice of you," Eileen said, "but I'm okay, really. Thank you."

"As long as you're all right," he said, and smiled, and turned swiftly from the table and began walking toward—

"Hey!" Eileen yelled and shoved back her chair, knocking it over. "Hey, you!"

She was on her feet and running, shoving past a waitress carrying a trayload of sandwiches, throwing open the front door and racing after the man, who made an immediate right turn on the sidewalk outside. Teddy could not hear Eileen shouting, "Police, stop!" but she did see the man as he came past the restaurant's plate glass window, and she did see Eileen come up fast behind him, both of them running, and she saw Eileen leap at the man in a headlong tackle that sent something flying out of his gloved hand, and only then did she realize that the something was a woman's handbag, and the handbag was hers.

They went down in a jumble of arms and legs, Eileen and the man, rolling over on the sidewalk, Eileen on top now, her right arm coming up, no gun in her hand, her gun was still in her shoulder bag on the floor under the table. Her right fist was bunched. It came down hard on the side of the man's neck. The man stiffened as if a nerve had been struck. A uniformed cop was suddenly on the scene, trying to break them apart, Eileen screaming she was on the job, which Teddy did not hear but which she guessed the officer understood because all at once his gun was in his hand and he was cuffing the man on the sidewalk and having a nice friendly chat with Eileen who just kept nodding at him impatiently.

She picked up Teddy's handbag from where it lay beside the handcuffed man. The cop wanted the bag. Eileen was telling him no, shaking her head. The conversation seemed to get very heated. Eileen began using her hands, the bag in one hand, both hands waving around in the air. Finally, she turned away from the cop, the bag still in her hand, and started back for the restaurant, automatically shooing away the crowd that had gathered outside, a holdover from the days when she herself had been a uniformed cop.

She came back to the table.

"How do you *like* that guy?" she said, shaking her head in amazement.

Teddy nodded.

She was thinking how strong Eileen had been, how brave and—

But Eileen, noticing everyone looking at her, flushed a red the color of her hair, and said in embarrassment, "Could we get out of here, please?"

And to Teddy she suddenly seemed like a little girl standing in front of a mirror in her mother's dress and shoes.

IN CALM'S POINT, there was a Jamaican neighborhood called Camp Kingston. In Riverhead, the Jamaican section was called Little Kingston. In other parts of the city, there was a Kingston North and even a Kingston Gulch, though how that name had originated was anyone's guess. Here in the Eight-Seven, the Jamaican section ran for several blocks from Culver Avenue to the River Harb, where what was still officially called Beaudoin Bluff was now familiarly called Kingston Heights. In any of these neighborhoods, whenever a cop broke up a street fight and asked the participants where they were from, the proud answer was "Kingston." Not a single Jamaican in this city was from Montego Bay or Savannala-Mar or Port Antonio. Every Jamaican in this city came from Kingston. The *capital*, man. The same way every Frenchman in the

world came from Paris. *Mais je suis* Parisien, *monsieur!*
The raised eyebrow. The indignant tone. Kingston,
mon, where you tink?

Kling had not been in this part of the precinct since it
was Puerto Rican. Before that, it had been Italian. And
before that, Irish. And if you went back far enough,
Dutch and Indian. But there was no sense of history in
these streets. There was merely a feeling of a transient
population inhabiting a decaying slum. The buildings
were uniformly gray here, even though there was red
brick beneath the ageless soot. The streets had been
only partially cleared of snow; in this neighborhood—
as was the case in most of the city's ghettos—garbage
collection, snow clearance, pothole repair, and most
other municipal services were provided at a rather
leisurely pace. The streets here looked dirty at any time
of the year, but particularly so during the winter
months. Perhaps because of the soiled snow. Or perhaps
because it was so goddamn cold. In the summer
months, for all its poverty, a slum looked extravagantly
alive. During the winter, the deserted streets, the vain
bonfires in vacant lots, the wind sweeping through narrow gray canyons, only exaggerated the ghetto's mean-
ness. Here is poverty, the ghetto said. Here is dope.
Here is crime. Here is only the thinnest thread of hope.

The mayor seemed not to know that the snow up
here hadn't been cleared yet.

Perhaps because he rarely went to dinner in the 87th
Precinct.

337 South Eustis Street was in a line of tenements on
a street that dropped swiftly toward the river. There

was ice out there today. The sky over the high-rises in the next state glowered with clouds threatening more snow. Kling walked with his head ducked against the fierce wind that blew in over the choppy gray water. He was thinking that what he'd hated most as a patrolman was a family dispute, and here he was a detective about to march into somebody's house to settle a marital problem. Call used to come in over the radio, 10-64, Family Dispute, a non-crime incident, and the dispatcher would almost always tag it with "See the lady," because it was usually the wife who'd called 911 to say her husband was batting her around the apartment. Today, he was about to see the man; it was Dudley Archibald who'd made the complaint about his wife Imogene.

He entered the building.

The stench of urine.

He wondered if there was a building in the entire 87th Precinct that did not stink of piss in the entrance hallway.

Broken mailboxes. Jimmied for the welfare, Social Security or Medicare checks.

A naked lightbulb overhead. Miraculously unbroken and unscrewed; victimizers normally preferred waiting in the dark.

An inner door with a missing doorknob. Stolen for the brass. You unscrewed enough brass doorknobs, you sold them to the junkman, you picked up the five bucks you needed for your vial of crack.

Kling put his palm flat against the door, a foot and a half above the hole left by the missing doorknob, shoved the door open, came into the ground-floor vestibule, and began climbing.

Cooking smells.

Alien.

Exotic.

Tile floors on the landings. Cracked, chipped, faded, worn. But tile nonetheless. From a time when the city's North Side was flourishing and apartments here were at a premium.

Television sets going behind every door. The afternoon soaps. A generation of immigrants learning all about America from its daytime serials.

Apartment 44, Archibald had told him.

He kept climbing.

The tile on the fourth-floor landing had been ripped up and replaced with a tin floor. Kling wondered why. The staircase wound up for another flight, dead-ending at a metal door painted red and leading to the roof. Four apartments here on the fourth floor. Forty-one, two, three, and four, count 'em. No light here on the landing. He could barely make out the numeral forty-four on the door at the far end of the hall. Not a sound coming from behind that door. He stood in the near-darkness, listening. And then, because he was a cop, he put his ear to the wood and listened more intently.

Nothing.

He looked at his watch. Squinted in the gloom. Ten minutes past three. He'd told Archibald he'd be here at three.

He knocked.

And the shots came.

He threw himself instinctively to the floor.

His gun was already in his hand.

There were two bullet holes in the door.

He waited. He was breathing very hard. The only sound in the hallway. His breathing. Harsh, ragged. Those two holes in the door right at about the level of where his head had been. His heart was pounding. He waited. His mind raced with possibilities. He'd been set up. Come talk to my wife, mon, she bought herself a .22-caliber pistol, and she has threatened to shoot me with it. Come help me, mon. A woman named Gloria told me about you. You did a burglary for her. A fat lady. Set the cop up because he's been talking to a man who knows that a huge shipment of cocaine will be coming into the city nine days from now. Kill the cop here in Kingston Heights where life is cheap and where those holes in the door did not look as if they'd been drilled by a mere—

Bam, bam, bam, three more shots in rapid succession and more wood splintering out of the door, showering onto the air like shrapnel.

And Archibald's voice.

"You crazy, woman?"

Kling was on his feet.

He kicked at the door where the lock was fastened, followed the door into the room as it sprang open, gun fanning the room, eyes following the gun, eyes swinging with the gun to where a skinny woman the color of whole-wheat bread stood near the kitchen sink opposite the door. She was wearing only a pink slip. A substantial-looking piece was in her right hand, a thirty-eight at least, the hand sagging with the weight of it, and Dudley Archibald over there on Kling's left, five shots gone now, Archibald balancing on his feet like a boxer trying to decide which way to duck when the next punch came.

Kling wished he knew how many bullets were in that gun, but he didn't.

There were thirty-eights with five-shot capacities.

There were also thirty-eights with nine-shot capacities.

"Hey, Imogene," he said softly.

The woman turned toward him. Gray-green eyes. Slitted. The big gun shaking in her tiny fist. The big gun shaking but pointed at his chest.

"Why don't you put down the gun?" he said.

"*Kill* the bastard," she said.

"No, you don't want to do that," Kling said. "Come on. Let me have the gun, okay?"

Jesus, don't shoot me, he thought.

"I told you," Archibald said.

"Just stay out of this," Kling said. He did not turn to look at him. His eyes were on Imogene. His eyes were on her eyes.

"Put down the gun, okay?" he said.

"No."

"Why not? You don't want to get yourself in trouble, do you?"

"I'm in trouble already," she said.

"Nah, what trouble?" Kling said. "Little family argument? Come on, don't make things worse than they are. Just let me have the gun, nobody's going to hurt you, okay?"

He was telling the truth.

But he was also lying.

He did not plan on hurting her. Not physically. Not he himself.

But neither he nor the police department were about to forget a lady with a gun. And the criminal justice system *would* hurt her. As sure as he was standing there trying to talk her out of firing that gun again.

"What do you say, Imogene?"

"Who tole you my name?"

"He did. Put the gun there on the table, okay? Come on, you're gonna hurt yourself with that thing."

"I'm gonna hurt *him,*" she said, and swung the gun from Kling toward her husband.

"Hey, *no!*" Kling said at once.

The gun swung back again.

One of us is gonna get it, he thought.

"You're scaring hell out of me," he said.

She looked at him.

"You really are. Are you gonna shoot me?"

"I'm gonna shoot *him!*" she said, and again the gun swung onto her husband.

"And then what? I'm a police officer, Imogene. If you shoot this man, I can't just let you walk out of this apartment. So you'll have to shoot me, too, am I right? Is that what you want to do? Shoot me?"

"No, but . . ."

"Then come on, let's quit this, okay? Just give me the gun, and . . ."

"No!"

She shouted the word.

It cracked into the apartment like another pistol shot. Archibald winced. So did Kling. He had the sudden feeling that his watch had stopped. The gun was pointed at him again. He was drenched in sweat. Nineteen degrees out there, he was covered with sweat.

He did not want to shoot this woman.

But if she turned that gun toward her husband again, he would make his move.

Please don't let me shoot you, he thought.

"Imogene," he said, very softly.

The gun was trained on his chest. The gray-green eyes watching.

"Please don't let me hurt you," he said.

Watching.

"Please put the gun down on the table."

Watching, watching.

"Please, Imogene."

He waited for what seemed forever.

First she nodded.

He waited.

She kept nodding.

Then she walked to the table, and looked down at the table top, and looked at the gun in her hand as if first discovering it, and then she nodded again, and looked at Kling, and put the gun on the table. He walked to the table slowly, picked up the gun, slipped it into his coat pocket, and said, "Thank you."

He was putting the handcuffs on her when Archibald, safe now, shouted, "Bitch!"

* * *

KLING MADE the phone call from the super's apartment downstairs.

People had gathered in the hallway. They all knew there'd been shooting on the fourth floor. Some of them seemed disappointed that no one had been killed. In a neighborhood where violence was commonplace, a shooting without a corpse was like scrambled eggs without onions. It would have been nice, in fact, if the cop had been killed. Not many people in this neighborhood liked cops. Some of the people in the hallway began jeering Kling as he led Imogene out.

At that moment, he didn't feel very good about himself, anyway. He was thinking that the system would wring Imogene out like a dirty dishcloth. Ninety-six pounds if she weighed a nickel, the system would destroy her. Not twenty minutes ago, all he'd been thinking about was his own skin. Heard shots, figured they were meant for him. Ambush for the big detective. A genuine family dispute erupting into a lady-with-a-gun situation, and all he could think at the time was that someone had set him up. Maybe he deserved to be jeered.

They came out of the building into the bitter cold.

Imogene in handcuffs.

Archibald on one side of her, looking penitent now that it was all over, Kling on the other side, holding her elbow, guiding her toward the patrol car at the curb.

He did not notice a tall, thin black man standing in a doorway across the street.

The man was watching him.

The man was Lewis Randolph Hamilton.

9.

IT WAS Fat Ollie Weeks who came up with the lead on Doctor Martin Proctor.

Fat Ollie was not an informer; he was a detective working out of the Eight-Three. Fat Ollie was not as fat as Fats Donner; hence Ollie's obesity was in the singular whereas Donner's was in the plural. The men did have two things in common, however: they were both very good listeners and nobody liked either one of them. Nobody liked Fats Donner because his sexual preferences ran to prepubescent girls. Nobody liked Fat Ollie because he was a bigot. Moreover, he was that rare sort of bigot who hated everyone.

The cops of the Eight-Seven still remembered Roger Havilland, who'd been an Ollie Weeks sort of person before he got thrown through a plate glass window to his final reward. No one—well, hardly anyone—wished such a dire fate would befall Ollie, but they did wish he would bathe every now and again. On a fair day with a brisk wind, you could smell Ollie clear across Grover Park.

On Monday morning, the sixteenth day of January, Ollie walked into the Eight-Seven's squadroom as if he owned the joint. Pushed his way familiarly through the slatted rail divider, his beer barrel belly preceding him as surely as did his stench, wearing only a sports jacket over his open-collared shirt, despite the frigid temperature outside. His cheeks were rosy red, and he was puffing like a man actively seeking a heart attack. He walked directly to where Carella was typing at his desk, clapped him on the shoulder, and said, "Hey, Steve-arino, how you been?"

Carella winced.

"Hello, Ollie," he said unenthusiastically.

"So you're looking for the Doctor, huh?" Ollie said, and put his finger to the side of his nose like a Mafia sage. "You come to the right person."

Carella hoped Ollie didn't mean what he thought Ollie meant.

"Martin Proctor," Ollie said. "Sounds like a Jew, don't he? The Martin, I mean. You ever heard of anybody named Martin who wasn't a Jew?"

"Yes, Martin Sheen," Carella said.

"He's *worse* than a Jew," Ollie said, "he's a fuckin' Mexican. His son's name is Emilio Estevez, so where does he come off usin' an American name like Sheen? There was this bishop in New York, his name was Sheen, wasn't it? So who's this fuckin' Mexican using a Jewish first name and an Irish last name?"

Carella was suddenly sorry he'd brought it up.

But Ollie was just gathering steam.

"You get these fuckin' immigrants, they change their names so nobody can tell they're foreigners. Who do they think they're kiddin'? Guy writes a book, he's a fuckin' wop, he puts an American name on the book, everybody knows he's really a wop, anyway. Everybody says You know what his real name is? His real name ain't Lance Bigelow, it's Luigi Mangiacavallo. Everybody knows this. Behind his back, they laugh at him. They say Good morning, Lance, how are you? Or Good evening, Mr. Bigelow, your table is ready. But who's he kidding? They all know he's only a wop."

"Like me," Carella said.

"That's true," Ollie said, "but you're okay otherwise."

Carella sighed.

"Anyway, you got me off the track with your fuckin' Martin Sheen," Ollie said. "You want what I got on Proctor, or you want to talk about Mexicans who put makeup on their faces to earn a living?"

Carella sighed again.

He did not for a moment doubt that Ollie Weeks had a line on Martin Proctor. But he did not want favors from Ollie. Favors had to be paid back. Favors owed to a bigot were double-edged favors. However good a cop Ollie Weeks was—and the sad truth was that he happened to be a very good cop—Carella did not want to owe him, did not want Ollie to come back later to say the note he'd signed was due. But a six-month-old baby and her sitter had been murdered.

"What've you got?" he asked.

"Ah yes, the man is interested," Ollie said, doing his world-famous W. C. Fields imitation.

Carella looked at him.

"Very definitely interested, ah yes," Ollie said, still doing Fields. "Let us say for the sake of argument that there is a certain lady who frequents a bar, ah yes, in the Eighty-Third Precinct, which some of us mere mortals call home, ah yes. Let us further say that this lady has on occasion in the past dispensed certain favors and information to certain detectives in this fair city who have looked the other way while the lady was plying her trade, do I make my point, sir?"

Carella nodded.

Weeks was banging a hooker in the Eight-Three.

"What's her name?" he asked.

"Ah yes, her name. Which, may I say, sir, is none of your fucking business, ah yes."

"Could you please drop the Fields imitation?" Carella said.

"You knew it was him, huh?" Ollie said, pleased. "I also do Ronald Reagan."

"Don't," Carella said.

"I do Ronald Reagan after they cut off his legs."

"What about this hooker?"

"Who said she was a hooker?"

"Gee, for some reason I thought she was a hooker."

"Whatever she may be, let us say she got to talking the other night . . ."

"When?"

"Saturday night."

"And?"

"And seeing as I am a law enforcement officer, and seeing as how we were sharing a few intimate moments together . . ."

"Get to it, Ollie."

"The lady inquired as to whether I knew why the police were looking for Martin the Doctor. This was like a strange situation, Steve. Usually, *I'm* the one pumping *her*. But there we were . . ."

His sex life, no less, Carella thought.

". . . both of us naked as niggers in the jungle, and *she's* the one tryin'a get information outa *me*. Can you see how peculiar that was?"

Carella waited.

But Ollie hadn't intended the question rhetorically.

"Do you see how peculiar that was?" he repeated.

"Yes," Carella said. "Very peculiar."

"I mean, she is riding me bareback like a fuckin' Indian on a pony and she wants to know why the cops are lookin' for Proctor, who I don't know from a hole in the wall."

"So?"

"So I get outa bed afterward, and I go wipe my dick on the drapes . . . do you know that joke?"

"No."

"It's what a Jewish guy does to get his wife excited after he comes. He wipes his dick on the drapes, you get it? To get his wife excited. Because Jewish girls . . ."

"I get it," Carella said.

"I didn't *really* wipe my dick on the drapes," Ollie said. "I mean, I know I'm a fuckin' slob but I'm not *that* big a slob."

"What *did* you use?" Carella asked. "Your tie?"

"That's very funny," Ollie said, but he didn't laugh. "Anyway, while she's squatting over a basin rinsing herself out, she tells me this friend of hers is a friend of Proctor's, and he was wonderin' why the cops were snoopin' around Proctor's old address, lookin' for him. And if I knew anything about it, she would appreciate it if I would tell her, seeing as we were old friends and all. So she could pass the information on to her friend. Who I guess, but she didn't say, would then pass it on to Proctor, saving his ass from whatever terrible thing we had in mind for him, the cops. I told her I would sniff around."

"So where is he?"

"Proctor? One thing at a time. Don't you want to hear what a brilliant detective I am?"

"No."

"Okay, then I won't tell you how I went to this spic snitch named Francisco Palacios, who is also known as The Gaucho, or sometimes The Cowboy, and who runs a little store that sells in the front medicinal herbs, dream books, religious statues, numbers books, tarot cards and such, but in the back French ticklers, open-crotch panties, vibrators, dildoes, benwa balls and the like, not that this is against the law. I won't tell you how The Cowboy mentioned to me that another stoolie named Donner had been in asking about this very same Doctor Proctor who it seems the boys of the Eight-Seven have been inquiring about. I won't tell you how it occurs to me that perhaps it was somebody from up here who was nosing around 1146 Park Street, which was Proctor's last known address, who according to The Cowboy he has busted parole and is being very cautious, anyway. I will not tell you all this, Steve-arino," Ollie said, and grinned.

"What will you tell me?"

"Not where Proctor is, 'cause I don't know."

"Terrific," Carella said. "So what are you doing up here?"

"My friend? This lady I was telling you about?"

"Yeah?"

"I know *her* friend's name."

EILEEN HADN'T SAID a word for the past twenty minutes.

Just kept sitting there staring at Karin.

Karin hadn't said anything either.

It was a staring contest.

Eileen looked at her watch.

"Yes?" Karin said.

"Nothing."

"You can leave whenever you want to," Karin said. "This isn't violin lessons."

"I didn't think it was."

"What I mean is . . ."

"Yes, I . . ."

"No one's forcing you to do this."

"I'm here of my own free will, I know."

"Exactly."

"But that doesn't . . ."

Eileen caught herself, shook her head.

"Doesn't what?"

"Doesn't mean I don't know you're sitting there waiting to *pounce* on whatever I might say."

"Is that what you think?"

Eileen said nothing.

"That I'm waiting to pounce on you?"

"That's your job, isn't it? To take whatever I say and make a federal case out of it?"

"I never thought of my job as . . ."

"Let's not get into *your* job, okay? The reason I'm here is I want to quit *my* job. And so far I haven't had any help in that direction."

"Well, we've only seen each other . . ."

"So how long does it take to write a resignation letter?"

"Is that what you want me to help you with? A resignation letter?"

"You *know* what I . . ."

"But I don't know."

"I want to *quit,* damn it! And I can't seem to do it."

"Maybe you don't want to quit."

"I do."

"All right."

"You know I do."

"Yes, that's what you told me."

"Yes. And it's true."

"You want to quit because you killed a man."

"Yes."

"And you're afraid if you stay on the job . . ."

"I'll be forced into another situation, yes, where I'll have to use the gun again."

"Have to fire the gun again."

"Yes."

"Kill again."

"Yes."

"You're afraid of that."

"Yes."

"What else are you afraid of?"

"What do you want me to say?"

"Whatever you're thinking. Whatever you're feeling."

"I know what you'd *like* me to say."

"And what's that?"

"I know *exactly* what you'd like me to say."

"Tell me."

"You'd like me to say rape."

"Uh-huh."

"You'd like me to say I'm afraid of getting raped again . . ."

"Are you?"

". . . that I want to quit before some son of a bitch rapes me again."

"Is that how you feel?"

Eileen did not answer.

For the remaining five minutes of the hour, she sat there staring at Karin.

At last, Karin smiled and said, "I'm sorry, our time is up. I'll see you on Thursday, okay?"

Eileen nodded, slung her shoulder bag, and went to the door. At the door, she hesitated with her hand on the knob. Then she turned and said, "I am. Afraid of that, too."

And turned again and went out.

SAMMY PEDICINI was used to talking to cops. Whenever a burglary went down in this city, the cops paid Sammy a little visit, asked him all kinds of questions. Sammy always told them the same thing. Whatever it

was they were investigating, it wasn't Sammy who did it. Sammy had taken a fall ten years ago, and now he was outside again, and he had learned his lesson.

"Whatever this is," Sammy told Carella now, "I didn't do it."

Carella nodded.

"I learned my lesson up at Castleview, I been clean since."

Meyer nodded, too.

"I play saxophone in a band called Larry Foster's Rhythm Kings," Sammy said. "We play for these sixty-year-old farts who were kids back in the Forties. They're very good dancers, those old farts. All the old Glenn Miller stuff, Harry James, Charlie Spivak, Claude Thornhill. We have all the arrangements. We get a lot of jobs, you'd be surprised. I learned how to play the sax in stir."

"You must be pretty good at it," Meyer said. "To earn your living at it."

"Which, if that's supposed to be sarcastic, happens to be true. I *do* earn my living playing saxophone."

"Just what I said," Meyer said.

"But what you *meant* is I'm still doing burglaries on the side. Which ain't true."

"Did I say that?" Meyer asked. He turned to Carella. "Steve, did I say that?"

"I didn't hear you say that," Carella said. "We're looking for Martin Proctor. Do you know where he is?"

"Is he a musician?" Sammy asked. "What does he play?"

"The E-flat jimmy," Meyer said.

"He's a burglar," Carella said. "Like you."

"Me, I'm a saxophone player. What Proctor is, I don't know, because I don't know the man."

"But your girlfriend knows him, doesn't she?"

"What girlfriend?"

"Your girlfriend who's a hooker and who was asking a detective we know why the police were snooping around Proctor's old address."

"Gee, this is news to me. I'll tell you the truth, I wish my girlfriend *was* a hooker. Teach me a few tricks, huh?" Sammy said, and laughed. Nervously.

"Proctor did a job on New Year's Eve," Carella said, "in a building on Grover. Two murders were also done in that same building, the same night."

Sammy let out a long, low whistle.

"Yeah," Carella said.

"So where is he?" Meyer asked.

"If I don't know the man, how can I tell you where he is?"

"We're going to bust your girlfriend," Carella said.

"What for?"

"For prostitution. We're going to get her name from this detective we know, and we're going to haul *her* ass off the street and ask *her* about Martin Proctor. And we'll keep busting her until . . ."

"Oh, you mean *Martin* Proctor. I thought you said *Marvin* Proctor."

"Where?" Meyer said.

HAMILTON FOLLOWED KLING from the station house on Grover Avenue to the subway station three blocks away, and then boarded the downtown train

with him. Stood right at the man's elbow. Bertram A.
Kling. Detective/Third Grade. Isaac had got the information from the court records. Isaac was very good at
gathering information. He was, however, somewhat
dim when it came to comprehending the complexities
of high-level business arrangements. Which was why
Hamilton had not told him about the telephone call last
month from Carlos Ortega in Miami. Or the necessity
of employing a fool like José Herrera, who had turned
out to be a fucking crook as well. Isaac would not have
understood. But, giving the devil his due, he had done
well on the cop. Bertram A. Kling. Who had testified at
the arraignments of Herbert Trent, James Marshall, and
Andrew Fields. Bertram A. Kling. Who did not know
that the man standing next to him hanging on a subway
strap was Lewis Randolph Hamilton, who would kill
him the moment he could do it conveniently and vanish
like smoke.

There were perhaps forty blacks on the subway car.

This was good for Hamilton.

Even if there were recent pictures of him in this
city's police files—which he knew there were not—but
even if there were, a white cop like Kling wouldn't have
recognized him, anyway. Kling—with his blond hair
and his peachfuzz appearance—looked like the kind of
white cop who thought all black criminals looked alike.
Only thing that was different on the mug shots was the
numbers. Otherwise, they all looked like gorillas. He
had heard too many white cops say this. Actually, it
would give him great pleasure to kill Kling.

He liked killing people.

Blowing them away with the big mother Magnum.

He particularly liked killing cops.

He had killed two cops in L.A. They were still look-ing for him out there. Black man with a beard. Gorilla with a beard. He didn't have a beard, anymore, he'd shaved in Houston before the posse took that big ship-ment coming up via Mexico. Wore his hair Rastafarian down there in Houston.

Hamilton hated cops.

Not even knowing Kling, he hated him. And would have enjoyed killing him even if Herrera hadn't told him a goddamn thing. Which was possible, after all, because how could Herrera have learned anything about the Tsu shipment coming up next Monday? When not even Isaac knew as yet.

Hamilton stood by Kling's side on the subway, a black man invisible among other black men, and smiled when he wondered how many people on this train even imagined that he and the big blond man were both wearing guns.

KLING GOT OFF the train at Brogan Square, and came up out of the tunnel into a day that was still cold but beginning to turn a bit sunny. He had called Karin Lefkowitz first, to make an appointment with her, and now he hurried along High Street to her office in what used to be the Headquarters Building. Linked to the Criminal Courts Building by a third-floor passageway through which prisoners going to court could be moved, the old gray building looked like a Siamese twin to the one beside it. He came up the low flat steps out front, entered through the huge bronze doors, showed his identification to a uniformed cop sitting behind a desk in the marbled ground-floor corridor, and then took the elevator up to the fifth floor. A sign hand-lettered PSAS indicated by way of a pointing arrow that the office was to the right. He followed the corridor, spotted another sign and yet a third one, and then found a door with a glass paneled top, lettered with the words Psychological Services and Aid Section.

He looked at his watch.

Five minutes to two.

He opened the door and went in.

There was a small waiting room. A closed door opposite the entrance door. Two easy chairs, a lamp, a coat rack with two coats on it, several back issues of *People* magazine. Kling hung up his coat, sat in one of the chairs and picked up a copy with Michael Jackson on the cover. In a few moments, a portly man with the telltale veined and bulbous nose of a heavy drinker came through the inner door, went to the rack, took his coat from it, and left without saying a word to Kling. He looked like a thousand sergeants Kling had known. A moment after that, a woman came through that same door.

"Detective Kling?" she said.

"Yes."

He got to his feet.

"I'm Karin Lefkowitz. Won't you come in, please?"

Short brown hair, blue eyes. Wearing a gray dress, with pearls and Reeboks. Twenty-six or -seven, he guessed. Nice smile.

He followed her into her office. Same size as the waiting room. A wooden desk. A chair behind it. A chair in front of it. Several framed degrees on the wall. A framed picture of the police commissioner. Another framed picture of the mayor.

"Please," she said, and indicated the chair in front of the desk.

Kling sat.

Karin went to the chair behind the desk.

"Your call surprised me," she said. "Did you know that Eileen was here this morning?"

"No."

"I thought she may have . . ."

"No, she doesn't know I called. It was entirely my idea."

"I see."

She studied him. She looked like the kind of woman who should be wearing glasses. He wondered if she had contacts on. Her eyes looked so very blue. Sometimes contacts did that.

"What was it you wanted to discuss?" she said.

"Has Eileen told you that we've stopped seeing each other?"

"Yes."

"And?"

"And what?"

"What do you think about it?"

"Mr. Kling, before we go any further . . ."

"Confidentiality, I know. But this is different."

"How?"

"I'm not asking you to divulge anything Eileen

may have told you in confidence. I'm asking *your* opinion on . . ."

"Ah, I see. *My* opinion. But a very thin line, wouldn't you say?"

"No, I wouldn't. I want to know whether this . . . well, separation is the only thing I can call it . . . whether you think it's a good idea."

"And what if I told you that whatever is good for Eileen is a good idea?"

"Do you think this separation is good for Eileen?"

Karin smiled.

"Please," she said.

"I'm not asking you to do anything behind Eileen's . . ."

"Oh? Aren't you?"

"Miss Lefkowitz . . . I need your help."

"Yes?"

"I . . . I really want to be with Eileen. While she's going through this. I think that her wanting to . . . to . . . stay apart isn't natural. What I wish . . ."

"No."

Kling looked at her.

"No, I will not advise her to resume your relationship unless that is what she herself wishes."

"Miss Lefkowitz . . ."

"Period," Karin said.

HAMILTON SAW HIM coming down the steps of the old Headquarters Building, walking at a rapid clip like a man who was angry about something. Blond hair blowing in the sudden fierce wind. Hamilton hated this city.

You never knew from one minute to the next in this city what was going to happen with the weather. The sun was shining very bright now, but the wind was too strong. Newspapers rattling along the curbs, people walking with their heads ducked, coattails flapping. He fell in behind Kling, no chance of a shot at him here in this crowded downtown area, courthouses everywhere around them, cops moving in and out of them like cockroaches, Christ, he was walking fast.

Hamilton hurried to keep up.

Where the hell was he going, anyway?

He'd already passed the entrance to the subway.

So where was he headed?

THE POCKET PARK was an oasis of solitude and quiet here in the city that normally paid only lip service to such perquisites of civilization. Kling knew the park because on days when he'd had to testify in one case or another, he'd buy himself a sandwich in the deli on Jackson, and then come here on the lunch break. Sit on one of the benches, eat his sandwich in the sunshine, think about anything but a defense attorney wagging his finger and wanting to know if he'd *really* observed the letter of the law while making his arrest.

The park was virtually deserted today.

Too windy for idlers, he guessed.

Set between two office buildings on Jackson, the space was a long rectangle with a brick wall at its far end. A thin fall of water cascaded over the top of this wall, washing down over the brick, even in the dead of winter; Kling guessed the water was heated. The park was dotted with trees, a dozen of them in all, with benches under them.

Only one of the benches was occupied as Kling came in off the street.

A woman reading a book.

The sounds of the streetside traffic suddenly vanished, to be replaced by the sound of the water gently running down the brick wall.

Kling took a seat on a bench facing the wall.

His back was to the park entrance.

In a little while, the woman looked at her watch, got up, and left.

HAMILTON couldn't believe it!

There he was, sitting alone in the park, his back to the entrance, no one in the place but Bertram A. Kling!

This was going to be too simple. He almost regretted the sheer simplicity of it. Walk up behind the man, put a bullet in the back of his head, gangland style. They might even think the Mafia had done it. This was delicious. He could not wait to tell Isaac about it.

He checked the street, eyes swinging right, then left.

And moved swiftly into the park.

The Magnum was in the right-hand pocket of his overcoat.

Patches of snow on the ground.

Water rolling down the brick wall at the far end.

The park silent otherwise.

Ten feet away from him now.

Careful, careful.

The gun came out of his pocket.

* * *

KLING SAW the shadow first.

Suddenly joining his own shadow on the ground in front of him.

He turned at once.

And saw the gun.

And threw himself headlong off the bench and onto the ground just as the first shot boomed onto the air, and rolled over, and reached in under his overcoat for the gun holstered on the left side of his belt, another shot, and sat upright with the gun in both hands and fired at once, three shots in succession at the tall black man in the long gray coat who was running out of the park.

Kling ran after him.

There were only three hundred and sixty-four black men on the street outside the park.

But none of them looked like the man who'd just tried to kill him.

MARTIN PROCTOR had just come out of the shower and was drying himself when the knock sounded on his door.

He wrapped the towel around his waist, and went out into the living room.

"Who is it?" he asked.

"Police," Meyer said. "Want to open the door, please?"

Proctor did not want to open the door.

"Yeah, just a second," he said. "I just got out of the shower. Let me put on some clothes."

He went into the bedroom, took a pair of under-shorts from the top drawer, slipped them on, and then hastily put on a pair of blue corduroy trousers, a blue turtleneck sweater, a pair of blue woolen socks, and a pair of black, seventy-five-dollar French and Shriner shoes with some kind of synthetic soles that gripped like rubber.

From outside the apartment door, he heard the same cop asking, "Mr. Proctor? You going to open this door for us?"

"Yeah, I'll be with you in a minute," he yelled and went to the closet and took from a hanger the eleven-hundred-dollar Ralph Lauren camel hair coat he had stolen on New Year's Eve, and then he went to his dresser and took from the same top drawer containing his undershorts and handkerchiefs a .22-caliber High Standard Sentinel Snub he had stolen last year some-time from a guy who also had a stamp collection, and then he yelled to the door, "Just putting on my shoes, be there in a second," and went out the window.

He came down the fire escape skillfully, not for nothing was he a deft burglar with the courage of a lion tamer and the dexterity of a high wire performer. There was no way he was going to have any kind of discussion with any representative of the law, not when he was looking at a renewed stretch in the slammer for break-ing parole. So he came down those fire-escape ladders as fast as he knew how, which was *damn* fast, because he knew that the cop in the hallway would be kicking in the door if he hadn't already done it, and him and his partner, they always traveled in pairs, would be in that apartment in a flash, and the minute they went in the bedroom—

"Hello, Proctor," the man said.

The man was looking up at him from the ground just below the first-floor fire escape. The man had a gun in one hand and a police shield in the other.

"Detective Carella," he said.

Proctor almost reached for the gun in the pocket of the coat.

"Just lower the ladder and come on down," Carella said.

"I didn't do anything," Proctor said.

He was still debating whether he should go for the gun.

"Nobody said you did. Come on down."

Proctor stood undecided.

"My partner's up there above you," Carella said. "You're sandwiched."

Proctor's hand inched toward the coat pocket.

"If that's a gun in there," Carella said, "you're a dead man."

Proctor suddenly agreed with him.

He lowered the ladder and came on down.

10.

THE Q & A BEGAN in Lieutenant Byrnes's office that Monday evening at ten minutes past six. Present were the lieutenant, Detectives Carella and Meyer, Martin Proctor, a lawyer named Ralph Angelini who'd been requested by Proctor, and a stenographer from the Clerical Office, as backup to the tape recorder. The detectives did not know as yet whether Proctor had asked for a lawyer because he was facing a return trip to Castleview on the parole violation, or whether he knew that the subject about to be discussed was murder. Twice.

The lawyer was Proctor's very own and not someone supplied by Legal Aid.

A nice young man in his late twenties.

Carella knew that even thieves and murderers were entitled to legal representation. The thing he couldn't understand was why honest young men like Ralph Angelini *chose* to defend thieves and murderers.

For the tape, the lieutenant identified everyone present, and then advised Proctor of his rights under Miranda-Escobedo, elicited from him his name and present address, and turned the actual questioning over to his detectives.

Carella asked all of the questions.

Proctor and his lawyer took turns answering them.

It went like this:

Q: Mr. Proctor, we have here a report from the . . .

A: Just a minute, please. May I ask up front what this is in reference to?

Q: Yes, Mr. Angelini. It is in reference to a burglary committed on New Year's Eve in the apartment of Mr. and Mrs. Charles Unger at 967 Grover Avenue, here in Isola, sir.

A: Very well, go ahead.

Q: Thank you. Mr. Proctor, we have here a report from the Detective Bureau's Latent Print Unit . . .

A: *Your* police department?

Q: Yes, Mr. Angelini.

A: Go ahead then.

Q: A report on latent fingerprints retrieved from a window and sill in the Unger apartment, and those . . .

A: Retrieved by whom?

Q: Retrieved by the Crime Scene Unit. Now Mr. Proctor, the fingerprints retrieved from the Unger window and sill match your fingerprints on file downtown. Can you tell me . . . ?

A: Do you have a copy of that LPU report?

Q: Yes, Mr. Angelini, I have it right here.

A: May I see it, please?

Q: Yes, sir. And may I say, sir, that in this Q and A so far, your client has not been allowed to give a single answer to any of the questions I've put. Pete, I think maybe we ought to call the D.A., get somebody here who can cope with Mr. Angelini, because I sure as hell can't. And I'd like that left on the record, please.

A: I believe I have every right asking to see a report purporting to . . .

Q: You know damn well I wouldn't *say* we had a report if we *didn't* have one!

A: Very well then, let's get on with this.

Q: You think maybe your client can answer a few questions now?

A: I said let's get on with it.

Q: Thank you. Mr. Proctor, how did your fingerprints get on that window and sill?

A: Is it okay to answer that?

A: (from Mr. Angelini) Yes, go ahead. Answer it.

A: (from Mr. Proctor) I don't know how they got there.

Q: You don't, huh?

A: It's a total mystery to me.

Q: No idea how they got on that window and sill just off the spare bedroom fire escape.

A: None at all.

Q: You don't think you may have left them there?

A: Excuse me, Mr. Carella, but . . .

Q: Jee-sus *Christ!*

A: I beg your pardon, but . . .

Q: Mr. Angelini, you are perfectly within your rights to

ask us to stop this questioning at any time. Without prejudice to your client. Just say, "That's enough, no more," you don't even have to give us an explanation. That's Miranda-Escobedo, Mr. Angelini, that's how we protect the rights of citizens in this country of ours. Now, if that's what you want to do, please do it. You realize, of course, that on the strength of the LPU report, the D.A. will undoubtedly ask for a burglary indictment, which he'll undoubtedly get. But I think you should know there's a more serious charge we're considering here. And . . .

A: Are you referring to the parole violation?

Q: No, sir, I'm not.

A: Then what charge are you . . . ?

Q: Homicide, sir. Two counts of homicide.

A: (from Mr. Proctor) What?

A: (from Mr. Angelini) Be quiet, Martin.

A: (from Mr. Proctor) No, just a second. What do you mean homicide? You mean murder? Did somebody get murdered?

A: (from Mr. Angelini) Martin, I think . . .

A: (from Mr. Proctor) Is that what you're trying to hang on me here? Murder?

Q: Mr. Angelini, if we could proceed with the questioning in an orderly manner . . .

A: I wasn't aware that this Q and A would concern itself with homicide.

Q: Now you are aware of it, sir.

A: I'm not sure my client should answer any further questions. I'd like to consult with him.

Q: Please do.
  (Questioning resumed at 6:22 P.M. aforesaid date)

Q: Mr. Proctor, I'd like to get back to those fingerprints we found in the Unger apartment.

A: I'll answer any questions about the alleged burglary,
  but I won't go near whatever you plan to ask about
  homicide.

Q: Is that what Mr. Angelini advised you?

A: That is what he advised me.

Q: All right. Did you leave those fingerprints on the
  Unger window and sill?

A: I did not.

Q: Were you surprised in the Unger apartment by Mr.
  and Mrs. Unger at approximately one-thirty A.M. on
  the first of January?

A: I was home in bed at that time.

Q: For the record, I would like to say that we have a
  sworn statement from Mr. and Mrs. Unger to the
  effect that . . .

A: May I see that statement, please?

Q: Yes, Mr. Angelini. I didn't plan to read it into the
  record, I merely . . .

A: I would like to see it.

Q: I wanted to explain the content so that your client . . .

A: Just let me see it, okay, Mr. Carella?

Q: Okay, sure, Mr. Angelini.

A: Thank you.
  (Questioning resumed at 6:27 P.M. aforesaid date)

Q: Do I now have your permission to summarize the
  content of that statement for your client and for the
  tape?

A: (inaudible)

Q: Sir?

A: I said go ahead, go ahead.

Q: Thank you. Mr. Proctor, the Ungers have made a statement to the effect that at one-thirty A.M. on the first of January, they entered their spare bedroom . . . what they use as a TV room . . . and surprised a young man going out the window onto the fire escape. They described him as having blond hair . . . excuse me, but what color is your hair?

A: Blond.

Q: And they said he was thin. Would you describe yourself as thin?

A: Wiry.

Q: Is that thin?

A: It's slender and muscular.

Q: But not thin.

A: He's answered the question, Mr. Carella.

Q: They also said he had a mustache that was just growing in. Would it be fair to say that you have a new mustache?

A: It's pretty new, yes.

Q: And they said that the young man pointed a gun at them and threatened he would be back if they called the police. I show you this gun, Mr. Proctor, a High Standard Sentinel Snub, .22-caliber Long Rifle revolver, and ask if it was in the pocket of your overcoat when you were arrested this afternoon.

A: It was.

Q: Is it your gun?

A: No. I don't know how it got in my pocket.

Q: Mr. Proctor, when you were arrested tonight, were you wearing a camel hair coat containing a Ralph Lauren label?

A: I was.

Q: Is this the coat?

A: That's the coat.

Q: Where did you get this coat?

A: I bought it.

Q: Where?

A: At Ralph Lauren.

Q: Mr. Angelini, we have a list of goods stolen from the Unger apartment on the morning of January first—I'm showing you the list right this minute before you ask for it—and one of the items on that list is a Ralph Lauren camel hair overcoat valued at eleven hundred dollars. I wish to inform your client that the Ungers in their statement said the man going out their window was wearing the camel hair coat described in the list of stolen goods. Mr. Proctor, do you still claim you were not in the Unger apartment that night?

A: I was home in bed.

Q: Mr. Proctor, the Ungers said that the man going out their bedroom window was also wearing a black leather jacket, black slacks and white sneakers. I show you this black leather jacket, these black slacks, and these white sneakers and ask you if these articles of clothing were found in your closet this afternoon at the time of your arrest.

A: They were.

Q: I also show you this emerald ring which was found

in your apartment at the time of your arrest, and I refer you again to the list of goods stolen from the Unger apartment. An emerald ring and a Kenwood VCR are on that list. Mr. Proctor, would you now like to tell me again that you were not, in fact, in the Unger apartment at the time and on the night in question, and that you did not, in fact . . .

A: I would like to talk to my lawyer, please.

Q: Please do, Mr. Proctor.

(Questioning resumed at 6:45 P.M. aforesaid date)

A: In answer to your question, yes, I was in the Unger apartment that night.

Q: Thank you. Did you commit a burglary in that apartment on the night in question?

A: I was in the apartment. Whether that's burglary or whatever, it isn't for me to say.

Q: How did you enter the apartment?

A: I came down from the roof.

Q: How?

A: Down the fire escapes.

Q: And how did you get into the apartment?

A: By way of the fire escape.

Q: Outside the spare bedroom window?

A: Yes.

Q: Did you jimmy the window?

A: Yes.

Q: How did you leave the apartment?

A: The same way.

Q: The Unger apartment is on the sixth floor, isn't that so?

A: I don't know what floor it's on. I just came down

from the roof and when I saw an apartment looked empty, I went in.

Q: And this happened to be the Unger apartment.

A: I didn't know whose apartment it was.

Q: Well, the apartment where you stole the Ralph Lauren coat and the Kenwood VCR and the . . .

A: Well . . .

Q: That apartment.

A: I guess.

Q: Which was the Unger apartment.

A: If you say so.

Q: Now when you went out of this sixth-floor window onto the fire escape, did you then go up to the roof or down to the street?

A: Down to the street.

Q: Down the ladders, floor by floor . . .

A: Yes.

Q: To the street.

A: Yes.

Q: Did you stop in any other apartment on your way down to the street?

A: No.

Q: Are you sure?

A: I'm positive. Oh, I get it.

Q: What do you get, Mr. Proctor?

A: Somebody was killed in that building, right? So you think I done the sixth-floor burglary and then topped it off with a murder, right?

Q: You tell me.

A: Don't be ridiculous. I never killed anybody in my entire life.

Q: Tell me what you did, minute by minute, after you left the Unger apartment at one-thirty A.M.

A: Really, Mr. Carella, you can't expect him to remember minute by *minute* what he . . .

Q: I think he knows what I'm looking for, Mr. Angelini.

A: As long as it's clear that you don't mean minute by minute *literally*.

Q: As close as he can remember.

A: May I ask on my client's behalf, is he correct in assuming that a homicide was committed in that building on the night of the burglary?

Q: *Two* homicides, Mr. Angelini.

A: What are you pursuing here, Mr. Carella?

Q: Let me level with you. Your client . . .

A: (from Mr. Proctor) Go hide the silver, Ralph.

Q: Well, I'm happy for a little levity here . . .

A: (from Mr. Proctor) You either laugh or you cry, am I right?

Q: I'm glad you have a sense of humor.

A: One thing you develop in the slammer is a good sense of humor.

Q: I'm happy to hear that, but I don't think there's anything funny about a dead six-month-old baby.

A: (from Mr. Angelini) So *that's* the case.

Q: That's the case.

A: Maybe we ought to pack up and go home, Martin.

Q: Well, Mr. Proctor isn't going anywhere, as you know. If you mean you'd like him to quit answering my questions, fine. But as I was about to say . . .

A: Give me one good reason why I should permit him to continue.

Q: Because if he didn't kill that baby and her sitter . . .

A: He didn't. Flatly and unequivocally.

Q: Before you even ask him, huh?

A: My client is not a murderer. Period.

Q: Well, I'm glad you're so certain of that, Mr. Angelini. But as I was saying, I wish you'd permit your client to convince *us* he's clean. We're looking for a place to hang our hats, that's the truth. Two people are dead, and we've got your client in the building doing a felony. So let him convince us he didn't do a couple of murders, too. Is that reasonable? That way we go with the burglary and the parole violation and we call it a day, okay?

A: I wish we were talking only parole violation here.

Q: There's no way we can lose the burglary. Forget it.

A: I was merely thinking out loud. You understand what I'm saying, don't you?

Q: You're asking me what's in it for you. The D.A. might want to bargain on the burglary charge, that's up to him. But it won't just disappear, believe me. We're looking at a Burglary One here. Two people in the apartment while he was doing the . . .

A: Not while he was in there. He was already out the window.

Q: He spoke to them. Threatened them, in fact. Pointed a gun at them and . . .

A: The gun is your contention.

Q: Mr. Angelini, we've got an occupied dwelling at nighttime, and a threat with a gun. I don't know what else you think we need for Burglary One, but . . .

A: Okay, let's say you do have a Burg One. How can the D.A. help us?

Q: You'd have to discuss that with him.

A: I'd be looking for a B and E.

Q: You'd be looking low.

A: Would he go for Burg Two?

Q: I can't make deals for the D.A. All I can tell him is that Mr. Proctor was exceedingly cooperative in answering whatever questions we put to him about the double homicide committed in that building. Which is of prime importance to a lot of people in this city, as I'm sure you must realize. On the other hand . . .

A: Tell him what he wants to know, Martin.

A: (from Mr. Proctor) I forgot the question.

Q: Minute by minute. Starting with one-thirty when you went out on that fire escape.

Minute by minute, he had come down the fire escapes until he reached the one outside the first-floor window, and then he had lowered the ladder there to the cement area in the backyard, and had gone down it and jumped the four, five feet to the ground, and then he'd come around the side of the building carrying the VCR under his arm and wearing the camel hair coat with the emerald ring in one of the pockets. He'd walked up to Culver and dumped the VCR right away, sold it to a receiver in a bar named The Bald Eagle, which was still open as this must have been a little before two in the morning by now.

"Better nail it down closer," Carella advised.

"Okay, a movie was just starting on the bar TV. A Joan Crawford movie. Black-and-white. I don't know the name of it, I don't know the channel. Whatever time the movie went on, that's what time I got to the bar."

"And sold the VCR . . ."

"To a fence who gave me forty-two bucks for it. I also . . ."

"His name," Carella said.

"Why?"

"He's your alibi."

"Jerry Macklin," Proctor said at once.

He'd also showed Macklin the emerald ring, and Macklin had offered him three bills for it, which Proctor told him to shove up his ass because he knew the ring was worth at least a couple of grand. Macklin offered him fifty for the coat he was wearing, but Proctor liked the coat and figured he'd keep it. So he'd headed out, still wearing the coat with the ring in the pocket, looking for somebody he could score a coupla vials off . . .

"What time did you leave The Bald Eagle?" Meyer asked.

"Exact?"

"Close as you can get it."

"I can tell you what scene was on in the movie, is all," Proctor said. "I didn't look at a clock or anything."

"What scene was on?"

"She was coming out a fancy building."

"Who?"

"Joan Crawford. With an awning."

"Okay, then what?"

Proctor had gone out of the bar and cruised Glitter Park, which was the street name for the center-island park on Culver between Glendon and Ritter, where he'd run across . . .

"Oh, wait a minute," he said, "I can pin the time down closer. 'Cause this guy I made the buy from, he told me he had to be uptown a quarter to three, and he looked at his watch and said it was already two-twenty. So you got to figure it took me five minutes to walk from the Eagle to Glitter, so that puts me leaving the bar a quarter after two."

"And his name?" Carella said.

"Hey, come on, you got me doin' a snitch on half the people I know."

"Suit yourself," Meyer said.

"Okay, his name is Fletcher Gaines, but you don't have to mention the crack, do you? You can just ask was I with him at twenty after two."

"So according to you," Meyer said, "you . . ."

"Can you do that for me, please? 'Cause I'm cooperating here with you, ain't I?"

"Does this guy deliver all the way upstate?" Meyer asked.

"What do you mean?"

"You broke parole, Proctor. You're heading back to Castleview to see all your old buddies again. You don't have to worry about where your next vial's coming from."

"Yeah, I didn't think of that," Proctor said.

"But let's try to nail this down, okay?" Meyer said. "You were in the Unger apartment at one-thirty . . ."

"Just *leaving* at one-thirty . . ."

"And you came down the fire escapes . . ."

"Right."

"No stops on the way down . . ."

"Right."

"No detours . . ."

"Right."

"And you walked to The Bald Eagle on Culver and . . . *where'd* you say it is?"

"All the way up near Saint Paul's."

"Why'd you go all the way up there?"

" 'Cause I knew Jerry'd be there."

"Jerry Macklin."

"Yeah."

"Your fence."

"Yeah. Who I knew would take at least the VCR off my hands. So I could buy some vials to tide me over, you know?"

"You walked all the way up there, huh?"

"Yeah, I walked."

"That's a long walk, cold night like that."

"I like the cold."

"And you got there just as the Joan Crawford movie was coming on."

"A few minutes before. We were just beginning to talk price when it went on. It musta gone on about two o'clock, don't you think? I mean, they start them on the hour, don't they?"

"Usually. And you left there at a quarter after."

"Yeah."

"And took another little walk. This time to Glitter."

"Well, that wasn't too far. Five minutes is all."

"You like walking, huh?"

"As a matter of fact, I do."

"So if all this is true . . ."

"Oh, it's true."

"Then you can pretty much account for your time between one-thirty and a quarter past two. Provided Macklin and Gaines back your story."

"Unless you scare them with shit about receiving stolen goods and dealing controlled substances, they should back my story, yes. Look, I'm going back to jail, anyway, I got no reason to lie to you."

Except maybe a couple of dead bodies, Carella thought.

THEY FOUND MACKLIN at a little past nine that night.

He corroborated everything Proctor had said.

He even remembered the name of the Joan Crawford movie that had gone on at two in the morning.

And he remembered looking up at the clock when Proctor left the Eagle; he'd been invited to a New Year's Eve party, and he was wondering if it'd still be going at this hour. Which was a quarter past two in the morning.

It took them a while longer to find Fletcher Gaines.

Gaines was a black man living all the way uptown in Diamondback.

When finally they caught up with him at five minutes to ten that Monday night, he told them he was clean and asked them if they weren't just a wee bit off their own turf. They told them they weren't looking for a drug bust, which news Gaines treated with a skeptically raised eyebrow. All they wanted to know was about New Year's Eve. Did he at any time on New Year's Eve run into a person named Martin Proctor?

No mention of time.

No mention of place.

Gaines said he had run into Proctor in Glitter Park sometime that night, but he couldn't remember what time it had been.

They asked him if he could pinpoint that a bit closer.

Gaines figured his man Proctor was looking for a net.

No way to lie for him, though, because he didn't know what time Proctor needed covered.

So he told them he wasn't sure he could be more exact.

They told him that was a shame, and started to walk off.

He said, "Hey, wait a minute, it just come to me. I looked at my watch and it was twenty minutes after two exact, is that of any help to you?"

They thanked him and went back downtown—to their own turf.

VISITING HOURS at the hospital were eight to ten.

The old man was in what was called the Cancer Care Unit, he'd been there since the third of July, when they'd discovered a malignancy in his liver. Bit more than six months now. A person would've thought he'd be dead by now. Cancer of the liver? Supposed to be fatal and fast.

They visited him every night.

Two dutiful daughters.

Got there at a little before eight, came out of the hospital at a little after ten. Said their goodbyes in the parking lot, went to their separate cars. Joyce was driving the old man's car now. Big brown Mercedes. Living in the big house all alone. Went back to Seattle in August, soon as she found out the old man was going to die. Visited him in the hospital every night. A person could've set his watch by her comings and goings. Melissa was driving the old blue station wagon. Waddled like a duck, Melissa did.

It was foggy tonight.

Big surprise. Fog in Seattle. Like London in all those Jack the Ripper movies. Or those creepy werewolf movies. Only this was Seattle. If you didn't get fog here in January, then you got rain, take your choice, that's all there was. In this city, rain was only thicker fog. You wanted to get rich in Seattle, all you had to do was start an umbrella factory. But he figured the fog was good for what he had to do tonight.

The gun was a Smith & Wesson Model 59, which was a nine-millimeter double-action automatic pistol. Same as the 39 except that it had a fourteen-shot magazine instead of an eight. Otherwise, you couldn't tell the two apart: bit more than seven inches long overall, with a four-inch barrel, a blued finish and a checkered walnut stock. It looked something like an army Colt .45. He'd bought it on the street for two hundred bucks. You could get anything you wanted on the street these days. He planned to drop the gun in the Sound after he used it tonight, goodbye, darling. Even if they found it, they'd never be able to trace it. A gun bought on the street? No way they could link it to him.

He'd had the gun sent to Seattle. Just sent it UPS second-day air. Carried it all wrapped and sealed to one of those post-office alternatives that sent things by Federal Express and UPS, even wrapped things for you if you asked them to, though he wasn't about to have them wrap a *gun* for him. Told the girl who weighed it that it was a toy truck. The weight, with the packing and all, had come to twenty-eight pounds. She'd marked on the shipping label TOY TRUCK and asked if he wanted to insure it for more than the already covered hundred bucks. He'd said, no, it had only cost him twenty-five. That easy to send a gun. This was a democracy. He hated to think what *real* criminals were getting away with.

There she came.

Down the hospital steps.

Wearing a yellow rain slicker and black boots, made her look like a fisherman. Melissa was wearing a black cloth coat, kerchief on her head. Fifteen years older than Joyce. Prettier, too. Usually. Right now, she was pregnant as a goose.

Two of them walking toward the parking lot now.

He ducked down behind the wheel of the car.

Fog swirling in around the car, enclosing him.

Watched the yellow rain slicker. A beacon. Joyce in the slicker, bright yellow in the gray of the fog. Melissa's black coat swallowed by the gray, a vanishing act. A car door slamming. Another one. Headlights coming on. The old blue station wagon roared into life. Melissa pulled the car out into the fan of her own headlights, made a right turn, heading for the exit.

He waited.

Joyce started the Benz.

New car, the old man had bought it a month before he'd learned about the cancer. You could hardly hear the engine when it started. The headlights came on. He started his own car.

The Mercedes began moving.

He gave it a respectable lead, and then began following it.

THE HOUSE SAT ON four acres of choice land overlooking the water, a big gray Victorian mansion that had been kept in immaculate repair over the years since it was built. You couldn't find too many houses like this one nowadays, not here in the state of Washington, nor hardly anywhere else. You had to figure the house alone would bring twenty, thirty million dollars. That wasn't counting the furnishings. God alone knew what all those antiques were worth. Stuff the old lady had brought from Europe when she was still alive. And her jewelry? Had to be a fortune in there. The paintings, too. The old man had been a big collector before he got sick, the art in there had to be worth millions. The old Silver Cloud in the garage, the new Benz, the thirty-eight-foot Grand Banks sitting there at the dock, those were only frosting on the cake.

He parked the car in a stand of pines just to the north of the service road. Went in through the woods, walked well past the house and then approached it from the water side. Huge lawn sloping down to the water. Fog rolling in, you couldn't even see the boat at the dock no less the opposite shore. Lights burning in the upstairs bedroom of the house. The shade was up, he saw her move past the window. Wearing only a short nightgown. House was so naturally well protected by water and woods, not another house within shouting distance, she probably figured she could run around naked if she wanted to.

He could feel the weight of the gun in the pocket of his coat.

He was left-handed.

The gun was in the left-hand pocket.

He could remember movies where they caught the killer because he was left-handed. Left-handed people did things differently. Pulled matches off on the wrong side of the matchbook. Well, wrong side for *right*-handed people. That was the old chestnut, the matchbook. More left-handed killers got caught because they didn't see all those movies with the missing matches on the left side of the matchbook. Another thing was ink stains on the edge of the palm, near the pinky. In this country we wrote from left to right and the pen *followed* a right-handed person's hand, whereas the opposite was true for a left-handed person. A left-handed person *trailed* his hand over what he'd already written. Live and learn. If you were left-handed and you'd just finished writing a ransom note in red ink, it was best not to let the police see the edge of your palm near the pinky because there'd surely be red ink on it.

He smiled in the darkness.

Wondered if he should wait till she was asleep. Go in, shoot her in the head. Empty the gun in her, make it look like some lunatic did it. Maybe smash a few price-less vases afterward. Cops'd think somebody went berserk in there.

In a little while, the upstairs bedroom light went out.

He waited in the dark in the fog.

IN HER DREAM, the wind was rattling palm fronds on some Caribbean island and there was the sound of surf crashing in against the shore. In her dream, she was a famous writer sitting in a little thatched hut, an old black Smith-Corona typewriter on a table in front of her, a little window open to a crescent-shaped beach and rows and rows of palms lining an endless shore. The sky was incredibly blue behind the palms. In the distance there were low, green-covered moun-tains. She searched the sky and the mountains for inspiration.

In her dream, she reached idly for a ripe yellow banana in a pale blue bowl on a shelf near the open window. Beautifully shaped bowl. Bunch of bananas in it. She pulled a banana from the bunch. And peeled it down to where her hand was holding it. And brought it to her lips. And put it in her mouth. And was biting down on it when suddenly it turned cold and hard.

Her eyes popped wide open.

The barrel of a gun was in her mouth.

A man was standing beside the bed. Black hat pulled low on his forehead. Black silk handkerchief covering his nose and his mouth. Only his eyes showed. Pinpoints of light glowing in them, reflections from the night light in the wall socket across the room.

He said, "Shhhhh."

The gun in his left hand.

"Shhhhh."

The gun in her mouth.

"Shhhhh, Joyce."

He knew her name.

She thought, How does he know my name?

He said, "Your baby is dead, Joyce."

His voice a whisper.

"Susan is dead," he said. "She died on New Year's Eve."

All whispers sounded alike, but there was something about the cadence, the rhythm, the slow, steady spacing of his words that sounded familiar. Did she know him?

"Are you sorry you gave the baby away?" he said.

She wondered if she should say Yes. Nod. Let him know she was sorry, yes. The gun in her mouth. Wondered if that was the answer he was looking for. She would give him any answer he wanted, provided it was the right answer. She was not at all sorry that she had given the baby away, had never for a moment regretted her decision, was sorry now that the baby was dead, yes, but only because she'd have been sorry about the death of *any* infant. But if he wanted her to say—

"I killed the baby," he said.

Oh Jesus, she thought.

"Your baby," he said.

Oh Jesus, who *are* you? she thought.

"And now I'm going to kill *you*," he said.

She shook her head.

He was holding the gun loosely, allowing it to follow the motion of her head. Her saliva flowed around the barrel of the gun. There was a metallic taste in her mouth. The barrel was slippery with spit.

"Yes," he said.

And turned her head so that she was facing him.

Used the gun to turn her head.

A steady pressure on the gun in her mouth, turning her head so that the left side of her face was on the pillow, his arm straight out, his hand and the gun perpendicular to the bed.

She began to whimper.

Small whimpering sounds around the barrel of the gun.

She tried to say Please around the barrel of the gun. Her tongue found the hole in the barrel of the gun, and pushed out against it as if to nudge it gently and unnoticed from her mouth. The barrel clicked against her teeth. She thought at first that he had moved the gun because he'd discovered she was trying to expel it from her mouth. But she realized all at once that the reverse was true. The gun was steady in her mouth; it was her trembling jaw that was causing her teeth to click against the barrel.

"Well . . ." he said.

Almost sadly. And paused. As if trying to think of something else to say before he pulled the trigger. And in that split second, she knew that unless she herself said something brilliantly convincing, unless she spit that gun barrel out of her mouth and pleaded an eloquent—

The first shot took off the back of her head.

11.

THE PERSON Carella spoke to at the Coast Guard's Ship Movement Office was named Lieutenant Phillip Forbes. Carella told him he was trying to locate a ship.

"Yes, sir, which ship would that be, sir?" Forbes said.

"I don't know exactly," Carella said. "But I'll tell you what I *do* know, and maybe you can take it from there."

"Who did you say this was, sir?"

"Detective Carella, 87th Squad."

"Yes, sir. And this is in regard to?"

"A ship. Actually a person *on* that ship. If we can locate the ship."

"Yes, sir. And you feel this ship may be in port here, is that it?"

"I don't know where it is. That's one of the things I'd like to find out."

"Yes, sir, may I have the name of the ship, please?"

"The General Something. *Are* there ships called the General This or the General That?"

"I can think of at least fifty of them off the top of my head, sir."

"Military vessels or what?"

"No, sir, they can be tankers, freighters, passenger ships, whatever. There're a lot of Generals out there on the ocean."

"How about a General Something that would have been here fifteen months ago?"

"Sir?"

"Do you keep records going back that far?"

"Yes, sir, we do."

"This would've been October a year ago."

"Do you mean October of last year?"

"No, the year before that. Can you check it for me?"

"What is it you want to know, exactly, sir?"

"We have good reason to believe that a ship named the General Something was here in port fifteen months ago. Would you have any record of . . . ?"

"Yes, sir, all ships planning to enter the port must notify us at least twelve hours in advance of arrival."

"*All* ships?"

"Yes, sir, foreign or American. Arrangements for docking are usually made through the ship's agent, who contracts for a berth. Or the owner-operator can do it. Or sometimes the person who chartered the ship. But we also get captains who'll radio ahead to us."

"What information do they give you?"

"Sir?"

"When they notify you. What do they tell you?"

"Oh. The name of the ship, its nationality, the tonnage. Its cargo. Where it's been. Where it's going when it leaves here. How long it plans to be here. Where it'll be while in port."

"Do they usually dock right here in the city?"

"Some of them do, yes, sir. The passenger ships. But not too much of anything else, anymore. There're plenty of berths, you know, the port covers a lot of territory. All the way from Hangman's Rock to John's River."

"If a ship *did* dock here in the city, where would that be?"

"The Canal Zone, most likely. Nothing on the North Side, anymore. It'd be the Canal Zone, over in Calm's Point. Well, the Calm's Point Canal is its right name. That's the only place I can think of where they'd dock. But more than likely—well, this wouldn't be a passenger ship, would it?"

"No."

"Then most likely it'd head for Port Euphemia, over in the next state."

"But you said there *would* be a record . . ."

"Yes, sir, in the Amber files."

"Amber?"

"Amber, yes, sir. That's what the tracking system is called. Amber. Anytime a ship notifies us that it's coming in, all that information I told you about goes right into the computer."

"Do you have access to that computer, Lieutenant? To the Amber files?"

"I do."

"Could you kick up an October eighteenth departure . . ."

"This wasn't *last* October, am I right?"

"October a year ago. See what you've got on a tanker named the General Something-or-Other. Possibly the General Putnam. Or a General Putney. Leaving for the Persian Gulf."

"Take me a minute, sir, if you'd like to hang on."

"I'd like to hang on," Carella said.

When Forbes came back on the line, he said, "I've got two Generals departing on the eighteenth of October that year, sir. Neither of them are tankers. And neither of them are either a Putney or a Putnam."

"What are they?"

"Freighters, both of them."

"And they're called?"

"One of them's the *General Roy Edwin Dean* and the other's the *General Edward Lazarus Kalin*."

"Which one of them was heading for the Persian Gulf?"

"Neither one, sir. The *Dean* was bound for Australia. The *Kalin* was headed for England."

"Terrific," Carella said, and sighed heavily. Either Joyce Chapman's seaman had been lying in his teeth, or else she'd been too stoned to remember *anything* about him. "Well, Lieutenant," he said, "thank you very . . ."

"But you might want to run down there yourself," Forbes said.

Carella guessed he meant Australia.

"The Canal Zone," Forbes said. "The *Dean*'s in now. I know you're looking for a Putney or a Putnam but maybe your information . . ."

"Have you got a berth number?" Carella asked.

* * *

THE CALM'S POINT CANAL.

The police had long ago dubbed it the Canal Zone, and the label had seeped into the city's general vocabulary. For the citizens who had never seen it, the name conjured a patch of torrid tropicana right here in the frigid north, a glimpse of exotic Panama—which they had also never seen. The only thing Hispanic about the Zone was the nationality of many of the hookers parading their wares for seamen off the ships or men cruising by in automobiles on their way home from work. Much of the trade was, in fact, mobile. A car would pull up to any one of the corners on Canalside, and the driver would lean over and roll down his window, and one of the scantily dressed girls would saunter over, and they'd negotiate a price. If they both agreed they had a viable deal, the girl would get in the car, and the trick would drive around the block a couple of times while she showed him what an expert could accomplish in all of five minutes.

There were some thirty-odd berths on each side of the canal, occupied at any time of the year because docking space was scarce anywhere in this city. The *General Roy Edwin Dean* was in berth number twenty-seven on the eastern side of the canal. A sturdy, responsible-looking vessel that had weathered many a storm and always found its way back to safe harbor, it sat squarely on the water, bobbing on a mild chop that rolled in off the River Dix and the open water beyond.

Meyer and Carella had not called ahead; the truth was, they didn't know *how* to make a phone call to a ship. Lieutenant Forbes had given Carella the number of the berth, and he and Meyer simply showed up at five minutes past one that Wednesday afternoon. A fierce wind was blowing in off the water. Whitecaps crested as far as the eye could see. Carella wondered why some men felt they *had* to go down to the seas again, the lonely sea and the sky. Meyer was wondering why he'd forgotten to wear his hat on a day like today. There was a gangplank. Carella looked at Meyer. Meyer shrugged. They climbed to the deck of the ship.

Not a soul in sight.

"Hello?" Carella shouted.

Not a soul, not a sound.

Except for the wind banging something metallic against something else metallic.

A door beckoned. Well, a hatchway, Carella guessed you called it.

Darkness beyond it.

Carella poked his head inside.

"Hello?" he said again.

There was a staircase going up. Well, a ladder.

They climbed it. Kept climbing till they reached a small house on top of the ship. Well, a cabin. There was a man in the cabin. He was sitting on a stool behind a counter, looking at a map. A chart. Listen, the hell with it, Carella thought.

"Yes?" the man said.

"Detective Carella, my partner Detective Meyer," Carella said, and showed his shield.

The man nodded.

"We're investigating a double homicide . . ."

The man whistled.

He was, Carella guessed, in his late fifties, wearing a heavy black jacket and a peaked black cap. His sideburns were brown, but his beard had come in white, and he sat on his stool like a salty-dog Santa Claus, dark eyebrows raised now as his low whistle trailed and expired.

"May I ask who we're talking to, sir?" Carella said.

"Stewart Webster," he said, "captain of the *Dean*."

The men shook hands. Webster had a firm grip. His eyes were brown, sharp with intelligence. "How can I help you?" he asked.

"Well, we're not sure you can," Carella said. "But we figured it was worth a shot. We're looking for a ship we have as the General Putnam or the General Putney . . ."

"That's a long way from Dean," Webster said.

"Yeah," Carella said, and nodded. "Supposed to have departed for the Persian Gulf on the eighteenth of October, a year and three months ago."

"Well, I'm pretty sure we were in these parts around then . . ."

"But didn't you leave on that day?"

"I'd have to check the log. It would have been on or near that date. But, gentlemen . . ."

"We know," Meyer said. "You went to Australia."

"Haven't been anywhere *near* the Middle East since Reagan got those marines killed in Beirut. We were there when it happened. The owner cabled us to load our cargo and haul ass out. Afraid he'd lose his ship."

"We've also got a seaman named Mike," Carella said.

Webster looked at him.

"If that's his name," Meyer said.

Webster looked at *him*.

"We know," Carella said. "It's not much to go on."

"But it's all we have," Meyer said.

"Mike," Webster said.

"No last name," Carella said.

"Presumably on the *Dean*," Webster said.

"Or a ship with a General in its name."

"Well, let's take a look at the roster, see if we've got any Mikes," Webster said.

"Michael, I guess it would be," Meyer said.

There were no Michaels in the crew.

There was, however, a Michel.

Michel Fournier.

"Is he French?" Carella asked.

"I have no idea," Webster said. "Do you want me to pull his file?"

"If it's no trouble."

"We'll have to go down to the purser's office," Webster said.

They followed him down a different ladder from the one they'd climbed earlier, walked through several dark passageways, and came to a door that Webster opened with a key. The compartment resembled Alf Miscolo's clerical office back at the Eight-Seven. There was even the aroma of coffee on the air. Webster went to a row of filing cabinets—gray rather than the green in Miscolo's space—found the one he wanted, opened the drawer, began thumbing through folders, and then yanked one of them out.

"Here he is," he said, and handed the folder to Carella.

Michel Fournier.

Born in Canada, the province of Quebec.

When he'd shipped on, three years ago, he'd given his address as Portland, Maine.

No address here in the city.

"Was he with you in that time period we're talking about?" Carella asked.

"If he shipped on three years ago and his folder's still here in the active file, then yes, he was with us fifteen months ago, and he's still with us now."

"You mean he's aboard ship now?"

"No, no. The crew went ashore the moment we docked."

"Which was when?"

"Two days ago."

"When are they due back?"

"We won't be sailing again till early next month."

"Any idea where Fournier might be?"

"I'm sorry. I don't even know the man."

"Where does he sleep aboard ship?"

"Well, let's see, there ought to be a quarters-assignment chart someplace around here," Webster said, and began opening drawers in his purser's desk.

Fournier's quarters were in the forward compartment on B deck. His bunk was in a tier of three, folded up against the bulkhead now. Foot lockers ran along the deck under the bunks. All of the lockers were padlocked.

"This one is Fournier's," Webster said.

"What do we do?" Meyer asked. "Another goddamn court order?"

"If we want to see what's in there," Carella said.

"Think we'll even get it?"

Webster was standing there, but the men were thinking out loud.

"It'd have to include permission to bust open that lock."

"Boy, I don't know, Steve. Wouldn't she have mentioned a French accent? If the guy's French . . ."

"Canadian," Carella said.

"Yeah, but Quebec."

"We're close to downtown, you know. Right over the bridge."

"Kill the whole damn afternoon," Meyer said.

"And he may deny it, anyway."

"Yeah."

"So what do you think?"

"I don't know, what do *you* think?"

"I think the judge'll kick us out on our asses."

"Me, too."

"On the other hand, he may grant the warrant."

"I doubt it."

"Me, too. But *if* he does, we may find something in the locker."

"Or we may find only dirty socks and underwear."

"So what do you think?"

"Will we need a cop from Safe, Loft & Truck?"

"What do you mean?"

"If we get the search warrant. I mean, how the hell else are we going to open that lock? Those guys have tools can get into anything. They're the best burglars in this city."

"Mr. Webster," Carella said, "was your ship here in port on New Year's Eve?"

"Yes, it was," Webster said.

"Did the crew go ashore?"

"Well, certainly. New Year's Eve? Of course."

"We'd better go get that warrant," Carella said.

IF THE CASE had not concerned the murder of a six-month-old baby, the supreme court magistrate to whom the detectives presented their affidavit might not have felt they had probable cause for a search warrant. But the judge read newspapers, too. And he watched television. And he knew this was the Baby Susan case. He also knew it was the Annie Flynn case, but somehow the sitter's murder wasn't quite as shocking. In this city, sixteen-year-old girls got stabbed or raped or both every day of the week. But smothering an infant?

They went back to the ship with their search warrant and a pair of bolt cutters.

They were not bad burglars themselves.

It took them three minutes to cut through the lock.

They did indeed find a lot of dirty socks and underwear in Michel Fournier's foot locker.

But they also found a letter a girl in this city had written to him only last month.

The letter had a return address on it.

HERRERA WAS TRYING to explain to his girlfriend why there was a uniformed cop on the front stoop

downstairs. Consuelo didn't understand a word of it. It
had something to do with the police department owing
him protection because a detective had saved his life,
which made no sense at all. She sometimes thought
Herrera was a little crazy, which she also found tremen-
dously exciting. And confusing. All she could gather
was that a policeman followed Herrera everywhere he
went, to make sure nobody tried to kill him again. She
hadn't realized he was so important.

But now he was telling her that he had rented another
apartment and that they would be moving there. Temporarily. He would be losing the cop, and they would be
moving into this new apartment for just a little while.
Until he settled some business matters, and then they
would go to Spain. Live on the Costa Brava. Consuelo
had never been to the Costa Brava, but it sounded nice.

"When will we leave for Spain?" she asked, testing
him. This was Lenny asking George to tell about the
rabbits again. She hadn't believed Herrera's story the
first time around, but he sure made it sound better
every time he told it. He told her now that he'd already
booked the flight and would be picking up the tickets
very soon. First-class seats for both of them. Get out of
this city where no one would ever find him again. Not
the Chinks, not the Jakies, and not the cops, either.

"The Jakies?" she said.

"That's what they call them," he said.

Consuelo figured he probably knew.

She had never realized he was so smart.

He was, in fact, even smarter than he himself had
realized he was.

Street smart.

Which didn't only mean knowing how to kick the shit out of somebody. It also meant learning what was about to go down and figuring how to take advantage of it. For yourself. Playing for number one. Stepping out quicker than the other guy. Which came naturally if you grew up in these streets. Which the Jakies hadn't done, and which the Chinks hadn't done, either. Now maybe the streets of downtown Kingston or downtown Hong Kong were as mean as the streets here in this city, but Herrera doubted it. So whereas these small-town hoods could move in with their money and their muscle, there was something about this city that would always and forever elude them because they had not been born into this city, it was not in their *blood* the way it was in Herrera's.

This was *not* their city.

Fucking foreigners.

This was *his* city.

And he knew the stink of rotten fish, all right.

Had caught that stink the minute Hamilton approached him with the deal. Thought Uh-oh, why is he coming to me? Not coming to him in person, not going to where Herrera lived, but sending someone to get him. This was three days before Christmas. The deal was going down on the twenty-seventh. A simple dope buy, Hamilton explained. Very small. Fifty dollars for three kilos of cocaine. Close to seventeen grand a key. Hamilton needed someone to deliver the cash and pick up the stuff for him.

So why me? Herrera wondered.

All the while Hamilton talked, Herrera was thinking

This is bullshit, the man *wants* something from me. But what can it be?

Why is he asking *me* to pick up this cocaine for him?

Why doesn't he send one of his own people?

"You'll be carrying the money in a briefcase," Hamilton said.

Fifty fucking K! Herrera thought.

"This is the address."

He's trusting me with all that cash.

Never met me in his life, trusting me with all that money. Suppose I split with it? Straight to Spindledrift, I get on an airplane to Calcutta. Or else the coke. I give them the money in the briefcase, I pack the three keys, I disappear from the face of the—

"Don't get any ideas," Hamilton said.

But Herrera figured that was for show; the fish stink was very strong now.

"My people will be waiting for you downstairs," Hamilton said.

Then why don't you send your people *upstairs?* Herrera wondered.

Why send me instead? Who you never met in your life.

"You're probably wondering why I came to you," Hamilton said.

Now why would I be wondering such a thing, Herrera thought.

"You worked for Walter Chang some years ago, didn't you?" Hamilton said.

Herrera never admitted having worked for anyone at any time. To anybody. He said nothing.

"We need a man who understands the Chinese mentality," Hamilton said.

The word sounded so pretty on his Jamaican tongue.

"Men-tahl-ee-tee."

But why? Herrera wondered.

"Why?" he asked.

"The men making delivery are Chinese," Hamilton said.

Herrera looked at him.

This was the lie. He knew this was the lie, but he didn't yet know *what* the lie was. He knew only that he saw the lie sitting in Hamilton's eyes on Hamilton's impassive face, and the lie had something to do with Chinese making the delivery.

"Which Chinese?" he asked.

"That is for me to know, man," Hamilton said, and smiled.

"Sure," Herrera said.

"So do you think you might be interested?"

"You haven't yet mentioned how much this is worth to you."

"I thought ten dollars," Hamilton said.

Which was very fucking high.

High by about eight.

Especially high when you figured he could just as easily send someone on his payroll.

So why such rich bait?

It suddenly occurred to Herrera that this fucking Jakie was buying a fall guy.

"Ten sounds about right," he said.

* * *

THE RETURN ADDRESS on the flap of the envelope was 336 North Eames.

The woman had signed her letter *Julie*.

The mailboxes downstairs showed a J. Endicott in apartment 21. They climbed the steps to the second floor, stood outside the door listening for a moment, and then knocked. This was now a quarter to seven in the evening. Even if Julie had a job, she should be—

"Who is it?"

A woman's voice.

"Police," Carella said.

"Police?"

Utter astonishment.

"Miss Endicott?" Carella said.

"Yes?"

The voice closer to the door now. Suspicion replacing the surprise. In this city all kinds of lunatics knocked on your door pretending they were somebody else.

"I'm Detective Carella, 87th Squad, I wonder if you could open the door for me."

"Why? What's the matter?"

"Routine inquiry, Miss. Could you open the door, please?"

The door opened just a crack, restrained by a night chain.

An eye appeared in the crack. Part of a face.

"Let me see your badge, please."

He held up his shield and ID card.

"What's this about?" she asked.

"Is this your handwriting?" he asked, and held up the letter so that the envelope flap showed.

"Where'd you get that?" she asked.

"Did you write this?"

"Yes, but . . ."

"May we come in, please?"

"Just a second," she said.

The door closed. There was the rattle of the chain coming off. The door opened again. She was, Carella guessed, in her mid-twenties, a woman of medium height with long blonde hair and brown eyes. She had the look about her of someone who had just got home from work, still wearing a skirt and blouse, but she'd loosened her hair and undone the stock tie on the blouse, and she was barefoot.

"Julie Endicott?" Carella said.

"Yes?"

She closed the door behind them.

They were in a small entrance foyer. Tiny kitchen to the right. Living room straight ahead. In the living room, a young man sat on a sofa upholstered in a nubby blue fabric. There was a coffee table in front of the sofa, two drinks in tall glasses on it. A pair of medium-heeled women's shoes were on the floor under the coffee table. The young man was wearing jeans and a V-necked sweater. His shoes were under the coffee table, too. Carella figured they'd interrupted a bit of foreplay. Lady home from work, boyfriend or husband waiting to mix the drinks. She lets down her hair, they kick off their shoes, he starts fiddling with her blouse, knock, knock, it's the cops.

The young man looked up at them as they came in.

He was white.

Tall.

With dark hair and blue eyes.

Joyce Chapman's vague description of . . .

"Michel Fournier?" Carella asked.

His eyes opened wide. He looked at Julie. Julie shrugged, shook her head.

"Are you Michel Fournier?" Carella said.

"Yes?"

"Few questions we'd like to ask you."

"Questions?" he said, and looked at Julie again. Julie shrugged again.

"Privately," Carella said. He was thinking down the line. Thinking alibi. If Julie Endicott turned out to be Fournier's alibi, he'd want to question her separately later on.

"Is there anything you have to do?" he asked her.

"What?"

"Take a shower, watch the TV news . . ."

"Oh," she said. "Sure."

She went through the living room and opened a door opposite the couch. A glimpse of bed beyond. The door closed.

"We know the *Dean* was in port on New Year's Eve," Carella said. Straight for the jugular. "We know the crew went ashore. Where'd *you* go, Mike?"

First-name basis. Reduce him at once to an inferior status. An old cop trick that usually worked. Except when you were talking to a professional thief who thought you were calling him Frankie because you liked him.

"New Year's Eve," Meyer said.

"Where, Mike?"

"Why do you want to know?"

"Do you know a girl named Joyce Chapman?"

"No. Joyce Chapman. No. Who's Joyce Chapman?"

"Think back to October," Carella said.

"I was nowhere *near* this city in October."

"We're talking about October a year ago."

"What? How do you expect me to remember . . . ?"

"A disco named Lang's. Down in the Quarter."

"So?"

"Do you remember it?"

"I think so. What's . . . ?"

"A girl named Joyce Chapman. You did some dope together . . ."

"No, no."

"Yes, yes, this isn't a drug bust, Mike."

"Look, I really don't remember anyone named Joyce Chapman."

"Blonde hair," Meyer said.

"Like your friend Julie," Carella said.

"I like blondes," Fournier said, and shrugged.

"Green eyes," Meyer said.

"Pretty eyes."

"Her best feature."

"You went back to her apartment on North Orange . . ."

"No, I don't re . . ."

"She had a roommate."

"Asleep when you came in . . ."

"Still asleep when you left early the next morning."

"Angela Quist."

"I don't know her, either."

"Okay, let's talk about New Year's Eve."

"A year ago? If you expect . . ."

"No, Mike, the one just past."

"Where'd you go and what'd you do?"

"I was with Julie. I stay here with Julie whenever the *Dean*'s in port."

"How long have you known her?"

"I don't know, it must be six, seven months."

"She came after Joyce, huh?"

"I'm telling you I don't know anybody named . . ."

"Wants to be a writer," Meyer said.

"She was studying writing here in the city."

"Her father owns a lumber company out west."

"Oh," Fournier said.

Recognition.

"You got her now?" Carella said.

"Yeah. I think. A little tattoo on her ass?"

Nobody had mentioned a tattoo to them.

"Like a little bird? On the right cheek?"

"Picasso prints on the wall over the couch," Meyer said. "In the apartment on Orange."

"Like some kind of modern stuff?" Fournier said.

"Yeah, like some kind of modern stuff," Meyer said.

"I think I remember her. That was some night."

"Apparently," Carella said. "Ever try to get in touch with her again?"

"No. I'll tell you the truth, I didn't even remember her name."

"Never saw her again after that night, huh?"

"Never."

"Tell us about New Year's Eve, Mike."

"I already told you. I was with Julie. Did something *happen* to this girl? Is that why you're asking me all these questions?"

"You were here on New Year's Eve, is that it?"

"Here? No. I didn't say here."

"Then where?"

"We went out."

"Where?"

"To a party. One of Julie's friends. A girl named Sarah."

"Sarah what?"

"I don't remember. Ask Julie."

"You're not too good on names, are you, Mike?"

"All right, you want to tell me what happened to this girl?"

"Who said anything happened to her?"

"You come here, you bang down the door . . ."

"Nobody banged down the door, Mike."

"I mean, what the hell *is* this?"

The outraged citizen now. Guilty or innocent, they all became outraged at some point in the questioning. Or at least *expressed* outrage. People of Italian descent, guilty or innocent, always pulled the *"Conosce chi son'io?"* line. Indignantly. Roughly translated as "Do you realize who I am?" You could be talking to a street cleaner, he came on like the governor of the state. "Do you realize who I am?" Fournier was doing the same high-horse bit now. "What the hell *is* this?" Outrage on his face and in his blue eyes. The innocent bystander, falsely accused. But they still didn't know where he'd been on New Year's Eve while Susan and her sitter were getting killed.

"What time did you leave here?" Meyer asked.

"Around ten. Ask Julie."

"And got home when?"

"Around four."

"Where were you between twelve-thirty and two-thirty?"

"Still at the party."

"What time did you leave there?"

"Around two-thirty, three."

"Which?"

"In there. Closer to three, I guess."

"And went where?"

"Came straight back here."

"How?"

"On the subway."

"From where?"

"Riverhead. The party was all the way up in Riverhead. Something happened to this girl, am I right?"

"No."

"Then what happened?"

"Her daughter got killed," Carella said, and watched his eyes.

"I didn't know she had a kid," Fournier said.

"She didn't."

Still watching the eyes.

"You just said . . ."

"Not when you knew her. The baby was six months old."

Both detectives watching his eyes now.

"The baby was yours," Carella said.

He looked first at Carella and then at Meyer. Meyer nodded. In the kitchen, a water tap was dripping. Fournier was silent for a long time. When he spoke again, it was stop and go. A sentence, a silence, another sentence, another silence.

"I didn't know that," he said.

"I'm sorry," he said.

"I wish I'd known," he said.

"Will you tell her how sorry I am?" he said.

"Do you know where I can reach her?" he said.

The detectives said nothing.

"Or maybe you can give her the number here," he said. "If you talk to her. If she'd like to call me or anything."

In the kitchen, the water tap dripped steadily.

"You don't know how sorry I am," he said.

And then:

"What was the baby's name?"

"Susan," Meyer said.

"That's my mother's name," he said. "Well, Suzanne."

There was another long silence.

"I wish I'd known," he said again.

"Mr. Fournier," Carella said, "we'd like to talk to Miss Endicott now."

"Sure," Fournier said. "I really wish I could . . ."

And let the sentence trail.

Julie Endicott told them that on New Year's Eve they had left the apartment here at a little past ten o'clock. They had gone to a party at the home of a friend named

Sarah Epstein, who lived at 7133 Washington Boulevard in Riverhead, apartment 36. Julie Endicott went on to say that they had stayed at the party until ten minutes to three, had walked the two blocks to the subway station on Washington and Knowles, and had got back to the apartment here at a few minutes after four. They had gone straight to bed. Mike Fournier had been with her all night long. He had never left her side all night long.

"Did you want Sarah's phone number?" she asked. "In case you plan to call her?"

"Yes, please," Carella said.

Sarah Epstein corroborated everything they'd been told.

They were back to square one.

12.

CARELLA PLACED THE CALL to Seattle on Thursday morning, at a little after nine Pacific time. He tried the number for the Pines, and got no answer. He then called the Chapman Lumber Company, and spoke to the same woman he'd spoken to nine days ago. Pearl Ogilvy, his notes read. *Miss*. He explained that he had a message for Joyce Chapman, and couldn't reach her at the house. He wondered if she might pass the message on to her.

"Just tell her that Mike Fournier would like to talk to her. His number here is . . ."

"Mr. Carella? Excuse me, but . . ."

There was a sudden silence on the line.

"Miss Ogilvy?" Carella said, puzzled.

"Sir . . . I'm sorry, but . . . Joyce is dead."

"What?"

"Yes, sir."

"What?"

"She was murdered, sir."

"When?"

"Monday night."

Carella realized he was frowning. He also realized he was shocked. He had not been shocked in a long, long time. Why the murder of Joyce Chapman should now have such an effect on him . . .

"Tell me what happened," he said.

"Well, sir, maybe you ought to talk to her sister. She was out here when it happened."

"Could I have her number, please?"

"I don't have her number back east, but I'm sure it's in the phone book."

"Where would that be, Miss Ogilvy? Back east where?"

"Why, right where you're calling from," she said.

"Here? She lives here in this city?"

"Yes, sir. She came out because Mr. Chapman was so sick and all, and everybody was expecting him to die. Instead, it was poor Joyce who . . ."

Her voice caught.

"And she's back here now?" Carella asked.

"Yes, sir, they flew home yesterday, her and her husband. Right after the funeral."

"Which part of the city, would you know?"

"Does Calm's Point sound right? Is there a Calm's Point?"

"Yes, there is," Carella said. "Can you tell me what her married name is?"

"Hammond. Melissa Hammond. Well, it'd probably be under Richard Hammond."

"Thank you," Carella said.

"Not at all," she said, and hung up.

Carella immediately dialed Seattle Directory Assistance, asked for the Seattle P.D. and looked up at the clock. 9:15 A.M. their time. If it worked the way it did here, the day shift would have been in for an hour and a half already. He dialed the number. Identified himself. Asked to talk to someone in Homicide. A sergeant told him he was just passing through with some papers, heard the phone ringing, picked it up. Didn't seem to be anyone up here at the moment, could he have someone get back? Carella told him he was trying to reach whoever was handling the Chapman case. Joyce Chapman. The Monday night murder. He said it was urgent. The sergeant gave his solemn word.

The man who called back at one o'clock Carella's time identified himself as Jamie Bonnem. He said he and his partner were working the Chapman case. He wanted to know what Carella's interest was.

"Her daughter was murdered here on New Year's Eve," Carella said.

"Didn't know she was married," Bonnem said.

Sort of a Western drawl. Carella didn't know they talked that way in Seattle. Maybe he was from someplace else.

"She was single, but that's another story," he said. "Can you tell me what happened out there?"

Bonnem told him what had happened.

Killed in her own bed.

Pistol in her mouth.

Two shots fired.

Gun was a Smith & Wesson 59.

"That's a nine-millimeter auto," Bonnem said. "We recovered both bullets and one of the cartridge cases. We figure the killer picked up the other one, couldn't find the one he left behind. He couldn't do anything about the bullets 'cause they were buried in the wall behind the bed."

"Anything else involved?" Carella asked.

"What do you mean?"

"Was she raped?"

"No."

"What've you got so far?"

"Nothing but the ballistics make. What've you got?"

Carella told him what he had.

"So we've *both* got nothing, right?" Bonnem said.

"HE ASKS FOR PROTECTION, and then he disappears on me," Kling said.

He had the floor.

The detectives were gathered in Lieutenant Byrnes's office for the weekly Thursday afternoon meeting. The meetings were the lieutenant's idea. They took place at three-thirty every Thursday, catching the off-going day shift and the on-coming night shift. This way, he hoped for input from eight detectives, all of them airing their various cases. If he ended up with six of them in his office, what with vacations and people out sick, he considered himself lucky. The lieutenant called these meetings his Thursday Afternoon Think Tank. Detective Andy Parker called them the Thursday Afternoon Stink Tank.

There were only five detectives with Byrnes that

afternoon. O'Brien and Fujiwara were on stakeout and had relieved on post. Hawes was out interviewing a burglary victim. Parker wished he could have thought up some good excuse to miss the meeting. He hated these fucking meetings. He didn't like hanging around late if his shift happened to be the one getting relieved, and he didn't like coming in early if he was the one about to do the relieving. Anyway, he had enough problems with his own case load without having to listen to somebody else's troubles. Who *gave* a damn what was happening with Kling and this Herrera character? Not Parker.

He sat in a straight-backed chair, looking out the window. He was willing to bet anyone in the room that it would start snowing again any minute. He wondered if that blue parka was still downstairs in his locker. He was glad he hadn't shaved this morning. A two-day growth of beard kept you warm when it was snowing. He was wearing rumpled gray flannel trousers, unpolished black shoes, a Harris tweed sport jacket with a stain on the right sleeve, and a white shirt with the collar open, no tie. He looked like one of the city's homeless who had wandered into a warm place for the afternoon.

"Maybe he only needed cover till they turned off the heat," Brown suggested.

He was wearing a dress shirt and tie, the trousers and vest to a suit; he'd been in court all day, testifying on an assault case. His jacket was draped over the back of his chair. He was a huge man, his complexion the color of his name, a frown on his face as he tried to work through Kling's problem with him. The frown came out as a scowl.

"Okay, Artie," Kling said, "but why would the posse suddenly quit? Two weeks ago, three weeks, whenever it was, they tried to kill the man. So all at once all bets are off?"

"Maybe the color of blue scared them," Carella said.

"What'd you have on him?" Willis asked. "A round-the-clock?"

"No, sun-to-sun," Kling said.

"All we could afford," Byrnes said. "The man's small time."

He sat behind his desk in his shirt sleeves, a man of medium height with a compact bullet head and no-non-sense blue eyes. It was too damn hot in this room. Something wrong with the damn thermostat. He'd have to call Maintenance.

"Don't forget the one who came after me," Kling said.

"You think that's connected, huh?" Brown said.

"Had to be," Carella said.

"You get a make on him?"

"Nothing."

"What you got here," Parker said, turning from the window, "is a two-bit courier who gave you a story so you'd put some blues on him, and you fell for it hook, line and sinker. So now he disappears, and you're surprised."

"He told me a big buy was coming down, Andy."

"Sure, when?"

"Next Monday night."

"Where?"

"He didn't know where yet."

"Sure, you know when he's gonna know? *Never* is when he's gonna know. 'Cause there ain't no buy. He conned you into laying some badges on him till the heat cooled, Artie's right. Now he don't need you anymore, it's goodbye and good luck."

"Maybe," Kling said.

"Why would he have lied?" Byrnes asked.

"To get the blue muscle," Parker said.

"Then why didn't he lie bigger?" Carella said.

"What do you mean?"

"Give Bert the time, the place, the works. Why the slow tease?"

The room went silent.

"Which is why I figure he's really trying to find out," Kling said.

"Why?" Parker said.

"So we can make the bust."

"Why?" Parker said.

"So we'll put away the people who tried to kill him." Parker shrugged.

"That's a reason," Byrnes said.

"Bust up the posse," Brown said.

"Herrera walks away safe," Meyer said.

"But something's missing," Carella said. "Why'd they want him dead in the first place?"

"Ah-ha," Parker said.

The men looked at each other. Nobody seemed to know the answer.

"So what's next?" Parker asked. "I want to go home."

Brown scowled at him.

"You're scaring me to death, Artie," Parker said. "Can we get on with this, Loot?"

Byrnes scowled at him, too.

Parker sighed like a saint with arrows in him.

"This double on New Year's Eve," Carella said. "The baby's mother was killed Monday night, in Seattle. It may be linked, we don't know. I'll be seeing her sister later today."

"The sister lives here?" Byrnes asked.

"Yeah. In Calm's Point."

"They're originally from Seattle," Meyer explained.

"So have you got any meat at all?" Parker asked impatiently.

"Not yet. According to the timetable . . ."

"Yeah, yeah, timetables," Parker said, dismissing them as worthless.

"Let him talk," Willis said.

"You get six different timetables from six different people," Parker said. "Makes it look like the person got killed six different times of day."

"Just let the man *talk,*" Willis said.

"It's ten after four already," Parker said.

"The way we've got it," Carella said, "the sitter was still alive at twelve-thirty in the morning. The parents got home at two-thirty and found her and the baby dead. The father had been drinking, but he was cold sober when we got there."

"The girl was raped and stabbed," Meyer said.

"The baby was smothered with a pillow," Carella said.

"What was it in Seattle?" Brown asked.

"A gun."

"Mmm.

"How do you know she was still alive at twelve-thirty?" Kling asked.

"You want to look at this?" Carella said, and handed him the timetable he and Meyer had worked up.

"Twelve-twenty A.M.," Kling said, reading out loud. "Harry Flynn calls to wish Annie a happy new year."

"The sitter's father?" Willis asked.

"Yeah," Meyer said.

"Twelve-thirty A.M.," Kling read. "Peter Hodding calls to check on the baby . . ."

"Peter *who?*" Parker said.

"The baby's father."

"His name is Peter *Hard-On?*"

"Hodding."

"How would you like to go through life with a name like Peter Hard-On?" Parker asked, laughing.

"He tells the sitter they'll be home in a little while, asks if everything's okay."

"Peter Hard-On," Parker said, still laughing.

"*Was* everything okay?" Byrnes asked.

"According to Hodding, she sounded fine."

"No strain, no forced conversation, nobody there with her?"

"He said she sounded natural."

"And this was at twelve-thirty, huh?" Willis asked.

"Yeah. According to Hodding."

"Who'd had a little to drink, huh?" Brown said.

"Well, a *lot* to drink, actually," Meyer said.

"So there's your problem," Parker said. "One end of your timetable is based on what a fuckin' *drunk* told you."

Carella looked at him.

"Am I right?" he asked.

"Maybe," Carella said.

"So can we go home now?"

IT BROKE HER HEART sometimes, this city.

On a day like today, with the storm clouds beginning to gather over the river, gray and rolling in over the gray rolling water, the certain smell of snow on the air . . .

On a day like today, she remembered being a little girl in this city.

Remembered the playground this city had been, winter, summer, spring and fall. The street games changing with the changing seasons. A children's camp all year round. In the wintertime, on a day like today, all the kids would do their little magic dance in the street, praying that the snow would come soon, praying there'd be no school tomorrow, there'd be snow forts instead and snowball fights, the girls shrieking in terror and glee as the boys chased them through narrow canyons turned suddenly white. Eileen giggling, her cheeks red, her eyes flashing, bundled in a heavy parka, a woolen pom-pommed hat pulled down over her ears, her red hair tucked up under it because she was ashamed of her hair back then, made her look too Irish, whatever that was, too much the Mick, her mother used to say, We're American, you know, we didn't just get off the boat.

She loved this city.

For what it had inspired in her.

The need to compete, the need to excel in order to survive, a city of gutter rats, her father had said with pride in his voice. Michael Burke. They called him Pops on the beat, because his hair was prematurely white, he'd looked like his own grandfather when he was still only twenty-six. Pops Burke. Shot to death when she was still a little girl. A liquor store holdup. The Commissioner had come to his funeral. He told Eileen her father was a very brave man. They gave her mother a folded American flag.

Her Uncle Matt was a cop, too. She'd loved him to death, loved the stories he told her about leprechauns and faeries, stories he'd heard from his mother who'd heard them from hers and on back through the generations, back to a time when Ireland was everywhere green and covered with a gentle mist, a time when blood was not upon the land. Her uncle's favorite toast was "Here's to golden days and purple nights," an expression he'd heard repeated again and again on a radio show. Recently, Eileen had heard Hal Willis's new girlfriend using the same expression. Maybe *her* uncle had listened to the same radio comic.

Chances were, though, that Marilyn's uncle hadn't been killed in a bar while he was off duty and drinking his favorite drink and making his favorite toast, here's to golden days and purple nights indeed. Not when the color of the day is red, the color of the day is shotgun red, Uncle Matt drawing his service revolver as the holdup man came in, red plaid kerchief over his face, blew him off the barstool and later took fifty-two dollars and thirty-six cents from the cash register. Uncle Matt dead on the floor in a pool of his own blood. Another folded American flag for the family. The shooting took place in the old Hundred and Tenth in Riverhead. They used to call it The Valley of Death, after the Tennyson poem about into the Valley of Death rode the six hundred. How this applied to the Hundred and Tenth, God alone knew; the lexicon of cops was often obscure in origin.

She wondered if she should tell Karin Lefkowitz that the main reason she'd joined the force was so that someday she could catch that son of a bitch with the red plaid kerchief over his face, rip off that kerchief, and look him dead in the eye before she blew him away. Her Uncle Matt was the reason. Not her father who'd been killed when she was still too young to have really known him. Her Uncle Matt.

Who still brought tears to her eyes whenever she thought of him and his leprechauns and faeries.

This city . . .

It . . .

It taught you how to do something better than you'd ever done anything else in your life. Taught you how to be the *best* at it. Which was what she'd been. The best decoy cop in this city. Never mind modesty, she'd been the best, yes. She'd done her job with the sense of pride her father had instilled in her and the sense of humor her uncle had encouraged, never letting it get to her, balancing its risks and its rewards, eagerly approaching each new assignment as if it were an adventure, secure in the knowledge that she was a professional among professionals.

Until, of course, the city took it all away from her.

You either owned this city or you didn't.

Once upon a time, when she was good, she owned it.

And now she owned nothing.

Not even herself.

She took a deep breath and climbed the low flat steps in front of the old Headquarters Building, and went through one of the big bronze doorways, and wondered what she should tell Karin Lefkowitz today.

CARELLA DID NOT get to the Hammond apartment in Calm's Point until almost ten o'clock that night. He had phoned ahead and learned from Melissa Hammond that her husband usually got home from the office at seven, seven-thirty, but since he'd been away from work for almost a week now and since there was a lot of catching up to do, he might not be home until much later. Carella asked if she thought eight would be okay for him to stop by, and she told him they'd be having dinner as soon as her husband got home, so if he could make it a bit later . . .

It was five minutes to ten when he knocked on the door.

He'd been on the job since a quarter to eight that morning.

Before he'd left the office, he'd called a woman named Chastity Kerr, who'd given the party the Hoddings had attended on New Year's Eve. He'd made an appointment to see her at ten tomorrow morning. So if he got out of here by eleven, he'd be home by midnight. Have a snack with Teddy before they went to bed, wake up early in the morning so he could have breakfast with the twins before they caught their seven-thirty school bus, leave for the office at eight, catch up on the reports he hadn't got to yesterday *or* today, and then go see Mrs. Kerr. Just thinking about it made him more tired than he actually was.

The Hammonds were still at the dinner table, lingering over coffee, when he arrived. Melissa Hammond, a very attractive, pregnant blonde with the same green eyes her sister had listed as "Best Feature" on the Cooper-Anderson background form, asked Carella if he'd care for a cup. "I grind the beans myself," she said. He thanked her, and accepted the chair her husband offered. Richard Hammond—his wife called him "Dick"—was a tall, good-looking man with dark hair and dark eyes. Carella guessed that he was in his late thirties, his wife a few years younger. He had obviously changed from the clothes he'd worn to work this morning, unless his law office was a lot more casual than the ones Carella was accustomed to. Hammond worked for the firm of Lasser, Bending, Merola and Ross. He was wearing jeans, a sweat shirt with a Washington State University seal on it, and loafers without socks. He offered Carella a cigar, which Carella declined.

Melissa poured coffee for him.

Carella said, "I'm glad you agreed to see me."

"We're eager to help in any way possible," Melissa said.

"We were just sitting here talking about it," Hammond said.

"The coincidence," Melissa said.

"Of this baby getting killed."

"Joyce's baby, yes," Carella said and nodded.

"Well, you don't know that for sure," Hammond said.

"Yes, we do," Carella said, surprised.

"Well," Hammond said, and looked at his wife.

"I'm not sure I understand," Carella said.

"It's just that this *baby,*" Melissa said, and looked at her husband.

"You see," he said, "this is the first we're hearing of it. When you called Melissa earlier today and told her Joyce's murder might be linked to the death of her *baby* . . ."

"I mean, as far as I knew, Joyce never *had* a baby."

"But she did," Carella said.

"Well, that's your contention," Hammond said.

Carella looked at them both.

"Uh . . . look," he said. "It might be easier for all of us if we simply accept as fact . . ."

"I assume you have substantiating . . ."

"Yes, Mr. Hammond, I do."

"That my sister-in-law gave birth to . . ."

"A baby girl, yes, sir. Last July. At St. Agnes Hospital here in the city. And signed it over for adoption to the Cooper-Anderson Agency, also here in the city."

"You have papers showing . . . ?"

"Copies of the papers, yes."

"And you know for a fact that this baby who was murdered on . . . ?"

"Yes, was your sister-in-law's baby. Adopted by Mr. and Mrs. Peter Hodding, yes."

Hammond nodded.

"Well," he said, and sighed.

"This is certainly news to us," Melissa said.

"You didn't know your sister had this baby?"

"No."

"Did you know she was pregnant?"

"No."

"Never even suspected she might be?"

"Never."

"How often did you see her?"

"Oh, on and off," Melissa said.

"Every few months or so," Hammond said.

"Even though you lived here in the same city, huh?" Carella said.

"Well, we didn't move here till last January," Hammond said.

"And, anyway, we were never very close," Melissa said.

"When would you say you'd seen her last?"

"Well, in Seattle. All the while we were in Seattle. I saw her the night she was killed, in fact. We were at the hospital together."

"I meant before then."

"Well, we flew out together. When it looked as if my father might . . ."

"What I'm trying to ask . . . your sister gave birth in July. When did you see her *before* that?"

"Oh."

"Well, let's see, when was it?" Hammond said.

"We moved here last January . . ."

"So it must've been . . ."

"My birthday, wasn't it?" Melissa said.

"I think so, yes. The party here."

"Yes."

"And when was that?" Carella asked.

"February twelfth."

"March, April, May, June, July," Carella said, counting on his fingers. "That would've made her four months pregnant."

"You'd never have known, I can tell you that," Hammond said.

"Well, lots of women carry small," Melissa said.

"And she was a big woman, don't forget. Five-ten . . ."

"Big-boned . . ."

"And she always wore this Annie Hall sort of clothing."

"Layered," Melissa said. "So it's entirely possible we'd have missed it."

"Her being pregnant," Hammond said.

"She never confided it to you, huh?" Carella asked.

"No."

"Didn't come to see you when she found out . . . ?"

"No. I wish she would have."

"Melissa *always* wished they were closer."

"Well, there's the age difference, you know," Melissa said. "I'm thirty-four, my sister was only nineteen. That's a fifteen-year difference. I was already a teenager when she was born."

"It's a shame because . . . well . . . now there's no changing it. Joyce is dead."

"Yes," Carella said, and nodded. "Tell me, did she ever mention anyone named Michel Fournier? Mike Fournier?"

"No," Melissa said. "At least not to me. Dick? Did she ever . . ."

"No, not to me, either," Hammond said. "Is he the father?"

"Yes," Carella said.

"I figured."

"But she never mentioned him, huh?"

"No. Well, if we didn't know she was pregnant . . ."

"I thought maybe in passing. Without mentioning that she was pregnant, do you know what I mean? Just discussing him as someone she'd met, or knew, or . . ."

"No," Melissa said, shaking her head. "Dick?"

"No," he said. "I'm sorry."

"Did she have any boyfriends back in Seattle?" Carella asked.

"Well, no one recent," Melissa said. "She moved here right after high school, you know . . ."

"Graduated early . . ."

"She was only seventeen . . ."

"She was very smart . . ."

"Wanted to be a writer . . ."

"You should see some of her poetry."

"She was studying here with a very important man."

"So she came east . . . when?" Carella asked. "June? July?"

"It would've been two years come July."

"And we came here in January," Melissa said. "Dick had a good job offer . . ."

"I'd been practicing out there, but this was too good to refuse," Hammond said.

"So when you got here in January . . ."

"Yes, toward the end of . . ."

". . . your sister was already pregnant," Carella said.

"Was she?" Melissa said.

"Yes. She would've been three months pregnant," Carella said. "Did you look her up when you got here?"

"Yes, of course."

"But you didn't notice she was pregnant."

"No. Well, I wasn't looking for anything like that. And, anyway, what'd you say it was? Three months?"

"Three, yes."

"Yes," Melissa said. "So she wouldn't have been showing, would she? At least, not so *I* could notice."

"All the Chapman women carry small," Hammond said. "Melissa's eight months pregnant now, but you'd never guess it."

Carella had the good grace not to look at her belly.

"Who was Joyce's most recent boyfriend?" he asked. "Out there in Seattle?"

"I guess it would have been Eddie," Melissa said. "She was seeing a lot of him in high school."

"Eddie Gillette."

"Pretty serious?" Carella asked.

"Well, high school stuff," Hammond said. "You know."

"Have the Seattle police talked to him?"

"I really couldn't say."

"Didn't mention his name as a possible suspect or anything, did they?"

"Didn't mention *anyone's* name."

"They're pretty much scratching their heads out there," Melissa said.

"A thing like this . . . it's not too common out there," Hammond said.

"Well, people get *killed,*" Melissa said.

"Yes, but not like here," Hammond said. "Is what I meant."

"Big bad city, huh?" Carella said, and smiled.

"Well, it is, you know," Hammond said, and returned the smile.

"What sort of law do you practice?" Carella asked.

"*Not* criminal," Hammond said. "The firm I'm with now specializes in corporate law."

"And out there in Seattle?"

"General law. I had my own practice."

"He was his own boss out there," Melissa said, and smiled somewhat ruefully.

"Yes, but the opportunities were limited," Hammond said. "You make certain trade-offs in life. We may go back one day, Lissie, who knows?"

"Time we go back, there'll be no family there anymore," she said.

"Her father's very ill, you know," Hammond said.

"Yes," Carella said.

"Never rains but it pours," Melissa said, and sighed heavily.

Carella looked at his watch.

"I don't want to keep you any longer," he said. "Thanks very much for your time, I appreciate it."

"Not at all," Hammond said.

He walked Carella into the entry foyer, took his overcoat from the closet there, and helped him on with it. Carella thanked him again for his time, called "Good night" to Melissa, who was clearing the dining room table, and then went out into the hallway and took the elevator down to the street.

It was just beginning to snow.

13.

CHASTITY KERR was the sort of big-boned person Melissa had said her sister was. Tall, sturdy but not fat, she gave the impression of a woman capable of handling any physical task a man could, only better. Blonde and suntanned—she explained that she and her husband had just come back from two weeks at Curtain Bluff on Antigua—she offered Carella a cup of coffee and then sat with him at a small table in the kitchen alcove overlooking Grover Park.

It was still snowing outside.

"Two days ago, I was lying under a palm tree sipping a frozen daiquiri," she said. "Look at this, willya?"

Carella looked at it.

It did not make him happy.

The plows wouldn't come out until the snow stopped, and it showed no sign of doing that.

"Mrs. Kerr," he said, "the reason I'm here . . ."

"Chastity, please," she said. "If you have a name like Chastity, you either use it a lot, or else you ignore it or change it. My sisters and I *use* our names, I think to spite our father, who chose them. I should tell you that there are four girls in our family, and they're named, in order, Verity, Piety, Chastity—that's me—and guess what he named the fourth one?"

"Sneezy," Carella said.

"No. Generosity. Can you believe he had the *temerity?*"

Carella smiled. "Anyway, Mrs. Kerr," he said, "what I'm . . ."

"Chastity, please."

"Well, what I'm trying to do, I'd like to pinpoint the time Peter Hodding called home on New Year's Eve. To talk to the murdered girl."

"Oh, my, New Year's Eve," Chastity said, and rolled her eyes.

"Yes, I know."

"Not a night when one normally tracks comings and goings, is it?"

"Not normally."

"What time did he give you?"

"Well, I'd rather you told me."

"Big rush for the phone," Chastity said. "I know I tried to get through to my sister in Chicago shortly after midnight, but all circuits were busy. I don't think *any*-one was getting through to *any*where. At least, that's my recollection."

"When do you think Mr. Hodding placed his call?"

"I'm trying to remember."

Carella waited.

Chastity was thinking furiously.

"He was in the guest bedroom," she said, nodding, "that's right."

"Mr. Hodding?"

"Yes, he was using the extension in there."

"And this was when?"

"Well, that's what I'm trying to do, place the time. I know he told her he'd been trying to reach her, but the line was busy."

"Told who?"

"The sitter. When he finally got through."

"Told her the *line* had been busy? Or the circuits?"

"I'm sure he said the line."

"That would've been her father calling."

"Well, I don't know what you're talking about, so I can't really comment."

"I'm thinking out loud," Carella said. "How'd you happen to hear this conversation?"

"I was in the room next door. Checking on my daughter. I have an eight-year-old daughter. The door between the rooms was open, and I . . . well, there you are."

"Where?" Carella said, and smiled.

"I'd just got through to my sister, and she'd given me a hassle about not calling sooner. Said it was a tradition to call at midnight, and that was half an hour ago. And I went in to check Jennifer right after that. So it must've been a little past twelve-thirty."

"When you overheard Peter Hodding on the telephone."

"Yes."

"How much of the conversation did you hear?"

"Well, all of it, I suppose. From the beginning. From when he said, 'Annie . . .'"

"Then this definitely *was* the call to the sitter."

"Oh, yes. No question. 'Annie, it's me,' he said, and went on from there."

"'Annie, it's me.'"

"Yes."

"Not, 'Annie, it's Mr. Hodding'?"

"No, 'Annie, it's me.' I guess she knew his voice."

"Yes. Then what?"

"Then he said he'd been trying to get through but the line was busy . . ."

"Uh-huh."

"And then he asked how the baby was, little Susan."

"Yes."

"God, every time I think of what happened," Chastity said, and shook her head.

"Yes," Carella said. "Then what?"

"He told her they'd be home in a little while."

"A little while," Carella repeated.

"Yes."

"But they didn't leave until sometime between two and two-thirty."

"Yes. Well, I didn't look at the clock, but it was around that time."

"So that would've been at least an hour and a half later."

"Are you thinking out loud again?"

"Yes. If he called home around twelve-thirty, it would've been an hour and a half later when he and his wife left the party."

"That's what it would've been," Chastity said.

"But he told Annie he'd be home in a little while."

"Well, I didn't hear him say *exactly* that."

"What *did* you hear him say?"

"Just 'In a little while.'"

"Only those words?"

"Yes."

"'In a little while.'"

"Yes. She must have asked when they'd be home."

"Yes, I would guess so."

"Would you like more coffee?"

"Yes, please."

She got up, moved to the coffee-making machine, picked up the pot, carried it back to the table, and freshened Carella's cup. The snow kept coming down outside.

"Thank you," Carella said. "Why do you suppose he told the sitter they'd be home in a little while when actually they didn't leave until . . . ?"

"Well, he'd had a little to drink, you know."

"So I understand."

"I thought he was going to be sick, as a matter of fact."

"Uh-huh."

"Gayle was mad as hell. Told him she didn't enjoy the company of a drunken pig. Those were her exact words."

"This was when?"

"Actually, I think he was already drunk when he called home."

"Why do you say that?"

"Well, you know the way drunks sound. The way their speech gets? That's how he sounded."

"So when he made that call at twelve-thirty, he sounded drunk. While he was talking to Annie."

"Yes. *Very* drunk."

"How'd the conversation end?"

"Goodbye, so long, I'll see you, like that."

"And when did the argument with his wife occur?"

"Shortly after that. He'd spilled a drink on someone, and Gayle told him she was never going anyplace with him again . . . well, I told you what she said, except it was the company of a *fucking* drunken pig. Was what she said, actually."

"Pretty angry with him, huh?"

"Furious."

"But they stayed at the party, anyway, till sometime around two in the . . ."

"Well, *she* did."

"What do you mean?" Carella asked at once.

"Gayle stayed."

"I thought they left together at . . ."

"Yes, that was later. After he came back from his walk."

"What walk?"

"He went down for some air."

"When?"

"After Gayle tore into him."

"Are you saying he left the party?"

"Yes. Said he needed some air."

"Said he was going down for a walk?"

"Well, I assume he was. He put on his overcoat. He

didn't just go stand out in the hall, if that's what you mean."

"What time was this?"

"It must've been around one o'clock."

"Mrs. Kerr . . ."

"Chastity. Please."

"Chastity . . . what time did Peter Hodding come back from his walk?"

"At two o'clock. I know because I was in the hallway saying goodbye to some of my guests when the elevator doors opened and Peter stepped out."

"How do you know it was two o'clock?"

"Because I was asking these people why they were leaving so early, and the man said, 'It's already two,' and that's when the elevator doors opened and Peter stepped out."

"Did he look as if he'd been outdoors?"

"Oh, yes. His cheeks all ruddy, his hair all blown. Yes, very definitely."

"Was he sober?"

"He was sober," Chastity said.

FRANCISCO PALACIOS was surprised to see Bert Kling.

"Does this have to do with Proctor again?" he asked.

"No," Kling said.

"Because I had two fat guys in here asking about Proctor," Palacios said. "First one was an obnoxious snitch named Fats Donner, you know him?"

"I know him."

"He digs Mary Jane shoes and white cotton panties.

Second one was a fat cop from the Eight-Three, his name is Weeks. You know him, too?"

"I know him, too," Kling said.

"*He* digs a hooker works in his precinct. I gave Weeks the name of her boyfriend plays saxophone. But I don't know where Proctor is. I told Weeks, and I'm telling you the same. How come he's so hot all at once, this two-bit little jerk?"

"We already found him," Kling said.

"Thank God. 'Cause I don't know where he is, anyway."

"I'm looking for a guy named Herrera."

"Give me a hard one, why don't you? You know how many Herreras we got in this city?"

"Are they all named José Domingo?"

"Most of them," Palacios said.

"This one did work for the Yellow Paper Gang some years back."

"What kind of work?"

"Dope. Which is what he's into right now."

"Who isn't?" Palacios said, and shrugged.

"Which is the next thing I want to know."

"Uh-huh."

"There's a big shipment coming in next week," Kling said. "I'd like details."

"You're hot stuff," Palacios said, shaking his head. "You give me a common name like Smith or Jones in Spanish, and you tell me there's a big shipment coming in next week, which there's a big shipment coming in *every* week in this city, and you expect me to help you."

"A hundred kilos of cocaine," Kling said.

"Uh-huh."

"Coming in on the twenty-third."

"Okay."

"By ship."

"Okay."

"Scandinavian registry."

"Uh-huh."

"Coming up from Colombia."

"Got it."

"The coke's going for ten grand per."

"A bargain."

"Earmarked for a Jamaican posse."

"Which one?"

"*Not* Reema."

"That leaves plenty others."

"I know. But a million bucks'll be changing hands, Cowboy. There's got to be somebody whispering about it."

"A million bucks is not so much nowadays," Palacios said. "I hear stories about twenty-, thirty-million-dollar dope deals, they're commonplace."

"I wish you'd tell *me* some of these stories," Kling said.

"My point is, a million-dollar deal nowadays you don't have people wetting their pants. It won't be easy getting a line on something like this."

"That's why I came to you, Cowboy," Kling said.

"Yeah, bullshit," Palacios said.

"Because I know you like the hard ones."

"Bullshit, bullshit," Palacios said, but he was grinning.

* * *

THE DOORMAN at 967 Grover Avenue was a roly-poly little person wearing a green uniform with gold trim. He looked like a general in a banana republic army. The people in the building knew him only as Al the Doorman, but his full name was Albert Eugene Di Stefano, and he was proud of the fact that he used to be one of the doormen at the Plaza Hotel in New York City. He immediately told Carella that he'd once given the N.Y.P.D. valuable information that had helped them crack a case involving some guy who was breaking into rooms at the Plaza and walking off into Central Park with bags full of jewelry. He would be happy to help Carella now in solving this terrible crime he was investigating. He knew all about the fourth-floor murders. Everybody in the building knew about them.

It so happened that he had, in fact, been working the midnight to eight A.M. shift on New Year's Eve, which he happened to pull because he'd drawn the deuce of clubs instead of the three of diamonds or the four of hearts. That was how the three doormen here at the building had decided who would work this particular shift on New Year's Eve, it being not what you would call a choice shift. He had drawn the lowest card, and he'd got stuck with it. So, yes, he was on that night. But he didn't see anyone suspicious coming in or going out of the building, if that was what Carella wanted to know.

"Do you know Mr. Hodding personally?" Carella asked.

"Oh, yes. A very nice man. I suggest a lot of commercials to him, he's a copywriter at an advertising agency. I told him one time I had a good idea for a Hertz commercial. The car rental people, you know? I thought they could show an airport with a lot of people waiting on lines at all these other car rental counters, but this guy goes right up to the Hertz counter, and he's walking off with a car key in ten seconds flat, and as he's passing all those people still waiting on the other lines, he busts out laughing and he says, 'I only laugh when it's Hertz.' They could even have a jingle that goes 'I *own*-lee *laugh* when it's *Hertz,* bom-bom.' Mr. Hodding told me his agency don't represent Hertz. So I gave him . . ."

"Do you know what he looks like? Mr. Hodding?"

"Oh, sure. I gave him this other idea for a Blue Nun commercial, this is a wine, you know, it's got a picture of a little blue nun on the label, well it's *called* Blue Nun. I told him the headline they should use on their commercial is 'Make a little Blue Nun a habit.' They could have a jingle that goes 'Make a *litt*-el *Blue* Nun a *ha*-bit.' Mr. Hodding told me his agency don't represent Blue Nun. So I gave him . . ."

"Would you recognize Mr. Hodding, for example, if he walked up the street right this minute?"

"Oh, sure. I gave him this other idea for a Chrysler Le Baron commercial. We see this World War I German fighter pilot with the white scarf, you know, and the goggles . . ."

"Did you see him at any time on New Year's Eve?"

"Who?"

"Mr. Hodding."

"As a matter of fact, I did, yes."

"When would that have been?"

"Around one o'clock. Well, a little after one. Ten after one, a quarter after, around then."

"Where did you see him?"

"Well, *here*," Di Stefano said, sounding surprised. "This is where I *was*. Remember when I told you I caught the low card? Which was how come I . . ."

"You saw him here in this building sometime between one and one-fifteen, is that correct?"

"Not only *saw* him, but also *spoke* to him. Which is the irony of it, you know? He comes here to check on the baby . . ."

"Is that what he said? That he was going to check on the baby?"

"Yes. So he's up there a half-hour, and right after he leaves there's this terrible thing happens. I mean, he must've missed the killer by what? Ten, fifteen minutes? Something like that?"

"You saw him when he came downstairs again?"

"Yes. Came right off the elevator. I was watching TV in this little room we got over there," he said, pointing, "we can see the whole lobby from it if we leave the door open."

"What time was this? When he came down?"

"I told you. It must've been around a quarter to two."

"Did he say anything to you?"

"He told me everything was okay. I told him it never hurts to check. He said That's right, Al, and off he went."

"Did he seem sober?"

"Oh, yes."

"Sober when he got here?"

"Sober when he got here, sober when he left."

"Any blood on his clothing?"

"Blood?"

"Or his hands?"

"Blood?" Di Stefano said, appalled. "Mr. Hodding? Blood? No, sir. No blood at all. No, sir!"

"Were you still here when he came home with Mrs. Hodding?"

"I was here all night. Till eight in the morning."

"And what time was that? When they got home?"

"Around two-thirty. Well, a little before."

"Okay," Carella said. "Thanks a lot."

"Don't you want to hear the Le Baron commercial?" Di Stefano asked.

SHE COULD NOT GET Eileen Burke out of her mind.

"My wife says I drink too much," the detective was telling her. "Her father was a drunk, so she thinks anybody has a few drinks, *he's* a drunk, too. She says I get dopey after a few drinks. It makes me want to punch her out. It's her goddamn upbringing, you can't grow up in a house with a drunk and not start thinking anybody takes a sip of elderberry wine is a fuckin' alcoholic.

"We were out last night with two other couples. I had the day shift, we're investigating this murder, somebody sawed off this woman's head and dropped it in a toilet bowl at the bus terminal. That is what I was dealing with all day yesterday. A fuckin' woman's *head* floating in a toilet bowl. From eight-thirty in the morning till six at night when I finally got outta that fuckin' squadroom. So I get home, we live in Bethtown, we got this garden apartment there near the bridge, I pour myself a Dewar's in a tall glass with ice and soda, I'm watching the news and drinking my drink and eating some peanuts and she comes in and says 'Do me a favor, don't drink so much tonight.' I coulda busted her fuckin' nose right then and there. She's already decided I'm a drunk, I drink too much, don't drink so much tonight, meaning I drink too much *every* night. Which I don't.

"I had a fuckin' heart attack last April, I can't *eat* what I want to eat, I have to walk two fuckin' miles every morning before I go to work, I used to smoke two packs of cigarettes a day and now I can't smoke any at all, and she's giving me no, no, no concerning a couple of drinks I allow myself when I get home after a head floating in a toilet bowl. Two fucking drinks! Was all I had before we left the house! So we meet these two other couples at this Chinese restaurant on Potter, one of the guys is an assistant D.A., the other one's a computer analyst, their wives I don't know what they do. We're sharing, you know, the way you're supposed to when you're eating Chinks, and we order a bottle of wine goes around the table once and it's empty. Well, there's six people there, you know. So we order another bottle of wine, and that makes two glasses of wine I have, which is what everybody at that table had, *including* my fuckin' Carry Nation wife with her hatchet.

"Now it's ten-thirty, and we're leaving the restaurant,

all of us together, and she takes her keys out of her bag and says so everybody can hear it, 'I'll drive, Frank.' So I say 'Why?' and she says 'Because I don't trust you.' The assistant D.A. laughs, this is a guy I work with, we call him in whenever we got real meat, make sure the case'll stick, you know, he's laughing at what my wife says. A guy I *work* with. The other guy, the computer analyst, he picks up on it, he says, 'I hope you've got the day off tomorrow, Frank.' Like they're all taking the cue from Cheryl, that's her name, my wife, and making Frank the big drunk who can't drive a car and who maybe can't even walk a straight *line* to the fuckin' car.

"On the way home, I tell her I don't want to start an argument, I'm tired, I worked a long hard day, that fuckin' head in the toilet bowl. She tells me I didn't work harder than any of the other men at the table, and I say 'What do you mean?' and she says 'You know what I mean,' and I say 'Are you saying I drank more than Charlie or Phil, are you saying I'm drunk?' and she says 'Did I say you're drunk?' and all at once I want to break every fuckin' bone in her body. All at once, I'm yelling. I'm supposed to avoid stress, am I right? It was stress caused the fuckin' heart attack, so here I am yelling like a fuckin' Puerto Rican hooker, and when we get home I go in the television room to sleep, only I can't sleep because I'm thinking I better throw my gun in the river 'cause if she keeps at me this way, I'm gonna use it on her one day. Or hurt her very bad some other way. And I don't want to do that."

Detective Frank Connell of the Four-Seven looked across the desk at her.

"I don't know what to do," he said. "It's like I've got an enemy for a wife instead of a friend. A wife is supposed to be a friend, ain't she? Ain't that why people get married? So there'll be somebody they can trust more than anybody else in the world? Instead, she makes me look like a fuckin' fool. I wouldn't do that to her in a million years, ridicule her in front of people she works with. She works in a law office, she's a legal secretary. I would *never* go in there and say she's this or that, she's no good at this or that, I would *never* hurt her that way. The way she hurts me when she says I'm a drunk."

"*Are* you a drunk?" Karin asked.

"No. I swear to God I am not."

"Do you want or need a drink when you get up in the morning?"

"Absolutely not. I go walk my fuckin' two miles, I eat my breakfast, and I go to work."

"Do you really have only two drinks when you get home at night?"

"Two. I swear."

"How big?"

"What do you mean? Like a regular drink. Some booze, some ice, some soda . . ."

"How *much* booze?"

"Two, three ounces."

"Which?"

"Three."

"That's six ounces."

"Which ain't a lot."

"Plus whatever wine you'll drink at . . ."

"Only when we go out. When we eat home, I usually have a Pepsi with dinner."

"Would you say you're a heavy drinker?"

"A moderate drinker. I know guys drink non-stop, day and night, I'm not one of . . ."

"Do you consider them drunks?"

"I consider them alcoholics. I rarely see them *drunk,* but I know they have drinking problems, I know they can't control their drinking."

"But you can."

"I do not consider two fucking drinks a day a *drinking* problem!"

"Now you're getting mad at me, huh?" Karin said, and smiled.

"I don't like being called a fuckin' drunk! It infuriates me! I'm not here because I have a *drinking* problem, I'm here 'cause I have a fucking *wife* problem. I love her to death, but . . ."

"But you've been talking about hurting her," Karin said.

"I know."

"Physically hurting her."

"Yes."

"Punching her out. Breaking her nose . . ."

Connell nodded.

"Breaking every bone in her body."

He nodded again.

"Even using your gun on her."

"This is what's tearing me apart," Connell said. "She's my wife, but when she starts on me I'd like to kill her."

"You said you love her to death," Karin said. "Do you?"

Connell thought about this for a moment.

"I guess so," he said, and fell silent.

Eileen Burke popped into her head again.

And do you love him?

Asking her about Bert Kling.

Eileen thinking it over.

And saying, "I guess so."

In which case, why had she stopped seeing him?

THE OFFICES OF the David Pierce Advertising Agency were midtown on Jefferson Avenue, where most of the city's advertising agencies grew like poisonous toadstools. Carella and Meyer arrived there together at seven minutes past three that Friday afternoon. Peter Hodding was still out to lunch. This was the twentieth day of January. His daughter would be dead three weeks tomorrow. They were wondering if he'd killed her.

They were sitting on a chrome and leather sofa in the waiting room when he came in. He was wearing a raccoon fur coat. Cheeks ruddy from the cold outside, straight brown hair windblown, he looked the way Chastity Kerr had described him looking after his early morning walk on New Year's Eve. He seemed happy to see them. Asked them at once if there was any news. Led them to his private office in the agency's recesses.

Two walls painted yellow, a third painted a sort of lavender, the last banked with windows that looked out over a city hushed by snow. Photocopies of print ads tacked to the walls with pushpins. A storyboard for a television commercial. A desk with an old-fashioned electric typewriter on it. Sheet of paper in the roller. Hodding sat behind the desk. He offered the detectives chairs. They sat.

"Mr. Hodding," Carella said, "did you at any time on New Year's Eve leave the party at the apartment of Mr. and Mrs. Jeremy Kerr?"

Hodding blinked.

The blink told them they had him.

"Yes," he said.

"At what time?" Meyer asked.

Another blink.

"We left at a little after two."

"To go home. You and your wife."

"Yes."

"How about before then?"

Another blink.

"Well, yes," he said.

"You left the Kerr apartment before then?"

"Yes."

"At what time."

"Around one o'clock."

"Alone?"

"Yes."

"Where'd you go?" Carella asked.

"For a walk. I was drunk. I needed some air."

"Where'd you walk?"

"In the park."

"Which direction?"

"I don't know what you mean. Anyway, what's . . . ?"

"Uptown, downtown, crosstown? Which way did you walk?"

"Downtown. Excuse me, but what . . . ?"

"How far downtown did you walk?"

"To the statue and back."

"Which statue?"

"The Alan Clive statue. The statue there."

"At the circle?"

"Yes. Why?"

"Are you sure you didn't walk *uptown*?" Carella said. Hodding blinked again.

"Are you sure you didn't walk uptown on Grover Avenue?" Meyer said.

"Four blocks uptown?" Carella said.

"To your apartment?"

"Getting there at ten after one, a quarter after one?"

"And staying there for a half-hour or so?"

There was a long painful silence.

"Okay," Hodding said.

"Mr. Hodding, did you commit those murders?" Carella asked.

"No, sir, I did not," Hodding said.

THE AFFAIR with Annie Flynn . . .

He couldn't even properly call it an affair because their love wasn't fashioned in the classic adulterers' mold, it was more like . . .

He didn't know what to call it.

"How about cradle-snatching?" Carella suggested.

"How about seducing a girl half your age?" Meyer suggested.

They didn't particularly like this man.

To them, he was a cut above Fats Donner—who dug Mary Jane shoes and white cotton panties.

He wanted them to know that he'd never done anything like this before in his life. He'd been married to Gayle for the past five years now, he'd never once even *looked* at another woman until Annie began sitting for them. Annie was the only woman he'd ever . . .

"A *girl*," Carella reminded him.

"A sixteen-year-old *girl*," Meyer said.

Well, there were girls who became women at a very early age, listen she wasn't a virgin, this wasn't what you'd call seduction of the innocent or anything, this was—

"Yes, what was it?" Carella asked.

"Exactly what would you call it?" Meyer asked.

"I loved her," Hodding said.

Love.

One of the only two reasons for murder.

The other being money.

It had started one night early in October. She'd begun sitting for them in September, shortly after they'd adopted the baby, he remembered being utterly surprised by Annie's maturity. You expected a teenage girl to be somehow bursting with raucous energy, but Annie . . .

Those thoughtful green eyes.

The subtlety of her glances.

Secrets unspoken in those eyes.

The fiery red hair.

He'd wondered if she was red below.

"Look," Meyer said, "if you don't fucking mind . . ."

Meyer rarely used profanity.

"I didn't kill her," Hodding said. "I'm trying to explain . . ."

"Just tell us what . . ."

"Let him do it his own way," Carella said gently.

"The son of a bitch was fucking a sixteen-year . . ."

"Come on," Carella said, and put his hand on Meyer's arm. "Come on, okay?"

"I loved her," Hodding said again.

In October, the middle of October, she'd sat for them while he and his wife attended an awards dinner downtown at the Sherman. He remembered that it was a particularly mild night for October, the temperature somewhere in the seventies that day, more like late spring than early fall. Annie came to the apartment dressed in the colors of autumn, a rust-colored skirt, and a pale orange cotton shirt, a yellow ribbon in her hair, like the song. She had walked the seven blocks from her own apartment, schoolbooks cradled in her arms against abundant breasts, smiling, and bursting with energy and youth and . . .

Sexuality.

Yes.

"I'm sorry, Detective Meyer, but you have to understand . . ."

"Just get the fuck on with it," Meyer said.

. . . there was an enormous sexuality about Annie. A sensuousness. The smoldering green eyes, the somewhat petulant full-lipped mouth, the volcanic red hair, lava erupting, hot, overflowing. The short skirt revealing long, lovely legs and slender ankles, French-heeled shoes, the short heels exaggerating the curve of the leg and the thrust of her buttocks and breasts, naked beneath the thin cotton shirt, nipples puckering though it was not cold outside.

They did not get home until almost three in the morning.

Late night. The dinner had been endless, they'd gone for drinks with friends after all the prizes were awarded—Hodding had taken one home for the inventive copywriting he'd done on his agency's campaign for a cookie company, he'd shown the plaque to Annie, she'd ooohed and ahhhed in girlish delight.

Three in the morning.

You sent a young girl out into the streets alone at three in the morning, you were asking for trouble. This city, maybe any city. Gayle suggested that her husband call down, ask Al the Doorman to get a taxi for Annie. Hodding said, No, I'll walk her home, I can use some air.

Such a glorious night.

A mild breeze blowing in off Grover Park, he suggested that perhaps they ought to take the park path home.

She said Oh, gee, Mr. Hodding, do you think that'll be safe?

Innuendo in her voice, in her eyes.

She knew it would not be safe.

She knew what he would do to her in that park.

She told him later that she'd been wanting him to do it to her from the minute she'd laid eyes on him.

But he didn't know that at the time.

Didn't know she wanted him as much as he wanted her.

It was only seven blocks from his apartment to where she lived with her parents. Well, seven and a half, because she lived in the middle of the block, off the avenue. He had seven and a half blocks to do whatever it was he planned to do . . .

He didn't have any plan.

. . . whatever it was he longed to do . . .

He yearned for her with every fiber in his being.

She began talking about her boyfriend. A kid named Scott Handler. Went to school up in Maine someplace. The asshole of creation, she said. She looked at him. Smiled. Green eyes flashing. Had she deliberately used this mild profanity? To tell him what? I'm a big girl now?

She said she'd been going with Handler since she was fifteen . . .

Rolling her eyes heavenward.

He guessed that at her age, dating someone for a year and more was an eternity.

. . . but that she was really beginning to feel tied down, you know? Scott all the way up there, and her down here, you know? They were supposed to be going *steady*, but what did that mean? How could you go *steady* with someone who was all the way up near the Canadian border? In fact, how could you *go* with him at *all*?

In the park now.

Leaves underfoot.

The rustle of leaves.

French-heeled shoes whispering through the leaves.

He was dying to slide his hands up her legs, under that rust-colored skirt. Open that cotton blouse, find those breasts with their erect nipples, teenage nipples.

You know, she said, a girl misses certain things.

His heart stopped.

He dared not ask her what things she missed.

Kissing, she said.

Scuffing through the leaves.

Touching, she said.

He held his breath.

Making love, she whispered.

And stopped on the path.

And turned to him.

And lifted her face to his.

That was the first time.

He had been with her a total of fourteen times since that October night, the fifteenth of October, the night he'd accepted the industry's coveted award, the night he'd been gifted, too, with this girl, this woman, this unbelievably passionate creature he'd coveted since September. Fourteen times. Including their hurried coupling on New Year's Eve.

His eyes brimmed with tears.

For Christmas he'd given her a small lapis pendant on a gold—

"You saw it," he said. "It was on the floor. Beside her. The chain must have broken when . . . when . . . do you remember it? A small teardrop-shaped piece of lapis with a gold loop holding it to the chain? I bought it in an antiques shop on Lamont. She loved it. She wore it all the time. I gave it to her for our first Christmas together. I loved her so much."

She had broken off with Handler by then.

Told him she no longer wished to see him. This was when he came down for the Thanksgiving holiday. Told him it was over and done with. Said she wanted nothing further to do with him. He accused her of having found a new boyfriend. Told her he'd kill them both.

Hodding was in bed with her when she reported this to him.

A room he'd rented in a hotel near the Stem.

Hookers running through the hallway outside.

They both laughed at Handler's boyish threat.

On New Year's Eve . . .

He covered his face with his hands.

Wept into his hands.

Meyer felt no sympathy.

Neither did Carella.

On New Year's Eve . . .

14.

THE ASSISTANT district attorney was a woman named Nellie Brand, thirty-two years old and smart as hell. Sand-colored hair cut in a breezy flying wedge, blue eyes intently alert. Wearing a brown tweed suit, a tan turtleneck sweater, and brown pumps with sensible high heels, she sat on the edge of the long table in the Interrogation Room, legs crossed, a pastrami sandwich in her right hand. A little cardboard dish of soggy French fries was on the table beside her, together with a cardboard container of Coca-Cola.

"Willing to risk a quickie, huh?" she said, and bit into the sandwich.

She was married, Carella noticed. Gold wedding band on the ring finger of her left hand. He was drinking coffee and eating a tuna and tomato on toast.

"According to what he told us," Meyer said, "he simply *had* to see her." He was still angry. Seething inside. Voice edged with sarcasm. Carella had never seen him this way. Nor was he eating anything. He was trying to lose seven pounds. This probably made him even angrier.

"Ah, *l'amour,*" Nellie said and rolled her blue eyes.

In some countries, women wore the wedding band on the right hand. Carella had read that someplace. Austria? Maybe Germany. Or maybe both. Nellie Brand was a married woman who, Carella suspected, might not appreciate a married man her age playing around with a sixteen-year-old kid. He further suspected she might have preferred dining with her husband to eating deli with two weary detectives who'd spent most of the afternoon and evening with a man who may have killed his own baby daughter and the sixteen-year-old who'd been sitting with her. But here she was at eight o'clock on a cold and icy Friday night, trying to determine whether they had anything that would stick here should they decide to charge him. They would have to charge him soon or let him go. Those were the rules, Harold. Miranda-Escobedo. You played it by the rules or you didn't play at all.

"Got there at?" Nellie said.

"Quarter past one at the outside," Carella said.

"Doorman told you this?"

"Yes."

"Reliable?"

"Seems so."

"And left when?"

"Quarter to two."

"Half-hour even," Nellie said.

"*Had* to see her," Meyer said. Steaming. About to

erupt. Thinking about his own daughter, Carella figured.

"How long did he say this'd been going on?"

"Since October."

"When?"

"The fifteenth," Carella said.

"Birth date of great men," Nellie said, but did not amplify. "Told you all this, huh?"

"Yeah. Which troubles *us,* too. The fact that he . . ."

"Sure, why would he?"

"Unless he's figuring . . ."

"Yeah, there's that."

"You know, the . . ."

"Sure, show 'em the death and they'll accept the fever," Nellie said.

"Exactly. If he thinks he's looking at murder, he'll settle for adultery."

"He gives us the old Boy-Meets-Girl . . ."

"Pulls a Jimmy Swaggart . . ."

"Tearfully begs forgiveness . . ."

"And walks off into the sunset."

Nellie washed down a fry with a swallow of Coke. "He knew what the autopsy report said, is that right?"

"About sperm in the . . . ?"

"Yeah."

"Yes, he was informed earlier."

"So he knew one of the possibilities was rape-murder."

"Yes."

"And now you've got him up here, and you're asking questions about New Year's Eve . . ."

"Oh, sure, he's no dummy. He had to figure we were thinking he was our man."

"Which you're *still* thinking," Nellie said.

"Otherwise we wouldn't have invited you here for dinner," Carella said, and smiled.

"Yes, thank you, it's delicious," Nellie said, and bit into the sandwich again. "So let me hear your case," she said. "You can skip means and opportunity, I know he had both. Let me hear motive."

"We'd have to wing it," Carella said.

"I've got all night," Nellie said.

Carella repeated essentially what Hodding had told them in this very room not an hour earlier.

If it had not been so cold on New Year's Eve, he would have planned to walk Annie home, the way he'd done that first time in October and several times since. Make love to her in the park. Annie standing under a tree with her skirt up around her hips and her panties down around her ankles, Hodding nailing her to the tree. His words. But it was so damn *cold* that night. He and his wife had virtually frozen to death just waiting for a taxi to take them over to the Kerr apartment, and Hodding knew that lovemaking in the park was out of the question, however strong his desire. He had it in his head that he and Annie had to usher in the new year by making love. An affirmation—

"Really gone over this kid, huh?" Nellie asked.

"Totally," Meyer said.

—an affirmation of their bond. To seal their relationship. Fuck her senseless at the start of the new year. His words again. And the more he drank—

"Was he really drunk? Or do you think that was an act? To get out of the place."

"I think he was really drunk," Carella said.

"Probably sobered up on the way over to the apartment," Meyer said.

"Doorman says he was sober."

"So you have him sober at the scene of the crime."

"Yes."

"Okay, go ahead."

The more he drank, the more the idea became an obsession with him. He had to get to his apartment, had to make love to Annie. When he talked to her on the phone at twelve-thirty, he whispered what he wanted to do . . .

"Did he tell you this?"

"Yes."

"That he whispered to her?"

"Yes."

"Said what?"

"Said, 'I want to fuck you.' "

"The son of a bitch," Meyer said.

"Uh-huh," Nellie said. "And she said?"

"She said, 'Good. Come on over.' "

"Precocious."

"Very."

"He told you all this?"

"We have it on tape."

"What was his response?"

"He said, 'In a little while.' "

"You've got all this on tape?"

"All of it. We've also got his hostess overhearing him. Chastity Kerr. We've got a statement from her."

"The exact words he gave you."

"Yes. Telling Annie, 'In a little while.' "

"Okay. Go ahead."

At one o'clock he leaves the Kerr party, ostensibly to clear his head. By the time he gets to his own building, four blocks uptown, he's cold sober. He goes upstairs, finds Annie waiting for him with nothing on under her skirt. They make passionate love on the living room couch, he goes in to kiss his baby daughter on her rose-bud cheek, and then he leaves. The doorman clocks him coming out of the elevator at a quarter to two.

"Wham, bang, thank you, ma'am," Nellie said.

"That's how *his* story goes," Meyer said.

"And your version?"

"I think the strain of the relationship was beginning to tell on him," Meyer said. "The very fact that on New Year's *Eve,* he would risk running back to his apartment for a quick assignation . . ."

"Well, you yourself said he was totally gone on her."

"Exactly my point. And getting in deeper and deeper. On Christmas, for example, he . . ."

"No puns, please," Nellie said, and smiled.

Carella returned the smile. Meyer did not.

"On Christmas, he gave her a gift. Our first *Christmas* together," Meyer said, bitterly repeating Hodding's words. "And he caused her to break up with a decent . . ."

"What kind of a gift?" Nellie asked.

"Lapis pendant on a gold chain."

"Expensive?"

"I would guess moderately expensive."

"Well, there's cheap lapis, too," Nellie said.

"He bought this on Lamont."

"Okay, expensive," Nellie said.

"What I'm saying, this was a man out of control . . ."

"Uh-huh."

"Falling in love with a teenager to begin with . . ."

"Uh-huh."

"Getting in way over his head, buying her expensive gifts, making love to her in the *park*, for Christ's sake, meeting her in cheap hotels off the Stem, hookers parading the halls, taking risks no man in his right . . ."

"Detective Meyer, excuse me," Nellie said. "Why'd he kill her?"

"Because he couldn't see any other way out."

"Where'd you get that?"

"From everything he said."

"He told you he was in over his head?"

"No, but . . ."

"Told you he couldn't handle this?"

"Well . . ."

"Couldn't see any other way out?"

"Not in those exact words."

"What words then?"

"Mrs. Brand, excuse *me*," Meyer said. "He was in that apartment making love to this girl between one-fifteen and a quarter to two. When he got home with his

wife, forty-five minutes later, the girl is dead. Stabbed.
Are we supposed to believe someone *else* got into that
apartment during those forty-five minutes? Isn't it more
reasonable to assume that Hodding either figured this
was a good time to end his goddamn *problems* with this
girl, or else he . . ."

"What problems? How did he indicate to you in any
way that he considered this relationship a problem?"

"He said he *had* to see her, had to . . ."

"I don't see that as a problem. In fact, he was seeing
her regularly. Seeing her was not a problem, Detective
Meyer."

"Okay, then let's say they *argued* about something,
okay? Let's say they made love and she told him she
didn't want to see him anymore. She'd bounced her
boyfriend in November, why couldn't she now do the
same thing with Hodding? Over and done with, goodbye. Only he wasn't having any of it. Not after all the
deception of the past few months. So he flies off the
deep end, goes out to the kitchen for a knife—he knows
where they are, he lives in this . . ."

"I've granted you means," Nellie said.

"And comes back and stabs her," Meyer said.

"Uh-huh," Nellie said.

"He was in that apartment for a half-hour," Meyer
said.

"Okay, let's say all this happened," Nellie said.
"They made love and she told him thanks, it was nice,
but that's the last dance, goodbye and good luck, and
he stormed out into the kitchen and grabbed the knife
and did her in. Okay? Is that your scenario?"

"Yes," Meyer said.

"Let's say all of that—which you can't prove, by the way—is true. Then answer me one other question."

"Sure."

"Why'd he *then* kill his own daughter?"

And to that, there was no answer.

HENRY TSU did not enjoy being bad-mouthed.

As far as he was concerned, he was a trustworthy businessman and he did not like people spreading rumors about him. That his business happened to be illegal had nothing to do with whether or not he conducted it like a gentleman. True, Henry had been forced on occasion to break a few collarbones and heads, but even when force had been called for, the business community understood that such action had been an absolute necessity. Henry had a good reputation. He hated to see it going down the toilet because of a little spic cocksucker.

José Domingo Herrera, who years ago used to do some work for the Chang people when they had what was called the Yellow Paper Gang in Chinatown. Henry had heard that Herrera was very good at what he did. What he did was a secret between himself and Chang Tie Fei, otherwise known as Walter Chang here in this city. Then again, Henry's full and honorable name was Tsu Hong Chin. How he had got to be Henry was a mystery even to himself. Perhaps it was because he looked very much like Henry Fonda when he was young. With Chinese eyes.

Putting together the pieces, Henry figured that Herrera had served as a liaison between the Chang people and certain Colombian interests eager to establish a foothold here in the city. The Colombians were sick to death of having to deal with the wops in Miami, who thought they owned the whole fucking world. They didn't want to start dealing with them all over again up here so they went to the Chinese instead. The Chinese needed somebody who could understand these people who looked and sounded either like sombreroed and raggedy-assed bandidos in a Mexican movie or else pinky-ringed and pointy-lapeled gangsters in a movie about Prohibition days. So they landed on Herrera as a go-between.

Was what Henry figured.

Little José Domingo Herrera, building himself a rep with the Chinese and the Colombians as well.

How Herrera had got involved with a *Jamaican* posse was another thing.

Which was why Henry on this bleak Saturday morning, the twenty-first day of January, was talking to a man named Juan Kai Hsao, whose mother was Spanish—*really* Spanish, from Spain—and whose father was from Taiwan. The two men were speaking in English because Henry had no Spanish at all and Juan's Chinese was extremely half-assed, his father having come to this country at the age of two.

"Let me tell you what I suspect," Henry said.

"Yes," Juan said. "Please."

He had exquisite manners. Henry figured the manners were from his Chinese side.

"I believe Herrera is spreading this rumor in order to serve his own needs. Whatever they may be."

"This rumor that around Christmastime . . ."

"The twenty-seventh."

"Yes. That on the twenty-seventh, your people intercepted a shipment earmarked for the Hamilton . . ."

"Not the shipment. The money intended to *pay* for the shipment."

"Coming from where, this shipment?"

"How do I know?"

"You said . . ."

"I said that's the *rumor.* That I *knew* about this shipment. Knew where it would be delivered, and intercepted the money for it."

"Stole it."

"Yes, of *course,* stole it."

"From the Hamilton posse."

"Yes."

"Was this supposed to be a big shipment? In the rumor?"

"In the rumor, it was supposed to be three kilos."

"Of cocaine."

"Of cocaine, yes."

"But you don't know from where?"

"No. That's not important, from where. It could be Miami, it could be Canada, it could be the West—up through Mexico, you know—it could even be from Europe through the airport in a suitcase. Three kilos is a tiny amount. Why would I even *bother* with such a small amount? Three kilos isn't even seven fucking pounds. You can buy a Thanksgiving turkey that weighs more than that."

"But which doesn't cost as much," Juan said, and both men laughed.

"Fifty thousand," Henry said. "In the rumor."

"That you are supposed to have stolen."

"Not the cocaine."

"No, the money."

"Yes."

"From Herrera."

"Yes, this little . . ."

Henry almost said "spic," but then he remembered that his guest was half-Spanish.

"This little person Herrera, who by the way used to do work for the Chang people. When they had the Yellow Paper Gang. This was before your time."

"I've read a lot about Walter Chang," Juan said.

He was only twenty-four years old and still making a rep. He figured it didn't hurt to say he'd read a lot about every famous gangster this city had ever had. Make everyone think he had gone out of his way to learn such things. Actually, though, he did know about the Yellow Paper Gang because his father had once leaned on some people for them. Juan's father was six feet three inches tall and weighed two hundred and forty pounds, which was very large for a Chinese. Everybody joked that there must have been a eunuch in his ancestry someplace. Juan's father found this comical. That was because he had a keen reputation as a ladies' man.

"So as I understand this," Juan said, wanting to get the entire story straight before he went out of here on a wild pony, "you'd like to know what *really* went down on the night of December twenty-seventh."

"Yes. And why Herrera is saying we cold-cocked him."

"And stole the fifty."

"Yes. The story on the street is that Herrera went to take delivery of this lousy three keys . . ."

"Where? Do you know where?"

"Yes, in Riverhead. Where isn't important. Herrera is saying he *went* there with fifty dollars of Hamilton's money, to make the buy and take delivery, and as he was going in the building he was jumped by two Chinese men he later . . ."

"Your people? In the rumor?"

"Yes," Henry said. "I was about to say that he later identified them—this is all in the rumor that's going around—as two people who work for me."

"And none of this is true."

"None of it."

"And you think it's Herrera who's spreading the rumor?"

"Who else would be spreading it?"

"If it's someone else, you want to know that, too."

"Yes. And *why?* There has to be a reason for such bullshit."

"I'll find out," Juan promised.

But he wasn't sure he could.

It all sounded so fucking *Chinese.*

THE WAY HAMILTON had found out was through a person he'd done a favor for in Miami three years ago. The favor happened to have been killing the man's cousin. The man was a Cuban heavily involved in dealing dope. His name was Carlos Felipe Ortega. You kill a man's cousin for him, without charging him anything for it, the man might be grateful later on, if he could find an opportunity. Or so Hamilton thought at first.

The information was that the Tsu gang up here was going to take delivery on a million-dollar shipment of coke.

A hundred keys.

On the twenty-third of January.

The reason Ortega was calling—this was two weeks before Christmas—was that he'd found out the Miami people were insisting on a very low profile. They had gone along with Tsu's bullshit about testing and tasting five keys of the stuff in one place and taking delivery of the rest someplace else, but they didn't want a big fucking Sino-Colombian mob scene up there. In the first instance, they were insisting that one guy from the Chinese side meet one guy from their side, fifty grand here, five keys there. You test, you pay, you take the high road, we take the low, it was nice seeing you. If the stuff tested pure, you sent two other guys to pay for and pick up the rest of the shit. No *more* than two guys. No crowds from the Forbidden City. Two guys who'd come and go in the night, thank you very much, and so long. Tsu had agreed to the terms. Which meant, Ortega said, that instead of a thousand guys standing around with automatic weapons in their hands and threatening looks on their faces, you had a one-on-one in the first instance, and only two people from each side when the later exchange took place.

"Which sounds very thin to me," Ortega had said.

"Very," Hamilton said.

"Unless, of course, there are no thieves in your city."

Both men chuckled.

"Do you want to know where all this is going to take place, Lewis?" Ortega asked.

"That might be nice to know," Hamilton said.

"But no messing with the Miami people, please," Ortega said. "I live here."

"I understand."

"Whatever you decide to do is between you and the Chinese."

"Yes, I understand."

"And if a little happens to fall my way . . ."

Ortega's voice shrugged.

"How much do you think should fall your way, Carlos?" Hamilton asked, thinking You cheap bastard, I *killed* somebody for you. As a fucking *gift*.

"I thought ten percent," Ortega said. "For the address of where the big buy is going down."

"You have a deal," Hamilton said.

"Ten keys, correct?"

"No, that's more than ten percent."

"No, it's ten percent of a hundred keys."

"You told me five keys would be someplace else."

"I know. But ten keys is the price, Lewis."

"All right."

"Do we have a deal?"

"I said all right."

"You deliver."

"No. You pick up."

"Certainly," Ortega said.

"The address," Hamilton said.

Ortega gave it to him.

This was back in December.

Two weeks before Christmas. The tenth, the eleventh, somewhere in there.

Ortega had told him that the shipment would be arriving in Florida on the twenty-first of January. In Florida, there had to be at least eight zillion canals with private boats on them. A lot of those boats were Cigarette types—high-powered speedboats like an Excalibur or a Donzi or a Wellcraft Scarab that could outrun almost any Coast Guard vessel on the water. Zipped out to where the ship was waiting beyond the three-mile limit, zipped back in to their own little dock behind their own little house. Did it in broad daylight. Safer in the daytime than at night, when the Coast Guard might hail you and stop you. During the daytime, you were just some pleasure-seeking boaters out on the water to get some sun. Out there on the briny, you sometimes wouldn't see another vessel for miles and miles. Your ship'd be standing still out there, you lay to in her shadow, you could load seven *tons* of cocaine, there'd be nobody to see you or to challenge you. Coast Guard? Come suck my toe, man. What you needed to stop dope coming into Florida on *either* of its coasts was a fleet of ten thousand U.S. Navy destroyers and even *then* they might not be able to do the job.

The shipment would be coming up north by automobile.

No borders to cross, no Coast Guard vessels to worry about.

You drove straight up on interstate highways with the shit in the trunk of your car. You obeyed the speed limit. You drove with a woman beside you on the front seat. A pair of married tourists on vacation. *White* people, both of them, pure Wonder Bread. No blacks, no Hispanics. Nothing to raise even the slightest eyebrow of suspicion. You later met these people at a pre-arranged place in the city, usually one of the apartments you rented on a yearly lease for the specific purpose of using it as a drop, you paid them the money, you walked off with the shit.

This big shipment coming up was the reason Hamilton had hired Herrera.

What Herrera hadn't known, of course—

Well, maybe he *had* known, considering it in retrospect.

"I *still* don't know why you trusted that fucking spic with fifty dollars," Isaac said.

This was language the gangs had picked up from fiction.

It was funny the way life often imitated art.

None of the gangs in this city had ever read a book and they would never have heard of Richard Condon's *Prizzi's Honor* if there hadn't been a movie made from it. They liked that picture. It showed killers in a comical light. It also introduced real-life gangs to something Richard Condon had made up, the way his hoodlums talked about money in terms of singles instead of thousands. If Condon's crooks wanted to say five *thousand* dollars, they said *five* dollars. It was very comical. It was also an extension of real-life criminal parlance where, for example, a five-dollar bag of heroin became a nickel bag. That was when heroin was still the drug of choice, later conceding the title to cocaine and then crack, admittedly a cocaine derivative. A five-dollar vial was now a nickel vial. And when a thief said fifty dollars, he meant fifty *thousand* dollars. Which was the sum of money Lewis Randolph Hamilton had entrusted to José Domingo Herrera on the twenty-seventh day of December last year.

"Why?" Isaac asked now.

He knew he was risking trouble.

Hamilton was angry this morning.

Angry that Herrera had run off with fifty dollars belonging to him. Angry that Andrew Fields, who'd been sent out once *again* to dispatch the little spic, had been unable to find him anywhere in the city. Angry that he himself, Lewis Randolph Hamilton, had bungled the execution of the blond cop. Angry that the cop had taken a good look at him. All of these things were like a cluster of boils on Hamilton's ass. Isaac should have known better than to ask about Herrera at a time like this. But Isaac was still somewhat pissed himself over the way a week, ten days ago Hamilton had appropriated both of those German hookers for himself.

In many ways, Isaac and Hamilton were like man and wife. They each knew which buttons to push to get

the proper response from the other. They each knew
what the kill words were. Unlike most married couples,
however, they did not fight fair. A marriage was
doomed when either partner decided he or she would
no longer fight fair. Hamilton had never fought fair in
his life. Neither had Isaac. They weren't about to start
now. But this was not threatening to their relationship.
In fact, they each respected this about the other. They
were killers. Killers did not fight fair.

"Not of the blood," Isaac said, shaking his head in
exaggerated incredulity. "To have chosen someone not
of the blood . . ."

"There's Spanish in you, too," Hamilton said.

"East Indian maybe, but not Spanish."

"A Spanish whore," Hamilton said.

"Chinese maybe," Isaac said, "but not Spanish."

"From the old days," Hamilton said. "From when
Christopher Columbus was still there."

"That far back, huh, man?" Isaac said.

"Before the British took over."

"Oh my, a Spanish whore," Isaac said. He was letting all this roll off his back. This wasn't dirty fighting,
it wasn't even fighting. Hamilton was just feinting, seeing could he get a rise without exerting too much
effort. Isaac was the one with the power to punch
below the belt today. Isaac was the one who insisted on
knowing why Hamilton had handed fifty big ones to a
spic.

"I thought you knew the Spanish were not to be
trusted," Isaac said.

Of course, Hamilton might just tell him to fuck off.

"A race that writes on walls," Isaac said.

"You are not making sense, man," Hamilton said.

"It's a cultural thing," Isaac said. "Writing on walls. They also stare at women. It's all cultural. Go look it up."

"Come look up my asshole," Hamilton said.

"I might find a dozen roses up there," Isaac said.

Both men laughed.

"With a card," Isaac said.

Both men laughed again.

This was a homosexual joke. Neither of the men was homosexual, but they often made homosexual jokes, exchanged homosexual banter. This was common among heterosexual men, Harold. It happened all the time.

"To have trusted a *spic*," Isaac said, shaking his head again. "Whose credentials you never thought to . . ."

"He was checked," Hamilton said.

"Not by me."

"He was *checked*," Hamilton said again, hitting the word harder this time.

"If so, he was . . ."

"Thoroughly," Hamilton said.

And glared at Isaac.

Isaac didn't flinch.

"If *I* had checked the man . . ." he said.

"*You* were in Baltimore," Hamilton said.

"It could have waited till I got back."

"Visiting your *Mama*," Hamilton said.

"There was no urgency . . ."

"Running home to Mama for Christmas."

He was getting to Isaac now. Isaac did not like to

think of himself as a Mama's Boy. But he was always running down to see his mother in Baltimore.

"Running home to eat Mama's *plum* pudding," Hamilton said.

Somehow he made this sound obscenely malicious.

"While *you*," Isaac said, "are having a spic checked by . . . who checked him, anyway?"

"James."

"James!" Isaac said.

"Yes, James. And he ran the check in a very pro . . ."

"You picked *James* to do this job? James who later used *baseball* bats on this very same . . ."

"I didn't know at the time that James would later fuck up," Hamilton said frostily. "*You* were in Baltimore. Someone had to do the job. I asked James to check on him. He came back with credentials that sounded okay."

"Like?"

"Like no current affiliations. A free-lancer. No police record. A courier once, long ago, for the Chang people. I figured . . ."

"Chinks are not to be trusted, either," Isaac said.

"*No* one is to be trusted," Hamilton said flatly. "You didn't know what the situation was, you were in *Baltimore*. I had to operate on my instincts."

"That's right, I didn't know what the situation was."

"That's right."

"And I *still* don't."

"That's right, too."

"All I know is Herrera stole the fifty."

"Yes, that's all you know."

"Do you want to tell me the rest?"

"No," Hamilton said.

THE BA TWINS had been Hamilton's idea, too.

They were named Ba Zheng Shen and Ba Zhai Kong, but people outside the Chinese community called them Zing and Zang. They were both twenty-seven years old, Zing being the oldest by five minutes. They were also extraordinarily and identically handsome. It was rumored that Zing had once lived with a gorgeous red-headed American girl for six months without her realizing that he and his brother were taking turns fucking her.

Zing and Zang knew that if the Chinese ever took over the world—which they did not doubt for a moment would happen one day—it would not be because Communism was a better form of government than democracy; it would be because the Chinese were such good businessmen. Zing and Zang were young and energetic and extremely ambitious. It was said in Chinatown that if the price was right, they would kill their own mother. And steal her gold fillings afterward. The very first time the Ba twins had killed any-one was in Hong Kong five years back when they were but mere twenty-two-year-olds. The price back then had been a thousand dollars American for each of them.

Nowadays, their fee was somewhat higher.

Back in December, for example, when Lewis Randolph Hamilton first contacted them regarding a courier named José Domingo Herrera, he'd offered them a flat three thousand dollars for messing up the little Puerto Rican and retrieving the fifty thousand dollars he would be carrying. Zing and Zang looked Hamilton straight in the eye—they were more inscrutable-looking than most Chinese, perhaps because they carried their extraordinary good looks with a defiant, almost challenging air—and said the price these days for moving someone around was four thousand for *each* of them, a total of eight thousand for the job, take it or leave it. Hamilton said he wasn't looking for God's sake, mon, to *dust* the little spic, he only wanted him *rearranged* a trifle. Eight thousand total, the Ba boys said, take it or leave it. Hamilton rolled his eyes and sighed heavily. But he took it.

Which made them wonder.

What they were wondering was the same thing Herrera had wondered when he'd been hired by Hamilton to carry the fifty K: Why is this man not using one of his own people to do this job? Why is he paying us eight thousand dollars for something his own goon squad can handle?

They also wondered how they could turn this peculiar situation to their own advantage.

The first way they figured they could pick up a little extra change was to contact the intended victim, this José Domingo Herrera character, and tell him they were supposed to move him around a little on the twenty-seventh of December, which was two days after Christmas.

"New Year you be on clutches," Zing said.

They both spoke English like Chinese cooks in a Gold Rush movie. This did not make them any less dangerous than they were. Pit vipers do not speak English very well, either.

Herrera, who was already wondering why Hamilton had hired him as a courier, now began wondering why these two fucking illiterate Chinks were telling him about the plan to cold-cock him. He figured they were looking for money *not* to beat him up. Play both ends against the middle. Which meant that the possibility existed he would lay some cash on them and they would beat him up, anyway. Life was so difficult in this city.

Herrera listened while they told him they wanted eight thousand dollars to forget their little rendezvous two weeks from now. Herrera figured this was what Hamilton was paying them to ambush him and take back his money. He'd been planning to steal the fifty he was delivering for Hamilton. Vanish in the night. Fuck the goddamn Jakie. But now these Chinks presented a problem. If they beat him up, they would take the fifty and return it to Hamilton. Leaving Herrera cold and broke in the gutter. On the other hand, if he paid them the eight . . .

"We have a deal," he said, and they all shook hands.

He trusted their handshakes as much as he trusted their slanty eyes.

But, oddly, Herrera started wondering in Spanish the same things the Ba brothers began wondering in Chinese.

Out loud and in English, Herrera said, "Why is he setting me up?"

Out loud, and in his own brand of English, Zang said, "Why use-ah two *Chinee?*"

They pondered this together.

It was obvious to all of them that Herrera was indeed being set up. At least to take a beating. And even though he had to admit that ten thousand dollars was a good price for getting roughed up—in this city, prize-fighters had taken dives for less—he still wondered why. And why did the two men beating him up have to be Chinese?

Because . . .

Well . . .

They all looked at each other.

And then Herrera said, "Because something *Chinese* has to be coming down!"

"Ah, ah," Zing said.

Herrera was grateful he hadn't said, "Ah so."

"You want to go partners?" he asked.

The Ba brothers looked at him inscrutably. Fuckin' Chinks, he thought.

"You want to go in business together?"

"Ah, biz'liss, biz'liss," Zing said, grinning.

This they understood. Money. Fingers flying over the abacuses in their heads.

"Find out why he wants me hurt," Herrera said.

Everyone smiled.

Herrera figured the Ba brothers were smiling because maybe they'd stumbled on a way to become big players instead of handsome goons. Herrera was smiling because he was thinking he could maybe get out of this city not only alive but also rich.

Smiling, they shook hands all over again.

Eleven days later, the twins came back to him.

Frowning.

On Christmas Eve, no less.

No respect at all.

They were beginning to have misgivings about this new partnership. They had been to see Hamilton again, and he had paid them the agreed-upon fifty percent down payment for the job. But they were supposed to receive the remaining four thousand when they made delivery of the dope-cash Herrera would be carrying three nights from now.

"Now we no bling-ah cash, we no catchee monee!" Zang shouted.

"We lose-ah monee aw-relly!" Zing shouted.

"No, no," Herrera said patiently, "we can *make* money."

"Oh yeah how?" Zing asked.

The way he said it, it sounded like a Column B choice on a Chinese menu.

"If we can figure it out," Herrera said. "The deal."

The twins looked at him sourly and handsomely.

Fuckin' Chinks, Herrera thought.

"Did he say anything about *why?*" he asked patiently.

"He say we tell you Henny say hello."

A throw-away line.

"Henny?" Herrera asked.

"Henny Shoe."

Was what it sounded like.

He realized they were talking about Henry Tsu.

What they were saying was that when they beat him up on the twenty-seventh, they were supposed to give him Henry Tsu's regards, which would make it look as if two Chinks from Henry's big Chinatown gang had stolen Hamilton's money.

Ah so, he thought, and realized he was going native.

15.

SUNDAY WAS NOT a day of rest.

Not for the weary, anyway.

Jamie Bonnem of the Seattle P.D. was trying to sound patient and accommodating but he came over as merely irritated. He did not like getting called at home so early on a Sunday morning. Early for him, anyway. For Carella it was already ten o'clock. Besides, his case was still cold and Carella's call only reminded him of that bleak fact.

"Yes," he said brusquely, "we talked to the Gillette kid. We *also* talked to the other old boyfriend. Ain't that standard where you work?"

"It's standard here, yes," Carella said pleasantly. "How'd they check out?"

"We're still working Gillette."

"Meaning?"

"He's got no real alibi for where he was on the night of the murder."

"Where does he *say* he was?"

"Home reading. You know any twenty-year-old kid stays home *reading* at night? Eddie Gillette was home reading."

"Does he live alone?"

"With his parents."

"Where were they?"

"At the movies."

"Did you ask him where he was on New Year's Eve?"

"We asked *both* of them where they were on New Year's Eve. Because if this *is* tied to your kid kill . . ."

"It may be."

"The point ain't lost, Carella. We haven't been eliminating anyone just 'cause he was here in Seattle that night, but on the other hand, if somebody tells us he was roaming the Eastern seaboard . . ."

"What'd Gillette tell you?"

"He was right there on your turf."

"*Here?*" Carella said, and leaned in closer to the mouthpiece.

"Visiting his grandmother for the holidays."

"Did you follow up on that?"

"No, I went out to take a pee," Bonnem said. "You might want to check Grandma yourself, her name is Victoria Gillette, she lives in Bethtown, is there such a place as Bethtown?"

"There is such a place," Carella said.

"I talked to her on the phone, and she corroborated Gillette's story."

"Which was what?"

"That they went to the theater together on New Year's Eve."

"Gillette and Grandma?"

"Grandma is only sixty-two years old. And living with a dentist. The three of them went to see a revival of . . . what does this say? I can't even read my own notes."

Carella waited.

"Whatever," Bonnem said. "The dentist corroborates. The three of them went to see whatever the hell this is, Charlie's Something, and afterward they went out in the street with the crowd, and walked over to a hotel called the Elizabeth, is there such a hotel?"

"There is such a hotel," Carella said.

"To the Raleigh Room there, where Grandma and the dentist danced and Eddie tried to pick up a blonde in a red dress. All this according to Eddie and Grandma and the dentist, too, whose name is Arthur Rothstein. We do not have a name for the blonde in the red dress," Bonnem said drily, "because Gillette struck out."

"Where was he between one-forty-five and two-thirty?"

"Pitching the blonde."

"The dentist and Grandma . . ."

"Corroborate, correct."

"How about the other boyfriend?"

"Name's Harley Simpson, she dated him in her junior year, before she met Gillette. He has an alibi a mile long for the night she was killed. And he was here in Seattle on New Year's Eve."

"Mmm," Carella said.

"So that's it," Bonnem said.

"How's the old man taking this?"

"He doesn't even know she's dead. He's heavily sedated, on the way out himself."

"Is there anyone else in the family? Any other brothers or sisters?"

"No. Mrs. Chapman died twelve years ago. There were just the two sisters. And the husband, of course. Melissa's husband. You want my guess, they'll be out here settling a will before the week's out."

"He's that bad, huh?"

"Be a matter of days at most."

"How do you know there's a will?"

"Do you know any zillionaires who die intestate?"

"I don't know any zillionaires," Carella said.

"I know there's a will because I've been following an idea of mine out here. I'll tell you the truth, Carella, I don't think this is linked to your New Year's Eve case. I think what we have here are two separate and distinct cases. I guess you've been a cop long enough to know about coincidence . . ."

"Yes."

"Me, too. So while I ain't forgetting what happened there, I also have to treat this like a case in itself, you follow me? And I started thinking love or money, those are the only two reasons on God's green earth, and I started wondering if the old man has a will. Because you see, he was playing house with this younger woman before he got . . ."

"Oh?"

"Yeah, before he got sick. Her name's Sally Antoine, good-looking woman runs a beauty parlor downtown.

Thirty-one years old to his seventy-eight. Makes you wonder, don't it?"

"It'd make *me* wonder," Carella said.

"About whether she's in the old man's will, right? If there *is* a will. So I started asking a few questions."

"What'd you find out?"

"Miss Antoine told me she has no idea whether she's in the old man's will. In fact, she said she saw no reason why she *should* be. But when I get an idea in my head, I ain't about to let go of it that easy. Because if the lady *is* in his will, and if the younger daughter found out about it somehow . . ."

"Uh-huh."

". . . then maybe she came out here to pressure the old man into *changing* the will while he could still sign his own name. Get the bimbo *out* of it. Though she isn't a bimbo, I can tell you that, Carella. She's a decent woman, divorced, two kids of her own, came up here from L.A., been working hard to make a go of it. I can hardly see her pumping two shots into Joyce Chapman."

"Did you take a look at the will?"

"You ought to become a cop," Bonnem said drily. "What I did, I couldn't ask the old *man* if there's a will because he's totally out of it. So I asked his attorney . . ."

"Who's that?"

"Young feller who took over when Melissa and her husband moved east. Hammond used to be the Chapman attorney, you know. Got the job shortly before Melissa married him, little bit of nepotism there, hmm? Met her when he got back from Vietnam, used to be in the army there, next thing you know he's the old man's lawyer."

"Did he draw the will for him?"

"Hammond? No. Neither did the *new* lawyer. Said he had no knowledge of it. Protecting his ass, I suppose. So I asked him who *might* have knowledge of it, and he suggested that I talk to this old geezer here in town, name's Geoffrey Lyons, used to be Chapman's attorney, retired just before the son-in-law took over. He told me he'd drawn a new will for Chapman twelve years ago, yes, right after Mrs. Chapman died, but a will's a privileged communication between attorney and client, and there was no way I could compel him to waive that privilege."

"Does he know you're investigating a murder?"

"Tough."

"Does Chapman have a copy of the will?"

"Yes."

"Where?"

"Where do you keep your will, Carella?"

"In a safe deposit box."

"Which is where Miss Ogilvy told me the old man keeps his. So I go for a court order to open the box, and the judge asks me if I know what's *in* this will, and I tell him 'No, that's why I want to open the box.' So he says 'Do the contents of this will provide probable cause for the crime of murder,' and I tell him that's what I'm trying to find out, and he says 'Petition denied.' "

"Who typed the will?" Carella asked.

"What do you mean? How the hell do I know who typed it?"

"You might try to find out."

"Why?"

"Legal typists have long memories."

The line went silent. Bonnem was thinking.

"Find the secretary or whoever," he said at last.

"Uh-huh," Carella said.

"Ask *her* does she remember what's in the will."

"It'd be a start."

"And if she says the will *does* name Sally Antoine . . ."

"Then you've got to go see Miss Antoine again."

"Won't that be fruit of the Poison Tree?"

"Once the old man dies, which you say is any day now . . ."

"Any day."

"Then the will goes to Probate and becomes a matter of public record. In the meantime, you're working a murder."

"Yeah. But you know, the Antoine woman was here in Seattle on New Year's Eve. So that would let out any connection with your case. Even if she *is* in the will."

"Let's see what the will says."

"The husband's back east, you know. Why don't you ask *him?*"

"Hammond? Ask him what?"

"What's in the will."

"How would he know?"

"Well, maybe he won't. But if *I'm* going to bust my ass looking for a person typed a will God knows how many years ago, the least you can do is pick up a telephone. Which, by the way, are you guys partners with AT&T?"

Carella smiled.

"Let me know how you make out," he said.

"I'll call collect," Bonnem said.

THERE HAD BEEN TIMES during the past month when Herrera wished his partners were Puerto Rican, but what could you do? The roll of the dice had tossed him two Chinks who, as agreed, had *not* given him either a beating *or* Henry Tsu's regards on the twenty-seventh day of December. Instead, on that day, Herrera had disappeared with the dope money, and Zing and Zang had gone back to Hamilton—seemingly shame-faced—to return his deposit. By the twenty-eighth of December, the year was running out through the narrow end of the funnel and Herrera was still sitting on the fifty K, hoping to turn it into a fortune overnight. He knew that the only way to do that was through dope. Any other way of turning money into more money was dumb. In America, there were no streets of gold anymore. Nowadays, the streets were heaped with cocaine. Coke was the new American dream. Herrera sometimes figured it was all a Communist plot. But who gave a shit?

On the twenty-eighth day of December, the Ba brothers came to report what they had learned.

At peril to their own lives, they said.

"Velly dange-ous," Zing said.

"Henny Shoe fine out, tssssst," Zang said, and ran his forefinger across his throat.

"You want to be wimps or winners?" Herrera asked.

The Ba brothers giggled.

Somehow, their laughter made them seem even more menacing.

Zing had done most of the talking. His English, such as it was, sounded a bit better than his younger brother's in that he never said ain't. Herrera listened intently. Partly because Zing was difficult to understand if you didn't listen intently and partly because the content of Zing's report was causing Herrera's hair to stand on end.

Zing was talking about a million-dollar dope deal.

"Millah dollah," he said.

A hundred kilos at ten thousand per. Discounted because Tsu was making a quantity buy.

"Hunnah kilo," Zing said.

The shipment was coming up from Miami by automobile.

On the twenty-third of January.

"Tessa-tay one play, pee up-ah ress not same," Zing said.

"What?" Herrera asked.

"Tessa-tay one play, pee up-ah ress not same," Zing repeated, exactly as he had said it the first time. He showed Herrera a slip of paper upon which several addresses were written in English in a spider-like hand. "Tessa-tay play," he said, indicating the first address.

"What?" Herrera asked.

"Tessa-tay."

"What the fuck does that mean?"

Through a series of pantomimes, Zing and his brother managed at last to transmit to Herrera the idea that the first address on the slip of paper was an apartment where the testing and tasting would take place . . .

"Fi' kilo," Zing said, and held up his right hand with the fingers and thumb spread.

"Five kilos," Herrera said.

"Yeh, yeh," Zing said, nodding.

"Will be tested and tasted at this place . . ."

"Yeh, tessa-tay play."

"And if it's okay, the rest'll be picked up at this second place."

"Yeh," Zing said, "pee up-ah ress not same," and grinned at his brother, letting him know the benefits of a second language.

"Where only *some* of the bags will be tested at random."

"Yeh, ony some."

"What if the first stuff tests bad?" Herrera asked.

Zing explained that the deal would be off and the Miami people and the Tsu people would go their separate ways with no hard feelings.

"No har feeyin," he said, and nodded.

"But if the girl is blue . . ."

"Yeh," Zing said, nodding.

"Then they hand over the five keys and Tsu's people hand over fifty thousand."

"Fiffee tousen, yeh."

"And then they go to this next address to do some random testing and pick up the rest of the shit."

"Yeh, ressa shit."

Herrera was thoughtful for several moments.

Then he said, "These Miami people? Are they Chinese?"

"No, no, Spanish," Zing said.

Which was what Herrera figured.

"I need to know how to get in touch with them," he said. "And I need to know any code words or passwords they've been using on the phone. Can you get that information for me?"

"Velly har," Zang said.

"Velly dange-ous," Zing said.

"You wanna make velly big money?" Herrera asked.

The Ba brothers giggled.

Herrera was thinking that if he could buy those five measly keys set aside for testing and tasting . . .

Buy those five shitty little keys with the money he'd stolen from Hamilton . . .

Why then he could turn the pure into fifty thousand bags of crack . . .

At twenty-five bucks a bag . . .

Jesus!

He was looking at a million and a quarter!

Which if he split with the Chinks as they'd agreed . . .

"Velly big money, you bet," Zing said, laughing.

"You bet," Herrera said and smiled at them like a crocodile.

Now—at twelve noon on the twenty-second day of January—Herrera made a long-distance call. Just dialing the 305 area code made him feel like a big shot. Spending all this money to make a telephone call. Then again, it was Hamilton's money he was spending.

The person who answered was a Colombian.

The two men spoke entirely in Spanish.

"Four-seven-one," Herrera said. The code numbers the resourceful Ba brothers had supplied. Chinese magicians.

"Eight-three-six," the man said.

The counter code.

Like spy shit.

"A change for tomorrow night," Herrera said.

"They're already on the way."

"But you can reach them."

"Yes."

"Then tell them."

"What change?"

"For the test. A new address."

"Why?"

"Heat."

"Give it to me."

"705 East Redmond. Apartment 34."

"Okay."

"Repeat it."

The man read it back.

"See you tomorrow," Herrera said.

The man said, "And?"

"And?" Herrera said, and realized in a flash that he'd almost forgotten the sign-off code. "Three-three-one," he said.

"*Bueno,*" the man said, and hung up.

THE COWBOY'S SHOP was closed on Sundays, and so he met Kling in a little tacos joint off Mason Avenue. At a quarter past one that afternoon, the place was packed with hookers who hadn't yet gone to sleep. Palacios and Kling were both good-looking men, but none of the women even glanced in their direction. Palacios was eager to get on with the business at hand. He did not like having his Sunday ruined with this kind of bullshit. Besides, he was not at all happy with what he'd come up with.

"There is no ship coming in tomorrow," he told Kling. "Not with dope on it, anyway. You said from Colombia?"

"That's my information."

"Scandinavian registry?"

"Yes."

"Nothing," Palacios said. "I talked to some people I know, the ports are dead right now. Not only for dope. I'm talking bananas, grapefruits, automobiles. There's people saying a strike's in the wind. Ships are holing up at home, afraid to make the trip, they get here there's nobody to unload."

"This one would be unloading outside."

"I know, you told me. A hundred keys. A million bucks' worth of coke. Aimed for a Jamaican posse."

"That's what I've got."

"Who gave you this? Herrera? Who, by the way, I know where he is."

"You do?" Kling said, surprised.

"He's shacked up with a chick named Consuelo Diego, she works for you guys."

"She's a cop?"

"No, she answers phones down 911. Civil service. She used to work in a massage parlor, so this is better. I

guess. They moved into a place on Vandermeer a coupla days ago."

"Where on Vandermeer?"

"Here, I wrote down the address for you. After you
memorize it, swallow the piece of paper."

Kling looked at him.

Palacios was grinning.

He handed Kling the slip of paper upon which he'd
scrawled the address and apartment number. Kling
looked at it and then slid it into the cover flap of his
notebook.

"How reliable is this guy?" Palacios asked.

"I'm beginning to think not very."

"Because something stinks about this, you know?"

"Like what?"

"You say this is a Jamaican buy, huh?"

"That's what he told me."

"A hundred keys."

"Yes."

"So does that ring true to you?"

"What do you mean?"

"The Jamaicans aren't into such big buys. With them,
it's small and steady. A kilo here, a kilo there, every
other day. They step on that kilo, they've got ten thousand bags of crack at twenty-five bucks a bag. That's a
quarter of a million bucks. You figure a key costs them
on average fifteen thou, they're looking at a profit of
two-ten per. Still want to be a cop when you grow up?"

Palacios was grinning again.

"So what I'm saying, you get a Jamaican posse making even a *five*-kilo buy, that's a lot for them. But a *hun-*

dred keys? Coming straight up the water instead of from Miami? I'll tell you, that stinks on ice."

Which was why Kling liked hearing stuff that didn't come from police bulletins.

HENRY TSU was beginning to think that Juan Kai Hsao would go far in this business. Provided that what he was telling him was true. There was an ancient Chinese saying that translated into English as "Even good news is bad news if it's false." Juan had a lot of good news that Sunday afternoon—but was it reliable?

The first thing he reported was that the name of the Hamilton posse was Trinity.

"Trinity?" Henry said. This seemed like a very strange name for a gang, even a Jamaican gang. He knew there were posses called Dog, and Jungle, and even Okra Slime. But Trinity?

"Because from what I understand," Juan said, "it was started in a place called Trinity, just outside Kingston. In Jamaica, of course. This is my understanding."

"Trinity," Henry said again.

"Yes. And also it was three men who started it. So trinity means three. I think. Like in the Holy Trinity."

Henry didn't know anything about the Holy Trinity. And didn't *care* to know.

"Was Hamilton one of these three?" he asked.

"No. Hamilton came later. He killed the original three. He runs the posse now, but he takes advice from a man named Isaac Walker. Who has also killed some people. In Houston. They are both supposed to be very vicious."

Henry shrugged. From personal experience, he knew that no one could be as vicious as the Chinese. He wondered if either Hamilton or Walker had ever dipped a bamboo shoot in human excrement and stuck it under the fingernail of a rival gang leader. Shooting a gun was not being vicious. Being vicious was taking pleasure in the pain and suffering of another human being.

"What about Herrera?" he asked. He was getting tired of all this bullshit about the Hamilton posse with its ridiculous religious name.

"This is why I'm telling you about Trinity," Juan said.

"Yes, why?"

"Because Herrera has nothing to do with it."

"With what? The posse?"

"I don't know about that."

"Say what you *do* know," Henry said impatiently.

"I do know that it's not Herrera who's spreading this rumor. It is definitely not him. He has nothing to do with it."

"Then who's responsible?" Henry asked, frowning.

"Trinity."

"The Hamilton posse?"

"Yes."

"Is saying we ambushed Herrera and stole fifty thousand dollars from him?"

"Yes."

"Why?"

"I don't know why," Juan said.

"Are you sure this is correct?"

"Absolutely. Because I talked to several people who were approached."

"What people?"

"Here in the Chinese community."

Henry knew he did not mean legitimate businessmen in the Chinese community. He was talking about Chinese like Henry himself. And he was saying that some of these people . . .

"Who approached them?" he asked.

"People in Trinity."

"And said we'd stolen . . ."

"Stolen fifty. From the posse. That a courier was carrying for them. Herrera."

"How many people did you talk to?"

"Half a dozen."

"And Hamilton's people had reached all of them?"

"All of them."

"Why?" Henry asked again.

"I don't know," Juan said.

"Find out," Henry said, and clapped him on the shoulder and led him to the door. At the door, he reached into his pocket, pulled out a money clip holding a sheaf of hundred-dollar bills, peeled off five of them, handed them to Juan and said, "Go buy some clothes."

Alone now, Henry went to a red-lacquer cabinet with brass hardware, lowered the drop-front door on it, took out a bottle of Tanqueray gin, and poured a good quantity of it over a single ice cube in a low glass. He sat in an easy chair upholstered in red to match the cabinet, turned on a floor lamp with a shade fringed in red silk, and sat sipping his drink. In China, red was a lucky color.

Why bad-mouth him?

Why say he'd stolen what he hadn't stolen?

Why?

The only thing he could think of was the shipment coming up from Miami tomorrow night.

A hundred kilos of cocaine.

For which he would be paying a million dollars.

In cash, it went without saying. In this business, you did not pay for dope with a personal check.

Did the Hamilton posse have its eye on that shipment? Trinity, what a ridiculous name! But assuming it did . . . why bad-mouth Henry? Assuming the worst scenario, a Jamaican hijack of a shipment spoken for by a Chinese gang, why spread the word that Henry had stolen a paltry fifty thousand dollars?

And suddenly the operative words came to him.

Jamaican.

And Chinese.

If Hamilton had planned to knock over a shipment destined for another *Jamaican* gang, say the Banton Posse or the Dunkirk Boys, both far more powerful than his shitty little Trinity, he'd have done so without a by-your-leave. Go in blasting with his Uzis or his AK-47 assault rifles, Jamaican against Jamaican, head to head, winner take all.

But Henry was *Chinese.*

His gang was *Chinese.*

And if Hamilton's *Jamaican* people started stepping on *Chinese* toes, Buddha alone knew what reverberations this might cause in the city.

Unless.

All thieves understood retaliation.

In all cultures, in all languages.

If Henry had actually stolen fifty thousand dollars from the Hamilton posse, then Hamilton would be well within his rights to seek retaliation.

The fifty K plus interest.

A whole hell of a *lot* of interest when you considered that the stuff coming up from Miami was worth a million bucks, but honor among thieves was costly.

Hence the bullshit running around the city.

Hamilton setting up his excuse in advance: Tsu did *me* and now I am going to do *him*.

That's what *you* think, Henry thought, and reached for the telephone and dialed the same Miami number Herrera had called not five hours earlier.

IT WAS ALREADY DARK when they got to Angela Quist's apartment that Sunday evening. She had been rehearsing a play at the Y all day, she told them, and was exhausted. She really wished this could wait till morning because all she wanted to do right now was make herself some soup, watch some television, and go to sleep.

"This won't take long," Carella said. "We just wanted to check a lead the Seattle cops are following."

Angela sighed heavily.

"Really," Meyer said. "Just a few questions."

She sighed again. Her honey-colored hair looked frazzled. Her star sapphire eyes had gone pale. She was sitting on the couch under the Picasso prints. The detectives were standing. The apartment was just chilly enough to make overcoats seem appropriate.

"Did Joyce ever mention a woman named Sally Antoine?" Carella asked.

"No. I don't think so. Why?"

"Never mentioned that her father was seeing a woman? Any woman at all?" Carella asked.

"I don't recall her ever saying anything like that."

"Did she ever mention her father's will?"

"No."

"When she went out to Seattle, did she say *why* she was going?"

"Yes. Her father was very sick. She was afraid he might die before she saw him again." Angela looked at them, her eyes puzzled now. "Why don't you ask Joyce all this?" she said.

And they realized all at once that they hadn't told her.

She didn't know.

"Miss Quist," Carella said gently, "Joyce is dead. She was murdered last Monday night."

"Oh, shit," Angela said.

And bowed her head.

Sat there on the couch under the Picasso prints, head bent.

Nodding.

Saying nothing.

At last she sighed heavily and looked up.

"The same person?" she asked.

"We don't know."

"Boy."

She was silent again.

Then she said, "Does her sister know?"

"Yes."

"How's she taking it?"

"Okay, I guess."

"They were so close," Angela said.

Both detectives looked at her.

"Saw each other all the time."

They kept looking at her.

"*All* the time?" Meyer said.

"Oh, yes."

"Even *after* she got pregnant?"

"Well, sure. In fact, it was Melissa who did all the groundwork for her."

"*What* groundwork?" Carella asked.

"Finding an adoption agency," Angela said.

16.

THEY DID NOT get to Richard and Melissa Hammond until eleven o'clock on Monday morning because they'd had to make another stop first. The Hammonds were packing when the detectives got there. Melissa told them she'd received a call from Pearl Ogilvy in Seattle, who had advised her that her father had passed away that morning at seven minutes to eight Pacific time. The two were planning to catch an early after-noon flight to the Coast.

Carella and Meyer expressed their condolences.

"There'll be a lot to take care of, won't there?" Carella said.

"Pearl will be a big help," Hammond said.

"I'm sure," Carella said, and smiled pleasantly. "I know this is a bad time for you . . ."

"Well, it was expected," Hammond said.

"Yes. But I wonder if we can ask a few questions."

Hammond looked at him, surprised.

"Really," he said, "I don't think this is . . ."

"Yes, I know," Carella said. "And believe me, I wish three people hadn't been murdered, but they were."

Something in his voice caused Hammond to look up from his open valise.

"So, I'm sorry, really," Carella said, not sounding sorry at all, "but we would appreciate a few more minutes of your time."

"Certainly," Hammond said.

On the other side of the bed, Melissa was neatly arranging clothing in her open bag. The detectives stood just inside the door, uncomfortable in a room as intimate as the bedroom, further uncomfortable in that no one had asked them to take off their coats.

"The last time we spoke to you," Carella said, "you mentioned that you hadn't seen Joyce since February sometime . . ."

"The twelfth of February," Meyer said, consulting his notebook.

"That's right," Melissa said.

Head still bent, packing.

"When she would've been four months pregnant," Carella said.

"Yes."

"But you didn't notice she was pregnant."

"No."

"Because all the Chapman women carry small, isn't that so, Mr. Hammond?"

"I'm sorry, what . . . ?"

"Isn't that what you said, Mr. Hammond? That all the Chapman women carry small."

"Yes."

"Which Chapman women did you have in mind?"

"I'm sorry, I really don't know what you're . . ."

"Your wife had only one sister. Joyce. You couldn't have meant Joyce because you'd never seen her pregnant. And the last time Melissa's *mother* was pregnant was twenty years ago. You didn't see *her* pregnant, did you?"

"No, I didn't."

"So which Chapman women did you mean?"

"Well, Melissa, of course . . ."

"Yes, of course. And who else?"

"What I *meant*," Hammond said, "was that everyone in the family always *said* the Chapman women carried small."

"Ah," Carella said. "Well, that explains that, doesn't it?"

"Mr. Carella, I'm not sure what you're going for here, but I know I don't like your tone. If you have anything you . . ."

"Mrs. Hammond," Carella said, "isn't it true that you suggested the Cooper-Anderson Agency to your sister?"

Melissa looked up from her suitcase.

"No," she said.

Flat out.

A flat-out lie.

"Before coming here this morning," Carella said, "we went to see a man named Lionel Cooper, one of the partners in the Cooper-Anderson . . ."

"What is this?" Hammond said.

"Mr. Cooper distinctly remembers having had several telephone conversations with you . . ."

"My wife never spoke to anyone named . . ."

". . . regarding your sister's pregnancy and the placement of her baby after it was born."

"Do you recall those conversations?" Meyer asked.

"No, I don't," Melissa said.

"But you do understand that if you *did* have those conversations, then we'd have reasonable cause to believe you *knew* your sister was pregnant."

"I did *not* know she was pregnant," Melissa said.

"So you told us. Because you weren't very close and you rarely saw her."

"That's right."

"Her roommate, a young woman named Angela Quist, seems to think you were *very* close and that you saw each other all the time. *Especially* after Joyce got pregnant."

"Miss Quist is mistaken," Hammond said flatly.

"Mr. Hammond, where were you on New Year's Eve, New Year's *Day*, actually, between one-forty-five and . . ."

"He was here with me," Melissa said.

"You were both here between . . ."

"That's it, gentlemen," Hammond said.

"Meaning what?" Carella said.

"Meaning I'm a lawyer, and this is the end of the conversation."

"I thought you might say something like that," Carella said.

"Well, you were right. Unless you have . . ."

"We do," Carella said.

Hammond blinked.

"We have a match."

Hammond blinked again.

"A report from the Federal Bureau of Investigation," Carella said, "stating that the fingerprints recovered from the handle of the knife used to murder Annie Flynn match the U.S. Army fingerprints on file for Richard Allen Hammond. That's you."

He was lying.

Not about the F.B.I. files. Bonnem in Seattle had told him that Hammond had served in the army during the Vietnam War, and so he knew his fingerprints would be on file as a matter of course. But the foreign prints on the handle of the murder weapon had been too smudged for any meaningful search. He was hoping Hammond hadn't been wearing gloves when he'd jimmied open the window to the Hodding apartment. He was hoping a lot of things. Meanwhile, he was taking his handcuffs from his belt.

So was Meyer.

Melissa seemed to realize all at once that one pair of cuffs was intended for her.

"My father just died," she said. "I have to go to Seattle."

Carella looked her dead in the eye.

She turned away from his icy gaze.

AT TEN MINUTES past eleven that Monday morning, Herrera came down the steps of the stoop outside 3311 Vandermeer and began walking eastward toward Soundview Boulevard.

Kling was right behind him.

He had got here at seven, not figuring Herrera for an early riser, but not wanting to take any chances, either. Herrera was walking along at a brisk clip now; well, sure, he hadn't been freezing his ass off on the street for the past four hours. Good arm swinging, head ducked into the wind, racing along like a man with a train to catch. Kling hoped he didn't plan to walk all over the goddamn city. His ears were cold, his hands were cold, his feet were cold, and his nose was cold. It bothered him that Herrera had most likely woken up in a warm bed an hour or so ago, made love to Consuelo Diego, and then eaten a hot breakfast while Kling was standing in a doorway across the street waiting for him to put in an appearance.

Herrera stopped to talk to someone.

Kling fell back, turned toward a store window, eyes glancing sidewards toward where Herrera was obviously asking directions.

The man he'd stopped was pointing up the street now.

Herrera thanked him, began moving again.

Cold as the frozen tundra out here.

Kling fell in behind him, staying a good fifty feet back. Herrera knew what he looked like. One glimpse and—

Stopping again.

This time to look up at the number over one of the shops.

In motion again.

Kling behind him.

Then, obviously having seen the storefront window

ahead of him, recognizing it for what he'd been seeking, he turned immediately toward the door, opened it, and disappeared off the sidewalk.

The lettering on the window read:

GO, INC.
TRAVEL AGENCY

Kling was too cold to appreciate the pun.

He crossed the street, took up position in the doorway to a tenement building, pulled his head into his shoulders, and hunkered down to wait again.

An hour later, Herrera came flying out of Go, Inc. as though he were not only *going* but already *gone*. Big smile on his face, this was a man with tickets in his pocket, this was a man on his way to somewhere sunny and warm. Falling in behind him, Kling wished for a moment that he was going wherever Herrera was going. Get away from this city with the snow already turned soot black and the sidewalks slick with ice and the sky a gunmetal gray that seemed to threaten even more snow. Get away someplace. Anyplace.

So where are we going now? he wondered.

Where Herrera was going was right back to 3311 Vandermeer Avenue.

Climbed the front steps, walked directly inside, and poof.

Vanished.

Kling took up his position in the doorway across the street. The superintendent came out at a little after one to chase him away from the building. Kling went to the luncheonette several doors up, took a seat at a table near the front plate glass window, and sat eating a cheeseburger and a side of fries while he watched the building diagonally across the way. He was on his third cup of coffee when Herrera came out of the building, this time with a very pretty, dark-haired woman on his good arm. The woman was wearing a short fake fur over a micro miniskirt. Terrific legs. Smile all over her face. Consuelo, Kling figured. It was almost three P.M.

He followed them past the park on Soundview and then eastward to Lincoln and a movie theater complex named Gateway, where two different movies were playing in two different theaters, the Gateway I and the Gateway II. He could not get into line immediately behind Herrera because Herrera knew what he looked like. He waited until Herrera had bought two tickets to *something*, and then asked the girl behind the ticket-dispensing machine which movie the guy with his arm in a cast was seeing.

The girl said, "Huh?"

"The guy wearing the cast," Kling said. "Which theater did he go into?"

He did not want to flash the tin. Let the girl know he was a cop, everyone in the place would know it five minutes later. Herrera had eyes and ears.

"I don't remember," the girl said.

"Well, there are only two movies playing, which one did he buy tickets for?"

"I don't remember. You want a ticket or not?"

"Give me tickets to both movies," Kling said.

"*Both* movies?"

"Both."

"I never heard of such a thing," the girl said.

She was sixteen years old, Kling figured. One of the teenagers who nowadays were running the entire universe.

"How can you watch two movies at the same time?" she asked.

"I like to catch a little of each," Kling said.

"Well, it's your money," she said, her look clearly indicating that there were more nuts roaming this city than there were lunatics in the asylums. "That's fourteen dollars even," she said, punching out the tickets.

Kling took the tickets as they popped out of the machine. He gave her a ten and four singles. The girl counted the bills. "Ten and four make fourteen," she said, showing off.

Kling walked to where another teenager was standing beside a long vertical box, tearing tickets in half.

"Ticket, please," the boy said.

Kling handed him both tickets.

"Someone with you, sir?" the boy said.

"No, I'm alone."

"You have two tickets here, sir."

"I know."

"And they're for two different movies."

"I know."

The boy looked at him.

"It's okay," Kling said, and smiled.

The boy kept looking at him.

"Really," Kling said.

The boy shrugged, tore the tickets in half, and handed the stubs to Kling.

"Enjoy the show," he said. "Shows."

"Thank you," Kling said.

He tried Gateway I first. Waited at the back of the theater until his eyes adjusted to the darkness. Cautiously came down the aisle on the left, standing behind each row of seats so he wouldn't be made if Herrera was in here and happened to glance away from the screen. Checked each row. No Herrera. Went down the aisle on the opposite side of the theater, same routine. On the screen, somebody was saying he thought he was falling in love. His friend was saying something about him *always* falling in love, so what else was new? The two guys were teenagers. Who knew all about love, Kling guessed. One of the thousands of movies made for teenagers and starring teenagers. Kling tried to remember if there were any teenage stars when he was a teenager. He couldn't remember any teenage stars. He could only remember Marilyn Monroe's pleated white skirt blowing up over her white panties. Herrera was nowhere in the theater.

Kling came up the aisle, pushed open the door, turned immediately to the left, walked past the rest rooms and the concession and the video game machines, and then opened the door to Gateway II, and waited all over again while his eyes adjusted to the darkness. He spotted Herrera and Consuelo sitting in two aisle seats about midway down the theater on the right-hand side. He took a seat three rows behind them. The couple on the screen—both teenagers—were necking. The girl was struggling to keep her blouse buttoned. Kling remembered a time when unbuttoning a girl's blouse was tantamount to scaling Mount Everest. The boy on the screen unfastened an undoubtedly key button. The girl's breasts, contained in a white bra, popped out of her blouse and onto the screen. Kling figured she was supposed to be seventeen. She looked twenty-five. The boy looked twelve. Three rows ahead of him, Herrera was passionately kissing Consuelo. The position of his body seemed to indicate that he had his good hand up under Consuelo's skirt. Kling wondered why they didn't simply go back to the apartment. There was a new scene on the screen now. Two teenagers were fixing an automobile. The hood was up. They were talking about a girl named Mickey. Listening, Kling found Mickey somewhat less than fascinating. Herrera and Consuelo did not seem too interested in Mickey, either. Herrera looked as if he now had his entire *arm* up under Consuelo's skirt.

Kling kept looking at his watch.

An average film was about two hours long; he did not want to get caught sitting here when the movie ended and the lights came up. He kept checking the action on the screen against his watch. The movie seemed to have sixteen endings. Each time he thought it was close to over, another teenage crisis sprang up, demanding immediate resolution. Kling wondered how teenagers managed to get through an entire day, all the serious problems they had to solve. The movie seemed to be peaking at about an hour and fifty minutes. He got up, walked to the back of the theater, and stood there until the movie did finally and truly end. As the credits began to roll, he stepped outside and walked over to one of the video game machines. Stood there with his back to the theater's doors, but with a good sideward shot at the exit doors to the street. Herrera and Consuelo walked through those doors some ten minutes later. Kling figured they'd both made rest-room stops. He tried to remember when he himself had last peed. It was now twelve minutes past five o'clock.

Already dark on the street outside. Streetlamps on. He followed Herrera and Consuelo back to the apart-ment on Vandermeer. Waited until they were inside and the lights came on in the third-floor front apartment. He ducked into the luncheonette then, used the rest room, and immediately came out onto the street again. The lights were still on in the third-floor apartment. Kling settled down to wait again.

At seven minutes past six, two Chinese men entered the building.

To most cops, all Chinese looked alike.

But *these* two could have passed for twins.

HAMMOND REFUSED to say a word.

Advised his wife to remain silent as well.

But alone in the Interrogation Room with Nellie Brand and the detectives, Melissa finally burst into tears and told them everything they wanted to know. The time was a quarter past six. Until that moment, they'd been nervously watching the clock, aware of Miranda-Escobeda, knowing that time was running off down the drain. They figured Melissa's sudden outpouring was prompted by the presence of another woman, but they didn't give a damn about the why of it. All they wanted was a case that would stick; Nellie asked all the questions.

"Mrs. Hammond," she said, "do you now remember where your husband was between one-forty-five and two-thirty A.M. on the first day of January?"

"I don't know about the exact times," Melissa said. "But he left the apartment at . . ."

"By the apartment, do you mean . . . ?"

"*Our* apartment. In Calm's Point."

"Left it at what time?"

"Midnight. We toasted the New Year, and then he left."

"To go where?"

"To kill the baby."

The way she said those words sent a chill up the detectives' backs. Emotionless, unadorned, the naked words seemed to hover on the air. To kill the baby. They had drunk a midnight toast. He had left the apartment. To kill the baby.

"By the baby, do you mean Susan Hodding?" Nellie asked softly.

"Yes. My sister's baby."

"Susan Hodding."

"We didn't know what they'd named her."

"But you did know the adopting couple was named Hodding. Mr. and Mrs. Peter Hodding."

"Yes."

"How did you know that?"

"My husband found out."

"How?"

"Someone at the agency told him."

"By the agency . . ."

"Cooper-Anderson."

"The adoption agency."

"Yes."

"Someone at the agency revealed this information to him."

"Yes. He paid someone to get this information. Because, you see, the name of the people adopting the baby was only in two places. In the court records and in the agency records. The court records are sealed, you know, in an adoption, so Dick had to get the name through the agency."

"And, as I understand this, cash was given to . . ."

"Yes. Five thousand dollars."

"To someone in the agency."

"Yes."

"Who? Would you remember?"

Planning down the line. Getting her ducks in a row for when she had to prosecute this thing. Get the name of the agency person. Call him or her as a witness.

"You'll have to ask Dick," Melissa said.

"So once your husband had the name . . ."

"And address."

"Name and address of the Hoddings, he knew where to find the baby."

"Yes."

"And he went there on New Year's Eve . . ."

"Yes."

". . . to kill this infant."

"Yes."

"Specifically to kill this infant."

"Yes."

"How did he happen to kill Annie Flynn?"

"Well, I only know what he told me."

"What did he tell you, Mrs. Hammond?"

"He told me he was in the baby's room when . . . you see, what it was, he had the floor plans of the building. It's a new building, he went there pretending he was interested in buying an apartment. So he knew the layout of the apartment the Hoddings were in, do you see? There's a fire escape off the second bedroom, which he knew would be the baby's room, it's only a two-bedroom apartment. So he knew if he came down the fire escape from the roof, he could get right into the baby's room. And smother her. With her pillow. But the night he was there . . ."

"Why did he pick New Year's Eve?"

"He figured New Year's Eve would be a good time."

"Why? Did he say why?"

"No. He never told me why."

"Just figured it would be a good time."

"Well, yes. You'll have to ask him. Anyway, he was in there, and the girl . . ."

"Annie Flynn?"

"Yes, the sitter. You see, what he figured was that he'd just go in the baby's room, put the pillow over her face, and go right out again. I mean, this was a *baby*. There wouldn't be any resistance or anything, no noise, no yelling, he'd just go in and go out again. If the Hoddings were home . . . well, this was New Year's Eve, they probably would've had a few drinks, and anyway it was very late, they'd be sound asleep, he'd go in very quietly, do what he had to do and get out without them hearing a thing. This was a *baby*, you see. And if they were still out celebrating, there'd probably be a sitter, and if *she* wasn't asleep . . ."

"There *was* a sitter, as it turned out, wasn't there?"

"Well, yes, but Dick knew where the living room was, and the baby's room was all the way down the hall from it. So . . . what he figured, you see, was that either way it would be . . . well, *easy*. This was a *baby*. He wasn't expecting any problem at all."

"But there *was* a problem."

"Yes."

"What was the problem, Mrs. Hammond?"

"The mobile."

"The what?"

"The mobile. Over the crib. He was leaning in over the crib when he hit the mobile. It was one of these . . . almost like wind chimes, do you know? Except it didn't depend on wind. What it was, if you hit it, it would make these chime sounds. It was hanging over where the baby's hands would be, so the baby could reach up and hit it and make the chime sounds. But Dick didn't know it was there, he'd never actually been in the apartment, and when he leaned in over the crib, his head hit the mobile, and it went off like an alarm."

"What happened then?"

"He yanked the mobile loose from the ceiling, but it had already woken up the baby, the baby was screaming. And the sitter heard her crying, and that's when all the trouble started. Otherwise it would've gone smoothly. If it hadn't been for the mobile."

"So when Annie heard the baby crying . . ."

"Yes. Well, you have to understand we didn't know either of their names. Not the baby's and not the sitter's. Until we heard them on television."

"What happened when she heard the baby crying?"

"She yelled from the living room, wanted to know who was there, and then she . . . she just *appeared* in the doorway to the room. With a *knife* in her hand. A very *big* knife, in fact. And she came at Dick with it. So he had to defend himself. It was self-defense, really. With the sitter, that's what it was. She was really coming at him with that knife. He struggled with her for maybe three, four minutes before he finally got it away from her."

"And stabbed her."

"Yes."

"Did he tell you that?"

"Yes."

"That he stabbed her?"

"Yes. That he had to kill her. In self-defense."

"Did he say how many times he'd stabbed her?"

"No."

"And the baby? When did he . . . ?"

"The baby was still crying. So he had to work fast."

"The baby was awake . . ."

"Crying, yes."

". . . when he smothered her?"

"Well, put the pillow over her face."

"Smothered her."

"Well, yes."

"Was there blood on his clothing when he got home?"

"Just a little. Some spatters."

"Do you still have that clothing?"

"Yes. But I soaked out the stains. With cold water."

Nellie was still planning her case. Seize the clothing as evidence. Send it to the lab. It was almost impossible to soak out all traces of blood. Compare the bloodstains with those recovered from the knife's wooden handle. Get herself a match that would prove Annie Flynn's blood was on the murder weapon and on the clothes Richard Hammond had worn on New Year's Eve.

"Tell me what happened on Monday night, the sixteenth of January," she said.

"I don't want to talk about that."

"That's the night your sister was murdered, isn't it?"

"I don't want to talk about it."

"Did your husband kill her?"

"I don't want to talk about it."

"Did he?"

"You know, there are some things . . ." Melissa said, almost to herself, and shook her head. "I mean, we'd be getting half when Daddy died, so why . . . ?" She shook her head again. "Half to me, half to Joyce," she said. "Plus the trust. Which is why the baby was so important. So . . . why get so greedy? Why go for it *all*?"

"Mrs. Hammond, did your husband kill Joyce Chapman?"

"You'll have to ask him. I don't want to talk about it."

"Was he going for all of the *inheritance*? Is that what you're saying?"

"I loved my sister," Melissa said. "I didn't care about the baby, I didn't even *know* the baby, but my sister . . ."

She shook her head.

"I mean, the baby meant *nothing* to me. And my husband was right, you know. Why *should* all that money go to a child that was . . . well, a bastard? I mean, Joyce didn't even know who the *father* was."

"All what money?" Nellie asked.

"I could understand that, it made sense. But my sister . . . I didn't know he was going to do that to her, I swear to God. If I'd known . . ."

"But you *did* know he was going to kill the baby."

"Yes. But not my sister. I'd have been happy with half, I swear to God. I mean, there are *millions,* why'd he have to get so damn *greedy* all at once? The other money, okay. Why *should* it go to a baby my sister never wanted? But then to . . ."

"What other money?" Nellie asked again.

"It's all in the will," Melissa said. "You'll have to look at the will."

"Has someone already contacted you about it?"

"About what?"

"The will. I understand your father died early this morning. Has his attorney . . . ?"

"No, no."

"Then . . ."

Nellie looked suddenly puzzled.

"Are you saying . . . ?"

"We knew what was in the will," Melissa said. "We found out almost a year ago."

"How did you find out?"

"Mr. Lyons told my husband."

"Mr. Lyons?"

"Geoffrey Lyons. Who used to be my father's attorney."

Nellie looked appalled.

"Told your husband the provisions of his client's *will?*" she said.

"Well, he was very fond of Dick," she said. "His own son was killed in Vietnam, they'd grown up together, gone to school together, I suppose he looked upon Dick as a sort of surrogate son. Anyway, there was nothing illegal about what he did. Or even unethical. My father was trying to make sure the family wouldn't just die out. He was trying to provide some incentive. Mr. Lyons gave Dick a friendly tip, that was all. Told him what was in the will. Said we'd better get going, you know?"

"Get going?"

"Well, you know."

"No, I don't know."

"Well, get on with it."

"I still don't know what you mean."

"Well, you'll have to look at the will, I guess," Melissa said, and turned away from Nellie.

And then, for some reason Carella would never understand, she looked directly into his eyes, and said, "I did love her, you know. Very much."

And buried her face in her hands and began weeping softly.

* * *

THE APARTMENT Herrera was using for the testing and tasting was only three blocks east of the one he had rented on Vandermeer. Both apartments were normally rented by the hour to prostitutes turning quickie tricks, and so the separate landladies had been happy to let Herrera have them at weekly rates that were lower but more reliable than the come-and-go, on-the-fly uncertain hooker trade.

Herrera had walked here with Zing and Zang. He was carrying fifty thousand dollars in hundred-dollar bills in a dispatch case that made him feel like an attorney. The five kilos of cocaine would go into that dispatch case once the deal was consummated. The three of them would then go back to the apartment on Vandermeer, where Zing and Zang expected to take possession of their half of the coke. Two and a half keys for them, two and a half for Herrera. Just as they'd all agreed. Gentlemen. Except that Herrera planned to kill them.

It was all a matter of having been born in this city, he figured.

You take two pigtailed Chinks from Hong Kong, they did not know that the minute the door to the apartment on Vandermeer closed behind them, he would shoot them in the back.

They did not understand this city.

You had to be born here.

They stopped now at the steps to 705 East Redmond.

"I have to go up alone," Herrera told them.

"Yeh," Zing said.

"Because that's the way Miami wants it."

"Yeh," Zang said.

"It may take a while. Make sure they ain't selling us powdered sugar."

"We be here," Zing said.

KLING SAW HERRERA go into the building.

The two Chinese men stayed outside, hands in the pockets of their overcoats. Both wearing long dark blue coats. No hats. Sleek black hair combed straight back from their foreheads. Neither of them had ever seen Kling before, he could move in closer for a better look.

Walked right past them on the same side of the street.

Brothers for sure.

Twins, in fact.

Didn't even seem to glance at them. But got enough on them in his quick fly-by to be able to spot them later, anytime, anywhere.

He continued on up the street. Walked two blocks to the west, crossed over, came back on the other side, this time wearing a blue woolen watch cap that covered his blond hair. The one thing you could count on in any slum neighborhood was a dark doorway. He found one three buildings up from the one Herrera had entered. Across the street, the Chinese twins were flanking the front stoop like statues outside a public library. Ten minutes later, a man with a mustache walked past the Chinese and into the building. Like Herrera, he, too, was carrying a dispatch case.

* * *

THE MAN FROM MIAMI was a hulking brute with a Pancho Villa mustache. He said "Hello," in Spanish, and then "You got the money?"

"You got the shit?" Herrera asked.

No passwords, no code words, no number sequences. The time and the place had been prearranged. Neither of them would have known when and where without first having gone through all the security bullshit. So now they both wanted to get on with it and get it done fast. The sooner they got through with the routine of it, the safer the exchange would be.

There were people who said they could tell by a little sniff up the nose or a little speck on the tongue whether you were buying good coke or crap. Herrera preferred two simple tests. The first one was the old standby cobalt thiocyanate Brighter-the-Blue. Mix the chemical in with the dope, watch it dissolve. If the mix turned a very deep blue, you had yourself high-grade coke. The brighter the blue, the better the girl. Meaning if you got this intense blue reaction, you were buying cocaine that was purer than what you'd get with, say, a pastel blue reaction. What you had to watch out for was coke that'd been stepped on maybe two, three times before it got to you.

For the second test, Herrera used plain water from the tap.

The man from Miami watched in utter boredom as he scooped a spoonful of the white dust out of its plastic bag, and dropped a little bit of it into a few ounces of water. It dissolved at once. Pure cocaine hydrochloride. Herrera nodded. If the powder hadn't dissolved, he'd have known the coke had been cut with sugar.

"Okay?" the man from Miami said, in English.

"*Bueno,*" Herrera said, and nodded again.

"How much of this are you going to go through?" the man asked, in Spanish.

"Every bag," Herrera said.

FROM WHERE HE STOOD in the doorway across the street, Kling saw the man with the mustache coming out of the building, still carrying the dispatch case. He did not look at the two Chinese, and they did not look at him. He walked between them where they were still flanking the stoop, made a left turn and headed up the street. Kling watched him. He unlocked the door to a blue Ford station wagon, got in behind the wheel, started the car, and then drove past where Kling was standing in the doorway. Florida license plate. The numerals 866—that was all Kling caught. The street illumination was too dim and the car went by too fast.

He waited.

Five minutes later, Herrera came out of the building.

"NO TRUBBER?" Zing asked.

"None," Herrera said.

"You have it?" Zang asked.

"I've got it."

"Where?" Zing asked.

"Here in the bag," Herrera said. "Where the fuck you think?"

His eyes were sparkling. Just holding the dispatch

case with all that good dope in it made him feel higher than he'd ever felt in his life. Five kilos of very *very* good stuff. All his. Take the Chinks back to the place on Vandermeer, kiss them off, leave them there for the cops to find when somebody complained about the stink in apartment 3A. Take his time disposing of the coke, so long as he got rid of it by the fifteenth of February. Catch the TWA plane to Spain on the fifteenth. The plane to Spain is mainly in the rain, he sang inside his head. Christ he was happy!

The twins were on either side of him now.

Like bodyguards.

Zing smiled at him.

"Henny Shoe say tell you hello," he said.

FROM WHERE KLING STOOD across the street, he heard the shots first and only then saw the gun. In the hand of the Chinese guy standing on Herrera's right. There were three shots in rapid succession. Herrera was falling. The guy who'd shot him backed away a little, giving him room to drop. The other Chinese guy picked up the dispatch case from the sidewalk where it had fallen. They both began running. So did Kling.

"Police!" he shouted.

His gun was in his hand.

"Police!" he shouted again and watched them turn the corner.

He pounded hard along the sidewalk. Reached the corner. Went around it following his gun hand.

The street was empty.

His eyes flicked doorways. Hit doorways. Snapped

away from them. Nothing. Where the hell had they . . . ?

There.

Partially open door up ahead.

He ran to it, kicked it fully open, fanned the dark entrance alcove with his gun. Open door beyond. Went to that. Through the doorway. Steps ahead. Not a sound anywhere in the hallway. An abandoned building. If he went up those steps he'd be walking into sudden death. Water dripped from somewhere overhead. A shot came down the stairwell. He fired back blindly. The sound of footfalls pounding up above. He came up the steps, gun out ahead of him. Another shot. Wood splinters erupted like shrapnel on the floor ahead of him. He kept climbing. The door to the roof was open. He came out into sudden cold and darkness. Flattened himself against the brick wall. Waited. Nothing. They were gone. Otherwise they'd still be firing. Waited, anyway, until his eyes adjusted to the darkness, and then covered the roof, paced it out, checking behind every turret and vent, his gun leading him. They were gone for sure. He holstered his gun and went down to the street again.

As he approached Herrera lying on his back on the sidewalk, he saw blood bubbling up out of his mouth. He knelt beside him.

"José?" he said. "Joey?"

Herrera looked up at him.

"Who were they?"

They won't let you live in this city, Herrera thought, but they won't let you out of it, either.

His eyes rolled back into his head.

* * *

SITTING IN THE AUTOMOBILE, Hamilton and Isaac watched the two Chinese men from the Tsu gang entering the building.

Hamilton smiled.

The thing about the Chinese, he thought, is that they know business but they have no *passion*. They are cool lemon yellow. And tonight, they were going to get *squeezed*.

The two men from Miami were waiting upstairs in apartment 5C.

This according to what Carlos Ortega had told him.

For ten percent, the ungrateful bastard.

The two men from the Tsu gang were now on their way upstairs to make payment and take delivery. The earlier testing and tasting, wherever the hell *that* had taken place, had apparently gone off without a hitch. Hamilton had no interest whatever in those shitty five keys that had vanished in the night. Upstairs in apartment 5C, there were ninety-five keys of cocaine and only four people to look after all that dope.

He nodded to Isaac.

Isaac nodded back and then flashed his headlights at the car up the street. He still didn't understand all the details of the deal. He only knew that tonight they were making a move that would catapult them into the big time where posses like Spangler and Shower roamed at ease. He was confident that Hamilton knew what he was doing. You either trusted someone completely or you didn't trust him at all.

Together, they got out of the automobile.

Up the street, the doors on the other car opened. Black men in overcoats got out. The doors closed silently on the night. The men assembled swiftly, breaths pluming on the frosty air, and then walked swiftly to the front steps of the building. Eight of them altogether. Hamilton, Isaac and six others. Hamilton knew the odds would be two to one in his favor.

Together they climbed to the fifth floor of the building.

Hamilton listened outside the door to apartment 5C.

Voices inside there.

Three separate and distinct voices.

There now.

A fourth voice.

He kept listening.

He smiled. Held up his right hand. Showed four fingers. Isaac nodded. Four of them inside there. As promised by Ortega. Isaac nodded to the man on his right.

A single burst from the man's AR-15 blew off the lock on the door.

The Jamaicans went in.

Hamilton was still smiling.

There were not four people in that apartment.

There were a dozen Colombians from Miami and a dozen Chinese from right here in the city.

Henry Tsu was one of those Chinese.

In the first ten seconds, Isaac—who still did not completely understand all the details of this deal—took seventeen slugs in his chest and his head. Hamilton turned to run. His way was blocked by the Jamaicans behind him. They, too, had realized all at once that they had walked into an ambush, and they were now scrambling in panic to get out of the trap. They were all too late. A second wave of fire cut them down before they reached the door. It was all over in thirty seconds. The only shot the Jamaicans had fired was the one that took off the lock.

Hamilton, still alive, started crawling over the bodies toward the doorway.

One of the Chinese said, "Henny Shoe say tell you hello."

Then he and another Chinese who looked remarkably like him fired twelve shots into Hamilton's back.

Hamilton stopped crawling.

Henry Tsu looked down at him.

He was thinking it was all a matter of which was the oldest culture.

17.

CARELLA SIGNED for the Federal Express envelope
at ten minutes past nine the following morning. It was
from the Seattle Police Department and it contained a
sheaf of photocopied pages and a handwritten memo.
The memo read: *Thought you might like to see this.* It
was signed: *Bonnem*. The pages had been copied from
Paul Chapman's will. They read:

My daughters are Melissa Chapman Hammond and Joyce Chapman.

I give and bequeath to my trustee hereinafter
named the sum of one million dollars
($1,000,000) to hold same in trust for the
benefit of the first child born of my said
daughters, and to manage, invest and rein-
vest the same and pay all costs, taxes . . .

"He was making sure the family line would continue after he was gone," Carella said.

"If his daughters were still childless at his death, he was giving them a good reason to change the situation," Meyer said.

"To get on with it."

"To get going."

"Melissa's words."

"Here's the motive," Carella said, tapping the page of the will that spelled out the firstborn provision.

"He was signing little Susan's death warrant," Meyer said.

"Because if she'd never been born . . ."

"Melissa's baby would be the firstborn child . . ."

"And that's where the million-dollar trust would go."

Both men continued reading in silence.

All the rest, residue and remainder of my estate, of whatsoever nature and wheresoever situated, which I may own or to which I may in any way be entitled at the time of my death, including any lapses or renounced legacies or devises, is referred to in this, my will, as my residuary estate.

"Defining his terms," Carella said.

"The rest of his estate."

"Millions of dollars, isn't that what she said?"

I give, devise and bequeath any residuary estate in equal shares to my daughters living at my death . . .

"Just what she told us."

. . . or if a said daughter shall predecease me . . .

"Here comes the motive for *Joyce's* murder . . ."

. . . then I give, devise and bequeath all of my residuary estate to my then surviving daughter.

"Kill Joyce and Melissa gets it all," Carella said.

"Love or money," Meyer said and sighed. "It never changes."

There was more to the will.

But they already had all they needed.

And the phone was ringing again.

THERE WERE NO WINDOWS in the room.

This was the first time Eileen noticed it.

Neither was there a clock.

Must be Las Vegas, she thought.

"Something?" Karin asked.

"No."

"You were smiling."

"Private joke," Eileen said.

"Share it with me."

"No, that's okay."

She was wearing a digital watch. Nothing ticked into the silence of the room. She wondered how many minutes were left. She wondered what the hell she was doing here.

"Let's play some word games," Karin said.

"Why?"

"Free association. Loosen you up."

"I'm loose."

"It's like snowballing. Cartoonists use it a lot."

"So do cops," Eileen said.

"Oh?"

"In a squadroom. You take an idea and run with it," she said, suspecting Karin already knew this. If so, why the expression of surprise? She wished she trusted her. But she didn't. Couldn't shake the feeling that to Karin Lefkowitz, she was nothing but a specimen on a slide.

"Want to try it?"

"We don't have much time left, do we?"

Hoping she was right. Not wanting to look at her watch.

"Twenty minutes, anyway," Karin said.

Christ, *that* long?

"I'll give you a word, and you give me the first word that pops into your head, okay?"

"You know," Eileen said, "I really don't enjoy playing games. I'm a grown woman."

"Yes, so am I."

"So why don't we just skip it, okay?"

"Sure. We can skip the whole damn thing, if you like."

Eileen looked at her.

"I think we're wasting each other's time," Karin said flatly. "You have nothing to say to me, and if you don't *say* anything, then I can't help you. So maybe we ought to . . ."

"The only help I need . . ."

"Yes, I know. Is quitting the force."

"Yes."

"Well, I don't think I can help you do that."

"Why not?"

"Because I don't think it's what you really want."

"Then why the hell am I here?"

"You tell me."

Eileen folded her arms across her chest.

"Here comes the body posture again," Karin said. "Look, I really don't think you're ready for this. I don't know why you came to me in the first place . . ."

"I told you. Sam Grossman sugg . . ."

"Yes, and you thought it was a good idea. So here you are, and you have nothing to tell me. So why don't we call it a day, huh?"

"You want to quit, huh?"

"Just for now, yes. If you change your mind later . . ."

"Too bad *I* can't quit just for *now*, huh?"

"What do you mean?"

"The force. Leaving police work is for*ever*."

"Why do you say that?"

"Come on, willya?"

"I really don't know why you feel . . ."

"Don't you ever talk to cops? What do you do here? Talk to architects? Bankers? I mean, for Christ's sake, don't you know how cops *think*?"

"How do they think, Eileen? Tell me."

"If I quit now . . ."

She shook her head.

"Yes?"

"Never mind, fuck it."

"Okay," Karin said, and looked at her watch. "We've got fifteen minutes left. Have you seen any good movies lately?"

"I just don't like having to explain the simplest god-damn *things* to you!"

"Like what?"

"Like what everyone would think if I quit!"

"What would they think?"

"And why it would be impossible to . . ."

"What would they think, Eileen?"

"That I'm *scared*, goddamn it!"

"Are you?"

"I told you I was, didn't I? How would *you* like to get raped?"

"I wouldn't."

"But try to explain that to anyone."

"Who do you mean?"

"People I've worked with. I've worked with cops all over this city."

"Men?"

"Women, too."

"Well, surely the *women* would understand why you'd be afraid of getting raped again."

"Some of them might not. You get a certain kind of woman with a gun on her hip, she's sometimes worse than a man."

"But *most* women would understand, don't you think?"

"I guess so. Well, Annie would. Annie Rawles. She'd understand."

"Rape Squad, isn't that what you told me?"

"Annie, yeah. She's terrific."

"So who do you think might not understand? Men?"

"I've never heard of a man getting raped, have you? Except in prison? Most cops haven't been in prison."

"Then it's *cops* you're worried about. Men cops. You don't think they'd understand, is that it?"

"You should work with some of these guys," Eileen said.

"Well, if you quit, you wouldn't have to work with them anymore."

"And they'd run all over the city saying I couldn't cut it."

"Is that important to you?"

"I'm a good cop," Eileen said. "Was."

"Well, you haven't quit yet. So you're *still* a cop."

"But not a good one."

"Has anyone said that to you?"

"Not to my face."

"Do you think anyone has said that behind your back?"

"Who cares?"

"Well, you do, don't you?"

"Not if they think I'm scared."

"But you are scared. You told me you were scared."

"I know I am."

"So what's wrong with that?"

"I'm a cop."

"Do you think cops aren't scared?"

"Not the way I'm scared."

"How scared are you, Eileen? Can you tell me?"

She was silent for a long time.

Then she said, "I have nightmares. Every night."

"About the rape?"

"Yes. About giving him my gun. He has the knife to my throat, and I give him my gun. Both guns. The thirty-eight and the little backup pistol. The Browning. I give him both guns."

"Is that what happened in reality?"

"Yes. But he raped me, anyway. I thought . . ."

"Yes?"

"I don't know what I thought. I guess that . . . that if I . . . I cooperated, then he . . . he wouldn't cut me . . . wouldn't rape me. But he did."

"Cut you. And raped you."

"So fucking *helpless!*" Eileen said. "A *cop!*"

"What did he look like, do you remember?"

"It was dark."

"But you saw him, didn't you?"

"And raining. It was raining."

"But what did he look like?"

"I don't remember. He grabbed me from behind."

"But surely, when he . . ."

"I don't remember."

"Did you see him after that night?"

"Yes."

"When?"

"At the trial."

"What was his name?"

"Arthur Haines. Annie made the collar."

"Did you identify him at the trial?"

"Yes. But . . ."

"Well, what did he look like?"

"In the dream, he has no face."

"But while he was raping you, he had a face."

"Yes."

"And at the trial, he had a face."

"Yes."

"Which you identified."

"Yes."

"What did he look like, Eileen?"

"Tall. Six feet. A hundred and eighty pounds. Brown hair and blue eyes."

"How old?"

"Thirty-four."

"How old was the man you killed?"

"What?"

"How old was . . . ?"

"What's *he* got to do with this? I don't have nightmares about him."

"Do you remember how old he was?"

"Yes."

"Tell me."

"Early thirties."

"What'd he look like?"

"I already told you this. The second time I was here. We've been through all this."

"Tell me again."

"Blond," Eileen said, and sighed. "Six-two. Two hundred pounds. Eyeglasses. A heart-shaped tattoo with nothing in it."

"What color were his eyes?"

"Blue."

"Like the rapist."

"The eyes, yes."

"His size, too."

"Well, Bobby was heavier and taller."

"But they were both big men."

"Yes."

"You said you were alone with him in a room . . ."

"Bobby, yes."

"Because you'd lost your backups. By the way, do you always think of him as Bobby?"

"Well . . . I guess so. That's what he called himself. Bobby."

"Uh-huh."

"Is there anything wrong with that? Calling him Bobby?"

"No, no. Tell me how you lost your backups."

"I thought I already did."

"No, I don't think so. How many were there?"

"Two of them. Annie and a . . . Annie Rawles . . ."

"Yes."

". . . and a guy from the Seven-Two in Calm's Point. Mike Shanahan. Big Irishman. Good cop."

"How'd you lose them?"

"Well, Bert got it in his head that I needed help. So he drove out to the Zone . . ."

"Bert Kling."

"Yeah. Who I was still seeing at the time. I told him I

didn't want him coming out there, but he came anyway. And . . . he's blond, you know. Did I mention he's blond? And there was a mix-up on the street, Shanahan saw Bert and thought he was the guy we were looking for, because Bobby was blond, too, you know, and about the same size. So by the time they straightened it out—it was the Feather in the Hat thing, you know, only nobody was wearing feathers—by the time Shanahan realized Bert was on the job, Bobby and I were gone."

"Gone?"

"Around the corner. On our way to the room."

"Did they ever catch up to you?"

"No."

"Then you really *did* lose them. I mean, permanently."

"Yes."

"Because Bert stepped into the play."

"Well, it wasn't his fault."

"Whose fault was it?"

"Shanahan's."

"Why?"

"Because he mistook Bert for the suspect."

"Didn't know Bert was a cop."

"That's right."

"But if Bert hadn't been there . . ."

"But he was."

"But if he *hadn't* been there . . ."

"There's no sense thinking that way. He *was* there."

"Eileen, if he hadn't been there, would there have been a mix-up on the street?"

"Well, no."

"Would you have lost your backups?"

"Probably not."

"Do you think they might have helped you in your situation with Bobby?"

"Who?"

"Your backups."

"I suppose so. If they'd got to me in time."

"Well, you said they're both good cops . . ."

"Oh, sure."

". . . who undoubtedly knew their jobs . . ."

"I'd have trusted my life with either of them. In fact, that's exactly what I *was* doing. Trusting them to get there on time if I needed them."

"But they weren't there when you needed them."

"Yes, but that wasn't *their* fault."

"Whose fault was it?"

"Nobody's. It was one of those dumb things that happen all the time."

"Eileen, if it *hadn't* happened—if there *hadn't* been the mix-up, if you *hadn't* lost Shanahan and Annie—do you think you'd have had to shoot Bobby?"

"I don't know."

"Well, think about it."

"How can I possibly . . . ?"

"Well, if they'd been following you . . ."

"Yes, but they weren't."

"*If* they'd been there behind you . . ."

"But you see . . ."

". . . *if* they'd seen where Bobby was taking you . . ."

"Look, there's no use crying over . . ."

". . . and *if* they'd got to you in time, would you have shot and killed Bobby Wilson?"

"I'd shoot him all over again," Eileen said.

"You didn't answer my question."

"Man with a knife? Coming at me with a knife? Of *course* I'd shoot the son of a bitch! I got cut *once*, thanks, and I don't plan to . . ."

Eileen stopped dead.

"Yes?" Karin said.

Eileen was silent for several moments.

Then she said, "I wasn't trying to get even, if that's what you think."

"What do you mean?"

"When I shot Bobby. I wasn't . . . I didn't shoot him because of . . . I mean, it had nothing to do with the rape."

"Okay."

"Nothing at all. In fact . . . well, I already told you."

"What was that?"

"I was beginning to like him. He was very charming."

"Bobby."

"Yes."

"But you killed him."

"I had to. That's the whole *point*, you know, the whole reason I'm here."

"Yes, tell me the reason."

"I already told you this, I don't know why I have to tell you every fucking thing a hundred times."

"What was it you told me?"

"That I want to quit because I'm afraid I'll . . ."

"Yes, I remember now. You're afraid . . ."

"I'm afraid I'll get so angry I'll kill somebody else."

"Angry?"

"Well, Jesus, if somebody's coming at you with a knife . . ."

"But I thought you were beginning to like him. Bobby."

"The man had already killed three other women! He was ready to kill me! If you think that doesn't start the adrenaline flow . . ."

"I'm sure it does. But you say it made you angry."

"Yes." She hesitated a moment, and then said, "I emptied the gun in him."

"Uh-huh."

"Six shots."

"Uh-huh."

"A big gun. A Smith & Wesson forty-four."

"Uh-huh."

"I'd do it again. In a minute."

"And that's what you're afraid of. That's why you want to quit the force. Because someday you might get angry all over again, and . . ."

"He had a knife!"

"Is that what made you angry? The knife?"

"I was all alone up there! I'd lost my . . . you know, I *told* Bert to stay out of it. I told him I could take care of it just fine, I had two backups who knew what they were doing, I didn't need any more help. But he came out there, anyway."

"And caused you to lose your backups."

"Well, that's what he did, didn't he? I mean, *I* didn't lose them! And Shanahan was only doing his job. It was

Bert sticking his nose in that caused all the trouble. Because he thought I wasn't any good anymore. Thought I'd lost it, you see. Couldn't take care of myself. Couldn't do the job. When I found out later what'd happened out there on the street, I could've *killed* him!"

"So you were angry with him, too," Karin said.

"Well, later, yes."

"Yes. When you realized that if he hadn't inter- fered . . ."

"I wouldn't have been alone up there with Bobby. Yes."

The room went silent.

Karin looked at her watch.

Their time was up.

"But you told me you'd kill Bobby again," she said. "In a minute."

"I'd never killed anyone before, you know," Eileen said. "I used to . . . you know, my father and my Uncle Matt both got killed on the job . . ."

"I didn't know that."

"Well, yeah. And . . . I used to think I'd . . . if I ever caught that guy with the red handkerchief over his face, I'd . . . blow him away without batting an eyelash. For what he did to . . . but . . . you know . . . when I . . . the third shot knocked him onto the bed, Bobby, he was lying flat on the bed, I'm sure he was already dead. But I . . . I fired the rest of the . . . three more bullets into . . . into his back . . . along the spine. And then I threw the gun across the room and began screaming."

Karin looked at her.

You're *still* screaming, she thought.

"Our time is up," she said.

Eileen nodded.

Karin rose from behind her desk. "We have a lot of work to do," she said.

Eileen was still sitting. Looking at her hands. Head bent, hands in her lap. Without looking up, she said, "I hate him, don't I?"

"Which one?" Karin asked, and smiled.

"Bert."

"We'll talk about it, okay?" Karin said. "Will I see you on Thursday?"

Eileen stood up.

She looked directly into Karin's eyes.

She did not say anything for several seconds.

Then she said, "Yes."

It was a beginning.

SIMON & SCHUSTER
PROUDLY PRESENTS

HARK!

ED McBAIN

Now available in hardcover
from Simon & Schuster

Turn the page for a preview of
Hark! . . .

1.

GLORIA KNEW that someone was in her apartment the moment she unlocked the door and entered. She was reaching into her tote bag when a man's voice said, "No, don't."

Her fingertips were an inch away from the steel butt of a .380 caliber Browning.

"Really," the voice said. "I wouldn't."

She closed the door behind her, reached for the switch to the right of the doorjamb, and snapped on the lights. He was sitting in an easy chair across the room, facing the entrance door. He was wearing gray slacks, black loafers, blue socks, and a matching dark blue, long-sleeved linen shirt. The throat of the shirt was unbuttoned two buttons down. The cuffs were rolled up on his forearms. There was a hearing aid in his right ear.

"Well, well," she said. "Look what the cat dragged in."

"Indeed," he said.

"Long time no see," she said.

"Bad penny," he said, and shrugged almost sadly.

It was the shrug that told her he was going to kill her. Well, maybe that and the gun in his right hand. Plus the silencer screwed onto the muzzle of the gun. And their history. She knew he was not one to forget their history.

"I'll give it all back," she said at once. "Whatever's left of it."

"And how much is that, Gloria?"

"I haven't been frugal."

"So I see," he said, and with a slight arc of the gun barrel indicated her luxurious apartment. She almost reached into the tote again. But the gun regained its focus at once, steady in his hand, tilted up directly at her heart. She didn't know what kind of gun it was; some sort of automatic, it looked like. But she knew a silencer when she saw one, long and sleek and full of deadly promise.

"What's left of the thirty million?" he asked.

"I didn't get nearly that much."

"That was the police estimate. Thirty million plus."

"The estimate was high."

"How much *did* you get, Gloria?"

"Well, the smack brought close to what they said it was worth . . ."

"Which was twenty-four mil."

The gun steady in his fist. Pointing straight at her heart.

"But I had to discount it by ten percent."

"Which left two-sixteen."

Lightning fast calculation.

"If you say so," she said.

"I say so."

A thin smile. The gun unwavering.

"Go on, Gloria."

"The police sheet valued the zip at three mil. I got two for it."

"And the rest?"

"I'm not sure I have all this in my head."

"Try to find it in your head, Gloria," he said, and smiled again, urging her with the gun, wagging it encouragingly. But not impatiently, she noticed. Maybe he didn't plan to kill her after all. Then again, there was the silencer. You did not attach a silencer to a gun unless you were concerned about the noise it might make.

"The rocks brought around half a mil. The lucy was estimated at close to a mil. I got half that for it. The ope, I had a real hard time dealing. The cops said eighty-four large, I maybe got twenty-five for it. If I got another twenty-five for the hash, that was a lot. The gage brought maybe one-fifty large for the bulk. The fatties, I smoked myself." She smiled. "Over a period of time," she said.

"Over a *long* period of time," he said. "So let me see. You got two-sixteen for the heroin and another two for the coke. Half a mil for the crack and another half for the LSD. Twenty-five for the opium and the same for the hashish. Another one-fifty for the marijuana. That comes to two hundred and nineteen million, two hundred thousand dollars. The cigarettes are on the house," he said, and smiled again. "You owe me a lot of money, Gloria."

"I spent a lot of it."

"How much is left?"

"I haven't counted it lately. Whatever's left is yours."

"Oh, you bet it is," he said.

"Maybe two mil, something like that? That's a lot of cash, Sonny."

The name he'd used on the job was Sonny Sanson. Sonny for "*Son'io*," which in Italian meant "I am." The Sanson was for "*Sans son*," which in French meant "without sound." I am without sound. I am deaf. Maybe.

"Where's the money?" he asked.

"In a safe deposit box."

"Do you have the key?"

"I do."

"May I have it, please?"

"And then what? You kill me?"

"You shouldn't have done what you did, Gloria."

"I know. And I'm sorry. Put down the gun. Let's have a drink, share a joint."

"No, I don't think so. The key, please. And let me see your hands at all times."

He followed her into a lavishly decorated bedroom, a four-poster bed, a silk coverlet, a chest that looked antique Italian, silk drapes to match the bedspread. From a drop-leaf desk that also looked Italian, hand-painted with flowery scrollwork, she removed a black-lacquered box, and from it took a small, red, snap-button envelope. The printing on the envelope read FIRSTBANK.

"Open it," he said.

She unsnapped the envelope, took out a small key, showed it to him.

"Fine," he said. "Put it back, and let me have it."

She put the key back into the envelope, snapped it shut, and held it out to him. He took it with his left hand, the gun steady in his right, and slipped it into his jacket pocket.

"So here we are in my bedroom," she said, and smiled.

"Took me a long time to find you, Gloria."

"Thought you'd never get here," she said. Still smiling.

"Didn't even have a last name for you," he said.

"Yes, I know."

"All I knew was you'd been a driver since you were sixteen, that your end of a bank job in Boston enabled you to buy a house out on Sand's Spit . . ."

"Sold it the minute I came into some money."

"*My* money."

"Well, actually the ill-gotten gains from narcotics the police were going to burn anyway."

"Still *my* money, Gloria."

"Well, yes, it *was* your plan, so I suppose the dope was rightfully yours. And we all got paid for what we did, so it wasn't really right of me to . . . well . . . run off with the stash, I know that, Sonny. The plan was a brilliant one, oh, *God*, what a plan! First the diversion in the Cow Pasture . . ."

"I see you remember."

Smiling.

"How could I forget? And then the heist itself, at the Department of Sanitation incinerator . . ."

"Yes."

Nodding. Remembering.

"Houghton Street on the River Harb Drive," she said. "Remember, Sonny? Me driving the truck, you sitting right beside me?"

"Went off like clockwork," he said.

Still smiling, remembering.

"Like clockwork," she said. Smiling with him now. Beginning to feel this would go all right after all.

"I found the house you used to live in, Gloria. Took me a while, but I found it."

"What took you so long?"

"Recuperating. You almost did me in. A doctor named Felix Rickett fixed me up. Dr. Fixit, I called him," he said, and smiled again.

"Yeah, well, like I said, I'm sorry about that."

"I'm sure you are," he said, and glanced knowingly at the gun in his hand. "The present owner of the house told me he'd bought it from a woman named Gloria Anstdorf."

"Yep, that was me, all right."

"German ancestry?"

"I suppose so. I know the *dorf* part means 'village' in German. My grandmother thinks the 'anst' may have come from *bade*ans*talt,* which means 'baths' in German. A village where they had thermal baths, you know? She thinks the Customs people at Ellis Island shortened it when her parents got to America. To Anstdorf, you know?"

"But that's not the name in your mailbox, Gloria."

"No, it isn't."

"You bought this apartment as Gloria Stanford."

"Yes. What I did was rearrange the letters a little. From Anstdorf to Stanford. Made the name a little more American, you know?"

"A *lot* more American."

"Never hurts to rearrange the letters of your name here in the land of the free and home of the brave, does it? Especially when someone might be looking for you."

"It's called an anagram, Gloria."

"What is?"

"Rearranging the letters to form another word."

"Is that right?"

"Anstdorf to Stanford. An anagram."

"Is that what I did? An anagram? I'll be damned."

"Never hurts to use anagrams here in the land of the free and home of the brave."

"I suppose not."

"But I found you, anyway, Gloria."

"So you did. So why don't we make the most of it?"

"Was that your German ancestry, Gloria?"

"Pardon?"

"Tying me to the bed that way?"

"I thought you liked that part."

"The Hamilton Motel, remember, Gloria?"

"Oh, *how* I remember."

"In the town of Red Point. Across the river."

"And into the trees," she said, and smiled.

She was feeling fairly confident now. She sat on the edge of the bed, patted it to indicate she wanted him to sit beside her. He kept standing. Kept pointing the gun at her chest. She took a deep breath. Never hurt to advertise the breasts here in the land of the free and home of the brave. He seemed to notice. Or maybe he was just searching for a spot on her chest to shoot her.

"Was that German, too?" he asked. "Little bit of Nazi heritage there?"

"I don't know what you mean, Sonny."

"Shooting me twice in the chest that way?"

"Well . . ."

"Leaving me tied to the bed that way?"

"Speaking of beds . . ."

"Leaving me there to bleed to death?"

"I'm really sorry about that, I truly am. Why don't you let me show you just how sorry I am?"

"Turnabout is fair play," he said.

"Come over here, honey," she said. "Stand right in front of me."

"Fair is foul, and foul is fair," he said.

"Unzip your fly, honey," she said.

"*Macbeth*," he said. "Act One, Scene One."

And shot her twice in the chest.

Pouf, pouf.

2.

"NOW THAT IS what I call a zaftig woman," Monoghan said.

"How do you happen to know that expression?" Monroe asked.

"My first wife happened to be Jewish," Monoghan said.

Monroe didn't even know there'd *been* a first wife. Or that there was now a second wife. If in fact there was a second wife. The woman's skirt had pulled back when she fell to the expensive Oriental carpet, exposing shapely thighs and legs, which in concert with her ample breasts justified the label Monoghan had just hung on her. She was indeed zaftig, some five-feet-nine-inches tall, a woman of Amazonian proportions, albeit a dead one. The first bullet hole was just below her left breast. The second was a bit higher on her chest, and more to the middle, somewhere around the sternum. There were ugly blood stains around each bullet hole, larger stains in the weave of the thick carpet under her. The detectives seemed to be staring down at the wounds, but perhaps they were just admiring her breasts.

Today was Tuesday, the first day of June, the day after Memorial Day. The dead woman lying there at Monoghan's feet looked to be in her mid-thirties, still young enough to be a mother, though not what anyone would call a young mother, which was the juiciest kind. Monroe's thoughts were running pretty much along similar lines. He was wondering if the woman had been sexually compromised before someone thoughtlessly shot her. The idea was vaguely exciting in an instinctively primitive way, her lying all exposed like that, with even her panties showing.

Monoghan and Monroe were both wearing black, but not in mourning; this was merely the customary raiment of the Homicide Division. Their appearance here was mandatory in this city, but they would serve only in an advisory and supervisory capacity, whatever that meant; sometimes even they themselves didn't know what their exact function was. They *did* know that the actual investigation of the crime would be handled by the detective squad that caught the initial squeal, in this instance the Eight-Seven—which, by the way, where they hell were they? Or the ME, for that matter? Both detectives wondered if they should go down for a cup of coffee, pass the time that way.

The handyman who'd found the dead woman was still in the apartment, looking guilty as hell, probably because he didn't have a green card and was afraid they'd deport him back to Mexico or wherever. The super had sent him up to replace a washer in the kitchen faucet, and he'd let himself in with a pass key, figuring the lady . . .

He kept calling her the lady.

. . . was already gone for the day, it being eleven o'clock in the morning and all. Instead, the lady was dead on her back in the bedroom. The handyman didn't know whether or not it was okay to go back downstairs now, nobody was telling him nothing. So he hung around trying not to appear like an illegal, shifting his weight from one foot to the other as if he had to pee.

"So how do you wanna proceed here?" Monoghan asked.

Monroe looked at his watch. "Is there traffic out there, or what?" he said.

Monoghan shrugged.

"You wanna hear what happened yesterday?" he asked.

"What happened?"

"I go get some takee-outee at this Chinese joint, you know?"

"Yeah?"

"And I place my order with this guy behind one of these computers, and I tell him I also want a coupla bottles non-alcoholic beer. So he . . ."

"Why you drinking non-alcoholic beer?"

"I'm tryin'a lose a little weight."

"Why? You look okay to me."

"I'm tryin'a lose ten, twelve pounds."

"You look fine."

"You think so?"

"Absolutely."

Together, the detectives looked like Tweedledum and Tweedledee. But Monroe didn't seem to realize this.

"Anyway, that ain't the point of the story," Monoghan said. "I told him I wanted two non-alcoholic beers, and he told me I'd have to get those at the bar. So I go over to the bar, and the bartender—this blonde with nice tits, which was strange for a Chinese joint . . ."

"Her having nice tits?"

"No, her being blond . . . can you please pay attention here? She asks me, 'Can I help you, sir?' And I tell her I'd like two non-alcoholic beers, please."

"When you say 'nice tits,' is that what you really mean? 'Nice tits?'"

"What?"

"Is that a truly accurate description? 'Nice tits'?"

"Can you please tell me what that has to do with my story."

"For the sake of accuracy," Monroe said, and shrugged.

"Forget it, then," Monoghan said.

"Because there's an escalation of language when a person is discussing breast sizes," Monroe said.

"I'm not interested," Monoghan said, and looked down again at the breasts of the dead woman.

"The smallest breasts," Monroe said, undeterred, "are what you'd call 'cute boobs.' Then the next largest breasts are 'nice tits . . .'"

"I told you I'm not—"

". . . and then we get to 'great jugs,' and finally we arrive at 'major hooters.' That's the proper escalation. So when you say this blond bartender had nice tits, do you really mean—"

"I really mean she had nice tits, yes, and that has nothing to do with my story."

"I know. Your story has to do with ordering nonalcoholic beer when you don't even need to lose weight."

"Forget it," Monoghan said.

"No, tell it. I'm listening."

"You're sure you're not still distracted by the bartender with the great tits or the cute hooters or whatever the hell she had?"

"You're mixing them up."

"Forgive me, I didn't know this was an exact science."

"There's no need for sarcasm. I'm tryin'a help your story, is all."

"So let me tell it then."

"So tell it already," Monroe said, sounding miffed.

"I ask the bartender for two non-alcoholic beers, and a Chinese manager or whatever he was, standing there at the service bar says, 'We can't sell you beer to take home, sir.' So I said, 'Why not?' So he says, 'I would lose my liquor license.' So I said, 'This isn't alcohol, this is non-alcoholic beer. It would be the same as my taking home a Diet Coke.' So he says, 'I order my non-alcoholic beer from my liquor supplier. And I can't sell it to customers to take home.' So I said, 'Who *can* you sell it to if not customers?' He says, 'What?' So I say, 'If you can't sell it to *customers*, who *can* you sell it to? Employees?' So he says, 'I can't sell it to *anyone*. I would lose my liquor license.' So I say, 'This is *not* liquor! This is non-alcoholic! And he says, 'I'm sorry, sir.'"

"So did you get the beer or not?"

"I did not get it. And it wasn't beer. It was *non-alcoholic* beer."

"Which you don't need, anyway, a diet."

"Forget it," Monoghan said, sighing, and a voice from the entrance door said, "Good morning, people. Who's in charge here?"

The ME had arrived.

Detectives Meyer and Carella were just a heartbeat behind him.

YOU COULDN'T MISTAKE THEM for anything but cops.

Monoghan and Monroe might have been confused with portly pallbearers at a gangland funeral, but Meyer and Carella—although they didn't look at all alike—could be nothing but cops.

Detective Meyer Meyer was some six feet tall, a broad-shouldered man with China-blue eyes and a completely bald head. Even without the Isola PD shield hanging around his neck and dangling onto his chest, even with his sometimes GQ look—on this bright June morning, he was wearing brown corduroy slacks, brown socks and loafers, and a brown leather jacket zipped up over a tan linen shirt—his walk, his stance, his very air of confident command warned the criminal world at large that here stood the bona fide Man.

Like his partner, Detective Stephen Louis Carella exuded the same sense of offhand authority. About the same height as Meyer, give or take an inch or so, dark-haired and dark-eyed, wearing on this late spring day gray slacks, blue socks, black loafers, and a blue blazer over a lime green Tommy Hilfiger shirt, he came striding into the room like an athlete, which he was not—unless you counted stickball as a kid growing up in Riverhead. He was already looking around as he came in just a step behind both Meyer and the medical examiner, who was either Carl Blaney or Paul Blaney, Carella didn't know which just yet; the men were twins, and they both worked for the Coroner's Office.

In answer to Blaney's question, Monroe said, "We *were* in charge until this very instant, Paul, but now that the super sleuths of the Eight-Seven—"

"It's Carl," Blaney said.

"Oh, I beg your parmigiana," Monroe said, and made a slight bow from the waist. "In any event, the case is now in the capable hands of Detectives Meyer and Carella, of whose company I am sure you already have had the pleasure."

"Hello, Steve," Blaney said. "Meyer."

Carella nodded. He had just looked down at the body of the dead woman. As always, a short, sharp stab, almost of pain, knifed him between the eyes. He was looking death in the face yet another time. And the only word that accompanied the recognition was *senseless*.

"Nice jugs, huh, Doc?" Monoghan remarked.

"*Great* jugs," Monroe corrected.

"Either way, a zaftig woman," Monoghan said.

Blaney said nothing. He was kneeling beside the dead woman, his thumb and forefinger spreading her eyelids wide, his own violet-colored eyes studying her pupils. A few moments later, he declared her dead, said the probable cause of death was gunshot wounds, and ventured the wild guess that the lady had been shot twice in the heart.

Same words the handyman had used.

The lady.

We interrogate the "Grand Master of American Mystery,"

ED McBAIN

■ ・ ■ ・ ■ ・ ■ ・ ■

**ON WRITING AN
87th PRECINCT NOVEL:**

"I usually start with a corpse.
I then ask myself how the corpse
got to be that way and I try to
find out—just as the cops would.
I plot, loosely, usually a chapter
or two ahead, going back to make sure
that everything fits—all the clues are
in the right places, all the bodies are
accounted for... [I] believe strongly in the
long arm of coincidence because I know cops
well, I know how much it contributes
to the solving of real police cases."

2348

ON VIOLENCE IN HIS NOVELS:

"I am unflinching about the violence...If someone is getting killed, that person is getting killed and you know it, and it hurts, and it results in a torn body lying on the sidewalk. It's not pretty...it's horrible. But there's a way of doing violence that's salacious. And that's wrong...I have never, ever, ever in my books tried to make violence appealing. I've made it frightening and I've made it ugly, but never appealing."

ON POLICE REACTION TO 87th PRECINCT NOVELS:

"I get a lot of mail from cops pleased with the accuracy of my books, and if I ever need any help with any problems that may crop up while working on a book, I know who to turn to. After all, some of my best friends are cops."

ON WHAT HIS 87th PRECINCT NOVELS ARE ALL ABOUT:

"I think of the 87th as one big book, a changing portrait of a big city and of crime and punishment in our time."

The fiction of Ed McBain
Published by Pocket Books

We interrogate the "Grand Master of American Mystery," ED McBAIN

ON WRITING AN 87th PRECINCT NOVEL:

"I usually start with a corpse. I then ask myself how the corpse got to be that way and I try to find out—just as the cops would. I plot, loosely, usually a chapter or two ahead, going back to make sure that everything fits—all the clues are in the right places, all the bodies are accounted for... [I] believe strongly in the long arm of coincidence because I know cops well, I know how much it contributes to the solving of real police cases."

2348

ON VIOLENCE IN HIS NOVELS:

"I am unflinching about the violence...If someone is getting killed, that person is getting killed and you know it, and it hurts, and it results in a torn body lying on the sidewalk. It's not pretty...it's horrible. But there's a way of doing violence that's salacious. And that's wrong...I have never, ever, ever in my books tried to make violence appealing. I've made it frightening and I've made it ugly, but never appealing."

ON POLICE REACTION TO 87th PRECINCT NOVELS:

"I get a lot of mail from cops pleased with the accuracy of my books, and if I ever need any help with any problems that may crop up while working on a book, I know who to turn to. After all, some of my best friends are cops."

ON WHAT HIS 87th PRECINCT NOVELS ARE ALL ABOUT:

"I think of the 87th as one big book, a changing portrait of a big city and of crime and punishment in our time."

The fiction of Ed McBain
Published by Pocket Books

We interrogate the "Grand Master of American Mystery,"

ED McBAIN

▪ ▬ ▪ ▬ ▪ ▬ ▪

**ON WRITING AN
87th PRECINCT NOVEL:**

"I usually start with a corpse.
I then ask myself how the corpse
got to be that way and I try to
find out—just as the cops would.
I plot, loosely, usually a chapter
or two ahead, going back to make sure
that everything fits—all the clues are
in the right places, all the bodies are
accounted for... [I] believe strongly in the
long arm of coincidence because I know cops
well, I know how much it contributes
to the solving of real police cases."

2348

ON VIOLENCE IN HIS NOVELS:

"I am unflinching about the violence...If someone is getting killed, that person is getting killed and you know it, and it hurts, and it results in a torn body lying on the sidewalk. It's not pretty...it's horrible. But there's a way of doing violence that's salacious. And that's wrong...I have never, ever, ever in my books tried to make violence appealing. I've made it frightening and I've made it ugly, but never appealing."

ON POLICE REACTION TO 87th PRECINCT NOVELS:

"I get a lot of mail from cops pleased with the accuracy of my books, and if I ever need any help with any problems that may crop up while working on a book, I know who to turn to. After all, some of my best friends are cops."

ON WHAT HIS 87th PRECINCT NOVELS ARE ALL ABOUT:

"I think of the 87th as one big book, a changing portrait of a big city and of crime and punishment in our time."

The fiction of Ed McBain
Published by Pocket Books